I0678985

THE
HANGMAN
OF PARIS

CLAUDE CUENI

THE
HANGMAN
OF PARIS

Translated by
LEE CHADEAYNE

SCRIPT AVENUE
PUBLISHING

The Hangman was first published in 2013 by Lenos Verlag Basel.
Translated from German by Lee Chadeayne.
Last Chapter by Lisa Reinhardt.
First published in the U.K. in 2017 by Script Avenue Publishing.

Cover design by Hauptmann & Kompanie, Zürich, Dominic Wilhelm
Interior design by Andreas Seebeck
Cover Painting by Pierre-Antoine Demachy
(une éxecution capitale place de la revolution, 1793)

Copyright © 2017 Script Avenue Publishing, Switzerland
English translation copyright © 2017 by Lee Chadeayne

All rights reserved.

No part of this book may be reproduced, or stored in a retrieval system,
or transmitted in any form or by any means, electronic, mechanical,
photocopying, recording, or otherwise, without express
written permission of the publisher.

Published by Script Avenue Publishing Switzerland
www.scriptavenue.ch

For Lee Chadeayne

From Lisa Reinhardt to Lee Chadeayne

In grateful memory of Lee Chadeayne, the friend and mentor I never met. He was a great admirer of Claude Cueni's work and wished for his translation of this book to be completed.

From Claude Cueni to Lee Chadeayne

My collaboration with Lee began in 2013, when he translated my novel about John Law, the inventor of paper money, *The Great Gambler*. Sometimes I wouldn't hear from Lee for a while and start to worry—all the greater my joy whenever I received an email from him. Other times, he wouldn't hear back from me, as I was in and out of hospital myself due to leukemia treatment. That way, we gradually learned more about each other's lives, became closer, and took a profound liking to one another. We had both lost loved ones and adopted a somewhat humble attitude to life.

I was surprised when he told me last year that he had started translating the hangman's novel I'd sent him years ago. He said he loved the book. Unfortunately, the breaks in communication grew longer—from his end as well as mine—but all the happier we were each time we received a sign of life, reassurance the other had managed to overcome yet another health crisis.

Sadly, I never met Lee in person, but thanks to our correspondence throughout the last four years I feel like I've lost a dear friend. Lee was a very sensitive man with a big heart, and he'd be happy to know that his daughter was able to keep her promise to have the final chapter translated with the help of Lisa Reinhardt. Thus the publication of this book is fraught with emotions and will forever be a reminder of a great person and translator.

Claude Cueni, November 2017

CHAPTER 1

It was the year 1737, and around midnight a huge storm swept over Normandy. The rain streamed down, and a bolt of lightning followed by a mighty roll of thunder struck in the forest, revealing for a fraction of a second a lone horseman galloping through the night. He whipped his horse madly as if trying to escape the deluge engulfing the countryside. One flash of lightning after the other split the night sky and thunder echoed through the hills. Trees bent and snapped like matchsticks and the black stallion whinnied loudly as they passed a small farmyard whose weathered paint shone blood red. Again the rider applied his spurs to the exhausted beast. It raised its head in protest as white foam appeared on its lips and was at once washed away in the night by the rain. The horseman pressed ahead on the flooded road toward Neufchâtel in the Pays de Bray as the storm raged and the rain beat down. Finally, he saw a flickering yellow light between the trees, the vague outlines of a tavern. At the same moment his horse 's front legs buckled and the rider flew forward head over heels, landing with a splash and sliding forward another few yards before banging his head against a tree trunk blown down by the storm. It took him a while to realize he had survived the fall uninjured. Then came the pain. His steed lay exhausted and whinnying at the side of the road, trying in vain to stand up. Helplessly, the animal flailed the air with its legs, tried to raise its head one last time, then fell back with a loud splash into the mud and was silent. It was pitch black.

The rider struggled to his feet slowly and paused for a while, stooped over, panting and looking at the horse. Then he noticed the saddlebag that had evidently been torn away from its leather strap and lay on the ground in front of him. He opened it and took out a heavy, double-barreled, wheel lock pistol that he'd won in a game of Pharo. Suddenly he fell again and slid through the mud. He got to his knees to search for the weapon that had fallen from his hands, found it, and with relief crawled back toward his horse. Almost tenderly he passed his hand over the horse's nostrils, then placed the pistol against its temples and pulled the trigger. The impact of the hammer was audible, but the powder was wet. Once again a roll of thunder interrupted the silence of the night and several bolts of lightning struck nearby. The rider got back to his feet again. The rain poured down his soaked uniform in buckets but he hadn't travelled this far just to give up.

He stomped down the muddy road and step by step approached the yellow light. A smile passed over his lips. Had God heard his prayers? He pushed open the tavern door and saw inside a few grim-looking men sitting at a long table. The other tables were unoccupied. Except for one. At a small, round table in the corner sat a huge man all alone holding a wooden cup in his hands.

The rider shut the door behind him, and now all eyes turned toward him. He himself was unusually large. He had a proud bearing and long, brown hair. Now he noticed the tavern keeper behind the counter who was eyeing him suspiciously. The men at the long table looked at his trousers, which despite being spattered with mud were—from his belt down to the mud-splattered boots—unmistakably the colors and uniform of an officer in the regiment of the Marquis de La Boissière.

"Where am I?" the rider asked. No one answered.

Then he turned to the innkeeper. "Give me something to drink."

"We have nothing to offer," replied the innkeeper after a while.

"Wine. Red wine."

The innkeeper picked up a bottle, filled a cup with wine, and the rider took a coin from his pocket and laid it on the counter. The innkeeper examined the unfamiliar piece.

"It was coined in New France," the officer continued, seeking to be shown the proper respect, adding, "I am Lieutenant Chevalier de Longval, Jean-Baptiste Sanson de Longval."

The innkeeper lowered his head uncertainly, and took a respectful step backward as he slowly handed the cup across the counter and asked: "Did you fight in India?"

"We call it America but we call the natives Indians. I don't know which is correct, but the main thing is we understand each other."

The innkeeper nodded, adding after a while: "We don't like strangers here."

"I was never really gone, a year at most."

The innkeeper shook his head. "I've known some people who were over there, and they weren't the same when they came back. They just talk a lot of nonsense. There are no kings over there, and everyone calls himself king, I've heard."

"Yes," Lieutenant Sanson murmured, "there are men there who want to break away from France, and for that they go to war and die. They want freedom."

The innkeeper eyed him skeptically and then turned away to serve another jug of wine to the guests at the long table.

"Where is the rest of your army?" sneered one of the men, showing the blackened stump of a tooth, and all his drinking friends broke out in loud, disrespectful laughter. Like a group of enemy soldiers, they sat at their table, awaiting his answer.

"Did you desert?" one of them asked, "or are you coming to make war on us?"

The lieutenant emptied his cup in one gulp and approached the long table. "Messieurs, my regiment, that of the Marquis de La Boissière, is stationed near Dieppe. I am on a mission in behalf of my commander with an urgent message for Paris." He straightened up and placed his right hand on the iron hilt of his long sword. "I need a fresh horse," he added, looking sternly at the innkeeper.

"Do you see any horses here?"

"He has nothing but us," one of the men added in a raucous voice. The others giggled drunkenly.

"How did you get here?" the innkeeper asked.

"My horse is lying outside in the mud. He broke his leg." His impatience was growing. "I tried to put him down, but my gun powder is wet."

Now everyone turned to look at the bald-headed man sitting all alone at a round table in the corner. He didn't look up, but stared into his cup.

"Ask him," the innkeeper said gruffly, "perhaps he has a horse for you. You can't stay here. We have no guest rooms."

"I need a weapon, too. My horse needs to be put out of its misery."

"Do I look like an arms dealer?" the innkeeper grumbled. "Ask him. He knows something about animals and how to dispatch a dying horse."

The men at the long table broke out in laughter again.

"Five sous," the huge man in the corner grumbled.

Lieutenant Sanson pulled a few coins out of his pocket and put them down on the counter.

"Give it to him yourself," replied the innkeeper with a strange tone of contempt in his voice.

"No," the huge man asked, "leave it on the counter, and in return he can bring me another cup of wine."

The lieutenant pushed an empty cup across the counter.

"Give him some wine."

The innkeeper took the cup and turned it upside down. "He'll drink from his own cup."

The lieutenant looked over at the men sitting at the long table. They stared at him silently. He picked up the carafe of wine and walked slowly over to the man in the corner, stopping at his table and pouring him some more wine.

"Where's the animal?" the man asked in a hoarse voice.

"Head toward the forest, and you'll see him."

The man nodded. "I'll take care of the horse, but the cadaver belongs to me. Go back the way you came. Did you see the little red cottage? Behind it you'll find a chapel, and you'll find me there. You can spend the night in my barn, Chevalier." The lieutenant looked at him in annoyance.

"You can go on ahead. I'll stay and drink the wine, and take care of the horse later."

"Can't you take care of it right away?"

The man looked up at him with cold, piercing eyes. His face looked like a heavy iron anvil—angular yet inflexible, as if it could be beaten without incurring the slightest damage. The lieutenant took the carafe back to the counter and told the innkeeper "I'd like to wash up," pointing to his dirty hands. Only now did the innkeeper notice the blood on his left hand.

"You'll find a trough in the back of the building," said the innkeeper, nodding in the direction of the door behind the counter. Outside, boards lay on the muddy ground. The lieutenant washed his hands and face and tidied up his uniform. He had no idea where the blood came from.

When he returned to the inn, the huge man had vanished.

"I'll go now and spend the night in this red farmhouse."

The men at the long table laughed, and one announced: "We call it the condemned farmhouse." They all laughed.

"Well," the innkeeper grumbled, "no one likes to go there." Again, laughter. One of them added: "It's very quiet

there, especially in the barn." Now the men again broke out in raucous laughter and pounded their fists on the table. The innkeeper's face was emotionless.

Jean-Baptiste Sanson pulled up his collar as he went out the door and marched back with determination into the darkness. He was still shaking. Along the way, he saw his horse lying dead in a pool of blood which kept growing even as the rain kept washing it away. Now he remembered the saddlebag and though he looked for a while, he couldn't find it in the darkness.

After a while he arrived at the cursed farmyard. There was a light flickering inside and he could see that the house was really painted red, and glittered like fresh blood in the rain. Behind the house he found a barn with a small chapel behind it. The entrance was lit by a lantern clattering in the wind. He slowly climbed down a little stairway, carefully setting one foot after the other on the slippery steps. When he reached the bottom, he stopped for a while in the entrance, staring at the little altar of Mary and the candles flickering atop it. He could sense he was not alone, and then he saw the man in front of him. He walked slowly across the creaking wooden floor and knelt down beside the man he had spoken to earlier in the tavern. He propped his elbows on the altar rail and folded his hands. Though he tried to pray, no prayer crossed his lips. The years had worn him down and perhaps even God had tired of hearing his prayers. The huge man turned and looked at him. His prayers in the chapel seemed to have changed him. He now seemed gentle and calm, though perhaps it was the wine. Praying or drinking—both seemed to have the same effect, Sanson thought.

"Did you find my saddlebag?" he asked, directing a piercing gaze at the man as if warning him not to lie.

"Chevalier, your saddlebag is over in the barn. I opened it. After all, I want to know who's spending the night in my barn. But there was no message for Paris, and I fear you are

traveling in a personal matter. In your eyes I can see the fear that is consuming you. Misfortune is at your heels, perhaps it's a curse. Some men are cursed and spend their lives fleeing from it. But the fear pursues them like a shadow and they lose the blessing of God who cursed the serpent that seduced Eve, as well as Cain for the murder of his brother, and he cursed the earth and men."

"Enough of this nonsense! I don't believe in curses."

"Why then do you ride like a madman through the night? In this weather? If you believe in God, then you also believe in the devil, and if you believe both in God and the devil, you also believe in curses. So what are you running away from?"

Jean-Baptiste Sanson was silent.

"Some men know their fate, but cannot escape it. That is the curse."

Jean-Baptiste put his hand to his right side, and when he put it up to his eyes he saw it was bloodied.

"Come to the barn," the huge man said, "we must clean the wound or you will never make it to Paris."

He lit the way with a lantern. The horses were restless in their stables, and some got to their feet and raised their heads, smelling the odor of the stranger and the blood. The huge man laid out fresh straw beyond the last stall, then threw a brown horse blanket over it and told Jean-Baptiste to strip to the waist.

"I'll get some clean water," he said as he set the lantern on the floor.

Jean-Baptiste lay down and waited. The only sounds were the pawing of the horse's hoofs. After a while, the man returned with fresh rags, followed by a young maid with a mortar in her hand. She knelt down and crushed some herbs in it. "This is *Symphyti radix*," the man declared. "It relieves inflammation and stops the formation of pus."

"Are you a doctor?" Jean-Baptiste asked.

The huge man was silent and appeared to be concentrating on cleaning the wound.

"Yes, he's a doctor," said the young woman after a while. "A good doctor." She placed more herbs in the mortar, crushed them with a practiced hand, then added water to the mixture and handed it to Jean-Baptiste to drink. It tasted terrible, but he didn't resist.

"This herb will help you," whispered the big man, "Rauwolfia serpentina takes away the fear. It calms your body and senses. You'll feel no more pain, and will sleep."

"I have no fear, I have fought in the New World and have seen a lot."

The giant did not seem impressed. "When you wake up tomorrow and look around in the barn, perhaps you will feel fear. You still have not seen all that fate has in store you."

Jean-Baptiste struggled to get to his feet. Maybe he should leave this place, he thought, but the strength had drained from his body, and he lay there motionless. His thoughts were lost in a dark place. He could still feel the fear coming on, then he fell asleep.

Outside it was gradually becoming light. A new day. The first rays of sunlight shone through the large opening in ceiling. Jean-Baptiste Sanson had awakened. He slowly got to his feet and studied his surroundings. He had slept next to the last horse stall. There were four of them in all with horses waiting impatiently to be led to pasture. Curious and impatient, they pushed their heads against the door to their stalls. He studied them. He liked horses, but they would hardly have been useful as cavalry horses. They were old and probably suited only to pull the wagon that stood in the yard. He looked around in the spacious barn. Harnesses were hanging on hooks in the wooden wall, and iron objects hung on hooks: tongs, shackles, crowbars, and wicker baskets on the floor holding leather straps, a rack, a medium-sized

wooden barrel holding fat, ointments, powder, charcoal, grease, soap, bran, sand and sawdust, and a large wheel. In the corner there was something on a table, with a cloth on top covering it. Sanson tugged on a corner of the cloth revealing bluish fingers, and when he'd pulled the cloth off completely, he was shocked to see a disembodied arm. The elbow had been skinned, revealing the bones, sinews and joints.

A wave of fear came over him, and he remembered the curse. He had to flee from this shed, at once. It was possible his life was cursed, but in this place it surely was. He decided to flee, panicked and feared something would stop him at the last minute. He walked hastily to the barn door. Outside in the courtyard he heard the hoof beats of at least a half-dozen horses. Opening the door a crack, he saw that the men were lightly armed dragoons, carrying muskets and wearing white tunics. By the color of their collars and cuffs he recognized them as members of the regiment of the Marquis de La Boissière. The door of the opposite house opened and the huge man stepped out into the yard.

"Do you need water for your horses?"

"We are looking for a deserter. Have you happened to see one?"

"No one comes wandering around here. And no one visits this farm of their own will."

The leader tugged at his reins, pulling the horse around. He was in a hurry. Then he turned around again. "We'll ride on to Paris, and on the way back we will visit you again. So be vigilant."

Then he spurred his horse on, and dashed across the yard toward the woods, with the others following him.

Jean-Baptiste had been holding his breath, but once the dragoons had left, he opened the barn door a crack. The big man was blocking his way, his powerful torso obscuring the sun and darkening the interior of the barn. "Do not do it," he

said, "this is the only place you are safe. Stay here for the winter with me and help me to replace the roof."

Jean-Baptiste rummaged in the straw. "Who are you?"

"Are you looking for your saddlebag?" asked the big man, walking across the straw. and pushing the bag with his foot over to Jean-Baptiste, who opened it at once. It was empty. He stared furiously at the giant. "And where are my papers?"

The giant took a document from his breast pocket and tore it in two with his big, powerful hands.

This man doesn't make a living working at a desk, Sanson thought.

"These were an officer's papers, chevalier, and you won't need them anymore. You're a deserter and nowhere will you find work, warm soup, or a roof over your head. If you help me, I'll help you. Soon the first snow will fall and the straw in the barn will become wet and moldy. I will help you, but you must swear to remain here until the spring."

"I swear to you . . ."

"You must not swear to me, chevalier, you must swear to God. If you break your oath, I will kill you, but God's punishment is worse than death."

"I swear before God, I will do everything you ask if I may hide here until my regiment has withdrawn."

"That's easily said, but would you also make a pact with the Devil?"

"Yes," Jean-Baptiste said with a heavy tongue, "but you are not the Devil. You can relieve pain."

The giant stared down at him and after a while said: "I can relieve pain as well as inflict pain; I am like fire. It can heal wounds but can also inflict wounds. When you enter my world, you enter the world of pain."

Jean-Baptiste stared at the severed arm. The big man noticed, smiled, and walked over to the table. The young man

followed. "I will help you repair your roof before the first snow falls."

"You will serve as my apprentice, eat at my table and sleep under my roof until the first trees bloom. If your regiment is still in the area, you can also stay longer. I badly need an apprentice."

"Is it so difficult to find an apprentice? People are suffering and starving, and in these dark days everyone wants just one thing: work."

"But not this kind of work," the man replied. "We will not just repair the roof."

"What, then, is your line of work?" asked Jean-Baptiste with obvious distrust.

"I am a servant of the law, and you are now my assistant, chevalier. I am despised, and they will also despise you."

Jean-Baptiste turned white and gradually he began to suspect. "Why should an official of law should be despised?"

The giant reached out in the dark, seizing an object hanging on the wall. When he brought it out into the light, Jean-Baptiste could see it was a two-handed sword. The giant thrust the point of the sword in the wooden floor, supporting himself with both hands on the hilt.

"I am Master Pierre Jouenne, executioner of Caudebec-en-Caux and work for the city of Rouen and the vice-countship Dieppe."

"No!" Jean-Baptiste shouted in despair. "No, no no!"

He stormed out of the house past Jouenne, into the courtyard, grabbed the reins of a horse drinking at the trough, and mounted it. As he was about to spur the horse on, he heard a shrill whistle across the yard and the horse stopped suddenly, as if rooted to the spot. Jean-Baptiste flew forward over the horse's head and, shouting loudly, landed on the hard stone pavement.

Jouenne planted himself in front of him and warned him, "Don't do that again, or I will chase you to all the way to

Paris and torture you mercilessly. I know how to inflict pain without killing. Don't force me to do that, not now. I was just beginning to like you."

Jean-Baptists struggled to his feet, groaning, and instinctively reached for the wound that Jouenne had cleaned the evening before. It was bleeding again. "I did not flee to the New World just to become a hangman," he panted. "I joined the army to escape the curse that lies on her family. My father, my grandfather and all my ancestors were hangmen. We come from Abbeville in Picardy."

"You should be proud of having been born into such a family."

"That was not my world!"

"There is only one world, and each person must take the place in it that God has ordained. There is no other world. You must play the part that has been preordained for you."

"There was another ancestor, a cartographer . . ."

"Nicolas Sanson," Jouenne said. Jean-Baptiste was astonished.

"Did you think I was stupid and uneducated just because I am an executioner?"

"No, Master Jouenne," Baptiste lied.

"Listen to me, chevalier, you think there is a curse on your family. You wanted to escape it. You left your family, joined the army, traveled to the New World, and fought in the wars there. You survived and have returned. You deserted. You wanted to escape the curse on your family, and now you are my apprentice. Do you sense the curse? It follows you like your own shadow. You can recognize the curse, but you cannot escape it. The mighty pine defies the storm and is uprooted, but the wheat bends and survives. Accept this accursed life and learn to forget. The pain comes when you look back, fear comes over you when you think of the future. Try to live only in the present. Today you lack nothing. Come, I'll show you something."

Jouenne returned to the barn, took the disembodied arm from the table and showed it to Jean-Baptiste, then stepped back.

"Look more closely: this is where the shoulder joint begins. It consists of the head of the upper arm and the shoulder blade. They are not held in place by the bony structures, but primarily by musculature. Fascinating, isn't it? This is something you can only learn by dissecting the parts. And you can help only if you know how the joint functions. A simple inflammation can take up so much space when it swells up that the joint can no longer move. So you must wait for the swelling to go down and not try to manipulate the arm. Any hangman knows more about the anatomy of the human body than most doctors in Versailles."

Jean-Baptiste nodded.

"There is much I can teach you, chevalier, but you must want it."

"I will be your apprentice, Master Jouenne, but in the spring, when my regiment leaves, I will also leave you."

Jouenne smiled briefly, then walked out into the yard. Jean-Baptiste remained behind alone in the barn, walked over to his bed of straw, and picked up his saddlebag. Inside there was a secret little pocket. He felt for it— it was empty as well. He ran out into the yard and shouted after Jouenne. "There was something else in the saddlebag. You stole it!"

"No," replied Jouenne without turning around, "I have kept it as security."

Furiously, Jean-Baptiste stomped back into the barn, threw the saddlebag down in the straw, and lay down.

"Master Jouenne is a student of anatomy," said a friendly woman's voice. Jean-Baptiste turned and squinted. Before him stood the maid with a cup of red wine. She was perhaps thirty years old and wearing shabby clothes beneath which the contours of her breasts stood out. She was tall and had long, dainty legs. He got up and approached her. He had not

had a good look at her the night before. She was very beautiful.

"In the morning he receives patients," she said, "and works in his little pharmacy. He knows the healing power of nature, but in the evening he carries out his criminal verdicts."

Jouenne entered the barn again. "Without me, order would give way to chaos—without me the throne would fall."

Jean-Baptiste leaned against a large beer barrel with undefinable things floating around in it that were strung together and looked like human fingers

"It's just what you think," said the maid, "Fingers. Fingers of hanged men. They improve the aroma of the beer. All disembodied limbs have magic powers, as do the plants that grow beneath the scaffold if they are plucked at night at the full moon."

Jean-Baptiste looked at her, horrified.

"That's magic. My name is Joséphine, and I am no witch," she replied with a smile. "I'm Master Jouenne's maid. There are many things we can't explain, we simply believe them. We believe in life after death, even though no one has ever returned, we believe in the immaculate conception even that doesn't exist in our world, we believe in the resurrection of the dead . . ."

"And we believe in charms, in the grace of God, in miracles and curses," Jouenne said, eyeing him severely. "You can lie there and drink one more day, Sanson, and then I'll expect you outside in the yard. Two o'clock sharp. At four o'clock we have an execution to carry out in the Place du Puits-Salé. by order of the king. I am the people's avenger, and starting tomorrow you are my assistant. Pull yourself together. The crowd will be large and they expect a dignified spectacle. There is a first, second, and third act, and

at the end the principal character loses his life. No theater in Paris can surpass its drama."

At the Place du Puits-Salé the rolling drums fell silent. A dense crowd of people stood around the six-foot high platform with the gallows in the middle. Some were perched up in the trees like bats or on the facades of house to get a good view of the action. Majestically, Master Jouenne walked up the steps and across the platform to the scaffold. This was his stage. He wore a tight, dark-red jerkin and a sleeveless leather coat over it that he had tied to his upper body like a cuirass. His black riding boots reached up to his knees. In addition, he was wearing a long, wide blood-red coat whose collar was turned up, making only a part of his angular face visible. The crowd applauded, then the drums started rolling again. Jouenne took his time, removed the written document from his pocket, unrolled it, then stopped to gaze imperiously over the heads of the crowd. The tension in the square was palpable. The spectators feared him, but they also loved the shudder of fear that this huge man unleashed in them. Again the drumroll fell silent and Jean-Baptiste Sanson led the unlucky Bouvier up the steps to the scaffold. The condemned man was wearing a red, sleeveless shirt and had his hands tied behind his back. The hangman's assistant was wearing a black helmet with two slits for the eyes and an opening for his nose and mouth. They had agreed on this masquerade because it enhanced the performance, but also so that Jean-Baptiste would not be recognized. Of course it was unlikely one of the nosy onlookers would recognize him, but if a curse lay on him anything was possible said Jouenne, who was now glancing at the dark clouds gradually gathering over the accursed farm.

In a strange, thundering voice, Jouenne read the judgement. Bouvier was to be branded, then hanged. He had stolen bread and then killed the furious baker who had

23

pursued him through the town. Once again, the drums started to roll. At this sign, Jean-Baptists dragged the condemned man to the post in the middle of the platform. He pushed Bouvier to his knees and ripped off his red shirt. The branding iron was already glowing in the brazier. Master Jouenne grabbed the iron, turned it a few times in the fire, then applied it to the right shoulder of the condemned man. The burned flesh hissed and the stench drifted over the Place du Puits-Salé while Bouvier let out a piercing scream and could barely be restrained by Jean-Baptiste. Master Jouenne now climbed down from the scaffold, holding his head high. The crowd applauded. Jean-Baptiste seized Bouvier from behind and lifted him to his feet. Suddenly, silence fell over the square as he tightened the noose around Bouvier's neck. Bouvier stood there looking almost apathetically at the trap door, then closed his eyes. When Jouenne asked him if he had any last words, Bouvier shook his head emphatically. He wanted to get it over with quickly. Jean-Baptiste checked that he himself was not standing on the trap door, and when Jouenne nodded calmly, without any apparent concern for Bouvier's fate, Jean-Baptiste released the door. It opened, and Bouvier plummeted down like a sack of flour until the rope suddenly stopped the fall. The weight of the falling body tightened the rope around his Adam's apple cutting off his breath and breaking his neck. Bouvier thrashed about for a few seconds, then turned limp and discharged a large amount of urine. as the crowd laughed and applauded. Jouenne was visibly pleased with the performance. He had prepared the length of the rope according to the weight and size of the body, and his calculations had been flawless. Just a small miscalculation could have caused Bouvier's head to be ripped off, and that was not in his instructions.

Suddenly, men on horseback appeared at the edge of the square, made their way forward and surrounded the scaffold. They were dragoons and wearing the white tunics of the

regiment of the Marquis de La Boissière. Jean-Baptiste stood alongside the open trap door and did not budge. The lifeless body of the hanged man was still dangling on the rope. Jouenne approached the commander, who was coming up the stairs and walked out onto the platform.

"We have an announcement to read," the commander said bluntly, walking past Jouenne. He unrolled the parchment and read the message to the crowd. The dragoons were searching for deserters. Some had already fled while they were in the New World, and others only after reaching French soil. Some were accused of stealing money in the New World belonging to the regiment and killing two men guarding it. The Marquis de La Boissière has personally offered a reward in the amount of two Louis d'or for information leading to the arrest of the suspects.

The commandant rolled up the parchment again, cast a suspicious eye at the disguised assistant, and looked questioningly at Jouenne.

"He's my son," Jouenne said in a firm voice.

The commandant left the scaffold and mounted his horse once again, then gave the other dragoons a sign to follow him. Slowly they made their way through the crowd, and left the field.

Jouenne and Jean-Baptiste sat silently on the wagon's coach box. After they had left the town, Jouenne asked, "Did you steal the regiment's money?"

"No," Jean-Baptiste replied, though it's possible someone did on the day I slipped away. But it wasn't me."

"Then where did you get the gold coins I found in your saddlebag?"

"Do you mean the money you stole from me? I won it in a card game."

"I wouldn't have thought of that," Jouenne grumbled, though he didn't believe a word of it. "And why did you

leave the army?" When Jean-Baptiste did not answer, he gave him a stern glance.

"I was stationed in the New World, on the Boeuf River. Together with the French missionaries we were trying to put an end to the trade of English merchants with the Indians. We captured the Indians and shipped them as slaves to our plantations in the Caribbean. Finally, we received the order to shoot them like rabbits. There were just too many of them. Then the Englanders came and made an alliance with some of the tribes. We fought the Chickasaw, the Natchez, and the English sent more ships full of soldiers to build forts. We paid other tribes to burn them down, but then many of them became sick and were dying like flies. They were scalped by bounty hunters who were paid a hundred pounds for an English scalp by the missionaries. It was like Sodom and Gomorrah. Our regiment was decimated, and the survivors turned to bounty hunting, mining for gold, or deserted and returned to France. I had never before witnessed such cruelty."

"Then you had no trouble getting through today's performance?" Jouenne grinned.

"In the New World you fire at fleeing Indians, burn down their villages, but you never know if you have mortally wounded them, and you never see a child burning. But on your scaffold, Master Jouenne, you can even smell the urine when the victim's neck breaks."

"There is another difference," said Jouenne. "In the New World you get decorations and honors for killing, but as a hangman you are despised and scorned even though you are only doing what the court ordered. How can one despise a man who is doing exactly what society demands of him? They want to see the robbers and murderers hanged, but they don't want to be involved themselves."

"Thank you," said Jean-Baptiste after a while.

"I didn't do it for you," Jouenne lied, "but if they hanged my assistant, then I would have none. And I think my assistant has finally come to realize that he's safe only if he stays with me until the Marquis de La Boissière dissolves his regiment."

"I'll stay with you and wear the black hood."

Jouenne laughed. "The people enjoyed it. That's all they have. They must work several days just to earn enough for a loaf of bread and their only distractions are the executions, and because of that their expectations are high."

Jean-Baptiste nodded. He could still feel the fear in the pit of his stomach at seeing the dragoons. "Why didn't we bring the corpse back with us?" he asked.

"That's the will of the city administration: they want it to serve as a deterrent. Only after the corpse has rotted do we take it down and bury it. But not in the cemetery."

Jean-Baptiste wondered if there wasn't some way, after all, to escape his fate. He could simply jump down from the wagon now. But then he remembered the dragoons and suddenly had the feeling that everything was coming together. He could run away, hide, try everything possible, but in the end he would wind up on the gallows. He had no choice. This terrible realization disturbed him, and he stared in a daze at the dirt road under the horse's hoofs.

"When we're back at the house I'll show you how to calculate the length of the rope. It's a mathematical calculation."

Jean-Baptiste was silent.

Jean-Baptiste Sanson was interested in the pharmacy, herbal medicine, and the preparation of medicines more than the dissection of the hanged men. Perhaps that was because Joséphine spent most of her time in the pharmacy. She knew many things about the healing power of plants and was glad to pass this knowledge along to Jean-Baptiste. Sometimes

they went into the forest together and picked herbs. Joséphine showed him where to look for the plants, how to recognize them and preserve them so they wouldn't lose their powers. He enjoyed being with her, and liked her quiet manner. She gave him rest, peace. It didn't matter to him that she told him nothing about her past. He never brought it up. Perhaps he feared once again losing his serenity and peace. Sometimes he was not really listening to what she said, he listened only to the melody of her voice, more than the meaning of her words.

On long winter evenings, Jouenne, Joséphine and Jean-Baptiste sat by the hearth playing cards and drinking wine. They were magical moments. It occurred to Jean-Baptiste that Jouenne and Joséphine had a very close relationship. but he couldn't figure out what it was. Did he have a fatherly concern for the maid? Was she his mistress? He didn't think much about it, as he was only waiting for the Marquis de La Boissière to finally dissolve his regiment. Sometimes the urge came over him to simply disappear, yet something inside him resisted. He feared violating a higher order. He had to accept his fate, and then there was Joséphine, always Joséphine. He didn't even know if she liked him. Perhaps her life as a maid appealed to her more than the uncertain fate of a deserter. It was not certain that she would ever leave Master Jouenne. She was one of those people who sacrifice their own life in order to serve others, who renounce a life of their own, and can't explain it. Evidently there was also a curse on doing good.

"The cards," said Jouenne, interrupting his thoughts. Jean-Baptiste realized he'd been shuffling the cards for an eternity. He smiled in embarrassment and dealt. They always played until about midnight, then they drank to each other one last time and the young man returned to the barn and quickly fell asleep.

In the spring, Jouenne received an offer to perform an execution by sword in the Pays d'Auge. It made him very proud. Secretly he was inspired by the thought of becoming a great hangman not unlike a great actor who performs at guest appearances in other cities and regions. For good money, of course. Since he didn't want to leave Joséphine alone on this allegedly cursed farm, he had informed the city authorities that he wanted to employ a hangman's assistant in order to go to the aid of the seriously ill hangman in the Pays d'Auge. Thus Jean-Baptiste could stay on the farm with Joséphine.

Before he left, Jouenne went to his pharmacy and crushed two artichokes, added apple brandy and the pulverized bark of a yohimbe tree that some soldiers had brought back from the New World. Finally, he added the powder of the maca root, a plant sacred to the Incas that Spanish sailors had brought back to Marseille. "Try it tonight," Jouenne told Jean-Baptiste, "and tell me how quickly it acts and how strong it is. It's good for the gall bladder and liver, and promotes circulation." When he saw the skepticism in Jean-Baptiste's face, he laughed. "It won't kill you, chevalier, and it won't harm you. At worst, it won't help you at all."

Jouenne noted exactly how he had mixed the drink and entered the information in a small black book; then he bade farewell.

After Jean-Baptiste had taken care of the horses for the evening, Joséphine entered the barn, looking happy and relaxed. He didn't know the reason, but somehow she looked more beautiful than before. Was he only now recognizing her beauty?

"Now we're alone," she said at once, and stopped in front of him. As usual, she invited him into the kitchen where she had cooked beans and baked them with ham and onions. They ate without saying a word.

"We understand one another with few words," Joséphine said.

CLAUDE CUENI

He nodded.

After a while she handed him the artichoke brandy. "Drink," she said with a smile. "For science."

Jean-Baptiste drank the whole cup in one gulp. It tasted a bit bitter, but the alcohol made the drink quite appealing. When he put the cup down again, she stretched out her hand. He took it, and she said, "Come and sleep in the house, Jean-Baptiste." He hesitated.

"The nights are still cool," she continued, smiling somewhat awkwardly, and stood up. She was still holding his hand. Gently she led Jean-Baptiste around the linen sacks hanging from the ceiling and separating the kitchen from the bedrooms. She untied her apron, took off her shirt, and looked at him expectantly. At almost the same time, he had also started to undress, first hesitantly, cautiously, then faster and more passionately. After removing each item of clothing, he stopped and waited for her to do the same. Her directness pleased him.

They sat together in the kitchen eating cabbage and the pigeon Jouenne had killed with a spade before his departure.

"I feel so full," said Joséphine.

Jean-Baptiste replied with a smile and looked at her for a long time.

"I would be a good wife for you," she whispered, as if she could read his thoughts.

"I know," he said. "You're very able and also very kind. You have a good heart."

Joséphine smiled contentedly. "And so are you. We would get along well."

"Perhaps it's still too soon to know," he mused.

"Too soon?" she said angrily. "Children must come in the early years. Why do you want to wait?"

"A sign from fate."

"I don't believe in fate. Everything lies in your own hands. You decided the path you will take."

Her words astonished him. He took her hand, nodded, and tenderly patted the back of her hand.

Their love was not without consequences. Joséphine became pregnant. One morning, on her way to the well between the house and the barn, she fainted. Master Jouenne ran to help her and carried her to her room in the house. After a while, he came out of the house again, stomped over to the barn and tore open the creaking wooden door. The light blinded Jean-Baptiste, who was lying on his straw bed. Jouenne seized the large battle-ax behind the door and approached his assistant.

"Joséphine is pregnant. Are you going to marry her?" Jean-Baptiste remained silent.

"Listen to me carefully, chevalier. I care for my assistants and household help. When they get sick, when they get old and frail, I keep them with me and give them a roof over their heads and a warm meal. That is the tradition of hangmen. We behead and hang criminals, but we take responsibility for the fate of our own people."

Jean-Baptiste felt threatened and coerced into complying. At that moment, he hated Jouenne. Once again, someone wanted to determine his fate. He thought again of the saddlebag, as well. Jouenne had stolen it. "Yes," he heard himself saying, "I will marry her." Then he added in a hushed tone, "After the birth I shall move to Paris with Joséphine and the child."

Jouenne laid the ax down on the ground. He was visibly annoyed. "It is good that you will marry her, but it is not good that you will leave the farm. What will you do in Paris? Starve? Steal? Paris is a cesspool of filth and garbage. At night, the narrow lanes are dangerous, men have no work, too little bread, and they are starving. Stay here. You can be my successor, and one day your son will be your successor."

"I want to spare my successors this curse. I want them to be free. The life of an outcast is not for everyone."

"Don't come to any hasty conclusions, chevalier, but think about it. After a few nights, perhaps you will change your mind. Hangmen are well paid, and here in the country you can always find a few potatoes. You won't need them, however, because you are the hangman. Here the law allows us the *havage*: in the town market you can take as much fruit, vegetables, meat and fish as you can carry in your two arms. Even eggs. Everything is free."

"I know. Have you not forgotten that I come from a hangman's dynasty? And have you forgotten that I've spent my life up to now trying to escape this fate?"

"Chevalier," said Jouenne in an unexpected, fatherly tone, "I can teach you everything you need to know about herbal medicine. We wouldn't just perform executions, we'd even plant potatoes."

"I thought those existed only in the New World."

"No," Jouenne said, laughing. "They've even started planting potatoes in Burgundy now. I have some in my garden. They have an excellent taste, and their skins relieve burns." His expression became soft and gentle. He wanted so much for Jean-Baptiste to remain and hoped they could together be a family. "Chevalier, don't forget what I told you then in the chapel. You can see your fate, but you cannot escape it. That is the curse. If you resist, it will ruin you."

"No, no," Jean-Baptiste insisted, "when a man perceives his fate, he can escape it. Man is free, Master Jouenne."

"Man was never free," Jouenne said in an ominous voice. "All his life man does things without understanding why he does them. He is like a beast tracking a scent and can't stop following it."

In February, 1739 the birth pangs began and Jouenne asked Jean-Baptiste to ride to town and bring the midwife.

"I thought the hangman could do that, too," Jean-Baptiste said, astonished.

"I lack practice," Jouenne replied. "If she were just any woman, I'd do it, but not with Joséphine. She needs the best midwife in town."

Jean-Baptiste rode to the neighboring town where they carried out the sentences in the Place du Puits-Salé. The scaffold had been taken down, as usual, a few days after the last execution, and the square was teeming with a meagre selection of fruit and vegetables. A number of men were loafing about the square, most of them drunk. They had received their pay early that morning and being discharged honorably from the army. The men belonged to the regiment of Marquis de La Boissière who had finally disbanded the regiment. Jean-Baptiste tried to comprehend. He was free! He didn't have to return to the accursed farm. He could decide. Free!

The best midwife in the town was named Monique, who lived with her considerably older brother in a new half-timbered building like the ones the settlers from the New World had built after their return home to France. The supporting beams were exposed and stained brown or black. The space between the beams was filled with clay or bricks. In contrast with the German half-timbered houses with almost geometrically aligned beams, the beams in the houses here seemed in disorder and chaotic, as if their builders had been permanently drunk.

Jean-Baptiste knocked on the door. He couldn't understand how a midwife could afford a house like this. A maid opened the door.

"I'm seeking midwife Monique. Does she live here?"

"Yes, she lives here with her brother, the doctor."

He was led into the roomy parlor, where a stooped, elderly gentleman was sitting in a wooden chair with wheels

on its legs. A complicated mechanism allowed him to move around independently.

Jean-Baptiste bowed slightly. "Good day. I'm looking for a midwife for Master Jouenne's maid."

"Master Jouenne," the old man replied with a grin, "is still living in the cursed farm?"

Jean-Baptiste nodded.

"Since when does he have a maid?" said a shrill female voice behind him. Jean-Baptiste turned around. In front of him stood a corpulent woman: Monique. She was so fat that she had trouble breathing when she spoke. "What's the woman's name?"

"Joséphine."

The old man began to laugh, but the laughter soon turned to a coughing fit.

"Please hurry," Jean-Baptiste cried. "Her birth pains have already started."

"So our Joséphine is pregnant." Monique laughed. "And who is the father?"

"I am." Jean-Baptiste was gradually getting impatient.

"I brought little Joséphine into the world myself." The old doctor shook his head cheerfully and beckoned to his sister. "Bring me some absinth, and one for the young man as well."

"Will you come now, or won't you?" Jean-Baptiste persisted.

"I won't help give birth to any hangman," said Monique.

"Indeed, sister. If you assist in the birth of a hangman's daughter, no one will ever enter this house again. So drink your absinth and leave." The maid brought two glasses.

"Are you suggesting that Joséphine is the daughter of Master Jouenne?"

"Suggest? Wasn't it clear enough? That sly old fox has been waiting for years for someone to come and impregnate his daughter. I know the Jouennes. All the women in that family become pregnant the first time they lie with a man. As

if nature knew that their kind had only one chance. And the men, yes, the men in that family all become hangmen. You will have to take over from him, Monsieur, and after you, your son. Such is the custom among the men you live among."

"You are mistaken, Monsieur!"

"No," said the old doctor, raising his empty glass for it to be filled again. "Just as I can look into someone's eyes and know he has jaundice, I can see in your eyes all the blood you have witnessed. No, young man, no one will leave this house in order to bring a hangman into this world."

Jean-Baptiste pushed Monique aside and fled into the yard, where he quickly mounted his horse.

On his way back, he rode past a group of former soldiers and heard someone call his name. Some wanted to follow him, but they were too drunk. They shouted in raucous voices and Jean-Baptiste hoped they would soon forget him. He rode as fast as he could back to the accursed farm, and as soon as he entered the yard he could hear the pitiful cries. He raced into house to Joséphine's bed. She was sleeping and her head was bathed in sweat. At the foot of the bed were some bloody sheets and wooden tub full of water. Master Jouenne was sitting on a chair, holding a little bundle in his arms. "I have a grandson," he whispered.

"I know, Master," said Jean-Baptiste. He wanted to take his son in his arms, but Jouenne turned away and continued holding the newborn child. "I have a grandson," he mumbled. Jean-Baptiste was not at all pleased. He was, after all, the father and not some stud called to ensure the continuation of the old man's dynasty.

"I want my son now," he said sharply.

Jouenne looked at him questioningly He was surprised to hear the chevalier speak that way. With a stern face, he handed the infant to Jean-Baptiste.

Jean-Baptiste and Joséphine married a few days later. It was a quiet wedding, without guests.

Their life was harmonious and marked by mutual affection.

For Master Jouenne, all his dreams had been fulfilled. His daughter had found a husband and given him a grandson, Charles-Henri, or Charles for short. The continuation of the dynasty was assured. Jouenne knew that his son-in-law had imagined his fate differently, but he believed men were not on the earth to be happy and realize their dreams. No, life consisted of pain and anguish, and happiness came in finding and fulfilling one's place in it.

"I want to take a ride with Charles and show him the river," said Jean-Baptiste as he entered Jouenne's pharmacy. Little Charles sat on the floor playing with some wooden toy animals that his grandfather had carved for him.

"Leave the boy here," said Jouenne, without turning around. "He's playing now."

"I want to take a ride with my son," Jean-Baptiste repeated.

Jouenne turned around slowly and shook his head.

"What is the trouble with you? The boy likes it here and doesn't want to go for a ride now."

"Must I ask you for permission to take my son for a ride?"

"Don't be so sensitive," said Jouenne, turning back to his work.

Jean-Baptiste picked the boy up. "He is my son," he said, "and so that it stays that way we will be leaving for Paris."

"He is a Jouenne," the old man shouted at him, "he is my own flesh and blood."

"He is a Sanson," Jean-Baptiste countered, "in him flows both my blood and the blood of Joséphine, and we will all

three go to Paris. Perhaps then I will finally gain back the contents of my saddlebag."

For a long time after that, neither spoke to the other. Joséphine tried to smooth things out between them, and after a few weeks persuaded both men to spend an evening playing cards, just as in former times. The mood was gloomy, and they didn't speak to one another. Shortly before bedtime, Joséphine poured some wine for them.

"I know," Jouenne grumbled after a while, "he is your son, but he is also my grandson."

Joséphine looked anxious and observed the two men with increasing nervousness. "What's the matter with you two?" she asked.

"We shall move to Paris," Jean-Baptiste replied.

Jouenne was appalled and raised his eyebrows. He hadn't reckoned with that. Like most people, he feared change. "I thought we'd discussed that and the matter was settled. If you go to Paris, you choose poverty. "What are you looking for in Paris?" he asked, visibly angered. "In Paris you can become a hangman, chevalier, but you can do that just as well here." By force of habit he still called his son-in-law chevalier.

"I want to make something of myself," Jean-Baptiste replied defiantly. A wood turner, merchant, a shoemaker— anything but a hangman."

Jouenne shook his head in disbelief. "I'm sorry to tell you, chevalier, but you have two left hands. You're a man fit for some dirty job. You must do what others can't. Any fool can sweep up animal feces in the streets of Paris, and the competition is greatest among those fools. There is much you can still learn, either in anatomy or botany, but first you'll have to stay here awhile. I won't live forever, chevalier. Then you can go to Paris," he concluded in a conciliatory tone, looking over at little Charles who was playing on the ground with his wooden soldiers. But the thought that his son-in-law might not give up almost drove him crazy. He would never

again be able to carve little animals for his grandson. "No, no," he said loudly, "you'll stay here and get used to this life."

Jean-Baptiste was visibly angered. He didn't want to be put off, to wait possibly to the end of his days.

"Do you seriously believe people in Paris will want to buy bread or wine from a hangman from the provinces?" Jouenne argued.

"I think he's right," Joséphine said cautiously. "You won't find work that pays better than the office of hangman, Jean-Baptiste. What will become of our little Charles? You must become a hangman, if only for your son's sake."

"But not here," Jean-Baptiste persisted. He knew for certain that Jouenne would never move to Paris. "If we don't go now, my longing will die down. I cannot live my life forever according to the wishes of other people. I didn't flee to the New World back then just to do that."

Jouenne threw his cards on the table and drank his cup in one long gulp, then reached for the jug and left the kitchen.

Jean-Baptiste wanted to go to Paris whatever the cost. He couldn't shake off the dream, it kept him awake at night. He stared wide-eyed into the darkness. His desire was insatiable.

Since that evening, things had become quieter in the haunted house. Jouenne tried hard to teach his son-in-law all about modern medical knowledge. It was the sacrifice he had to make so that his grandson could spend the time in the pharmacy. He introduced Jean-Baptiste to the secrets of herbal medicine. But in reality he was teaching little Charles, who had an insatiable thirst for knowledge and no end of questions. The child had a huge fascination for herbs and their effects. Soon he knew all healing herbs by name, and exactly when and where to pick them. Jean-Baptiste had no objection, but he envied his father-in-law's knowledge. He soon felt redundant in the pharmacy and only an excuse for

Jouenne and Charles to be together. Charles loved his grandfather. Since there were no playmates his age in the region, he was happy to spend most of his time in the pharmacy crushing all the herbs, spices, leaves, stalks, flowers, bark, and roots that his grandfather gave him. Charles had a good memory He remembered the fragrances, colors, consistency, and most importantly the proper dosages. His grandfather preached to him at every opportunity that all mixtures can heal, or kill. It depends completely on the dosage.

Grandfather Jouenne also taught him very early how to read and write, and showed him books on botany and pharmacy, in particular two great works with magnificent illustrations. Charles looked at the two books every day, and could talk about them with his mother for hours. Proudly and almost reverently she listened to her son's words, and did not reveal to him that it was all something she already knew. It was a peaceful tune during which Jouenne and Jean-Baptiste did not often have to visit the Place du Puits Salé, but it was unfulfilling for Jean-Baptiste. His desire to move to Paris remained constant, his longing strong and demanding. Sometimes he tried to speak with Joséphine about Paris, and then she would embrace him each time and smile at him with great affection. "We are well-off here, we lack nothing." In such moments, his love for Joséphine and unconditional concern for Charles were more important that Paris. He could understand that even as a married woman Joséphine wanted to obey her father, even if he had not ordered her to. His love for her was far too great to do anything that would make her sad. In a certain sense he was completely devoted to her. So he continued donning the black helmet and awaited Jouenne's death. At the same time, he realized he too was getting older, and at times even wished that Jouenne would

die. He wanted finally to become the father of Charles and have Joséphine for himself. But the old man would not die.

It was Joséphine who died, quite unexpectedly during the summer of 1744, shortly after little Charles's fifth birthday. Even Master Jouenne did not know what she died of. Perhaps even God didn't know. She seemed to have just peacefully gone to sleep. Jouenne thought that she perhaps had suffered some internal bleeding. Sometimes an artery could burst in the head, or in the heart. That happened frequently in his family. They would become tired, fall asleep, lose consciousness, and never wake up again.

Joséphine found her final resting place behind the chapel. Charles didn't say a single word, but tears flowed down his cheeks. He took Jean-Baptiste's hand firmly, as if trying to make sure his father wasn't also called back by the Dear Lord, and Jean-Baptiste was surprised that his little Charles still called the dear Lord the Dear Lord. Only the postman appeared for the burial—not out of sympathy, but because he had a letter for Jouenne. Jouenne stuck it inside his vest pocket without reading it. He wanted to drink wine, in the morning, at noon, at night, and all night long. Master Jouenne fetched his best wines from the cellar, and for days neither he nor Jean-Baptiste was really sober. Charles sat on the sofa leafing through his grandfather's valuable books on plants. Sometimes he looked up briefly, saw that the men were still drinking, and went back to reading his book.

One morning, Master Jouenne staggered across the courtyard and took two horses from the barn, hitched them to a wagon, and returned to the kitchen. Jean-Baptiste had fallen asleep at the table. When Jouenne took a seat, the jug of wine tipped over, and Jean-Baptiste jumped up with a start. His head was pounding, he knew something had happened, and then he remembered that Joséphine had died. Jouenne pulled the letter from his pocket and pushed it across the table to his

son-in-law. "Some time ago I wrote the court of justice in Paris and applied for a position there if one becomes available.

Now the hangman of Paris has died."

Jean-Baptiste read the letter carefully. He was speechless.

"It was supposed to be a surprise," Jouenne murmured, "I thought it would make you happy if we could all travel to Paris together. I did it for you."

"The Royal Committee of the Parisian Court of Law has appointed you as the new hangman?"

"Yes, and it has called you along with me. Grasp the hand that fate has offered you, and don't delay."

For Jean-Baptiste that all came quite unexpectedly.

"On the twenty-third of September you must be in Paris. Don't delay! September is wet and cold, and the roads are muddy."

Jean-Baptiste poured another cup of wine and asked, "Well?"

"I'm in the autumn of my life, and can feel how winter is approaching. But be glad, and don't worry about that. You will receive ten thousand pounds, the three-fold of what I make here."

Jean-Baptiste was silent. It took his breath away.

"Think of your son. Rents are high in Paris, and you will need a maid." Little Charles sat down on Jouenne's knee and looked at him anxiously Jouenne put him back down again. "Now that you have decided to leave, you should do it quickly," he said, without looking at Jean-Baptiste. "The wagon is waiting in the courtyard and I have hitched up the horses. I will have no more need for them. And don't forget the books when you go. They're for Charles. He's a smart boy, so send him to school when the time comes. Someday every curse comes to an end, and I don't think he will follow in your footsteps. Give him what you lacked." Jouenne took the bottle of wine and left the kitchen. Then he turned around

and stuck his head in the door again. "Your gold coins are on Joséphine's night table, and the saddlebag is in the barn. Now you can tell me how you got this gold. Was it stolen?"

"No, I took it from a dead officer on the battlefield in Terre Rouge, in the New World."

"A grave robber," Jouenne said disdainfully.

"A burial shroud has no pockets," said Jean-Baptiste. "I'll use the money for Charles's education."

Jouenne turned away, crossed the yard and disappeared behind the barn. Jean-Baptiste remained in the kitchen with Charles, warmed up the potatoes left over from the day before and fried them with fresh garlic, onions, basil and cheese. Master Jouenne did not return so Jean-Baptiste went to look for him. They would have one more meal together.

He crossed the courtyard, where Jouenne had already laid a horse blanket over the wagon bed along with some other things, including his pharmaceutical reference books neatly tied together. First there was a smell of something burning. Jean-Baptiste thought of the potatoes, but then he remembered having taken the casserole off the fire. Then he saw clouds of smoke behind the barn and Charles came running out of the house crying that there was a fire somewhere. Together, they ran behind the barn and saw that the smoke was coming from the chapel. Over the entrance there was a crossbeam with an inscription, and dangling from a rope was Master Jouenne.

"It's the curse," murmured Jean-Baptiste, taking Charles in his arms. "I hope someday you will have only girls, just not a son. The curse must have an end."

"And I? Must I also become a hangman?"

"When the time comes, you will know."

CHAPTER 2

Jean-Baptiste Sanson travelled to Paris with his grandson. He'd already packed the most useful tools belonging to Master Jouenne and loaded them onto the wagon along with all the medications, the valuable books, and a huge pile of clothing stained by blood that could no longer be washed out. Someday the spots would no longer be visible, Jean-Baptiste mused as he drove the horses on, because everything would be red with blood. He no longer noticed the blood that spurted out from his victims' body when he severed the head from the torso with his sword. In Jouenne's cellar he found a few small kegs of apple brandy, which he also had loaded onto the wagon. He'd need the brandy. Ever since leaving the accursed farm with Charles, he was plagued with gloomy thoughts. Did this curse exist, or not? If he believed in God, Jouenne had said, he'd have to believe in curses as well, and if the curse was a creation of God, it was almost blasphemous to fight against it. He actually doubted that everything that happened on earth was derived from a cleverly conceived divine plan, but he dared not to dig deeper into the matter, fearing retaliation if he did. Silently, they continued on through the forest. A few times, Charles said in a quiet voice, "That's a chestnut tree" or "That's an acacia," and then looked up at his father and waited for him to nod. His grandfather had taught them all those things. Charles knew the beech trees—the white and the red ones, he knew the maple, the mountain ash, the Norway maple and the sycamore, the yew and the oak. They were all beginning to

shed their leaves, covering the forest floor with a -brownish yellow layer of leaves as if trying to protect the trail from the frost of the approaching winter. They stopped briefly because Charles had to relieve himself. He wandered around dreamily and bent down to pick up something he spotted in the leaves. "A worm," Charles said, showing it to his father. "I've never seen such a big one."

Jean-Baptiste smiled wearily and gave Charles a sign to get back on the wagon. "Let the worm go about its own business. Along with the mite and woodlouse it works the leaves and turns them into humus. Everything has its purpose."

Charles nodded and climbed back into the wagon. As they came out of the forest, he asked his father why he wanted to become a hangman in Paris. He never had wanted to be a hangman, after all. Jean-Baptiste looked at his son, wondering, and finally back over the heads of the horses trotting in front of them. "I don't want to, Charles, but I must. I have no other choice."

"But you can do something else. No one is watching you, no one will know."

"You're greatly mistaken," Jean-Baptiste replied bitterly. "Does a river have a choice? It flows in its river bead. Sometimes it overflows its banks, but it cannot change its course and ends up in the great ocean."

They rode along beside the apple farms in the direction of Paris. Now and then, Jean-Baptiste told about his younger years and the New World, but Charles remained silent. Jean-Baptiste was certain, however, that his son was listening attentively and that his voice comforted him.

Suddenly, Jean-Baptiste said "I'm becoming a hangman so you will never have to become one. I love you, Charles. You are more important than my own life, and I will do anything to make sure you have a better life. In a few years, if you still want to be a doctor, then you will be one."

In the distance they saw two men standing at the side of the road, and instinctively Jean-Baptiste placed his hand on the hilt of his sword. When the wagon had caught up with the two strangers, they asked if they could ride along with them in the wagon. They were laborers going to Paris to search for work there. They were shabbily dressed and their bodies emaciated from hunger, but as soon as they had climbed onto the wagon and seen the hangman's tools, they jumped back down in horror. "He's a hangman," shouted one of them. "Why didn't he tell us who he was?" the other cried angrily. Jean-Baptists drove on, undeterred, as a few stones flew over his head. "You see," he told Charles, "you do your duty and people despise you for it. We will live in disgrace."

His son looked up at him and took him by the arm.

"Once I have become a doctor, Father, you will no longer need to work. I will find a potion that would have cured Mother and made her proud of me."

"Plans are good, Charles, they give you a goal, a direction to follow, but when men make plans, God laughs, all of Heaven laughs, because up there we are scorned."

Charles nodded, though he couldn't really understand the melancholy that had come over his father. He wrapped his father's arm around his neck and pressed his hand on his father's chest. "Promise me you will never leave me."

"I promise you, Charles, as God is my witness."

Two days later, in the morning, they drove through one of the many city gates of Paris and waited for a customs officer in the yard of the tax building. Jean-Baptiste showed them his pass from the court of justice and they were waved through. Some farmers made use of the very early morning hours to drive their cattle to market, as this became almost impossible after daybreak. Jean-Baptiste stopped to ask for directions and realized with mixed feelings that he was being directed farther and farther into the worst part of town. "You are

"Can I see the shed?" Jean-Baptiste asked.

"Just don't ask me what the old hangman stored there. I just don't know, though sometimes it stank terribly." With a discreet glance at Charles, Jeanne indicated that what they would see in the shed was not suitable for children's eyes. She placed her hand in front of Charles's face and stepped back with him. "We'll wait outside."

When Jean-Baptiste entered, a dreadful stench came wafting toward him— the sweet, penetrating odor of decomposing bodies. Beneath the open window was a bed with a decapitated body lying on it. The head was place between the knees. Evidently his predecessor had the same passion as Master Jouenne, Jean-Baptiste thought, and had dissected the men he hanged before taking the body to the cemetery for burial the next day. Jean-Baptiste approached the corpse. It was always strange to see a body without a head. It was unnatural, but nothing could shock him anymore. He knew that fate had no pity. He had seen how men died, in the New World and in the Old World, and they didn't die differently from dogs or birds. He had witnessed immeasurable suffering, and hardly anything could move him anymore. Only little Charles could now and then bring a smile to his face. He loved his son, in whose eyes Joséphine lived on. He felt closest to her when Charles snuggled up to him.

"I would be glad to take care of you two," said Jeanne when Jean-Baptiste came back into the courtyard. "Your predecessor was very happy with me. He liked my cooking, and after an execution he would wolf down everything he could, like an animal. He was so fat that the undertaker had to order a larger coffin."

Jean-Baptiste nodded "Yes" he said, as if to himself, "Charles will need someone. He's become withdrawn, retreating into another world that is beyond me, and that I can't understand. It's frightening and dark."

"I have some eggs, ham, and vegetables," said Jeanne. Jean-Baptiste looked at her gratefully. There was warmth and tenderness in her voice, and when she was silent, her expression seemed even gentler and softer, and one couldn't help but think how wonderful her embrace would be.

The new household proved to be extremely harmonious and peaceful, but little Charles was not able to escape the dark prison of his soul. He could speak as well as most boys his age, but he remained silent. He simply had nothing to say, though from time to time he had to take his father by the arm. Most of all he liked spending his time in the pharmacy in the courtyard where everything was just the same as Jean-Baptiste's predecessor had left it. Charles loved the smell of the pharmacy, the aroma of the healing herbs, and the smell of the dusty old books.

In the meanwhile, Jean-Baptiste went about his work and carried out sentences with the assistants he had inherited from his predecessor. He was highly praised by the justice officials. In the evening he enjoyed sitting in the kitchen watching Jeanne cook. But he usually didn't stay long, as her kindness made him think of his beloved Joséphine and how much he missed her. Just the same, he had increasing trouble remembering how she looked, and her image faded, like a yellowed piece of paper. He had started to forget, and that grieved him deeply. It was like a betrayal of his great love, but time was stronger. His memories floated past like clouds in the sky, dissolved, and rarely returned. Only in his dreams was he still able to see her face, hear her voice, and in this secret world he kissed her and they made love again. But Paris displaced the memories of Normandy. In his thoughts he was often with his corpses, which assumed in his mind the proportions of gigantic machines that one could take apart piece by piece and understand. He never spoke with Jeanne

about the corpses, and she didn't even know he was dissecting them.

When she asked him one day if he wanted more cabbage soup, he answered he would marry her if she wanted. He considered marriage a practical idea, as Jeanne then wouldn't leave her position. "Only if you want, of course," he added.

"But Monsieur Sanson," she added with feigned indignation, beaming from ear to ear, "you never even kissed me, and you want to marry me?"

He looked up from his plate and stared into space. "Must I kiss you in order to marry you?"

"Yes," she said with great determination and smiled.

He pushed his chair back from the table, slowly walked toward her, took her in his arms and held her tight.

Jeanne squeezed him as hard as she could and closed her eyes. "Now you must kiss me, Monsieur Sanson," she said softly. When he didn't react, she pulled away and looked at him suspiciously. "Are you crying?" she asked in a soft voice.

"No," he whispered in a flat tone, "I'm not crying. The human body consists not just of skin and bones, but also water, and sometimes it loses its water. It's nothing but water, Jeanne. It washes out the old so the new can begin."

"So do you love me, Monsieur?" she asked.

"I will care for you, Jeanne."

For the young woman that was worth more than a declaration of love. Every maid in Paris wished for a husband who would provide financial security. That was much more important than love. Love was not out of the question, but it was no prerequisite for a good life-long marriage. Age differences didn't matter. Older men were calmer and more reliable, and didn't run after every woman they saw. And they weren't as violent in bed.

After a discussion with her mother, Jeanne married Jean-Baptiste in the church of Notre Dame de Bonne Nouvelle.

The mother was ecstatic. Finally, her daughter had found stability and she wouldn't have to worry who would care for her someday.

Charles was not at all happy about this marriage. He didn't begrudge his troubled father the new woman at his side, but he felt he was losing the last thing he had to hold onto in life. He didn't want to share his father with anyone, not even with Jeanne, whom he had come to love when she was still a maid. His relationship with her became noticeably worse. She tried to be a good stepmother, but Charles rejected her. Until then, he and his father had had a maid, and now the maid was number two in the house. If she asked him something, he didn't respond, and if she persisted he told her to her face she wasn't his mother. This enraged her so much that she wanted even more to make clear to the boy that she was in charge here. What angered her even more, however, was her husband's ambivalent attitude. She wanted Jean-Baptiste to reprimand the fresh boy now and then so he understood who was in charge here in the Sanson house.

One day, Jeanne expressed the wish to move to another house—one in which the blood of beheaded men didn't drip down between the wooden planks of the scaffold into the living room. She no longer wanted to live in the Hangman's Hotel, but in a good, middle-class house in a good, middle-class neighborhood, like other decent people. And she made Jean-Baptiste promise to buy a piano.

He yielded to her wishes and rented out the Hangman's Hotel for an unbelievable amount of five hundred ninety pounds, more than a laborer could earn in a year. Then he bought a house in the Rue d'Enfer, a stately home with a garden. With that, Charles lost the last of his roots. In the new house he had the feeling he could no longer breathe. It wasn't a home for him. There was no pharmacy, his

grandfather's books were up in the attic and no herbs grew in the garden—only berries and vegetables.

He had lost significance in any case through the birth of three half-sisters. Now the center of everyone's attention were the cute little girls who kept him awake at night with their crying. The Sanson family was now father Sanson, stepmother Jeanne, and their children together.

He, on the other hand, felt like the offspring of a past time, a forgotten love, a stranger whose past nobody wanted to think about. He hated this house, he hated this life, he yearned for his grandfather, Master Jouenne to return and put things back in order.

But his grandfather did not return. Instead, there was an insistent pounding on the door one day just as they were having supper. It was still light outside. Jeanne opened the door, and before her stood a resolute older lady who pushed the astonished wife aside and entered the house.

"Where is my boy?" she cried in a rough voice.

Jeanne closed the front door and followed the stranger, who was already standing in the kitchen.

"I knew I'd find you one day!" she shouted, planting herself in front of Jean-Baptiste, who eyed her in shock. She sat down at the table and reached for the wine glass at his place. She drank it in one gulp and briefly looked up at the three little children who were playing on the kitchen floor and had smeared marmalade all over each other's faces. "Are they yours?"

Jean-Baptiste nodded and stared in embarrassment at Jeanne who appeared startled and had sat down at her place again.

"Are you hungry, Madame?" Jeanne asked politely.

"Yes, hurry up and get me something to eat." Then she turned back to Jean-Baptiste. "Do you have any idea all the worry you caused me back then? Hm? And why? Because you didn't want to become a hangman! And look what has

become of you— a God-damned hangman! You could have spared yourself the whole odyssey, and all the grief you caused me. Was life any better for you in the army? In the New World you slaughtered the Indians by the dozens, something your father never got over. I had to promise him on his deathbed that I'd find you, in order to continue the family heritage. He said I should tell you that you cannot escape the curse. It is the original sin of the Sansons."

Jeanne served the woman a plate of soup and sat back down at her place. "Are you his mother?" she asked timidly.

"And he never told you about me? That sounds just like him." She cast a withering glace at her son as she continued to shovel in her vegetable soup. Briefly, she looked up and demanded bread and more wine, and then she noticed Charles standing in the doorway. "Who is that?"

"He's my son Charles. His mother died. She was the daughter of Master Jouenne . . ."

"Ah, the huge man from Normandy. You'll see, the little one will also be huge. I can see that by his wrists. Come here, boy." Charles approached hesitantly. She took him by the wrist and murmured "Indeed, he'll become a giant." Then she looked Charles in the eye. "I am your grandmother. Don't you want to give me a kiss?" Charles didn't budge. She shrugged slightly and continued eating.

"When your father died, I married again, the hangman Dubut. He drank like a fish, insisting that no one could engage in this vocation when sober. He, too, had lost his wife. He was a tender man looking for a firm hand. One ice-cold winter day he slipped on the wooden Saint Louis Bridge and fell into the river. When they fished him out and laid him out in the Bear Inn, he looked like an icicle. I told them they didn't have to thaw him out but could put him in the ground right away. Since then, I'm fed up with men. When they are young, they are quite entertaining, but later they become annoying, and when they get old and don't work anymore,

they just stand around like imbeciles trying to tell you how to manage a household, while they themselves don't even know how to cook an egg." She glanced up at Jeanne. "Give me more to eat. I've had a long trip. Do you even know how to cook?"

Jeanne nodded and poured her some more soup. "You have good child-bearing hips, girl and will give me many more grandchildren. You'll need help."

Jean-Baptiste, Jeanne and Charles were shocked. Grandmother Dubut was offering her help, but it sounded like a threat. She realized that none of them was pleased by her arrival, but it didn't matter to her.

"Mother," Jean-Baptiste began in a soft but very determined voice, "I am no longer your little boy. I served over there in the war as an officer and commanded a battalion, so don't tell me what to do."

"Yes, yes, but even if you were a general, you're still my child, and I'll tell you something. I'm not one of those old women who crawl silently into a corner and are a drain on the family. You need someone here who has experience and can help you out."

From that day on, Grandmother Dubut managed the Sanson's house. Despite her advanced age, she was a bundle of energy and treated her fellow men like prisoners on her imaginary galley that had to be driven by the beating of her imaginary drum. Grandmother Dubut had descended on Paris like an enemy cavalry. She was here how, and here she would remain. Strangely, Jean-Baptiste couldn't stand up to the old woman. His respect and obedience toward his family were too firmly ingrained. The family was sacrosanct, like God and His archangels. One could not rebel against them. Charles felt something approaching sympathy for his stepmother Jeanne, who never had a say in decision-making anymore. Her role once again was that of a maid, a woman to

make babies. The new general in the house had demoted her to that position.

Jeanne died after the birth of the seventh child, as if trying to escape the rule of grandmother Dubut. Now, finally, Charles wanted to leave this dreadful house. He gradually understood what kind of family he had been born into. All of them hangmen— a dreadful family. One by one he got to know them all, the aunts and uncles and all his cousins. Grandmother Dubut summoned them all to come to Paris, and together they applied pressure to Charles and glorified the office of hangman. They considered it an affront to the family that Charles wanted to become a doctor. Charles hated them all. He hadn't chosen this family, but it was all he had, he mused. Without a family he was like a deserter in the New World who had gone off to the forests in the far north or somewhere along the shore of Hudson Bay to hide in a wigwam, alone among savage tribes with strange customs. Completely on his own. The family, on the other hand, was like a fortress, but also a dark dungeon, and the only light that penetrated it was music, the melodies that he could coax out of his piano. His sister Dominique had opened up the world of music to him and taught him how to play the piano. They often sat side by side on a wooden bench, enticing tender, warm sounds from the instrument. Sometimes it appeared they could talk to one another through the piano keyboard. They told one another things they couldn't have expressed in words. Music became Charles's constant companion, and wherever he was he could always hear the beautiful melodies and feel close to his favorite sister Dominique.

When the time had come, Charles asked his father to send him to a school to study medicine. Even though a private school was expensive, Jean-Baptiste consented at once,

because he hoped it would bring more peace and quiet to the house, but also because he had a bad conscience. If he was honest with himself, he had to confess he had paid too little attention to his son and consequently they had drifted apart since Joséphine's death.

Grandmother Dubut, however, was not at all in favor, she considered it a complete waste of money, but perhaps, too, she was afraid that someday Charles would return with a better education than she'd ever had. She had opinions about everything, but this knowledge was so shallow that she could have things her way only in resorting to hardness, pressure and terror. In general, she considered knowledge useless and would say that a tree in Jesus's time was still just a tree. What else was there to discover? For her, all that counted was physical work, discipline, and performance of one's duty. She castigated any expression of emotions as a weakness.

Jean-Baptiste got his way, and decided to send Charles to the monastery school in Rouen, founded in 1605 as the Collège de médecine. Here the doctors of the future received their education.

CHAPTER 3

Charles liked Rouen at once. It was a gateway to strange worlds, other continents, new knowledge. The padres were more easy-going than the angry men of God who shouted down at their impoverished and frightened parishioners from their pulpits in the churches of Paris. In Rouen, everyone listened, exchanged opinions, and valued the conversations even if their opinions differed. There was no place here for someone like Grandmother Dubut, Charles thought with relief every morning. He slept with sixty other pupils in a large room and was awakened early in the morning by a bell. The students had to go silently to the courtyard where they washed themselves in the fountain, then gathered in the chapel for morning prayers, and finally went together to the dining hall. Everything was strictly regulated and every deviation was punished, but even the punishments were not angry confrontations, but friendly discussions that didn't disturb the rhythm of Charles's day. He wanted to learn, he wanted to know, he wanted to understand the human body.

And then there was something else in Rouen which immediately awakened Charles's passion. In the dining hall was a piano that the pupils were allowed to use after supper, though no one used it, and Charles didn't dare to. One evening, however, when everyone had finished supper and the priest had rung a bell as a sign that everyone could leave, Charles remained seated. He couldn't take his eyes off the piano. A slender boy sat down on the bench and began running his hands up and down he keys tenderly and

gracefully, but as soon as the room had emptied, the boy started playing louder and louder and stamping wildly on the pedals. Charles got up, walked over to him, and stood alongside, watching closely. The boy had seen Charles right away but seemed to enjoy the attention. Suddenly, without looking up, he cried out, "Come over and sit down. I know you can play. I'm Antoine."

Charles didn't have to be asked twice. Antoine slid down the bench to make room for Charles, then Charles began to play, too. Antoine grimaced, played more wildly and impulsively, and now both of them started playing away with great concentration and seriousness. Now and then they glanced at each other, laughed loudly and began playing faster and faster. It was wonderful.

"Where did you learn how to do that?" Antoine asked.

"My sister Dominique taught me everything."

"Does she have big tits?"

They continued playing for more than an hour until finally the gong sounded telling the students it was time to return to the dormitory. Antoine jumped up from the bench. "What's your name?"

"Charles."

"Do you have a last name?"

"Just Charles."

"Very well, Charles, let's play again tomorrow— or would you rather go over to the chapel and pray?"

"No, we can play."

"Fine," Antoine replied, grinning, "the dear Lord is no doubt sick of hearing our continual blabbering. By the way, I'm Antoine Quentin Fouquier de Tinville. What was your last name again?"

Charles was annoyed. He wasn't used to this sort of humor.

Music brought the two of them together, even though Antoine, in contrast to Charles, had little interest in anatomy

and pharmacy. What interested him were music, the money his parents sent him every month, and advertisement from a Paris printer's bringing news every month from the Paris Community Market— these were markets in which more than a hundred small vendors sold their goods under one roof, among them many useless things, but Antoine was fascinated by any useful new machine with a complicated mechanism. He could pour over them for hours, as he loved to hear himself talk and since he had taken a liking to Charles, who was a silent, patient listener, he didn't let his new friend out of his sight. The two were a strange duo. Charles was more than a head higher than any of his fellow pupils and stood out among the crowd of pupils like the Colossus of Rhodes. Despite his reticent manner, he had great physical strength and bearing that seemed to impress the rather short and slender Antoine. When he was with Charles he had the courage to mock his fellow students. That didn't escape Charles's notice, and it didn't please him. Just the same, he overlooked it, because in the evening they were together again at the piano. For a friendship it isn't absolutely necessary that both share all the same interests and opinions, he thought. One passion suffices, and with them it was music, the piano.

"I don't like it when you make fun of the poverty of some of your classmates," Charles said one evening after their piano playing.

"Oh," replied Antoine laughing, "I'm just joking."

"No one can help it if he's born poor. The parents of these pupils deserve great praise for making sacrifices so their sons can go to school."

"Doesn't that bring tears to your eyes," Antoine scoffed, feigning despair. "They'd be better off if they didn't send their sons to schools like this, because later they won't have enough money to buy a position. What has the school taught them except privation?"

"There's no merit in being born rich."

"There's certainly a difference whether my name is Antoine Quentin Fouquier de Tinville or Charles . . . what was your name again?"

"I'm the son of the chevalier Sanson de Longval" Charles replied, and immediately regretted having said it. "My father is a doctor," he lied, in addition.

"Sanson de Longval? Never heard of it." Antoine put on a face as if he'd just swallowed something bitter. "But your father never sends you money. Doesn't he have any, or does he spend it all on whores?"

"I have enough," said Charles. "I'm here to learn."

"Your heart seems to bleed for poor people, Charles. Is it because your family has no money? Only hunger, and your sister's big tits."

"We're a family of doctors. Our job is to relieve suffering, and we love people whether they are rich or poor."

"You're the only one I like here, Charles. I like your quiet manner. I talk a blue streak, and you listen to me, I offend you sometimes, and you stay silent. Sometimes I ask myself what I have to do to you to get you angry. Don't you ever blow up?"

Charles was silent.

"See what I mean? Nothing makes you angry. Sometimes I'm itching to punch you in the face just to see what you would do. But my arms are too short." Antoine laughed. "And I'm not a courageous person. I'm an anxious person, and though I have a big mouth, deep inside I'm crapping my pants. Can you understand that?"

Charles nodded.

Antoine patted him on the shoulder. "But don't tell anyone. I've just shared a secret with you."

Charles nodded again.

"Saturday evening I'm going to dine at the Golden Keg tavern. They have fresh game on the menu. Will you come along? As my guest?"

Charles hesitated.

"Please, Charles, I have plenty of money, but I need a friend." Antoine gave him another encouraging pat on the shoulder. "Antoine Quentin Fouquier de Tinville requests the honor of your presence at supper."

Charles couldn't suppress a smile.

From that time forward, Antoine regularly showered his friend with presents. He even bought Charles expensive medical books. "For my future private physician," he was accustomed to saying, and he would need one, as he always suffered from one or another ailment: shooting pain in the thigh, shortness of breath, bloated intestines, whistling in his ears, diffuse back pains, or simply nightmares. Charles had an answer to almost all his questions, and in this way Antoine became more and more dependent on him. Charles became engrossed in every organ, thanks to Antoine, and in this way Antoine's hypochondria, along with music, strengthened the bonds between the two very different young men. Soon Charles had assembled a whole library of books on the human body. Antoine pleaded with his mother for more money and gave it out generously, as if it was just worthless scrap paper. In school, all the money did him no good. He was a dreadful student, and without Charles's help he wouldn't have even lasted through the first year. He knew it, and sometimes it angered him so much that he felt the need to say nasty things to Charles. But Charles just took it all in stride, as he had never learned to fight back. Resistance was not in his repertory. He was accustomed to suffer his fate with all its daily adversities in silence. He concentrated on school and was a good pupil, but his achievements did not inspire Antoine, in whom jealousy festered like a malignant tumor.

"Medicine is not the right field for you," said Charles one day as the two were studying the circulation of the blood.

"I need to be honest with you, Antoine, you have too little love for your fellow men. You love only yourself, and that is not enough for a doctor."

"That really hurts," Antoine groaned, his face contorted in pain. "What should I do then?"

"I've been thinking about that," said Charles, as they were sitting one evening at the piano. "You must think about what you are really good at. What can you do that others can't, or can't do as well?"

"Talk, put words in other people's mouths, mock them. Do you think I should become an actor?" Antoine bore down on the keys and stomped on the pedals. "Suicide would also be a solution, or I could find a nice bordello in Paris and wait there until I get my inheritance. Mother wrote and told me recently that my old man is coughing up blood. She wanted me to talk with the doctor. Let her ask him herself how long our money will last."

"A lawyer!" Charles said suddenly, "you should become a lawyer. You could defend murderers as well as victims with the same meticulousness, because all you are interested in is winning, not justice."

Antoine smiled. "You have seen through me, big fellow, my weapon is the language, my brain, my memory. I enjoy humiliating men, especially in public, with a large audience. I crave prestige, I want to be important, I admit it, and I accept it. And so? Is that embarrassing? Who cares?"

"Do you never have the need for peace . . . for rest . . .?"

"Just don't say harmony. What a horrible word. I love arguments, conflicts, quarrels. The heat of battle is my life's blood, it spurs me on. Even more than a naked woman. Every play on words means more to me than a good friend. But tell me, can you really get that nasty disease in a bordello, I mean fungus and skin infections on your prick?"

"These sores appear three to four weeks after you visit a bordello, and they're painless."

"Then I feel better," said Antoine, breathing a sigh of relief. "Later I'll really need a private physician, Charles."

"Then your lymph nodes will swell up . . ."

"Oh, you mean that's just the beginning? Where the hell are the lymph nodes?"

"Then there will be rashes, and a colorless liquid will be excreted."

"But not through my penis, I hope? Just stop, this is all too disgusting."

"Then there will be symptoms like a bad cold, your hair falls out, and your body will be covered with welts. If the brain is affected, there is loss of ability to speak and think, and you revert to the level of a four-year-old. You can no longer control your bladder or your bowels, your optic nerve withers and dies, and your body becomes paralyzed."

"Just don't tell me I'll never get it up again."

"With that attitude, anything is possible."

"Very well then," he said, waving him off, "then I'll probably become a lawyer, Charles, and you a little country doctor. Or perhaps you won't quite make it and will become a veterinarian poking around in the anuses of starving cows, and you'll stink like shit all day." He slapped Charles on the shoulder and laughed loudly. It wasn't an especially friendly slap, but rather hard and aggressive, and his eyes sparkled maliciously. Charles sensed that another, dark soul was lurking in his heart.

Because of his excellent grades, Charles was allowed to go to Le Havre with Father Collin to buy new herbs. Along the way, the priest told him how the Vikings once attacked Rouen, and how Normandy fell to England, and showed him, as they made their way across the market square to the

western city gate, the place where Joan of Arc was burned at the stake in May 1431.

Merchant ships with huge sails lay at anchor in the harbor of Le Havre. They needed a heavy hull so they wouldn't tip. It was scarcely believable all the things that came out of the holds of these ships: people, wild animals in cages, exotic woods, colored fabrics, porcelain, expensive silk, statues, barrels and wooden crates with half-withered plants hanging out of them. Tea, coffee, herbs and herbal medicines were in great demand. These merchant ships belonged mostly to the French East India Company, which was established as a publicly traded corporation. Anyone could purchase stocks, and the holders of the shares participated in the earnings of the corporation. It was a very important company with rights guaranteed by the king to engage in overseas trade with Africa, Arabia, Madagascar, China, and the New World. The French crown had vested the merchant's corporation with enormous privileges. They had not just a monopoly in all conquered regions outside of France, but also the right to build their own warships and call up their own troops. They had their own judiciary and minted their own coins.

Charles looked at it all, wide-eyed. Behind the merchant ships, the company-owned warships that traveled with them lay at anchor equipped with canons, as the merchants had to fend off not just foreigners, but the competing Dutch and English who now and then would hoist the jolly roger on the open ocean, far from civilization, to rob and plunder the ships on behalf of their kings.

Charles and Father Collin strolled along the wharf where the ships were tied up, one after the other. They stopped in front of an imposing merchant ship with a huge coat of arms on the sails, the golden fleur- de-lis of the king on a blue background and the crown on top.

The words *"Florebo quocumque ferar"* appeared on one sail. "I flower wherever I am planted." The father laughed. "I

believe the merchants some day will be more powerful than the crown, as they are at home on all the oceans of the world."

"And the church?" Charles asked

"The church? It will have a hard time. Libraries will replace the faith, and when there are no more questions to answer, there will be no more need for a God. Religion is nothing but ignorance."

Black Africans were being led in chains down the quay. Charles had never seen people like that, and they aroused his curiosity and fear.

"Look at the people coming off the ships," said Father Collin. "Do you notice anything?"

"They have bad teeth. Some of them are bleeding from the mouth and have sores on their lips, and many are limping and have a peculiar gait."

"They're suffering from scurvy. If they have been traveling longer than three months and have had no fruits or vegetables, their body lacks something. The mucous membranes begin to bleed, and their teeth fall out. If someone can figure out someday a better way of preserving food, that will be a revolution in the history of mankind."

"That will prolong the wars, however. Many wars come to an end today due to lack of food."

The Father smiled. He liked Charles. He waved at someone standing at the railing of a gigantic merchant ship armed with fifty canons. It was modeled after the Dutch *fluit* and had an enormous carrying capacity. Ships like these were slow and had little chance in a fight with pirates in the Indian Ocean. For this reason, they were always accompanied by smaller, maneuverable warships. The stranger at the railing waved back and beckoned for them to come on board. He was wearing an orange, oriental-style wrap made of light material. Charles followed Father Collin as they pushed their way past dock workers, and boarded the ship.

"This is Father Gerbillon," Collin said. "He's returning from a visit to the Kingdom of Siam on behalf of our king. He's a Jesuit priest from Paris."

The two padres embraced warmly. Gerbillon was tanned and had a cheerful disposition. His movements were somewhat affected, as was considered good form at the Court of Versailles. In his cloak which reached down to his ankles, he looked something like a bird of paradise.

"This is Charles, my best pupil," said Father Collin, not without pride. Gerbillon looked at the tall boy approvingly, but with a strange smirk on his lips. It wasn't just the mischievous look in his eyes—it was more. Something conspiratorial, and it irritated Charles. He'd never before met a man like Gerbillon. Gerbillon was different.

"What have you brought us?" asked Collin. Gerbillon pointed toward the bow where a dozen youths dressed in long robes were standing, and beckoned to them. They came running toward Gerbillon, made a circle around Father Collin and Charles, placed their hands together over their chests and lowered their heads respectfully. "These are my little friends from the Kingdom of Siam," Gerbillon explained. "They will be studying in Paris at the Collège Louis-le-Grand. In return, young French children will be studying in Siam. The king desires this exchange program."

"Aren't they a bit young?" asked Collin.

"Looks are deceiving. They are all over sixteen, but they look like twelve-year-olds."

Charles looked at them, fascinated by their dark skin and long, black hair. They had delicate facial features and their lips were sensuous and full.

"Will you be returning to Siam?" Collin asked.

"Certainly," Gerbillon replied with a smile, "the weather is warm, Siamese cooking is a dream, and the King of Siam is an enthusiastic student. I've taught him everything I know about astronomy as we practice it here, but he wants to learn

more. He's delighted with the scientific instruments we brought him from Paris, and there's much work to do. First, we must prepare exact maps of the oceans, which will shorten the trade routes. And if it gives us an advantage over the Dutch and English, it will all have been worth it."

"And God?"

Gerbillon gestured coyly. "That will be a bit more difficult. God has a hard time competing with Buddha. They are one and the same, of course, but their Buddha is simply a more kindly figure. I think if we want to conquer Siam, we'll need to let them keep their religion. That's the way the Romans were, and they were successful. Buddha is not as prudish as our God," Gerbillon said with a laugh. "They have no inhibitions, they feel no shame when they make love."

"How do you know so much about that?"

"That's what I've been told." Gerbillon's air of innocence spoke volumes. Like many men who had lived for a long time in the colonies, he had largely given up the customs and conventions of his homeland and adopted the foreign culture.

Workers were carrying cages full of animals that looked like huge cats from the belly of the ship. Their fur had yellow and black stripes, and when one of them snarled, their terrifying jaws became visible full of huge teeth that could rip any other animal apart.

"These are tigers," said Gerbillon. "Supposedly, you can tame them, though I have never tried. I hope they will please our king. He wanted something bizarre for his zoo."

"Do you understand our language?" Charles asked one of the girls. She was the smallest of them all, yet she seemed to be their leader. She had a gorgeous face with fine cheek bones and a full mouth. Her eyes were as black as night and her piercing gaze seemed to cut Charles to the quick. She exuded warmth and affection, but it was clear that she was endued with toughness and a great deal of energy. The girl pointed at herself and said "*Lan Na Thai.*"

"This is our little Dan-Mali," Gerbillon declared not without pride, "and she is the smartest of them all. She has a memory like a library, and forgets nothing. She will learn our language quickly."

"What does *Lan Na Thai* mean?" Charles asked.

"Kingdom of a million rice fields— that's what the Siamese people call their language."

Charles smiled and nodded excitedly at Dan-Mali. He had understood. He couldn't stop looking at her. Her slightly protruding chin fascinated him. There was something about it that was animalistic, dangerous, and erotic.

"Have you brought us some cinnamon?" asked Collin, at the same time glaring at Charles to try to get his eyes off the Siamese girl.

"Not just that." Gerbillon smiled ambiguously. "For the first time I've brought back some turmeric, a plant used by the monks. They crush the yellow root into a powder that fights the black ulcers that grow like cauliflower in women's breasts. It is supposed to help also in curing other forms of putrescent ulcers. It grows wild in the mountains, but only those growing in the vicinity of teak trees are effective. Try some, and let me know next spring how it worked."

The young people went to get some boxes and baskets and returned to their places behind Father Gerbillon. "This is the bark of a laurel tree," he said, taking a piece of it from a basket and turning to Charles. "It's dry, and you can crush it into a powder."

"It promotes digestion," Father Collin said. "I tried it myself. You can also make it into a sauce that gives the food a very special taste. In Siam we spread it on meat before we grill it. The entire king's court is wild about it, and for that reason the price has already increased three-fold." Gerbillon laughed.

Charles nodded and furtively turned his head. He just had to look at Dan-Mali again. She fascinated him like no other

young woman ever had, and he returned her shy smile. Though she came from a culture completely foreign to him, he felt magically attracted to her. He sensed that she, too, had been uprooted and lonesome among men and yearned for peace and security.

Father Gerbillon turned back to Charles, for whom he'd seemed to take a liking. "When you are finished with your studies you must visit us in Paris," he said. "I'll show you all the herbs from the Kingdom of Siam."

"But don't be so fast," Collin joked, "or in the end he won't want to be a doctor any more, but a cook."

No, Charles still wanted to be a doctor for the sake of his mother. He could still keenly feel his helplessness on standing by her death bed, and somehow he imagined he could do some good belatedly by becoming a doctor. At the same time, he was quite aware that his mother was long dead and he could not undo anything. It was a completely illogical connection that he'd made in his mind, but Charles did not always act rationally. He was driven. He was haunted by aromas that reminded him of his mother. He had loved, for example, the smell when she tenderly pressed him against her soft breasts. It was no special aroma, but simply the aroma of his mother.

Charles pressed forward eagerly in his studies. His zeal never flagged, but he always feared something would intervene, that fate would strike and could end it all. No sooner had he found something he cared for, fear would creep over him, fear of losing something he loved. In time he began to fear the fear and distrust good news so much that he scarcely took any pleasure in it.

Once a month he had to go with Antoine Quentin Fouquier de Tinville to visit the hospitals and look for corpses. They were cheap and could be taken to the school in a pushcart. This job always fell to Charles and Antoine.

"You're right, Charles," said Antoine as they pushed the carts along over the bumpy pavement. "Medicine is probably not the right field for me. But try to tell that to my mother! She's told everyone I'm going to become a doctor, so I have no choice if I don't want to disappoint her. But she knows very well I'm so clumsy when it comes to practical things that I'd be a danger to my patients. When God made me, he concentrated on my brain and left me by accident with two left hands. I'm not going to criticize Him for that— the brain is superior to the hands. Even in a wheel chair you can command an army, which leads me to the next problem. I can't bear it when people tell me what to do. I could never be a soldier, or at best I could be a general."

"But you obey your mother," said Charles in his usual unemotional way.

"We all obey our mothers, and especially me, since when my old man returns to his Creator, I'll inherit his earthly goods. And then where I come from really matters. You know, Charles, you're an outstanding student, but you probably come from a very simple background," he said with a malicious grin. "Your father was perhaps the first in his family . . . oh, what am I saying, you certainly don't have a family bloodline . . . so he was the first to acquire a middle-class profession: doctor. In Paris, however, only your parentage and wealth count. How will you buy yourself a profession? Isn't it tragic—the best pupil in Rouen ends up in the gutter and I, a pampered, lazy scion of nobility . . ."

Charles stopped the cart. A corpse's arm had slipped from under the sheet and was dangling over the side. Antoine grabbed it and shoved it back under the sheet. They moved along.

"Even the corpses try to run away from me," Antoine said morosely. "I hope my words didn't depress you too much, Charles. The truth is sometimes bitter. You are the better pupil, but later I will have the better life."

"If I become a doctor," said Charles, "I'll be happy. I don't need to have a better life."

"Oh, how you amaze me, Charles. Man always yearns for something better, that's what separates us from animals. We never have enough, we're always hungry, and if someday you have enough money, you'll yearn for fame, recognition, and power. You'll want the world to set up monuments and name public squares after you."

"I don't want anyone to put up a monument to me," Charles mumbled. "Why?"

"Don't worry, that won't happen, but one thing I can promise you: someday when you knock on my door, sick and impoverished, I'll see that my servants give you a warm bowl of soup. I won't give you money because I'll never forgive you for being a better student than me." He laughed. "Actually, I wanted to make you my private physician, but I couldn't bear having to see every day the man who here in Rouen showed me how mediocre I am." Then he put a friendly arm around Charles's shoulder.

"You're my best friend, Charles. Without you, I'd never be able to stand it here. I'm mean sometimes, but I like you." Again he broke out laughing and watched two young women who had just walked past.

"Oh, the black-haired one really turns me on. What do you think, Charles, which one of us would the two women prefer, the rich Antoine or the good Samaritan Charles?"

"You have some visitors," said Charles in a soft voice.

Antoine recognized the seriousness in Charles's voice at once, and looked ahead of them. They had just turned into a narrow lane, and at the end stood three young men about their own age.

"Do you know them?" asked Charles, slackening his pace.

"Only fleetingly." Antoine couldn't conceal his nervousness. "I only know the fellow in the middle. I called

his sister a whore and told him he was the scum of creation. Do you think that was a mistake?"

"Why do you always have to insult people?"

"You'll help me, Charles, won't you? You know God gave me two left hands."

Now the three young men were standing in front of the cart, blocking their way. "We want an apology," said one of them.

"Get out of our way," said Antoine, "or my friend will lose his patience." He was afraid, and he looked up at Charles with pleading eyes.

"We're going to beat you so bad your friend will have to carry you away in his cart." The three charged at Antoine. Two of them grabbed him and the third punched him so hard he fell to the ground. Now Charles let go of the cart and ran to help Antoine. He knocked the first one to the ground, punched the second one in the face, and grabbed the third by the neck so hard that he fell to his knees, whimpering. As the first two ran off, Charles released his opponent. Antoine knelt on the ground staring at the blood on his hand.

"It's only your nose," said Charles.

"Only my nose!" shrieked Antoine. "Why did you take so long? They broke my nose."

"No," said Charles calmly, "your nose isn't broken, it's just bleeding a bit."

"A bit! Are you making fun of me? I could bleed to death here." Antoine stood up and hurried down the lane without looking back at Charles. From then on, Antoine was a different person. He was ashamed that Charles had been a witness to his fear and helplessness, and started to hate him for that.

The corpses were dissected in the room over the gymnasium. Some pupils turned away in horror during this presentation, but Charles saw nothing unnatural in these lifeless bodies.

All that interested him as the structure of the bluish, bloated bodies. He inspected them as if they were strange machines, moving the limbs back and forth like door hinges. The only things that interested Antoine, however, were the penis or the breasts of the corpses. He made snide remarks about these parts of the body and tried to entertain the other pupils. When Charles ignored him he just said with feigned regret in his voice that Charles had to study because his father was an actor and still facing ten more years in the Bastille.

Charles concentrated on his studies. As time went on, he became convinced that there had to be a way to understand the human body, and if one could understand it, if one could "read" the code, then one could heal it as well. This thought plagued him day and night. But he was possessed by another thought, as well— he had to see the young Siamese woman Dan-Mali again. He knew she was only sixteen, but time would pass, and in a few years he would have completed his study of medicine and have to return to Paris. She was always in his thoughts, firmly settled in his imaginary world. He didn't really know the mysterious Siamese woman and had never had a real conversation with her, but a single glance from her had sufficed to say she'd be waiting for him.

One morning they received the body of a vagabond who had collapsed right in front of the school. The Padres had decided to lay out the corpse inside so the pupils could observe the physical processes that take place immediately after death. At first, the vagrant seemed to be sleeping, but soon his cheeks became hollow and a deep triangle appeared around his nose. The blood had stopped circulating and the blood pressure fell. Dark blue spots formed around the corpse.

"Is that Charles's father?" Antoine exclaimed with a pretense of horror, "the Chevalier Sanson de Longval?" He looked at Charles. "I thought your father was a doctor."

"What's gotten into you this time?" a fellow student asked.

"What's wrong with that? You know everything about where I come from . . ."

"We hear it often enough," Charles grumbled.

"Yes, because I have nothing to hide. But Charles, your silence is the fertile ground for the wildest speculation. Nobody's ever heard of a doctor named . . . what's your old man's name again?"

"Do you expect me to be running around all day with my family tree in hand?"

"That would be hard to do, very hard, for you have none."

It wasn't a good day for Charles. Nervously he asserted his family tree could be traced back to the fifteenth century. "One of my ancestors was the cartographer Nicolas Sanson d'Abbeville. He published a number of atlases and instructed King Louis XIV in geography."

"Don't tell me that," Antoine interrupted sullenly.

"Of course not," Charles sneered. "You're unteachable, you have no education."

The other students laughed.

"I see," Antoine replied. "If you have neither money nor a noble background, you need education, of course. When I take my friends out on a hunt, no one wants to hear about geography. We talk about our estates, our mistresses, our intrigues, and all the fine food we stuff into ourselves every day. But if you have nothing, you draw maps and bore everyone around you with your worthless knowledge."

"Just a while ago you weren't talking so big," said Charles. "Sooner or later someone's going to come along and punch you in the mouth."

"Have you noticed? We've found a sore point: his ancestry. Who knows, maybe he's descended from apes living in caves that eat raw bear meat. Next weekend is

visitor's day. I'm curious if your father will come. Is your sister with the big tits coming, too?"

Jean-Baptiste Sanson came. It was the day the parents came to sit in on the classes and meet with the Padres to talk about their child's progress in school. First, the parents assembled in the courtyard and greeted their children, then two nuns from the neighboring convent came to serve bread and apple cider. Charles's father had come too, along with grandmother Dubut. It was clear he felt uncomfortable among the other parents, as he couldn't conceal his lower status. Charles watched as Antoine greeted his father, who seemed to be in a bad mood and whispered something to Antoine. Something was bothering him. Antoine's mother, on the other hand, seem relaxed and having a good time. She embraced her son several times and kissed him on the forehead, which made Antoine uncomfortable. He pulled away from her and went over to Charles, who was speaking with his father.

"This is my father," said Charles. Antoine bowed slightly and reached his hand out to Jean-Baptiste Sanson.

"I am an admirer of one of your ancestors," Antoine said, and Charles knew right away that the poison punchline would follow. "It's so sad he met with such a tragic end. First he was the map maker for the king and instructed Louis XIV in geography, only to be stabbed to death later in a side street in Paris."

Jean-Baptiste showed no emotion. He was not accustomed to this kind of humor, this irony with its suspect ambiguity.

"And you are a doctor," said Antoine, nodding with feigned appreciation.

Jean-Baptiste glanced at his son in annoyance. Grandmother Dubut grimaced nervously and said "Let's go inside. I'll certainly catch a cold outside here."

In the classroom, Father Collin was giving a talk about dirt pharmacies in the Middle Ages, and how they used to pulverize dried toads, moles, and the excrement of goats. He spoke as well about the first books on medicine which had appeared as early as the 16th century as guidebooks for the collection of herbs, and criticized the practice of bleeding, enemas, and forced regurgitation as well humoral pathology based not on successful treatments or empirical data but on the word of authority, He spoke of a new era that had already begun and the necessity of learning more about the proper dosing of medicinal plants. "Research today can change the world of tomorrow," the Father said in conclusion.

The parents in the audience nodded appreciatively and were proud that their church provided such superior instruction even if they themselves understood very little of it.

Antoine nudged Charles. "That was a very moving moment when I could greet your father. Tell me, does he have a lot of patients, I mean regular patients who keep returning to him?"

Charles looked at him in annoyance. He was trying to figure out the point of the question.

"What I mean is," whispered Antoine, trying to sound concerned, "when your father chops a patient's head off, it becomes very difficult to keep him as a regular patient. Or do they return sometimes holding their severed head under their arms?"

It took Charles's breath away. He wanted to strike back, but just let it wash over him.

"I thought it wouldn't hurt to further my education, so I looked around a bit in the library. And an uncle of mine, a lawyer in Paris, also looked around a bit for me. Why did you keep it from me, Charles? We're friends, after all."

Charles instinctively tried to catch his father's eye and then saw that Antoine's father was approaching, looking very

angry. He said something undistinguishable and then tapped the floor with his cane for attention. Now all eyes were turned toward him and the other parents started to whisper to one another, forming a circle around Father Collin.

"Father Collin," Antoine's father suddenly shouted, "I am the Marquis Fouquier de Tinville and would like to let everyone know that the man over there is the hangman of Paris!" he said, pointing at Charles's father. A loud murmur rippled through the classroom. The students cast sideways glances at each other and tried to get a look at the hangman. "Is it possible that the son of the hangman is a student in this school?" another visitor asked. Antoine tried to look remorseful and stunned, but then he grinned broadly at his friend's misfortune.

"Dear parents," Father declared in a loud voice, "please quiet down. We will try to clarify the matter." Then he turned to Jean-Baptiste Sanson and asked "Can you confirm that, monsieur?"

Charles's father was speechless.

"He is an official of the Justice Ministry," said Grandmother Dubut as loudly as she could, her voice cracking.

"Messieurs," cried out one of the fathers, taking a defiant stance in front of the blackboard, "I won't pay for my son to be educated with the hangman of Paris."

"Gentlemen," Father Collin pleaded, trying to placate them, "we are educating the son and not the father. The son is studying medicine and has no intention of working for the Department of Justice."

There were more and more outraged cries among the group that finally turned into a general uproar. The fathers protested most vehemently as Pater Collin made his way through the angry crowd of visitors toward Jean-Baptiste Sanson, whispered something in his ear and quickly exited the class room. Charles anxiously observed the scene, and

when his father beckoned to him and nodded toward the door, he picked up his things and left. The crowd fled in all directions as if he had the plague, cholera and smallpox all at the same time.

"Father Collin," Charles asked as he left, "can there be such a thing as a curse over a whole dynasty?"

"Noah cursed his grandson Canaan, the son of Ham, but it says in Genesis that God first cursed the serpent and then the ground. If you believe in God, you believe in curses."

"And if I no longer believe in God?"

"Then there are no curses, and you will become a seeker in the endless desert."

In the interior courtyard, Antoine waited, having left the classroom unnoticed. Charles walked past, without even glancing up at him.

"Do you see?" Antoine shouted, following just a few steps behind him, "Money is everything. Without a pedigree, you're nothing. Make sure that they at least give you a warm bowl of soup."

Charles stopped and stared menacingly at Antoine. "You have no one to protect you now."

Antoine laughed. "Who would do anything to me?"

"I would," Charles said. "Me, for example!" He slapped him hard on the cheek.

Antoine was astonished and stepped back, holding his reddened cheek. "You'll be sorry you did that," he said, then hurried back into the school building.

Silently, the Sansons set out on the long trip home to Paris. Charles was furious that the curse on his family was his undoing, all the more so because he wanted nothing to do with them. Jean-Baptiste sat dejectedly in the coach, staring out the window. The first snow had fallen in the fields and icy drafts blew through the cracks into the interior. The floor was ice cold. Jean-Baptiste deeply regretted what had

happened and was offended at being scorned in that way—along with his entire family.

Later, Grandmother Dubut said she was very proud of being the mother of the hangman of Paris. "You are not just any hangman," she said indignantly, "you are the Monsieur de Paris." Jean-Baptiste was silent. Then she turned to Charles. "You should be proud of your father, as well as your grandfather and all the Sansons who have ever held this office. This heritage is no burden—or are ten thousand pounds perhaps a burden?"

Jean-Baptiste and Charles were silent, but they were both thinking the same thing. Why can't she ever shut her mouth?

"Ten thousand pounds a year, that's the monthly wage of three hundred workers," she continued. "Other hangmen in France earn two thousand four hundred to six thousand pounds a year, depending on the size of the city."

Charles wished she'd just fall over dead and be silent. He could hardly stand even the sound of her voice anymore.

"Think seriously if you still really want to become a doctor, Charles. People will never like you, you will always be the son of the hangman until one day you'll be a great hangman yourself—Monsieur de Paris."

"I want to be a doctor," Charles shot back defiantly. "I want to cure people, not kill them."

Grandmother Dubut waved him off angrily. "Where else can you get twenty-five pounds for chopping off a hand? All of Paris would like to have a job like that."

"Father," pleaded Charles, turning to Jean-Baptiste, who was still staring at the floor. "Can you send me to another school?"

Jean-Baptiste turned to his son and nodded.

"We'll find a solution, Charles, and the next time you'd better tell them you were an orphan."

"He's going to deny his heritage?" Grandmother Dubut snarled.

CHAPTER 4

Charles no longer felt welcome at home. Grandmother Dubut ruled the roost and ordered the kitchen maid and the children around like a little army. She stayed so close to her son that every female visitor was immediately aware there was no room for a second wife for widower Sanson. Jean-Baptiste had lost all interest in either physical intimacy or the fragrance of a woman. He had enough children and valued a stable family life and good food. His mother was an excellent cook, and the kitchen maid had learned from her, though whatever she did Grandmother Dubut was not pleased. Grandmother Dubut was not pleased with anyone. and Jean-Baptiste always let her have her way. When he was not performing executions, he slipped off to his library and read. His mother considered this just time wasted, because books only collected dust, but she let him have his way, as well. She looked after him as if he were a child.

As soon as Charles had returned to the Rue d'Enfer, he went to the Jesuit monastery. A friendly priest opened the door and asked him to wait to a moment while he went to look for Father Gerbillon who was probably still at prayers in the chapel. After a while, he returned and asked Charles to follow him. He led him into the square-shaped monastery garden laid out like a Roman atrium surrounded by arcades with beds of herbs and a fountain in the middle. A priest who was kneeling down alongside the garden heard steps on the

gravel path, stood up, and brushed off his hands on his overalls.

"What a joy!" Gerbillon beamed and approached Charles with wide-opened arms. "Look, my friend, this is ginseng. Even the ancient Egyptians used it as a sedative. It relaxes you, even if you know someone is about to chop your head off."

Chares was shocked, and wondered if the priest already knew he was the son of a hangman and had been expelled from the monastery school in Rouen.

"But the plant doesn't grow well here. We have more success with salves for a sore throat, fennel for coughs, belladonna for stomach aches, and plantain for headaches, though with headaches the better recommendation is to drink less," he explained, pointing proudly at the individual plants.

Then he led Charles into his pharmacy, where some Ginseng roots were lying on a large wooden table. "Ginseng," he said, "is the universal remedy in Siam. Some people take it for relaxation, others for better circulation." He giggled like a little girl. "It's supposed to increase a man's potency as well. We have much work to do. Since the invention of printing, more and more medical books have been appearing every year about the effects and benefits of the different plants. No one could live long enough to read all these books, to say nothing of classifying and using this knowledge. Book printing has opened the floodgates. Everyone in Europe can now read, check, improve, and republish the experimental results of others."

In his laboratory there were numerous porcelain dishes and jars along with mortars, sketches, and tables of experimental results.

"But tell me, what brings you to Paris?"

"I'm looking for a new school, and I thought you might have a recommendation for me."

"A new school?"

"My father is the hangman of Paris," Charles said with determination. "The father of one of my classmates recognized him on the day my parents came to visit, and for that reason I had to leave school."

Gerbillon didn't seem shocked. "No one can choose their parents, and every misfortune opens a door to new possibilities. Don't forget that. Enroll at the university at Leiden— that's where the revolution in medicine is taking place. No other university in Europe can measure up to the one in Leiden. It's much better than the monastery school in Rouen."

He invited Charles into his impressive-looking office and served him some black coffee with lots of cinnamon and sugar. The effect of the room and the coffee was unexpected. Charles suddenly felt wide awake and full of energy. The priest smiled. "Visit me again when things have worked out for you in Leiden and then I'll give you another tincture to try."

"Where are all these young women from Siam?"

Father Gerbillon was amused by Charles's interest. "During the day they attend the Collège Louis-le-Grand, in accordance with our arrangement with the King of Siam. They are learning French and studying science, and in the evening we try to teach them the Word of God. But it's hard to persuade them. They consider our God a militant, warlike God and fear him for that reason, though He is actually a God of love, isn't He? So they still love their Buddha. But Buddha and Jesus are one and the same, they are both sons of God, the God of light—the same wine in different flasks."

Charles sat waiting atop the wall of the monastery across from the Collège Louis-le-Grand wondering what to do. But he was too excited to organize his thoughts and develop a strategy. When he heard the school bell, he jumped down from the wall and paced back and forth like a caged animal.

Students came pouring out of the schoolyard, headed in all directions. Finally came the students from Siam. Laughing, they formed a group, and it was hardly possible to identify anyone in this joyful gathering. To a European, all Asians looked alike. The group stepped out into the street, and suddenly Charles saw that someone remained behind in the doorway, looking lost. Dan-Mali. She'd already seen Charles. Joyfully, she ran toward him, but then stopped abruptly, as if ashamed of having shown her feelings.

"I wanted to tell you I'm going to the university in Leiden to become a doctor. But I will be back."

Dan-Mali nodded. Charles wasn't sure she'd understood everything, but she suddenly looked so serious, almost sad, that he assumed she had understood.

"I will come back then," Charles said, adding hesitantly, "I will wait here for you." Dan-Mali nodded, holding her hands together over her chest, and nodding several time. Then she looked up briefly, and with a shy, almost mischievous smile added: "Dan-Mali will wait," before running after the others.

The Dutch University of Leiden was indeed the leading school for medical education. Founded in 1575, it had struck out in new, revolutionary ways. Instruction was at the bedside of the patient, and not taught by theologians, but scientists and specialists. Students thronged to Leiden from all over Europe, as well as well-to-do patients.

Charles took an immediate liking to this type of instruction. Together with other students, he followed Doctor Lacroix through the narrow corridors of the hospital. After passing through the ward for smallpox patients they started up the wide staircase leading to the third floor, where innumerable beds were lined up side by side along the wall. For lack of space, up to four people had to share the same bed—the sick patients, the dying, and those who had passed

away. Only pregnant women were treated separately. They were all thrown together and after a while all had the same symptoms. The adjoining ward was the recovery room for those freshly operated, and beyond that was the ward for the insane patients. The latter were not just cruelly chained together, but examined. That was something new, but some of them shouted or raved so much and thrashed around that no one on this floor could get a good sleep. In the last room, operations were performed. Legs were amputated with a saw, and the waiting patients could see with their own eyes what was in store for them. Another extremely painful operation performed here was the surgical removal of kidney stones. In such an operation, painful stones were surgically removed, and many men would bleed to death even after a successful procedure.

At the University of Leiden, students did not hide behind textbooks or study theoretical matters, but put their knowledge to immediate practical use. Classes were taught using a living patient. It was strenuous work, and all the young students had to pitch in and help. Every student had to use what he had learned while being observed by experts. They operated and bandaged, and the sick patients had to accept being manipulated like puppets. Some of the students tried to remain in the background, others blanched and sat down on one of the crowded beds as if they themselves needed medical aid, but Charles always stayed up in front. He could see the blood, and it never bothered or sickened him. It was simply a fluid in the human body that poured out now and then like wine from a tapped keg. He also didn't feel sick at the sight of contorted, dislocated limbs. He took them in his hand like a worker who had to check a door hinge. He also quickly understood how things worked and absorbed everything he saw or heard like a sponge. The University of Leiden agreed with him, and he was proud to be there. He was part of the new, experimental medicine that

was opening up new continents like the courageous seafarers. Father Gerbillon had been right, Charles thought. Luck, both good and bad, were close neighbors, and a blow of fate sometimes led to unexpected good fortune.

But sometimes luck is of short duration, and another blow of fate follows. This came in the form of a letter from Grandmother Dubut. Charles at once recognized her handwriting that reminded him of sharp bayonets and harpoons. The content of the letter was like a declaration of war. She wrote that Jean-Baptiste had suffered a stroke and was paralyzed on one side. Charles had to return to Paris at once and should pack his suitcase immediately on receipt of the letter and catch the next stage back home.

Charles hastily got his things together and headed for the next post station without saying good-bye to anyone. Before he left, he stole a dozen unused school exercise books on the spur of the moment. It was not really like him to do anything like that, but he was overcome with anger, and stole just to hold onto some of what would be taken from him. He was about to lose everything, and as a consolation he took along a few empty exercise books in which, from now on, he'd write down everything that happened until he finally reached his goal—to be a doctor. He stole these books because he knew there was no one in Paris to whom he could pour out his sorrow. Except for these empty exercise books. He knew that from now on he would be a stranger among men and decided to write about himself, because few men even suspect who they really are, and only the blows of fate will give us the sudden and painful revelation of who we are and what we can do. Most people claim they could never so much as hurt a fly, and suddenly they are surprised to find themselves ripping the flesh from the bones of another living person with red-hot tongs. Those are things that one cannot easily confide to another person, they are things that one can only write

down secretly in a book. Anyone with no friends should at least have an empty book to write in.

CHAPTER 5

As the post coach rumbled over the dusty country road, Charles was again overcome by an infinite sense of sadness. That was the curse, the inherited sin of the Sansons. First they became melancholy, later they suffered apoplexy and were paralyzed. They remained alive in order to suffer.

From far off, Charles could see the gray pall of haze hanging over Paris. Dozens of steeples emerged from under the dark cloud of smoke produced by hundreds of thousands of chimneys, but the monumental Gothic steeple of the Notre Dame Cathedral towered above more than one hundred steeples like a pope over his cardinals.

As they got closer to town, he became so anxious he could barely speak. He hated Paris; he had loved Leiden. Leiden was a city of culture and knowledge. Rembrandt had lived there, and so had Antoni van Leeuwenhoek, the discoverer of bacteria. From the very start, he was charmed by the open, uncomplicated manner of the Dutch compared with the somewhat rude and conceited manner of the Parisians. But he hated Paris also because it was the home of his grandmother, Marthe Dubut, who like these grotesque demons cast in stone on the balustrade of Notre Dame Cathedral was always watching and would continue to guide the destiny of her family, thereby ensuring that the curse of the Sanson dynasty would be passed on from generation to generation. She would ensure that her ambition was also their ambition. She alone knew what was right and what was not, though she'd never read a book or truly considered any

opinion than her own. That's the tragedy of people who always think they know everything. They have no idea how little they know.

One morning in March of the year 1757, the postal coach passed through the tariff wall of the City of Paris and stopped in the commercial center behind it, surrounded by hundreds of laborers, wounded war veterans, impoverished farmers and emaciated girls from the country. They weren't seeking their fortune in Paris, as they knew that people like them were always unfortunate. They were seeking to escape the misery of rural life. They were all rudely and loudly reprimanded by the visibly overtired soldiers, who screened them and drove them forward like cattle. Coaches from all parts of Europe came together in these custom stations and exchanged news and rumors. On this day, everyone was talking about Robert-François Damiens, who allegedly had injured King Louis XV with a knife—a deed everyone considered unthinkable. How could anyone dare to shed royal blood? Didn't the king stand at the right hand of God?

Anyone wanting to enter Paris had to pass through one of the fifty-four customs stations and allow the soldiers to question them and search them closely. Many merchants stood impatiently by their coaches, carts, and wagons awaiting inspection of their goods by tax officials. These men had bought their office from the king and could tax the contents as they saw fit. They could raise their fees shamelessly, driving food prices of so high that a laborer had to pay half of his wages to buy a single loaf of bread. For poor people, a doubling of food prices meant the end, while for a nobleman who paid no taxes, it didn't matter. He would always have enough.

There might be people who found the largest city in Europe beautiful, Charles thought, but if one had no money and was starving, any city was ugly.

After a wait of almost an hour, Charles and the other passengers could continue their trip along the Champs-Elysées. The small road had been transformed into the boulevard of the well-to-do nobility who had constructed stately townhouses surrounded by picturesque parks. The postal coach stopped close to the Palace of the Tuileries, the royal residence. From here, it was a long walk to the Rue d'Enfer.

Charles did not want to return; everything within him struggled against it. He could have screamed, but remained silent. At a loss, he stood in front of the royal palace and tried to figure out what to do. Some soldiers were chasing away a gathering of beggars, and also motioned to Charles to move along. He walked down to the Seine and strolled slowly along the banks of the river toward the Bastille. He could think of no way out—he had to return to his family. On his own he would never have the money to continue his medical studies in Leiden. Without his family he was like a fish out of water. A wolf without a wolf pack, he was nothing. His family ties were the only things offering him security, and whoever did not respect the authority of the alpha wolf brought down on himself the anger of the whole pack. Angrily and reluctantly, Charles decided to face the facts and return to the Rue d'Enfer. As if driven by an invisible hand, he moved on, wondering if there was such a thing as free will, or if he was merely being driven by forces he did not understand, carrying out some plan he knew nothing about. He wandered on, losing his way in the labyrinth of the narrow, winding streets. The road was covered by such a heavy layer of mud and garbage that in some dark corners he sank to his ankles. Stray dogs and cats fought over bloody scraps from the slaughterhouses that had simply been tossed out into the street. Merchants whipped their stubborn animals forward in the direction of Les Halles, while dung collectors collected the piles of excrement mixed with straw and

garbage and loaded them onto their donkeys. They needed approval to do that from the tax office. Paris even was selling its shit. The city had changed— now it was edgy, tired, and without hope. Tens of thousands of men were en route in the narrow streets, fighting their way through crowds of desperate people looking for a job, any job, to buy a loaf of bread. No one had any concern for others— their own fate was hard enough. Without any compassion, they trampled the legs of crippled beggars along the curb, unmoved they hurried past the steps of churches where abandoned new-born babies lay crying, helplessly waving their arms around, sniffed at and licked by stray dogs without any inhibitions. On the walls hung placards mocking Louis XV and his mistress, Madame de Pompadour.

The king's assassin Robert-François Damiens was the topic of the day in the streets and public squares. It was said he wanted to punish the king because the people were dying of hunger, and they asked whether it was possible to be king of a starving people without despising them. Damiens had hidden all day in the garden of Versailles, went the story, and when night fell he hid under a staircase to await the arrival of the king. When Louis XV descended the stairs with his entourage, Damiens jumped out of his hiding place, slipped through his guard of musketeers and injured the king slightly with his dagger. Some said that Robert-François Damiens had cried, *Long live freedom!* Others said he shouted *In the name of the people*, but nobody knew exactly, because none of the people telling the story had been there. Since then, weeks had passed, and Robert-François Damiens had been questioned and tortured daily in a dungeon in Paris.

Jean-Baptiste Sanson sat motionless in an armchair next to the stove, staring at his son in disbelief. For several weeks he had been paralyzed on one side. Charles had dared to say no to his father. Grandmother Dubut stood behind her son in a

majestic pose and glared at her grandson. With visible impatience, she waited for him to rescind what he'd just said. But he remained silent. Charles's favorite sister Dominique sat on the bench beside the stove, lowering her eyes, as she always did when trouble was in the air. His other siblings looked at him with mixed feelings. Some were sitting on the heavy wooden planks leaning against the warm, brown oven tiles. The low-hanging wood ceiling was supported by large beams with damp laundry put out to dry. Charles's three sisters were glad their eldest brother had returned, but his four brothers were angry at him for having drawn the ire of the father and the grandmother down upon them.

"That would be a serious act of betrayal," said Grandmother Dubut after a while. Charles did not respond. "Isn't it enough," she continued, "that we are hated and despised by society? Must our own flesh and blood now reject us?"

Charles's father was a pathetic sight in his worn arm chair, and Charles didn't dare look him in the eye. He appeared completely helpless. Charles's gaze wandered over the armchair's worn brown upholstery. As a child, he had counted the hounds and the hunters on horseback. There was a large hole in the fabric by the man with the hunting horn, and he was missing a head. "Don't I have enough brothers," Charles could hear himself saying. His voice faltered, he was ashamed, but if he gave in now, he would pay for it the rest of his life. He had to stand firm. Two of his brothers sat up proudly, as they would have given anything to wield the sword of justice, but they were too young to understand what the office really meant. They had never watched as a head was severed from a body and a fountain of blood spurted out.

"You're the eldest," Grandmother Dubut said bluntly, "and besides, there are enough cities in France for your brothers. They will marry the daughters of hangmen and they will beget other hangmen. You have no choice."

"Oh, but I do," Charles contradicted her. "Aunt Brigitte married a musician."

"Aunt Brigitte," said Grandmother Dubut with bitterness in her voice. "Do you know what became of her sons? They both became hangmen. That is the heritage of the Sansons. It is not a curse, Charles, it's simply your destiny."

"But I love music more than the sound of the trap door opening under the scaffold. I want to become a doctor and play the piano in the evening. That's how I want to spend my life."

"What have these Dutchmen in Leiden done to you? Are you rejecting your life? What are these new ideas? What a shameless brat you have become! Do you think you can decide your own destiny? God decides your fate and shapes your destiny, and you must accept it. The performance of duty determines your life, and there is no greater duty than obeying and serving your family."

"I will not," said Charles, "I cannot."

The withering gazes of his family weighed so heavily on him that his knees began to shake. He felt not just the pressure of his grandmother and all his brothers and sisters— he felt the pressure of all his uncles and aunts who lived in Orléans, Tours, Dijon, Nantes und Cherbourg and came every Christmas and Easter for family gatherings, and he felt the pressure of all his cousins who never questioned the law of the family. This law of uncompromising obedience to the family was stronger than the power of the church or even the crown, for it was the family that protected its members, and not the musketeers of the king.

"Come closer to me," said Jean-Baptiste in a grave tone, struggling in vain to raise his arms and embrace his son. Dominique was about to wipe away the spittle drooling from one corner of his mouth with the handkerchief she always carried with her, but Grandmother got to him first, and with a rough movement wiped the crippled man's slaver onto his

shoulder. She rested her hand there as if to demonstrate that this man belonged to her alone.

"At first I thought the way you do," said Jean-Baptiste in a drawling voice. "I thought the job would be too difficult for me. All the blood . . ."

"The blood doesn't bother me," said Charles. "A doctor must be able to bear the sight of blood."

"Then what is your problem?" Grandmother Dubut scolded him. "You are predestined to become a hangman."

Jean-Baptiste's face turned red, he tried to turn his head, and with a rough gesture beckoned for Grandmother Dubut to be silent.

"I'm not going to say a word," Grandmother Dubut said, passing her hand a few times over his shoulder.

"Charles," the sick man said in an almost tender voice, "I too was afraid of it. I fled to the New World to escape my destiny, but it caught up with me and brought me to that accursed house. There I met your mother, and her father, Master Jouenne, taught me everything I know, and helped me to do the impossible. And I must say I did it with pride and to the satisfaction of the judicial officials. And if this accursed illness hadn't . . ." Jean-Baptiste attempted to make another rough gesture, but his body did not obey him. Grandmother Dubut looked angrily at Charles, as if he were responsible for their misery.

"I want to become a doctor," Charles replied, not knowing where he got the strength to defy his entire family. "I want to heal men, Father, not strangle, hang, torture, behead them, and draw them in quarters. I want to heal, not kill."

"The hangman is also a doctor," Jean-Baptiste said. "He cuts off the sick parts of our society, he cures the society, and makes it healthy. On behalf of justice. On behalf of the king."

Charles feverishly tried to think of some response, but when confronted by his father's arguments, he was at a loss

for words. He understood that he couldn't bargain with his father, he wanted to convince him. He didn't want to debate him.

"Charles," Jean-Baptiste continued, "there are only two hereditary offices in this kingdom, that of the ruler, and of the hangman. You will get used to the blood, if not out of conviction, then for the sake of your family. Look at me, Charles, your father, your grandmother, and all your brothers and sisters. If you reject this office, you will condemn us to a life of poverty and hunger. If you are a Sanson, the world will always reject you. We have no other choice, Charles. All our hope, our entire future, lies in your hands. Your brothers are still too young to assume the office. You are the eldest. At least try it!"

Grandmother Dubut's face flushed with anger. She had been listening to her son with growing anger toward her grandson. "Outside in the streets, people are hungry and dying like flies," she now exclaimed, with contempt in her voice, "and if anyone can get work the most he receives is three hundred pounds a year—if the work lasts that long. Three hundred pounds, while the office of the hangman brings in ten thousand a year. Ten thousand! Because it's a special job that not everyone can do. If you turn down this work, tomorrow the hangmen in the provinces will hand in their applications. Everyone wants to be the Monsieur de Paris."

"But not you!" shouted one of his brothers angrily, and his other brothers joined in the chorus of contempt. Only Dominique remained silent. She always supported Charles.

"I cannot, Grandmother. I can't inflict pain on anyone . . ."

Suddenly an oppressive silence came over the room. Jean-Baptiste became restless, and Grandmother Dubut placed both hands on his shoulders apprehensively, and took a deep breath. He motioned to his mother to remain silent.

Then he turned again to his son. "Charles, life has not always treated us well. We have been through a lot together, and for that reason I respected your wish to become a doctor. I sent you to Rouen, then to the University of Leiden, and it wasn't cheap. We all saved the money for tuition by cutting back on our food budget. But now, God has decided differently. It was not our wish, Charles, it is not our fault. What will we have to live on now?"

Deathly silence reigned in the room.

"My assistants will do the filthy job," Jean-Baptiste continued after a while. But his voice sounded harder now, more determined, as if Charles had already consented. "You will not see the blood, Charles, you will not have to climb up any scaffold, you will stand at the bottom of the steps of the scaffold and affirm the legality of the sentences by your presence. Is that asking too much?" He literally shouted his final sentence, his mouth contorted into a grimace. Once again, Dominique went to discretely wipe the spittle from his chin, but Grandmother Dubut got there first.

"I've already spoken with Master Prudhomme," she said. "He is a master of his trade, and he will do the work in place of you until you are a grown man."

"Until one of my brothers is old enough?" Charles asked skeptically.

"Monsieur de Paris," Jean-Baptiste whispered. A smile darted across his face, then the face twisted again into a grimace as saliva ran from a corner of his mouth. Dominique, who had remained silent until that point, stood up, walked slowly toward Charles, and took him gently in her arms, much to the displeasure of Grandmother Dubut. Dominique patted Charles gently on the back. He loved his sister above everything else. Even when he was in Leiden, he yearned to be pressed to her warm breast and breathe in the fragrance of her body. She reminded him of his mother.

"My dearest Charles," she said in a tender voice, "the office will be presented to you by the king, and you will receive your pay directly from the chancellor. This is an honor bestowed only on the best officers in the army. Charles, it is a great honor to be allowed to assume this office at such a young age, and I promise you, now that you are living here with us again, that we'll play the piano together every evening. You have talent for music, something that will always be with you, and you will need it when you return home in the evening after a day's work."

Charles looked at his sister with pleading eyes, but her smile broke all his resistance. He simply loved her too much. She was still so young, and yet already so bright and well-read, that he could sit there all day listening to her talk. When he lay awake at night in Rouen or Leiden, he could hear the piano pieces she had taught him. His imagination was so strong that he thought he saw her sitting at the piano alongside the bed, playing only for him. Charles sometimes wondered if other people could create images and melodies in their heads that were so real they couldn't just be dismissed as fantasy. That was not an especially kind gift of nature, as horrifying visions could also rise up like terrifying monsters. Charles knew that was the curse of the Sansons—the enemy in their own minds.

"You are a Sanson," Grandmother Dubut screeched, and after the warm, melodious voice of his sister, it in fact sounded like a screeching demon. "The Sansons are strong, because they have to be," she said bitterly, "and they are called Sansons because they carry out their duties silently, *Sans son,* without a sound."

Everything Charles had lived for up to then suddenly fell apart in front of him. The roll of drums at the foot of the scaffold would now replace the lessons on bacteria and the circulatory system, and the screaming and pleading of condemned men would now drown out the music of

Vivaldi's *Stravaganza*. His siblings rushed toward him and embraced him, beaming at him with delight. He wasn't aware that he had given in. The affection of his brothers and sisters moved him, and their enthusiasm and excitement flattered him. This was his family— he was home again. There he stood now, Charles-Henri Sanson, the fourth in his dynasty, upright like Hercules, far taller than all of them, imposing, yet writhed inside and as helpless as a small child.

Early the next morning, Charles and Grandmother Dubut were standing before the cast-iron gates of the Paris police headquarters waiting to be admitted. Around nine o'clock, the general procurator sent an elderly gentleman in a blue livery to call them inside.

They climbed the broad stone stairway to the third floor and entered the office of the general procurator. He was a friendly, older gentleman dressed in a suit with wide epaulettes and stripes on his sleeves inspired by the prevailing military dress, and wide, bristling sideburns that were turning gray. Behind him, a large picture hung on the wall representing a bridge on the Seine. Bookshelves with glass-paned doors lined the wall on the opposite side. Charles had never seen such magnificent furniture. Even the table where the general procurator sat was elaborately carved. Colored pieces of marble were embedded in the top of the table, whose legs were very slender, slightly curved outward, and covered with metal decorations. The general procurator seemed to know Grandmother Dubut well. In any case, he smiled warmly as he shook her hand, holding it for a long time. His gaze was so conspiratorial that Charles immediately knew that the two had once had a love affair. Now, Grandmother Dubut was too old to pay with her body. The general procurator looked young Charles up and down, seemingly impressed by his athletic appearance.

"Have I promised too much?" Grandmother Dubut asked in a firm voice, proudly awaiting the general procurator's reply. After a moment of silence, he replied, "He's very big and strong-looking. Nobody would imagine he's so young."

"And he hasn't stopped growing yet," Grandmother Dubut replied. "He takes after his grandfather. My husband was huge, strong as a bear, and very even-tempered."

The general procurator smiled. "Many people from the provinces have applied," he said. "Monsieur de Paris is the best-paid hangman's post in all of France."

Grandmother Dubut waved scornfully and asked, "And what sort of people are they? Tramps? Criminals? Released galley slaves or people like the hangman of Montpellier who faints during every execution and on Assumption Day copulates with the saddler's goats?"

Secretly, Charles hoped Grandmother Dubut would have a quarrel with the general procurator, but he seemed rather amused. "They're distant relatives of yours, Madame, the Jouennes, the cousins of your grandson."

"The Jouennes?" Grandmother Dubut shouted. "But who the devil will stand at the scaffold: the Jouennes or the Sansons? We have the favor of the king. Nobody has ever complained about us, and my grandson Charles will be the best of them all. God has given him all the skill needed to assume this legacy and perform his services to the complete satisfaction of the king. The people will love him."

"The Jouennes have offered me twenty-four thousand pounds." He appeared unimpressed, and smiled.

Grandmother Dubut, with a brusque gesture, pulled a leather purse from her pocket book. "Twenty-four thousand pounds? That's ridiculous You can see how little the office means to them," she said, emptying the purse. Heavy gold coins tumbled out onto the table.

The general procurator stopped smiling, and suddenly appeared very earnest. "I've had the Jouennes tossed into the

dungeon at Châtelet," he mumbled sternly. Instinctively, Charles straightened up, took a deep breath, and held the air in to make his chest look bigger, not realizing he was thereby lending support to his grandmother's words. Offended, she put the gold coins back in her leather purse with a resolute expression. But she was not a woman to admit her error. In such situations she reacted with anger in order to deflect the disgrace of her failure. "I never asked you for anything," she said in a forceful, conspiratorial tone, leaning across the table.

"Look at me, Monsieur. God granted me a long life in order to allow me to preserve and pass along the bloody heritage of the Sansons. For the benefit of the Kingdom."

The general procurator nodded thoughtfully. It was impossible to guess what his decision might be. "Madame Dubut," he said dryly, "have you ever thought of applying for a job with the Comédie Française?"

She had no sense of humor, and responded in an almost solemn tone, "I respectfully ask you to offer my grandson, Charles-Henri Sanson, who is standing here before you, the office of his father Jean-Baptiste Sanson."

"You wish to extend the Sanson's legacy of the scaffold, Madame." It was not a question but a fact. "Very well, Madame, your grandson will wear the blood-red cloak and wield the sword of justice. The office will be entrusted to him temporarily, until your son, the esteemed Jean-Baptiste Sanson has died. Thereafter, your grandson Charles will be the official Monsieur de Paris." He rang the little bell on his desk, and a young man in a blue livery entered. He bowed deeply before the general procurator, who ordered him to prepare the certificate of appointment and announce the decision.

After the servant had left the room, the general procurator turned to Charles. "You returned to Paris just recently," he

said, "but I assume you know who Robert-François Damiens is?"

Charles nodded as Grandmother Dubut answered for him. "Of course he knows who Damiens is."

The general procurator gave Grandmother Dubut a stern look of disapproval. "I asked your grandson, not you, Madame! You are not yet employed in my office." He smiled. "Still the same big mouth!" She fell silent, and Charles was secretly happy that someone had dared to reprove this quarrelsome old woman. The general procurator took a document from the top drawer and handed it to Charles. Instinctively, Grandmother Dubut stared to reach out for it, but the general procurator shook his finger sternly at her and she backed off. He knew the text by heart, and recited it without taking his eyes off Charles. "Robert-François Damiens was found guilty yesterday by the Court of Justice in Paris and condemned to death. First, he will be subject to painful interrogation." He paused and stared intently at Charles. "Do you know what painful interrogation means?"

Charles nodded. These methods of torture included all the acts of cruelty that Christians had ever thought up since the time of the Inquisition.

"And moreover," the general procurator added, "Damiens is to be ripped by tongs, according to the judgment."

Now even Grandmother Dubut was speechless. Lacerating the victim by tearing off his flesh was so cruel that it was no longer in use. Who would study and practice this gruesome torture? She cast a sympathetic eye at Charles, who was at a loss for words, too, but barely batted an eyelid.

"You'll need help, young man," said the general procurator in a very serious voice. "Ask your Uncle Nicolas Sanson, the hangman of Versailles. He has never committed an error. His work is perfect—skillful and dignified, like all Sansons. And for the tearing of flesh with tongs there is a

qualified torturer in Brest by the name of Soubise, and you can engage him to do that. I expect an outstanding performance. All of France, indeed all of Europe will be watching. If you can accomplish this, your future is secure. Just don't faint—the people don't like that at all."

Charles spent that evening with Dominique at the piano, where they played Galanterien by Bach, the favorite pieces of their father, who sat peacefully in his brown armchair, his head on his chest and eyes closed. But he wasn't sleeping, he was enjoying the music. He was delighted at the appointment of his son Charles. A temporary appointment was common in the case of minors, and was at the same time an expression of respect for the previous officeholder, since it helped preserve his dignity despite his inability to hold the title himself.

Although Charles had every reason to be angry at his father, he had no greater wish than to sit down at the piano with his sister every evening. He played with much affection for the man who had first encouraged his dream and later destroyed it.

The next day, Charles ordered a servant to ride to Versailles and inform Uncle Nicolas, and a second rider to Master Soubise in Brest. Charles's siblings were extremely proud of their brother. He would execute the man that all of Paris was talking about, the man who had tried to assassinate the king. Through that act he would step out of the shadow of His Majesty and become a celebrity himself—the personal avenger of the king. And they were the siblings of the man who would carry out the judicial order.

A few days later, a court bailiff brought the written judgment describing so precisely the torture to be applied that people who read it felt their mouths turn dry and had to catch their breath. Charles felt he was going to vomit. It was like a blow to the pit of the stomach that simply took his

breath away. With anger and bitterness, he listened to his brothers and sisters whispering to one another while sitting on the long bench by the stove, while Uncle Nicolas placed his hand on his shoulder, apparently sensing how Charles felt. Jean-Baptiste also realized how he felt, but his paralysis prevented him from touching his son and trying to comfort him. Even though Jean-Baptiste cared for his brother very much, he also envied him for the close relation he had with his son. Dominique drove the other children away from the oven bench, and even the cat jumped down from the brown tiles. None of those who were so delighted with her brother's position would stand at the scaffold on the day of the execution and torture a living human being to death.

"We're not torturer's assistants," said Jean-Baptiste over and over, "we punish by hanging or by the sword, but we don't torture. Others do that."

Charles didn't believe a single word his father said, but he didn't dare contradict him. He was quite aware that his job was to carry out whatever punishment the court required. It was also clear to him that someone like Damiens would be tortured publicly with such cruelty as had not been seen for half a century. The people were starving, and if the perpetrator Damiens saw himself as the avenger of the people, then the king definitely wanted to make a cruel example of him. Charles wasn't so sure this example would suffice. He instinctively felt that Damiens had awakened a latent anger in the people. Some people secretly viewed Damiens as a hero, since they, too, were starving just like him and eking out a miserable existence, like rats in the gutter. Charles was convinced there were tens of thousands of Damiens, and it was hard to imagine what would happen if someday all these people stepped forth out of the darkness. Charles felt more affinity for Damiens than for the king. He honored the king, but if he had the same cynical attitude toward people as Antoine did, he was a bad ruler. Charles

gradually became obsessed with Damiens, but there was no one he could speak with about it. Only his diary.

Even though time was short, he felt a strong desire to see Dan-Mali, and decided to go to the Collège Louis le Grand. She saw him at once, ran across the street to him beaming with joy, and timidly touched him on the arm. Then she nervously took a piece of paper from her pocket and read: "I miss you. I'm learning French. Then we can talk."

Charles nodded earnestly. He searched his mind for simple words to express his feelings, but Dan-Mali's friends who were waiting for her on the other side of the street called to her, and she ran back to them. Before she disappeared behind the wall, she looked back and waved shyly.

"Tell him the truth," insisted Uncle Nicolas, "your boy will have to climb up on the scaffold—first comes his assistant, then he himself, then I follow with Damiens. Before the torture with the tongs begins, he can climb down to the foot of the steps, but at the beginning, he must appear before the public. He is your representative on the scaffold."

In horror, Charles looked at his father, who tried to avoid his son's gaze.

"Play something on the piano for me," said Jean-Baptiste. "I miss the piano more than I do the scaffold." Troubled, Charles and Dominique sat down at the piano and began to play. He played badly. It was terrible to force him to sit down at the piano when he was in this mood. He hated his father for that, but he couldn't disobey him. Grandmother Dubut saw the sorrow and conflict in his heart, but she had no sympathy. She advocated harshness like a religion, yet she had prepared a pork roast just the way Charles liked it. He found it touching, yet it was the only sign of affection he had ever known from her: a juicy slice of roast pork wrapped in bacon and with a creamy mushroom sauce that probably had more cognac in it than cream. His siblings also loved him,

because he also made possible this sumptuous meal by what he was ready to do the next day.

After the meal, Grandmother Dubut lay down and asked Charles to come to her bedside. Since the meeting with the general procurator, her behavior toward him had changed. She realized he'd figured out that she had once had an affair with the official, and her pride was injured. She had lost face in the presence of her grandson, and from now on she was less coarse when dealing with him, as if paying secretly for his discretion. The part about the money had also humiliated her, for that too had taken place in his presence. He had seen that his feared grandmother was insignificant outside the four walls of their house—she was nothing but an old woman. It was also significant that Charles from now on would help make the family financially secure. Before long he would be the head of the family and she would lose her power. She looked into his eyes for a long time, as if trying to read his thoughts. Finally, she took out a talisman in the shape of a cracked bell and placed it in his right hand.

"Charles," she said in a calm and earnest voice, "your great grandfather wore this little silver bell around his neck and passed it on to his son. That is still the custom—the cracked bell is the Sanson's coat of arms. It has no clapper, and it neither rings nor makes any sound. It is the bell of the Sansons. No matter how much grief or pain you suffer, no one will pay any attention to you. A Sanson stays silent and performs his duty."

She pressed the little amulet into her grandson's hand.

"Hold on to it tightly," she said softly. "Tomorrow when you are standing on the scaffold you will feel the power of the Sansons. Have no fear, Charles. Our imagination torments us more than reality. When you are plagued with gloomy thoughts, like all Sansons, go out into the forest. Riding and hunting have lifted the hearts of all your ancestors. Music and literature offer consolation, as well,

though I consider both of them worthless. But above all, beware of loneliness. It has been the undoing of many a Sanson. Find yourself a strong woman. Every Sanson needs one, for in the end they all become cripples."

"Grandmother," Charles said softly, "why are you speaking to me like that?" He suspected something ominous, and at that moment he hoped she would be there for him late the next evening when he returned home.

"It's possible you hated me sometimes," she said in a soft voice. "You never really cared for me, but I have secured for the Sansons control of the throne of death. Now you are inviolable, because from now on you will be the hangman of the kings and the avenger of the people. You will be the greatest of all the Sansons. Under you, your brothers and you will surely become respected members of society. I have watched you, and you are the strongest and most courageous of all. The dynasty of the Sansons has never had one such as you."

As she spoke the final words, she closed her eyes and released Charles's hand. Not wanting to wake her, he quietly got to his feet, left the bedroom, and went out into the yard where Dominique was sitting in the sun. He sat down beside her.

"Tell me, Dominique, is there a curse on our family?"

"I don't know, Charles. I think that most people in Paris believe they have been cursed, as they live in the most bitter poverty and without hope. I think the sin comes from just being born."

"Then what Damiens tried was right."

"Yes, Charles, the king lets his people die of hunger, but God loves him more than he does the simple people of Paris. He protected the king and sends Damiens to his death."

"Do you doubt the existence of God, Dominique?"

"Yes, Charles."

"If there is no God, then there is no curse."

Dominique nodded.

"When Father and Grandmother are no longer alive, I'll give up my position and become a doctor, Dominique."

She felt he needed someone to grant him absolution, and this would give him the strength to withstand the time on the scaffold. "Yes, Charles, someday you will become a good doctor," she said, stroking his hand tenderly with her finger. He opened his hand, and Dominique saw the amulet, and smiled. "Now you are the Monsieur de Paris, Charles."

"For the time being," he said. It sounded like a plea.

Monsieur de Paris, a fine-sounding concept, was nonetheless impossible to reconcile with the shocking things that the court had imposed on Charles. Monsieur de Paris sounded noble and elegant, it had the fragrance of fine linens, poetry, and almond soap. But on the twenty-eighth of March 1757 it would have the odor of burning human flesh.

At four o'clock in the morning, Charles put on his father's blue trousers and the red jacket displaying the embroidered gallows and steps. He carried his sword in his right hand, but did not don the red three-cornered hat, holding it folded under his arm. He climbed into the first wagon with his uncle, while in the second wagon fifteen assistants with fawn-colored leather aprons took their places. They were primarily hangmen from the provinces and had come from all parts of France for this occasion. Four horses were hitched to their wagons, powerful horses selected to rip a man to pieces. The men were on the way to the prison.

Without saying a single word, they started moving, slowly, like a funeral procession. Dawn was approaching, and Paris was awakening. The mighty, round towers of the Conciergerie were visible in the distance, radiating authority and power. Their steep black roofs rising to a point resembled monumental executioners awaiting the prisoners. Damiens had been locked up and tortured in one of these

towers for almost six months. This took place in Montgomery Tower, named for Count Montgomery who had mortally wounded Henry II at a tournament. Charles and his assistants passed the mighty iron gate leading to the castle courtyard. The Conciergerie was more than a prison, it was also the headquarters of the judicial court. In this way, the judges always had quick access to the prisoners being tortured in the subterranean levels of the towers. Heavily armed police stood in the yard. The concierge led the hangmen into an interior court which belonged to the Sainte Chapelle and together they descended the winding staircase carved out of stone which led down into the world of suffering.

The most heavily guarded prisoner in all of France was taken to the lowermost dungeon in the Montgomery Tower. It stank of mold and rot, the air became noticeably cooler, and the flickering light of torches added to the eerie feeling as every step echoed within these narrow stone walls. Suddenly, there was an ear-splitting scream followed by a silence so deep that one had to wonder if he'd actually heard it. Finally, they found themselves in front of a massive oaken door with iron hinges guarded by several gendarmes. As the door to Damiens's cell swung open, the stench of burning human flesh wafted toward them. The air in the dungeon was hot, oppressive, and dirty, and pressed like a fist on their lungs. There was not a single breath of air to offer relief. Damiens lay on a torture grill, bound to it by leather straps so he couldn't move. He'd been lying on this grill for weeks. Straw had been spread underneath it to catch his excrement. Dr. Boyer, the doctor appointed by the court, knelt alongside him and stripped the blood-soaked sheepskin from his legs. Damiens's lower legs had burst like sausages on a spit. His left leg was broken and badly dislocated. At the head end, four soldiers of the guards regiment sat staring at the motionless prisoner. With an almost fatherly concern, the

court physician examined the prisoner's body and gave one of the soldiers the order to replace the smoking torches with wax candles, fearing that Damiens would collapse in the sticky air and not be fully conscious for his execution, The court had given Dr. Boyer responsibility of assuring that Damiens lived long enough to suffer all the means of torture prescribed in his sentence. One of the soldiers had brought a dog along, and fed it with a greasy-looking gruel. He watched the dog very closely as it ate, and after a while stuck three fingers in the bowl. Now it was Damiens's turn.

The soldier had orders to make sure Damiens was not poisoned. He was to live, to suffer. Damiens wasn't moving, and the porridge remained stuck on his bloodless lips.

Robert-François Damiens was a completely emaciated, forty-two-year-old man It was said his father drank himself to death and his mother died of scurvy. He was raised by an uncle and given the opportunity to get an education, but Damiens was driven by unrest and headed out to see the world. He fought on the battlefields of Europe, it was said, served a Swiss officer for a while as a messenger boy, and finally, sick and exhausted, was stranded in Paris, where the good-looking young man, whom everyone called *the Spaniard* served in a number of homes of the nobility, was abused as an erotic plaything, and after his masters tired of him, thrown out onto the street. He pulled himself together again and found an appointment in the palace of a count. One night, however, the king had the count arrested because of the soirees in his palace at which Rousseau, Voltaire and Montesquieu were discussed, and sympathy was expressed by the noble attendees for the hungering people. The count often gave Damiens clothes and money, and eventually Damiens was able to open a little store near the Pont Neuf. But he was deeply moved by the count's revolutionary ideas, and ever since, the sight of the suffering and starving people

filled his heart with anger. When the great famine cast its shroud over Paris, Damiens closed his shop. No one knows why he made the decision to kill the king. It's possible Damiens had taken leave of his senses, but that doesn't change the fact that he acted out of pity for the French people who lived lives of misery while the king squandered the tax money he received from the farmers and workers and amused himself with his noble entourage. In the past few weeks, these noble friends at Versailles had been eagerly searching ancient manuscripts for especially cruel methods of torture for the would-be assassin Damiens. Their search even included examining practices in ancient Rome, but the cruelest ones ever conceived by the human mind were those of the papal inquisitor who cruelly tortured and killed everyone who doubted their vengeful God. The Christians had moved Paradise to the afterworld and established Hell on earth.

Dr. Boyer left the dungeon. A bailiff entered and prepared to read the sentence of the court to the unconscious Damiens. First he informed him he would now be led to Bonbec Tower to be tortured.

"He can't hear you," said Charles, "he's unconscious." He felt deeply sorry for Damiens.

"That doesn't matter," replied the bailiff defiantly. "We're just following orders. The rule is the rule."

The four soldiers untied Damiens from the roasting grill. As they untied the straps from his injured legs, he let out a dreadful scream and whimpered terribly. The bailiff ordered Damiens to kneel, but he did not react, so two bailiffs grabbed his shoulders and forced him to his knees. He collapsed at once, as it was impossible with his broken knee caps for him to stand. Two soldiers grabbed him by the shoulders, and his lower legs dangled down as if they didn't belong to him. A third soldier grabbed him by the hair and

pulled his head back so he could see the bailiff read him his sentences. He listened without batting an eyelash, even at the news he would be drawn and quartered into pieces by four horses. Damiens stared into space in a trance, seeing all the people around him. The white of his eyes was yellow, his skin had the color of concentrated urine, and he kept uttering strange words that sounded something like "Oh God, oh God, oh God," but the words were not really comprehensible.

When a police lieutenant entered the dungeon, he calmed down somewhat and the soldiers set him down in a corner. The man who had fed the dog offered Damiens a glass of wine, but he just closed his eyes. He didn't want anything.

The priest knelt down before the condemned man and dabbed the sweat from Damien's face with his gown. At that moment, Damiens's head collapsed onto his chest. He had lost consciousness again. The priest stood up, scrutinized the bailiff and Nicolas Sanson one after the other, then fixed his gaze on Charles. He seemed to know who the tall young man was. He nodded almost imperceptibly and smiled, as if suggesting he would stand by him, just as he stood by Damiens. His face was soft and kind. He seemed to be a stranger to discord and anger and filled with an unshakeable love for God and humankind. People called him Father Gomart. He was a priest who had joined a monastic order years ago and was now serving at executions, the last friend of the condemned.

The police lieutenant asked Father Gomart if he was ready. Ashamed, the priest lowered his gaze and said he would pray in the chapel of the Conciergerie and wait for the condemned man. At once, the lieutenant gave an order to the guards to take the unconscious man to the torture chamber in the Bonbec Tower. Together with Uncle Nicolas, Charles followed the soldiers into the tower. The members of the criminal chamber were already present in the gloomy vault. They wanted to interrogate him one last time, since no one

believed the man had acted alone. Everyone still believed Damiens to be a leader of a conspiracy planning a revolution. The judges sat behind a long table. A few beams of light fell on their heads, making them look as if they were illuminated by God in order to better fulfill their work. They were all there: Maupeou, Molé, Severt, Pasquier, Rolland and Lambelin, as well as Doctor Boyer. As Charles looked at the filth on the stone floor, he looked up at the vaulted ceiling from which hundreds of little bats were hanging, as if watching what was happening down below. The guards sat Damiens down on a bench and Dr. Boyer wrapped Damiens's head with cold, wet cloths. Damiens at once regained consciousness and examined his surroundings with a strange, other-worldly look. He shifted around restlessly, trying to keep his feet from touching the floor. Now his words were clear. He was praying to God for help. He kept saying the words in a monotonous voice, as if their constant repetition could help him forget. The presiding judge rose and explained to Damiens that he would have to submit to torture, as he had not confessed. Then he ordered the master torturer Frémy to put Damiens in the Spanish Boot. A man sitting on one of the benches in back who had remained unnoticed to that point stood up and slowly made his way toward the accused man, planting himself in front of him. In his hand he held two perforated iron plates. Damiens stared at him, restlessly rolling his eyes. Then he shouted that he was innocent, that he had been cursed by a witch. "She lives in the Rue du Bouclier. Write it down, because the street is so bewitched that one easily forgets the name: Rue du Boisseau. One night she sat down on my face with her naked ass and I saw black toads slipping out of her festering cunt." Torture Master Frémy turned briefly to the judges sitting behind their benches, listening intently. They nodded.

Then Frémy nodded as well, and three assistants appeared out of the half-darkness. Two of them held Damiens tightly

by the arms while the third fetched a stool and pressed Damiens's right foot down onto it. Damiens let out a piercing scream and started ranting and raving. He kept asking why he was there and swore he had done nothing wrong.

Frémy knelt down in front of Damiens and put his lower leg between two metal plates serving as a splint. He fastened them with ropes so that the lower leg was crushed as if in a vise. Once again, Damiens howled with pain as the scabs broke open again and the wounds started bleeding profusely. Frémy squeezed the leg even tighter between the plates as his helpers held Damiens firmly in their grip. Suddenly, Damiens's face turned white as chalk, the blood drained from his lips, and once again his head collapsed onto his chest. The presiding judge beckoned to Dr. Boyer who felt Damiens's carotid artery and lifted his eyelid with his thumb. "Nothing serious," he said. Then, one of the assistants handed Frémy a large nail, which he quickly pounded through the first hole of the iron plate The nail passed through the victim's flesh and bone until it came out the second hole on the other side. With the first blow of the hammer, Damiens quickly regained consciousness. He stared wide-eyed up at the vaulted ceiling and shouted, "Give me some wine." Frémy and his assistants turned around and looked at Nicolas Sanson. Charles didn't know if it was his job to bring wine to Damiens, but when his uncle nodded at him, he understood it was indeed his job. He was overcome with an indescribable weakness, and at the same time he his mouth felt furry. He tried to swallow, but every muscle in his mouth went into a spasm, as if Frémy had clamped the Spanish Boot to his throat. He staggered to the table, poured some wine from a carafe into a cup, and slowly went back to Damiens. His legs were leaden. He placed one hand on Damiens's shoulder and with the other hand put the cup to the prisoner's mouth. Damiens only touched it with his lips, but when Charles took his hand away, he shot forward and

opened his mouth. He wanted more to drink. As Charles prepared to give him some more, Damiens opened his eyes and stared directly into Charles's face. Rolling his eyes, he whispered, "Spare the wine for the people of Paris. Give it to the poor. I will gladly die for them. Death to the king and the monarchy!" No sooner had he spoken those words than Frémy hammered the second nail through the metal plate, pounding so hard that the shinbone splintered. Damiens screamed, howled, pleaded, but Frémy hammered the third and fourth nails into Damien's leg as well. His screams seemed to bounce off the high vaulted ceiling and rain down on everyone as if shot from a catapult. He didn't stay silent any longer, but began screaming and shouting like a madman, and Charles could see that even the Judge Molé who was approaching him to ask him the first question began to tremble all over. Molé wanted names, he wanted to know if there had been a conspiracy, if there were others involved. "Yes," Damiens shouted in an almost happy voice, "the streets of Paris are full of them. You don't have enough soldiers to kill them all, because there are hundreds of thousands of Damiens." Molé now looked very upset. He had hoped to hear names. "Names!" he insisted. But Damiens just laughed maliciously, and started talking again about the witch who had ridden not on a broom but on a giant penis, because he was Satan. "Satan!" he roared. "Go out into the streets and you will see I am speaking the truth. Everywhere you will see the toads that have come jumping out of their cunts, and you'll hear them from far away, because they fart like a brass band, and the wet air that blows out of their ass leaves death and destruction everywhere."

As the seventh nail was driven in, Damiens let out one long, unending scream and vomited over Frémy's neck. Damiens was trembling all over. "Take the boots off," said someone. It was Maupeou. Stunned, he sat behind his judge's bench staring into space. On his right sat Molé, who had

evidently fainted, and was being treated by Dr. Boyer. Frémy took off Damiens's Spanish boots, and his assistants put Damiens on a stretcher and carried him out into the courtyard.

There stood Sanson's two wagons pulled by horses. An enormous crowd had gathered in front of the gate to the Conciergerie waiting for the helpless bundle of what used to be a man being led to his execution in a long procession. The wagons were open, with rows of benches on each side. They were escorted by armed men, members of the Maréchaussée, the French National Police. They were all waiting for Damiens. Father Gomart was seated in the first cart with his head bowed, looking tired and troubled, as if his own last hour was at hand. The assistants tossed Damiens into the first wagon. Frémy wiped the blood off his trousers and said in a completely unemotional tone. "He's all yours now." Charles followed his Uncle Nicolas to the first cart, and some of the members of the court joined them. Damiens lay on the wooden bed of the wagon between their feet, and the hangman's assistants sat in the second cart. The wagons started to move, then stopped again, because the many members of the Maréchaussée were blocking the passage through the gate. Finally, they stepped back, making way for Damiens's route to the scaffold.

Thousands of people greeted the wagons, shouting, bawling, cheering, singing and laughing. Hundreds of soldiers, police, and an unbelievable crowd of onlookers lined the streets, as if word had gotten around that there would be bread that day at a reasonable price in Paris. The Rue du Pont Saint Michel, the Quai du Marché Neuf, the Rue du Marché Palu, were packed with people. All businesses were closed. All of Paris wanted to see the man who had dared to spill the blood of the king. The two wagons struggled to make their way through the restless throngs of people surging like a tidal wave through the streets.

Gendarmes were posted in front of the Notre Dame Cathedral, riding back and forth to keep the stairway into the cathedral open, but it was almost impossible to hold back the surging crowds. Again and again the men on horseback pressed into the crowd of onlookers, trying to force them back, but the crowd had almost nowhere to go, as they were being pushed forward by the tens of thousands of people behind them. The National Police who had accompanied the wagons formed a column and fired some shots into the air, and for a short while the crowd settled down.

The two wagons stopped before the steps of Notre Dame, and the bailiff instructed Nicolas Sanson with the help of some of his servants to lift Damiens out of the wagon. Damiens's legs were so badly torn and shredded that every movement caused unbelievable pain. Charles tried not to look at Damiens's legs, but it was impossible. The bailiff waited impatiently on the steps of the cathedral. "Fall on your knees!" he said, looking out at the crowd, but he couldn't bring himself to take another look at Damiens. The assistants attempted to put Damiens down and force him to his knees, but he let out such a piercing scream that the people suddenly fell silent. Almost reverently the crowd remained silent, as if they'd only just now noticed that there was a human being in front of them. The hangman's assistants pulled Damiens to his feet, holding him tightly by the arms. His feet didn't touch the ground, as he was not supposed to suffer unnecessarily. Damiens repeated the words of the bailiff in a quiet falsetto. They were words of penance, begging God and the King for forgiveness. As the servants brought him back to the wagon, he broke out into tears. He seemed now so shattered and nearly mad with pain that he no longer had any control over his body, wetting and soiling himself.

The wagon continued on its way. As they got closer to the Place de Grève, the crowd became more menacing, eager to

witness Damiens's last moments. Some cursed and jeered, others threw garbage at him, but there were also some who stood at the edge of the street and pitied him. A large number of police and soldiers guarded every intersection. When the convoy finally turned into the Place de Grève, they were met by a huge roar from the crowd that has been waiting there for hours to see them. Instinctively, Charles turned to look at his uncle Nicolas, and even he, the hangman of Versailles, had never seen such an enormous crowd. All around the square windows were thrown wide open, and behind them onlookers crowded around to see out. The clothes they were wearing made it clear that the best places were occupied by noblemen. A seat at the window cost fifty sous. Other men, whom one might expect to see in a literary salon to judge by appearances, had been waiting for hours on the balconies of their city mansions in order to witness the cruelest execution of the century. They read Voltaire, Rousseau, and Montesquieu, but still wanted to see this man Damiens suffer and die.

In front of the scaffold, the crowd parted, and two lines of soldiers cleared a passage. Nicolas Sanson gave a sign to his assistants waiting up on the scaffold in the midst of this unpredictable mob yearning for blood, and were visibly relieved at the arrival of the soldiers. Fearfully they climbed down the stairs from the scaffold, casting furtive glances into the wagons. Damiens was writhing like a worm with its head cut off.

"Carry him up," Uncle Nicolas ordered, taking his nephew aside. Again they could hear Damiens's screams desperately asking his wife for help and begging for forgiveness. "You can wait at the foot of the steps and give the sign," said Uncle Nicolas. He obviously had reconsidered what to do, but Charles shook his head. The new Monsieur de Paris wasn't going to run and hide from anyone. This hateful job had been forced upon him, but he wanted to show

everyone that he hadn't been broken. Holding his head high, Charles climbed the steps to the scaffold. When he had reached the top and looked out over the enormous crowd, he realized finally that he'd taken on the heritage of the Sansons and from now on he would be the master of the scaffold.

The assistants who had followed in the second cart spread out at the foot of the gallows, and some climbed the steps. They had set up a small platform in the middle of the scaffold the night before, a sort of wooden altar about one yard high, and now they laid Damiens down on it and tied him tightly. His head was resting on a straw sack exposed to the hot sulfurous fumes rising from a bed of coals. A grill lay over the glowing coals on which a pan with a beaked spout was heated.

The acrid fumes drifted over the entire square, bringing the crowd to an almost unbelievable level of excitement. Next to the bed of coals was a small serving table covered with a black velvet cloth, on which the pincers, long butcher knives, a saw, and an ax were displayed Barely visible was the fine, rolled-up rope just in case a mercy killing was granted. Father Gomart tried to calm down Damiens, who couldn't stop screaming. He dabbed the cold sweat from his pale brow and took out a small bottle of holy water, pronouncing absolution to the doomed man, who kept repeating certain words over and over in a fevered frenzy. As Father Gomart recited the prayer for the dead, court officials admonished him to hurry. Gray clouds were passing over the square, as if heaven was displeased with what was happening down here.

"Where is Soubise?" Nicolas Sanson asked, looking around uneasily. But the hangman's helpers who were supposed to assist the Sansons stood there silently in their leather aprons, looking around themselves, uncertain what to do. Suddenly there was a loud belching sound, and everyone looked reflexively toward the steps. The old man, who bore

the name of an onion sauce, struggled up the steps. "Soubise, Sir," he said, mumbling, as he walked across the wooden planks. He stopped in front of Damiens and reached for the pincers.

"Where is the oil?" asked Nicolas Sanson in a harsh voice. He glared menacingly as he walked toward the drunk Soubise, who waved the pincers around menacingly and by accident struck himself on the forehead. Charles ripped the pincers from his hands and ordered the assistants to take Soubise away. "Go get us some oil!" The assistants rushed off to find some. Father Gomart used the interruption to approach Damiens again and say a prayer. The court officials watched stone-faced, waiting. It began to rain.

More than an hour later the first assistant made his way through the crowd and appeared again on the scaffold with the oil, and by then the fire in the brazier had gone out. An assistant tried in vain to get the fire started again.

"We need dry wood," said Nicolas Sanson, who had become restless and worried. He stood there staring after the assistants for a long while as they made their way through the crowd again, on their way to get wood. After another half hour the first one returned and said that no one would give them dry wood.

"Why?" Nicolas Sanson wanted to know.

"I really don't know, but it appears the people don't approve of what we're doing here."

Now Charles ordered the assistants to take an ax and cut some wood from the palisade wall beneath the scaffold, start the fire again, and heat the oil. He was getting increasingly annoyed at the long delays. Damiens had regained consciousness again and was screaming in a hoarse voice like a madman. With a pleading look, he addressed his hangmen.

"Shall we try it again with Soubise?" Charles whispered to his uncle, who was pale as a sheet but knew Soubise wouldn't sober up until at least noon the next day. It wasn't

the hangman's job to torture the man with the pincers, but there was no one else there to do it. The court bailiff and Doctor Boyer glared at the Sansons, demanding to begin the cruel process.

Six assistants now stood around Damiens waiting silently for new orders. Charles simply nodded. At this sign, an assistant swiftly seized Damiens's right arm and stretched it until his hand protruded far over the edge of the wooden altar. A second assistant took the smoking pan from the grill, another one placed the brazier under Damiens's hand. Instinctively, Damiens tried to draw it back, staring wide-eyed at his hand, as if he didn't know what was going to happen next. Nicolas Sanson poured the hot oil over it, and Damiens let out a long scream unlike any one Charles had ever heard from a human being. Damiens's teeth wedged together and his lips burst as blood streamed from his mouth. After a few minutes, the hand that had struck the king was only a charred stump.

Nicolas Sanson stood in front of Damiens, horrified, still holding the glowing brazier in his hand, while Charles turned pale. and was breathing hard. He'd sworn to himself that he'd perform the execution at the foot of the ladder leading up to the scaffold, but now he was standing up above, observed by thousands of people. The huge crowd seemed to surround the scaffold like a dark and dangerous sea, and Charles knew there was no turning back until it was all over. He couldn't flee—the crowd would have lynched him for doing that. He had to go through with it. Reaching into his pocket, he took out the amulet that Grandmother Dubut had given him.

With determined strides he went over to one of the assistants, André Legris, the hangman of Orléans, and offered him one hundred pounds if he would perform the ripping of the flesh with the pincers. Even though André Legris was considerably older than Charles and very esteemed in his city, he accepted at once that he was here just

as an assistant, and that the under-aged minor Charles Sanson was in charge of the scaffold here. "Yes, Monsieur de Paris," he answered, nodding respectfully with a nod. Quickly he seized the long pincers and held them in the pan of glowing coals. Charles took the glowing pan from his uncle and put it back on the grill. Father Gomart appeared exhausted, and walked slowly back to Damiens, holding the edge of the wooden altar tightly. Once again he dabbed the cold sweat from Damiens's face that was contorted with pain. The Father said something that no one could hear. He too was choked with emotion. Doctor Boyer approached, as well, looking dizzy and panting like a horse. With a trembling hand he felt Damiens's pulse. He nodded to the bailiff, who in turn also nodded to the Sansons. Charles gave the signal to André Legris, who immediately placed the glowing pincers against Damiens's naked chest. The victim reared up, without making a sound, as the pincer ripped off a huge section of his flesh along with one nipple. The hangman of Lyon, also present here in Paris as an assistant, poured boiling oil into the bloody wound. The flesh hissed and burned, as the odor of charred human flesh spread across the square. The hangman of Orléans now tore gaping wounds in the victim's arms, stomach, and upper leg. and once again an assistant poured burning resin and sulfur in the wounds. Finally, the hangman clamped the pincer around Damiens's penis and ripped it out. As if in a frenzy, the assistants carried out the sentence imposed on the dying man while Damiens roared in pain. It soon sounded like the bellowing of a mating stag, and then like the heart-rending whimper of a newborn baby. But suddenly he screamed like a madman at the top of his voice. "More, give me more, I love it, I love it, give me more!" The voice echoed over the square like a tempest. There was nothing human about it now, and it caused the crowd to shudder. The voice was the howling of Satan from the realm of suffering and purgatory.

Damiens lost consciousness again, and a strange stillness descended over the square. The whinnying of the four horses at the base of the scaffold could be heard as four assistants each took a horse by the reins and led it to one corner of the scaffold. Now they threw the long dressage reins to their colleagues on the scaffold who caught them and attached them quickly to the arms and legs of the badly mutilated and dying Damiens. A deathly silence fell over the scene, and even a coughing sound in the square would have been audible. It had stopped raining. Charles gave the assistants standing next to the horses a sign to begin. They took the horses by the halter and led them away from the scaffold. After a few steps, the horses stopped. Damiens's body was resisting. They tried again. Four huge, eight-hundred-pound horses struggled to rip the arms and legs from the body of a dying man. Damiens's left leg was dislocated, but not detached, while the horse reined to the right leg buckled and fell. The crowd suddenly let out an ear-splitting cry of horror. How could Damiens's leg resist the strength of a horse? Again, the men whipped the horses on, but Damiens's right leg and both arms were still attached to his torso. But, as before, his body resisted. Again, the assistants tried to whip the horses forward. They started to move, but his limbs remained attached to his torso. Charles summoned up his courage and stared at Damiens, and noticed how his arms and legs had lengthened grotesquely, but the muscles and tendons were connecting his extremities to his torso. It was almost unbelievable. Charles nearly passed out at the sight of this mangled, torn, bloody, and twitching body, singed like meat on a grill. He felt like the boards were starting to give way beneath him. Father Gomart fell on his knees in front of the dying man, clutching a cross in his hands. praying in a louder and louder voice as if trying to drive away all his own thoughts with his own voice, and at the same time closing his eyes because he no longer wanted to see what they were

showing him. Tears ran down his face as he shouted his desperate prayers to heaven. Charles took the fine cord from the side table and asked the bailiff whether the court allowed the use of the retentum. That was a secret stipulation often contained in death sentences giving the hangman the right to strangle the condemned man secretly with a fine rope before breaking all his bones or putting him on the wheel. The bailiff remained silent, staring over Charles's head, and Charles realized too late that the bailiff was about to lose consciousness. Stiff as a board, he fell to the floor of the scaffold, landing right on his face. Blood came streaming out of his mouth and Charles laid him on his side on the wooden floor so the blood could flow off. Doctor Boyer knelt down alongside him, not to help him, but because his own legs were starting to give way. With both hands he propped himself up on the unconscious bailiff. For the crowd, it no doubt looked as if the doctor was treating him, but Doctor Boyer himself needed a doctor.

Now a low mumbling of dissatisfaction rose from the crowd, at first sounding like a distant murmur, but then getting louder and angrier. and sweeping over the scaffold like a whirlwind. "Cut the muscles and the tendons," Doctor Boyer gasped, nodding urgently at Charles. André Legris was already standing behind Charles with an ax. When Charles nodded at him, he quickly moved toward the dying victim and with powerful blows chopped the arms and legs from the body. The horses were driven forward again, tearing Damiens into pieces. His left leg sailed through air and struck the bailiff, who was struggling to his feet, in the face.

Damiens's torso was still breathing weakly, and his eyes were wide open, looking up into the cloudy sky.

Bloody foam had formed on his lips and his pitch-black head of hair had suddenly turned white as snow. All of Paris spoke about that in days to come, and all of Europe's great

daily newspapers mentioned the phenomenon on their front pages, but it was nothing but the ashes.

Timidly, the crowd began applauding. It was late, and Uncle Nicolas gave his nephew a sign to parade around the scaffold. Slowly, Charles walked the perimeter of the wooden structure while the crowd chanted "Sanson, Sanson." Then he paused at the west side and put his hands on the parapet like a Roman general gripping the front of his chariot while marching into Rome. Thunderous applause swept over the square. Charles face remained impassive, but he lowered his head slightly as if to express his humble thanks to the crowd. "Sanson, Sanson," they continued cheering. Now he seemed more like an obedient gladiator in ancient Rome who enthralled the crowd simply because of his size and athletic build. Charles gazed back and forth over the huge crowd in the Place de Grève, and realized gradually that Paris was celebrating him. He sensed a power surging through him and suddenly felt strong, invincible and powerful. He strode to the north side to receive another ovation, then to the east and finally to the south side. Here, too, he bowed slightly and then turned to the court officials, who also nodded their approbation. They were happy. His uncle, too, nodded, and seemed surprised at how the crowd took leave of the new Monsieur de Paris.

The assistants were tossing Damiens's remaining body parts into the fire as dusk settled like ashes over their heads. Slowly, the blood-hungry crowd began to disperse and vanish in the adjoining lanes and avenues, returning to their villas or their wretched dwellings. As it began to rain again, hundreds of onlookers were still standing around. Now that the execution was over and the assistants were dismantling the scaffold, some took the opportunity to have a closer look at the scaffold. Charles was still standing at the top of the steps as Damiens's corpse was consumed by the flames, engulfing the hangmen in pungent clouds of smoke.

Charles had entered a strange, new world, a horrible one, and sensed that from now on, the blood that his ancestors had shed was now flowing in his own veins and would forever besmirch the family name. He felt lonely and ashamed that he had secretly enjoyed the adulation of the crowd. His behavior sickened him, and at that moment he swore forever to shun human contact. He didn't want to live among them, he didn't want to be one of them, he wanted to be alone and avoid this dreadful race of humankind. He was shocked that he'd been able to do it and that secretly he had imagined it all to be much more horrible. And was that all? Do I have a heart of stone, or am I still too young to experience genuine sympathy and grief, he asked himself. Someone who cannot feel pain can also not appreciate the pain of others, he knew. Perhaps that was it, but perhaps it was something entirely different. He was torn back and forth between disgust and pride.

The square quickly emptied out, and then, in the scattering crowd, he discovered Dan-Mali. "Oh, my God," he said, and quickly descended the steps. He wanted to stop her and tell her everything. Would this god-damned curse destroy everything he encountered in his life from now on? Was the sacrifice he'd made that day not be enough? Did he now have to lose Dan-Mali before he had even won her? "Dan-Mali!" he shouted, but the little Siamese woman did not turn around and disappeared in the crowd. He was about to run after her when a man stepped out from beneath the scaffold and addressed him. He had obviously been waiting for him. "The cheers were for you. You are a celebrity." The young man was perhaps ten years older than Charles, short, slender, and very pale. He was wearing a light brown dress coat, an expensive piqué vest, mustard yellow buckskin trousers, top boots, and was drawing on his clay pipe. Pompously he announced, "I am from the *Courrier de Versailles*. Gorsas is my name." In so doing he stared up into

the sky as is he was an important man posing for a painting. "Surely you have heard of me, or read my dispatches? Or perhaps just read about me. I am Gorsas. I always sign my articles in the *Courrier de Versailles.*" He put his pipe back in his mouth. Everything about him was ridiculous, as if a child were trying to imitate a grown-up.

"Unfortunately I am busy, Monsieur Gorsas." Charles turned around and started walking away, but Gorsas ran ahead and once again was standing in front of him. Taking his pipe out of his mouth, he tapped Charles patronizingly on the shoulder.

"Not so fast, Monsieur de Paris. Tell our readers what you felt when Damiens was drawn and quartered."

"I hoped it would soon be over."

Gorsas nodded his head pompously and then put on a sorrowful face. "No doubt it wasn't easy for a young man like you," he said, "but the people love you. You cut a dashing figure, Monsieur, you are an impressive person. You know, most people here don't look like much even though they're dressed in the finest clothing, But you would be an impressive figure even if you were naked. We'll meet again, Monsieur de Paris, I have an eye on you now."

Once again, Charles searched for Dan-Mali, but after a short while gave up. What could he have said to her? She had probably watched the entire execution and not taken her eyes off him. What else could he say? She had no doubt long ago made up her mind about him, but he hadn't been able to get a good look at her face. Maybe it wasn't her, at all. After all, there were lots of women from the Kingdom of Siam in Paris. The fear that it might have been Dan-Mali, however, was so great that he was deeply troubled.

That evening, Charles wouldn't be able to go straight home. Uncle Nicolas said he would take charge of taking down the scaffold, and after that all the hangmen and their assistants were invited to a meal in Jean-Baptiste's house.

Grandmother Dubut had arranged for the hangmen to spend the night in the barn before leaving on their return home the next day. "You put on a magnificent performance, Charles," he told him, "and someday you'll be a great hangman. Your father never had the strength for this job, it was too much for him. But people feel respect for you."

Charles wanted to reply, because there was a lot to say on that topic, but he remained silent. He wasn't sure—perhaps he shouldn't disdain the praise just bestowed on him. When people speak, they act if they know the whole story, but he wasn't sure of anything now. Everything he thought he'd known had been consumed in the flames that evening along with Damiens's corpse, and the surprising presence of Dan-Mali made clear to him that he'd no longer have a chance of a normal life. It greatly troubled him that Dan-Mali had seen him.

Charles hurried aimlessly through the streets. Under no circumstances did he want to go home and see the joy in the faces of his father, grandmother, and all his brothers and sisters. That would be too humiliating, because what had brought them joy had shocked him to the core, indeed left him a broken man. He still couldn't understand how a person would ever be able to inflict such sorrow and pain on his fellow man, and he found it almost impossible to believe that all of Paris had wanted to be there to witness it. He had not wanted to see it, but he'd had no choice. Restlessly, he prowled around the area of the Jardin du Palais Royal, wondering whether to visit one of the gambling parlors, but he had no money with him, and he was in too much of a turmoil to take a seat in one of the great coffee houses. He didn't want to hear people gossiping about the execution. What had they really seen from such a distance? The scaffold on the Place de Grève, and men no larger than their thumb. They'd heard shouting, but they hadn't looked into Damiens's eyes or touched his mangled body. But he,

Charles Henri Sanson, had seen everything, right before his face. He had been involved.

As he walked along, he met men who evidently had witnessed the execution. They nodded respectfully at him, some walked over to the other side of the street, but not because they were afraid, but because he was now a great man. Charles gradually had to admit to himself that this all gave him some satisfaction. Despite being at odds with himself about Dan-Mali. People felt admiration, respect, esteem for him, and the feeling of power flattered him, the feeling of being untouchable, invincible.

Without noticing, he had come to the allée des Soupirs, and felt the desire to enter a bordello. He wanted a woman to abase him, to humiliate him, because he wanted to prove he didn't need Dan-Mali, and never had needed her. But then he lost heart and continued on. He was determined to walk around until he collapsed with exhaustion and went to sleep.

A great weariness came over him around midnight and his restlessness started to leave him. He slowed his pace and decided to leave the quarter he was in and set out for home. At that moment, a dark figure emerged from under an archway, blocking his path. At first he thought he was being attacked and instinctively reached for his sword, but then he found himself looking into a young, dark face with wide, beaming eyes, a mouth forming a gentle smile, and beautiful white teeth, a rarity in Paris. She signaled for Charles to follow her into the house. She must be from the New World, he thought. She was so lovely and warm, and had nothing in common with all the white people who had spent hours today out in the Place de Grève. She led him through a narrow, dimly lit hallway smelling of rancid butter and into a hot, sticky room where scantily-clad black girls were sitting around a large table. Over the table hung an oil lamp covered by a red lamp shade that deflected the reddish light up to the ceiling while the faces of the girls below remained in semi-

darkness. Behind the table sat an old, almost toothless woman. The black girl led Charles to the table. "Three pounds" said the old woman in a coarse tone. He placed the coins on the table, then the old woman handed him one of the dirty, patched hand towels stacked on the table. The black girl took Charles by the hand while the other girls looked on enviously. They went down a staircase into a cellar that smelled of old wine kegs and was illuminated only by a narrow air shaft and a dozen candles. Charles heard soft breathing—there were other people in the room. Most were lying on their back, like wounded men in a field hospital, enjoying the artistry of the women of the night, who almost silently surrendered themselves to the love act. The girl led Charles to a straw mat lying on the floor surrounded by litter, then knelt down. She gently drew him down to her, pulled her skirt over her head, and held it a while in front of her breasts. Then she smiled and lowered her arms. Charles had never before seen a naked black person. He'd only read about it in books. Their breasts were large and fat, and their nipples thick and black. She lay down slowly on her back without taking her eyes off Charles, then reached out for him. Hesitantly, Charles began removing his clothing. She reached out for his penis, which was already stiff, and pulled him toward her, then took him in her arms. He gently embraced her at the waist and felt her bottom that stood out from her body like a huge apple. As she took him in her arms, Charles began to cry, and lowered his head into her bosom. Tenderly she passed her hand over his head and whispered words he did not understand, rocking him like a child in her arms. He cried silently, without making a sound, and didn't know if he'd ever be able to stop. A human life was too short to wash away the tears and all the sorrow he'd seen that day. He gave free rein to his tears, and gradually the pain in him subsided. The girl stroked his penis until it turned stiff again, then lay down astride him. Charles wanted to get up, but she pushed

him gently back onto the mat, propping herself up on his chest with both hands. She moved her hips up and down in a slow rhythm while looking him directly in the eye, nodding as if to say that now everything would be all right.

CHAPTER 6

When Charles got home, his father was sitting alone at the kitchen table. The room smelled of burnt lard and pumpkin soup.

"Did they forget you?" Charles asked.

"No," Jean-Baptiste replied, "I insisted on waiting up for you. Afterward you can take me to my bed, but first I want to drink a glass of wine with my son, because I'm proud of him."

Charles sat down.

"I was worried because you stayed out so long," said Jean-Baptiste in a soft voice. "They told me everything—some things went wrong, but it wasn't your fault. You acted decisively and impressed the judicial officials."

"I am also responsible for errors of the others."

"For the last ten years or so, Soubise has always been drunk. I even wonder if he ever sobers up."

Charles poured two cups of wine from the carafe, and the men raised their glasses to each other. When Charles saw that his father could also drink without his help, he emptied his own cup in one gulp.

"When you come home after work you can grease the ropes or sharpen the sword. That helps, too. I always greased my ropes, and if there was still time left, I cut up the old, used ropes. You can get ten sous for just a small piece of rope, and a lot of people will come to buy them. I know people who always carry a piece of a hangman's rope around in their trouser pockets just for good luck. I don't know why.

I have a whole collection of ropes, and they never brought me any luck. In any case, it brings peace to my soul when I grease the ropes after my day's work is complete."

Charles nodded. He didn't believe a word Jean-Baptiste said, but he let him go on. After all, he was his son. Charles looked up briefly had suddenly had the urge to slap him in the face, because his father had destroyed everything he held dear. It was bad enough having to be a hangman, Charles was thinking, but to lose Dan-Mali was more than he could take. It was easy for his father to talk. After all, he'd gotten his own way, thus destroying the life of his son.

Jean-Baptiste suddenly seemed troubled. He looked Charles in the eye, lowered his head and said, "Sometimes when my soul found no peace, I went to a bordello." When Charles did not react to that, he continued: "The hangman of Marseille once told me that after an execution he always went to a bordello. The pressure is really too great." He pointed to the carafe of wine on the table. "Pour us some more wine, my son. It wasn't easy for any of us. Your grandmother told me to wait for you, and tell you that the wine was for you. You deserved it. The hangmen of Orléans and Lyon are famous hangmen, and they said someday you would be great, as well. You have the strength and the decisiveness that others don't have, the gift of action."

Charles filled the cups again.

"But not too much, or your grandmother will have to get up at night." Jean-Baptiste laughed. "She's already threatened that she'll make me pee in the bed if I don't stop drinking after supper. But that would be bad for my kidneys." He laughed again, and it was clear how relieved he was about the way things had gone. He was really proud, it was easy for him to laugh, but Charles wasn't having any of it. He hated him for that, too. And he hated himself even more because, like his father, he'd gone to the bordello. Without even

realizing it, he'd done exactly what all the Sansons before him had done. So was he a Sanson?

"Let me drink from your cup," said Jean-Baptiste in a jovial voice. "That's something the Sansons always did."

"But I still want to become a doctor," Charles replied defiantly. "Don't forget that. That is my destiny"

Jean-Baptiste drank from Charles's cup, then he said, "Charles, we don't know God's plans for us. If it's your destiny, you will become a doctor, but for now you are Monsieur de Paris."

"For now," Charles said, drinking reluctantly from his father's cup.

In the early morning hours, Charles took his father to his bed in the same room as Grandmother Dubut and four of Charles's siblings. The old woman was still awake, but didn't speak a word. Jean-Baptiste asked Charles to go over to the grandmother's bed and say good-night to her. Her bed was huge and sat enthroned on long wooden legs. As he stood before the bed, he could smell the rose oil. The old woman was struggling to stay awake. Her breathing was shallow, her skin ashen and shining from all the beeswax she'd applied earlier to protect her skin.

"From this day forth," she whispered, "the king is in danger. The whole world has seen how fragile the monarchy is, and when the first thread rips, the whole fabric unravels. One by one, men will come to tear at the threads until the royal robe is destroyed and the king will stand there naked."

Old people always think that when they pass, the whole world comes to an end, Charles thought, but it's really just their own life that ends, and the body slowly disintegrates. The rest of the world is unaffected. He didn't want to hear all that. He hoped she would say something else to him—thank him, congratulate him for securing the future of the family. But instead she was talking about the king. She had no concern for her grandson's spiritual anguish. She wouldn't

even give milk to a starving cat. She'd saved the empire of the Sansons and no doubt believed that everyone coming after her would be eternally grateful and honor her. She mumbled a few more words about the king, then fell asleep. She had struggled to stay awake, awaiting the return of her grandson, and now they were all here, now she could sleep. She had assured her control and no longer needed to stay awake. Charles swore that on the day of her death he'd shorten the legs of her bed.

Charles was dazzled by the bright sunlight. He had overslept, and after he got up, he saw the events of the day before in a different light. He had been thrilled at the adulation of the crowd, but that had not changed his resolve. As soon as one of his brothers was old enough, he would give up his position as a hangman and become a doctor. Last night, everything had seemed so hopeless, and he was surprised at how clear everything seemed now. But for Dan-Mali, there was still no solution. Sorrowfully he thought of the little Siamese girl and was deeply troubled that she'd seen him performing the duties of his office. Then he thought of Grandmother Dubut. It was strange she'd not awakened him. He walked out into the yard where his brothers and sisters were playing and washed off in the trough. One of his brothers mentioned that Grandmother hadn't made any breakfast that morning.

"Oh," Charles joked, "she's forgetting her duties, so she must be really sick."

He hurried back into the house and knocked on the bedroom door. Jean-Baptiste lay in bed reading a medical book. "She's still sleeping," he whispered, "Let her be."

Charles walked over to the bed and saw she was still lying just the way she was the night before, with her eyes open. When he touched her hand, a shudder ran down his spine. Her hand was ice cold. At once he felt her carotid artery, just as he had learned to do at the University of

Leiden. She no longer had a pulse—she was dead. He felt no grief, he'd never liked her for destroying his dream, and only wished she'd died earlier. You can burn down buildings and drown cats, but you shouldn't destroy dreams, he thought as he walked over to his father.

"She's just sleeping," said Jean-Baptiste, putting the book down. The title was *Nostalgia,* written by a doctor named Nicolai and published five years before. Charles sat down on the edge of the bed, staring at his feet.

"Father," he said, "Grandmother is dead."

Jean-Baptiste was deeply troubled by the death of his headstrong mother. Fortunately, the kitchen maid had learned the old woman's way of cooking, and the food and drink were the same, which pleased the sick man. He hired another maid, but the spirit of Grandmother Dubut had vanished.

The following day Charles received the thanks and best wishes of the justice department. A messenger delivered the message, along with a special reward for his exceptional talents. That was the first money he'd ever earned. The newspapers also praised the dignified and brilliantly staged execution, and the executioner's gentlemanly reserve. Gorsas, in particular, heaped praises on his name, writing that Charles's name was now forever connected with those of King Louis XV and his would-be assassin.

Charles was now of two minds. On the one hand, he was proud he had accomplished the task, and on the other hand, he was ashamed. He was happy that for the first time in his life he had earned his own pay, but he didn't want to become famous for being a hangman. Overnight he had advanced to the head of the Sanson family, but he had lost Dan-Mali.

The latter thought tormented him to such a degree that one evening while he was sitting at the piano with Dominique, he started talking about Dan-Mali. His sister seemed amused.

"Don't laugh at me," he scolded her.

"But that's wonderful! My big brother has fallen love."

"But the girl didn't know it," he said, mournfully, "and now that she has found out I am the hangman, she certainly won't want me anymore."

Dominique embraced him. "Charles, listen to me. Many people fail just by thinking too much. Just go and see her, and ask. Perhaps the girl you saw wasn't even her. You said that yourself."

They played another piece, and when they were done, Dominique asked, "Well, are you going to?"

He shook his head and said in a soft voice: "I must tell you something. She comes from the Kingdom of Siam."

Dominique made a long face. "Can't you find a woman from Paris, like most people do? Must it be someone from the other end of the earth? They have very different customs and traditions there, and they speak another language. How do you even talk to her?"

"Actually, we don't talk at all," he said, visibly embarrassed, "we just look at each other."

"Charles," Dominique sighed, "then you don't know each other at all."

Charles walked past the Jesuit Monastery several times, but didn't dare to knock on the door. He wanted to see Father Gerbillon again and to learn what he knew, but secretly he hoped to meet Dan-Mali there. Father Gerbillon was only a pretext, he had to admit to himself.

One morning he gathered up all his courage and knocked on the door. An elderly priest invited him in. The monastery seemed even more imposing to Charles than the way he remembered it on his last visit. It was a splendid building with high, vaulted ceilings, large windows, and wide staircases made of gleaming white stone. So this is where God's servants live who sermonize about poverty and live

here like kings, Charles thought. The old priest knocked on a two-winged door, opened it, and invited Charles to enter. Before him was the most luxuriously appointed study and the largest library that Charles had ever seen. It reminded him of a royal gallery in Versailles. Father Gerbillon sat behind a massive oak table composing a letter, and only looked up briefly. He didn't seem surprised to see him. "I've expected you, Charles. Do take a seat. I'll be ready in just a moment."

Charles sat down. This temple of knowledge was a true feast for the eyes. Everywhere there were books, newspapers, reports, drawings, paintings, and a gigantic globe of the world by the window that made clear to every visitor that the world did not end in Marseille or Normandy.

"Did someone tell you, or did you have a premonition?" Charles asked suspiciously.

"No, no," Gerbillon laughed, "Just experience and good common sense. You are a seeker. Here in Paris you can hardly expect to find anyone who can help you. Here we have only parrots. Have you ever seen a parrot?"

Charles shook his head and shifted around uneasily on his chair.

"Here in Paris they are kept as pets by eccentric noblemen, but in the Kingdom of Siam they are regarded as pests. Along with ravens, they are probably the most intelligent bird in the world.

These animals can remember words and their meanings and repeat them. If you ask me, that is deviant behavior. But what brings you to me?"

"Do you think that God has a plan for each of us that we are destined to fulfill, that there is such a thing as fate or a curse inflicted on men?"

Father Gerbillon laughed heartily, then turned serious. "Charles, you have come to me so early in the morning to ask me such an existential question. But it's still too early, and first I need a mug of Bordeaux."

"Is this question so hard to answer?"

"Charles, use your common sense. Do you seriously believe that God has individual plans for millions of people? If he had a plan just for the two of us, it would fill volumes. There wouldn't be enough trees in the world to put all these plans down on paper. There is no plan, Charles, but there is a need for men to feel they have greater significance and direction than a stupid parrot in the forests of Siam. If you were a mathematician, Charles, you'd believe in probability, but we men are not mathematicians. Mathematics offers no consolation, and thus we search for a divine meaning. When a poor fellow loses his wife three times, we believe we see a structure in his fate, and we call it a curse. But there is nothing to it, Charles—no god, no plan, no goal."

"And thus, no curse. I alone am the master of my destiny?"

"Not completely. There are practical constraints, family circumstances, financial circumstances, political circumstances. But man has the choice. If he doesn't believe that, then he has no choice."

Charles was silent for a while then said. "I would like to talk to the young girl from Siam. Her name is Dan-Mali."

Father Gerbillon raised an eyebrow. "Oh, that can be arranged, but at the moment she is praying in the chapel. Nonetheless, we will not succeed in redeeming her from her Buddha. She considers our Christ to be just another incarnation of Buddha, and I can understand that. I understand her completely. Buddha is a more compelling story. Buddha is tolerant, Buddhists can indulge in sex without having a bad conscience. We, on the other hand, keep staring at the crucifix over our bed and can't even get an erection."

Charles stared at him in disbelief.

"I am sorry if I've shocked you, Charles, but travel to foreign continents helps you revise your image of the world.

Once you have seen the Kingdom of Siam, you see everything differently."

"When can I speak with Dan-Mali?" Charles persisted. The priest's words didn't interest him now.

"That will be difficult. Her knowledge of French is still very limited, and she is returning to Siam with the next convoy. But she will come back. She loves Paris, and I like the young girl. I'd be happy to have her in our cloister. She's a wonderful cook. Let's just stay in touch, Charles, and someday you'll see Dan-Mali again."

"I thought I could see her right away."

"That's not a good idea," said Father Gerbillon.

For Charles, that was the end of the matter. Looking back, he was embarrassed. Probably he meant nothing to this young woman. It was all his imagination—desires, hopes, dreams He was ashamed of his naivety. In order to forget, he would from now on concentrate on people who praised him. During this period there were no spectacular executions, and they were done quickly, as Charles had always correctly calculated the length of the rope. Petty criminals, desperate, hungry thieves who stole a few eggs, a loaf of bread or an apple in the market square were branded with glowing irons, and after each performance Charles-Henri Sanson, the hangman of Paris, would bow to his public. Increasingly, he enjoyed the adulation of people who actually meant nothing to him. It's possible to shield oneself against many things, but rarely is one immune from praise. And Charles enjoyed the adulation defiantly. If Dan-Mali rejected him because of his profession, then his urge to be a great hangman became even greater. He would no longer hide and reject his trade— yes, he was the hangman, the hangman of Paris, and earned a lot of money. For anyone who had grown up in poverty and lived modestly all his life, that is a very special feeling. He knew that people like Antoine would never understand that.

Some people claim that money doesn't make you happy, something he couldn't judge, but it definitely doesn't make you unhappy.

Money means freedom and independence, and wasn't it a wonderful feeling to be able to go to a doctor? Charles achieved a certain inner peace. Or was it arrogance? He ordered himself an elegant, brightly colored suit from a tailor in the Rue de la Reine, and from then on he could stroll like a proud peacock through the parks of Paris, enjoying the yearning glances of young ladies and the admiration of simple people. Sometimes when he was home alone in his pharmacy, he was ashamed of how he had changed. It was hard for him to understand the change that had come over him, to say nothing of accepting it, but he had suffered too much during all the years in which he and his family had been shunned. His compulsion to live the life of a hangman in fine clothing was for him an act of revenge. He was the Monsieur de Paris and wore the same expensive clothes as the people who despised him. He wasn't content to exercise his office in silence and make himself otherwise invisible, like his father. He wanted Paris to see him. He was their hangman and killed for them. And at home, a freshly printed copy of the *Encyclopédie* awaited him. Who in Paris could afford Diderot's *Encyclopédie*?

Charles often took walks in the garden of the Palais Royal and over the years learned the secret language of women. One day, while sitting in a café, he noticed a woman from a noble family who kept glancing over at him while playing with her fan. She was no longer a young woman. He understood the coquettish language of the fan, and accepted the invitation to take a seat at her table. They had a pleasant chat about Diderot's *Encyclopédie,* thereby demonstrating not just that they could read, but also had money and a degree of education. From time to time they dropped discreet

words or cues revealing more about their own status, casually mentioning a hunting trip, a theater performance, or a dinner with influential people. Charles quickly learned that the lady was a marquise, and he responded, saying only that he was an official of the Justice Department. Then she quickly got to the point and asked if a woman was expecting him for supper. When he replied to the contrary, she appeared relieved and asked if he could accompany her home. The chairs in this café gave her back pains, she claimed, and with a smile she added she'd have to lie down for a while. They took a coach and drove to her mansion, and after she told the servants she did not want to be disturbed, they crossed the exquisitely appointed salon and entered the bedroom.

"Do you know anything about massages?"

"Yes," replied Charles, "I am familiar with human musculature. Shall I massage you, Madame?"

"Would you?" she asked with a painful expression.

"Naturally," Charles replied, "I can't bear seeing beautiful women suffer."

Now the marquise smiled. "What are you waiting for, monsieur?" she sighed, and lay down on the bed.

"Would it be better if I disrobed?"

"Much better," Charles said, leaning over her.

She kissed him briefly, touching her tongue to his lips. Then she reached for her crotch and whispered, "You're torturing me, monsieur. I thought you wanted to relieve my sorrow." Then she reached into Charles's trousers and said in a firm voice, "Take your pants off, Monsieur, we can't do it like that."

Charles undressed as she watched. "I like men like you. Any sculptor would be delighted to have you as a model. What was the dear Lord thinking when he created you?"

"He was thinking of you, Madame," Charles joked.

"Do you mean he wanted to drive us women crazy? Or are you the apple in the Garden of Eden? Am I embarrassing

you?" She abruptly turned onto her stomach. Charles started massaging her neck and shoulder blades.

"I like it from behind, Monsieur, like our ancestors ten thousand years ago, and do it violently, as if you were committing a crime or mounting a little slut. And if you shout and insult me as well, you can be my future lover."

As Charles descended the wide, curving staircase he met a young man who was visibly shocked to see him. He had without doubt recognized the young hangman. Charles stopped and looked up the stairway to the second floor. There stood the marquise, smiling in her pink dressing gown.

"My sister, the Marquise, has tea with the hangman of Paris?"

The marquise looked puzzled and stared at Charles. She took his silence as an affirmation. The young man walked past Charles without a greeting, then took the last steps with an amused look on his face, until he had reached his sister.

"You deceived me!" The marquise suppressed a shout and her voice cracked as she said "If I had known that you were the hangman! Mon dieu!"

"Did you suffer any harm because of it, Madame?" Charles asked in a gallant tone which did not conceal the smug undertone in his voice, and then he left.

"My lawyer will let you know, Monsieur de Paris, you can be sure of that," she said in a haughty voice before disappearing behind the balcony.

Once back home, Charles felt mean and hollow. It seemed to him he'd done this, too, just out of defiance, to take revenge on the nobles who despised him. In retrospect, the adventure with the marquise disappointed him. He had hoped for more gratification and happiness.

Charles went regularly to his pharmacy to read the books he had bought in the Paris print shops. It was a lofty feeling having the chance to buy this knowledge, and again and again he became engrossed in Diderot's *Encyclopédie*. He

immersed himself in the world of plants and healing substances and forgot what had troubled him so badly before that. But his dreams reminded him that he was deceiving himself. At night he still dreamed of Dan-Mali, and the next morning he could still remember what they were talking about. It was strange, for he was quite aware that the words in his dream were figments of his imagination.

Over time, Charles forgot the incident with the marquise and performed his work at the scaffold more and more as a daily routine. When Jean-Baptiste saw that Charles was able to cope with his new role, he decided to move to a small estate in the country at Brie-Comte-Robert along with the maid and the younger children. He felt death approaching, and had terrible visions, losing himself from time to time in bizarre thoughts. He said that if fate wanted to deliver a cruel blow, it wasn't enough to paralyze a man, it had to let him live as long as possible after that so he would learn to suffer and grieve.

Dominique had moved out, also. She had married and lived with her husband, a hardware dealer in Beaune. Only Charles remained in the house with his assistants Barre, Firmin, Desmorets and Gros. The four of them cared for the horses, the tools, made repairs, and went shopping. And Gros cooked—badly. But he was the only one considered for this work, as he used to work in a bakery. He was a small, friendly man with a round face, a good-natured fellow who always had a cheerful word for everyone in the house.

Barre and Firmin were young butchers who had worked in a slaughterhouse. The two spent all their free time together. Barre was also short, but with a broad build and powerful arms, like a sailor. He often seemed very grim, as if he were angry about something. He hung around in taverns, waiting for someone to treat him disrespectfully, then he'd suddenly lash out and start a fight. Firmin, on the other hand,

was skinny as a skeleton and had a strikingly narrow face and a receding forehead that made him look a little retarded. Barre and Firmin quarreled often, but when either was in a tight spot, they clung together like brothers. They sometimes seemed like a married couple after their golden wedding anniversary.

Desmorets, finally, was the grandson of the Bordeaux executioner, and the youngest of them all. Since he could write and was very good at numbers, Charles had entrusted him with the bookkeeping of income and expenses in the house. Desmorets also kept an inventory of the clothes taken from victims of a hanging or beheading and handled all the correspondence with the Justice officials.

Charles was fortunate in having good helpers, as it was difficult at that time to find decent people whom one could also trust. Just the same, with the possible exception of Desmorets, it was impossible to have an intelligent conversation with them, and they were often too coarse for Charles. Thus, once again, Charles started entrusting his thoughts to his diary. He wrote a great deal, never making corrections, trying to write away his bloody memories, and never re-read old entries. Writing for Charles became a cleansing ritual. After he'd closed the diary, he tucked it carefully between two thick books on medicine, and drank some wine before going to bed. He fell asleep quickly, but his sleep was neither long nor refreshing.

In the morning, he would care for the people who came to him seeking relief from their pain. To his surprise, word had gotten around that he was even more competent than his father, and even doctors sometimes sent their hopeless cases to him. He was soon considered a great authority on healing of joint pains and stiff shoulders. Afternoons he spent studying Diderot's *Encyclopédie* in his herb garden, where he planted medicinal herbs, or riding horseback in the nearby forests. After the death of Grandmother Dubut and Jean-

Baptist's departure the house seemed empty. The familiar voices of his noisy brothers and sisters had fallen silent, and he missed them.

One day, Charles had to execute a manservant from Versailles. As he sheared the condemned man's hair for the hanging, the man confessed he had had an affair with one of the mistresses of the king. "Why did God give me such good equipment if I'm not allowed to use it?" he asked Charles.

"Please sit quietly, or I'm afraid I'll cut you."

The manservant laughed. "With these little scissors?" He took a little book from his pocket. "I wrote this, monsieur, at the behest of the king." The little book was carefully bound in red leather. It was a guide to the bordellos of Paris. "I'll never need this again," he said in a melancholy tone, "but you, who knows, may find it to your taste. I've heard that hangmen after a particularly cruel execution go to a bordello to find relief from the tension. But be careful—if you go too often, the appeal begins to fade. At the end you'll need a whole opera house of naked bodies to make the little man stand up. In case you need a lawyer someday, you can find one at such places. Everybody who is somebody goes there, but unfortunately no one there wanted to defend me."

Charles stuck the guidebook in his vest pocket and thanked him with a nod.

"Thus my life hasn't been meaningless," the manservant said with a bitter laugh.

"Do you think that life sometimes has a meaning? Please stand up so I can tie your hands."

Two hours later, as Charles was wrapping the noose around his neck on the scaffold, the condemned man whispered his last words: "I was hung like a stag." Then the trap door opened beneath him.

When Charles returned home in the evening, he added the little book the manservant had given him to the collection of

curiosities he'd inherited from his father. He had little interest in looking at it.

A few days later Charles received a summons to appear in court. The marquise had actually brought charges against him. She demanded that Charles-Henri Sanson be ordered by the court to put a noose around his own neck and beg her for forgiveness. She further demanded that for the protection of the public he be required to wear a uniform and a badge on his chest in the future to identify himself as a hangman.

Now, Charles really needed a lawyer, and he remembered the guide that the manservant from Versailles had given him. The man had also noted the bordellos frequented by the best attorneys in Paris. Something within him struggled against the idea, and he never even took out the book. He wanted a serious lawyer and not one that frequented such places. He mentioned it at supper, and Desmorets said he knew of an attorney who frequented the Golden Keg Tavern and sat at the last table in the back of the room every morning drinking his coffee. One could simply join him at the table and present the problem.

The next morning, Charles entered the tavern and found the middle-aged man sitting at a table in the back.

"Do have a seat, young man. How can I help you?" He evidently hadn't taken a bath in a long time and stared constantly at Charles while slurping his dark coffee. His face was gaunt, his skin wrinkled and gray, and the odor coming from his mouth was foul, leaving the impression he had digestive problems.

"I'm looking for a lawyer," Charles said, taking a seat on the well-born bench.

"Yes, just as I assumed, so listen to me: for each half hour, or part of a half hour, I charge forty sous, and you pay for the coffee. Can you afford that? Do you have a job?"

Charles nodded.

"What kind of work?"

"I'm the hangman of Paris," Charles said outright.

"Don't say anything more," the lawyer said, "up to this point our conversation has been without charge. Now get up and leave. If word gets around that I'm defending the hangman of Paris, I'll lose all my clients."

"Can you recommend someone?"

"Even a recommendation would ruin me. What do you think my colleagues would think of me if I recommended you to them? Go to hell."

Charles got up and headed for the door.

"Try your luck at the Château of Madame Gourdan," the lawyer called after him.

The so-called château was in the Rue des Deux-Portes. Wealthy businessmen met there with influential politicians, lawyers, journalists, noblemen, artists, and clergymen, without any pretense that the customers were divided between the people, Royalists, and Republicans. They all wanted the same thing. Madame Gourdan's bordellos comprised many buildings. No such establishment in the world was larger or more luxurious. Charles went to the main building, where a huge assortment of ornately carved erotic toys was on display in the lobby. Madame Gourdan was the world's greatest supplier of godemichés, or dildos. Among her most faithful customers were the nuns and abbesses of Europe's nunneries. *Bijoux religieux* was the code name for this accessory.

Marie-Luce, a scantily-clad girl, led Charles into a little anteroom with erotic Gobelin tapestries decorating the walls. The rugs were heavy and dampened any sound. This was the seat of power of the most influential bordello owner in France. "Monsieur," she said, "I am pleased that you honor us with your visit and will do everything possible to satisfy your desires. Marie-Luce will introduce you at once to the

girls—and to our prices. We have a wide range of quirky things to offer, for example the satanic chambers." She smiled. "But our house also has some rules, among them discretion. In the salons you will meet well-known celebrities, but you will remain silent, just as the other guests will remain discrete. You will not injure our girls. Anal penetration and whipping are permitted, but only with the girl's permission, and for an additional charge."

Marie-Luce led Charles into a large, circular, glass domed room through which the starry sky was visible. Small tables with comfortable red sofas were arranged in a circle around the room. Far enough from each other that a confidential conversation was possible. The guests felt at home here. Some wore silk dressing gowns, others were in street clothes and appeared to have come there just to smoke their pipe, converse, and look at naked women. The young women stood in seductive poses along a counter covered in black material seeking to catch the eye of the guests with unambiguous gazes. Charles pointed at a woman in blue underwear and a transparent robe of the same color.

"Enjoy your stay, Monsieur," said Marie-Luce, introducing him to the woman in blue who led him behind the counters where heavy, red curtains along a wall concealed entrances to the separate rooms. The woman in blue chose the last room whose walls and ceiling were covered with beautiful mirrors. Charles stopped in front of one mirror, and it looked as if he had become part of a painting, as the mirrors were set in ornamental golden frames. Otherwise, the room was sparsely appointed—a wash basin, a hand towel, and a bed, all the color of gold. An oil lamp was reflected in mirrors on the walls.

"I'm looking for a lawyer," said Charles.

"Marie-Jeanne, but just call me Jeanne."

"Is that your real name?"

Marie-Jeanne laughed. It was a charming laugh.

"Marie-Jeanne Bécu, but here I'm just Marie-Jeanne."

She was eighteen, had large breasts, and a warm, round face. Her mouth was a rather small and her lips too narrow for such a wide face, but she was one of Madame Gourdan's favorite courtesans.

"What are you by profession, Monsieur? Or were you born rich?" Marie-Jeanne asked with a laugh. "I hope someday I'll meet my prince here. If he marries me, he'll save a lot of money that he'd otherwise squander in our establishment. And in addition, I'm a wonderful cook." She loosened her blue gown and let it slide over her shoulders to the floor.

"I'm looking for a lawyer, and that's all."

"You're not afraid, are you?"

"No," Charles replied impatiently, "but I need a lawyer to represent me in court."

"There are several in the domed hall outside. I'll take you there." Marie-Jeanne wrapped her gown around her shoulders again and accompanied Charles back into the hall. "And there won't be anything between us this evening?" she said, disappointed.

Charles shook his head, cordially. "No, Mademoiselle. I'm sorry."

"But don't forget my name—Marie-Jeanne!"

"Charles!" he suddenly heard a voice calling. A man holding a glass of champagne stood up from one of the sofas in the back of the room and walked toward him. At first, Charles didn't recognize him.

"Antoine?" Charles asked in disbelief. He was still slender and haggard. His long sideburns made his face look even narrower and the striking hooked nose even more prominent. "Antoine Quentin Fouquier de Tinville," Charles continued in a soft voice.

"What brings you here? Has it got to the point when I must offer you a warm bowl of soup?" Antoine laughed and

looked Charles up and down. "You have gotten even taller. And otherwise, have you become a doctor?"

"No," replied Charles, "and you?"

"I'm a lawyer, just as you predicted." Then, with a scornful voice, he added, "I don't like to have bloody hands, Monsieur de Paris."

"I'm looking for a lawyer to represent me in court."

"Tell me about the case," Antoine said, feigning interest. He led Charles to a free table where they sat down and Charles told him the story of his affair with the marquise. "Did you do it?" Antoine grinned.

"That's beside the point," Charles answered in a grave voice.

"I know the marquise—everybody knows her—so you screwed her." Antoine broke out in a fit of laughter. "The marquise in bed with the hangman—now I've heard it all."

"Can you defend me in court?"

"Of course. The trial is next Friday."

"How do you know that?" Charles gasped with astonishment.

"If you're born into the right family, there are no secrets from you in Paris. That's something you don't learn in Rouen, Charles, all you need are connections, old blue blood."

Charles nodded. At least he'd found a lawyer, even if he disliked Antoine even more that before.

"How tragic," Antoine said in a sarcastic tone. "Here we have a young, good-looking man with talent and ambition who wants to become a doctor and then he winds up on the scaffold."

"Are you married?" asked Charles, to change the topic.

"Not yet, but soon. I'm going to marry my cousin, who's very wealthy. Money attracts money, and she has the most beautiful feet in Paris. I'm attracted to feet, Charles, it arouses me tremendously. And you? Married?"

"I'm not married."

"That's probably pretty difficult for a hangman, but perhaps you'll find someone here. For these women, even a hangman is a good catch, don't you think?"

Antoine Quentin Fouquier de Tinville appeared punctually in the courtroom and Charles went straight to him. "How does it look?" he whispered.

Antoine beamed from ear to ear. "You are going to lose, Charles." At that moment, the marquise entered the courtroom with her entourage. "Because I am representing the marquise," he added. "Just admit it, and you'll get off easy. If you fight the charge, I'll crush you like a louse. That's what I'm paid for, Charles, it's nothing personal. I've got some plans for the marquise. You don't find such quarrelsome bitches as the marquise every day."

Charles was dumbfounded, and stared in consternation at Antoine.

"The world is a bad place, Charles. The day after our meeting I went right to the marquise and offered her my services. I mean my legal services," he whispered. He approached the marquise, greeted her with a gallant bow, and together they took their seats in the first row.

Charles was still speechless. He had relied completely on Antoine. Then he sat down and impatiently awaited the opening of the proceedings.

Two staircases led to a long table standing on a wooden platform. Behind the table, looking bored, sat the judge and a scribe. After a while, the court president tapped his gavel on the table top and gave a signal to the two soldiers standing next to the entryway to close the doors and allow no one else to enter the room. The benches for the opposing parties and the public were arranged like pews in the nave of a church. In the first row on the left sat the plaintiff, the proud marquise, her brother, and Antoine, and Charles sat on the right, all

alone. Behind the disputing parties sat dozens of onlookers, either acquaintances of the marquise or those who just wanted to see the hangman up close. As far as the incident was concerned, the marquise only said they had had tea together as a titter ran through the crowd.

Charles didn't deny his misdeeds but as a gentleman did not of course mention the amorous adventure. He'd gotten control of himself again, and insisted on presenting basic facts about his profession as he stepped up before the judge. Charles was an imposing figure, tall, proud, confident, unafraid, and he radiated calmness and composure. "Why do I kill people?" he asked in a loud voice. "For personal motives? For pleasure? No, esteemed members of the court, I carry out the sentence imposed by you yourselves according to our law. And what would happen, gentlemen, if I didn't carry out your sentences? The law would become the mockery of society because no one would carry out your sentences. May I say with all due respect, the criminals you convict do not fear your sentence, nor the ink you use to formalize the sentence, but they fear my hands, the hands of the hangman. And who, gentlemen, gives me the right to carry out the duties of this office? It's his majesty, the king in person. It is the historic responsibility of any king to punish crimes in his kingdom and protect the innocent. I carry out the sentences on behalf of the king, and am therefore a royal official. Yes, I kill, but in contrast with soldiers I do not kill soldiers in foreign uniforms, I kill criminals whom you have convicted and according to our laws have been condemned to death. Just as a soldier has the duty of maintaining external peace with other nations, I protect our internal peace. While our king requires hundreds of thousands of soldiers to maintain external peace, he needs only a single man to maintain the peace at home: the hangman. Whereas the soldier is honored for killing on the battlefield, I am despised. I did not come here to defend myself against the absurd

accusations of Madame la Marquise, I am here to demand recognition of my status as an official of justice."

The judges started murmuring among themselves and exchanging confused glances. The audience became restless, and Antoine appeared irritated. In any case, his sarcastic grim had vanished.

"I beseech the court to permit me and all my descendants henceforth to use the title of *de Longval* in my name based on the noble heritage of my father, the Chevalier Sanson de Longval."

The court was appalled. They had expected to see a timid hangman fighting for his life, and instead had before them a confident young man who had come here not to beg, but demand his due. If fate had destined him to be a hangman, then he intended to be one unlike any the world had seen before. In conclusion, Charles cried out to the judges, "If you condemn me, you condemn your own actions."

"Monsieur Charles-Henri Sanson," said the chief judge, "The hall is reserved for only one hour. Have you finished your presentation?"

Charles nodded respectfully.

"Your remarks," the judge continued, "are not the subject of the charges brought against you and are therefore irrelevant."

"I respectfully disagree. Madame la Marquise would not be sitting here today if I were an officer of the royal guards. Therefore, these remarks are clearly significant."

The judge replied in a monotone: "The court will recess for deliberation and the sentence will be announced in writing in half an hour." Then he rose and left the hall.

Charles was pronounced innocent on all charges. The marquise was aghast, and raged around the courtroom, shouting at Antoine and demanding he do something at once. As Charles left the courtroom and stepped out into the corridor, Dominique came running toward him and embraced

CLAUDE CUENI

him enthusiastically. She didn't know whether to cry, or cheer for joy, but pride showed in her eyes.

"You are in Paris?" Charles asked in astonishment.

"Of course, Charles. I've come here with my husband on business. Charles, the people in the hall were so impressed," she whispered, "they spoke of you with such admiration, how cleverly and elegantly you chose your words, how calm and certain your speech was, and how you presented everything so rationally. You convinced us all, Charles."

Charles embraced her firmly. At that moment, the marquise stepped out into the hall with her attorney. She was searching for the right words, but Antoine took her arm and gently but firmly led her toward the exit. As they walked past Charles, Antoine whispered to him: "This is the beginning, not the end."

Charles saw a short man in a light brown coat, an expensive piqué vest and mustard yellow deer-skin trousers leaving the courtroom. He immediately recognized the gaudy clothing. It was Gorsas, the newspaper writer.

"Brilliant" Gorsas said respectfully as he took his pipe from his mouth and knocked it out on one of the columns.

"But you have come a hundred years too soon. The times are not yet ready for it. Eventually the death penalty will be abolished, but we're not ready for that yet. Is this your wife?"

"No," Charles replied, "this is my sister Dominique."

Dominique curtsied politely.

"You are an interesting man; I have an eye on you," Gorsas said, nodding and bidding them farewell.

A few weeks later, Charles ordered a new suit from his tailor, this time in royal blue. The first time he wore it, he took a casual stroll in the garden of the Palais Royal where he promptly crossed paths with the marquise, who was flirting with a very young man. She stopped in her tracks and shouted: "Monsieur, blue is the color of royalty and it is

inappropriate for actors, Jews, hangmen or simple people to wear it."

"Thank you," Charles replied with a smile, "I should probably hire you as a nanny so you could assist me in the morning in choosing my clothes."

"Are you just as skillful with your sword as with your big mouth?"

"I thought you were going to thank me for my discretion in court, Madame. After all, we didn't just drink tea together at our meeting in your house."

Her face flushed with anger. She took her companion's arm and tugged at it so hard that he understood they had to move along. "Shall I challenge him to a duel?" the young man asked in a trembling voice.

"You are more useful in bed, monsieur," she whispered, but loud enough that Charles could hear it.

Once again, Charles had time to think about his future, and decided to pay another visit to the Jesuit cloister. He felt he had to, it was an internal compulsion. Father Gerbillon received him cordially and led him directly into his pharmacy where some young Siamese women were busily grinding herbs in mortars. Charles recognized Dan-Mali at once and was beside himself with joy. Father Gerbillon watched with a knowing smile and said he'd have to leave briefly and be right back. Charles got up his courage and went over to her. She smiled, lowered her head respectfully, and placed her hands together in greeting. They stood there simply looking at each other, and even if they didn't exchange a single syllable, it seemed to Charles as if they were exchanging a shower of words.

After a while, she said she'd been studying French hard since they returned. He'd be glad to help her, he replied. If she had someone to talk to, it would be much easier to learn. She nodded eagerly. Clearly, she had understood everything.

Then she looked over her shoulder, and her laughter froze. Father Gerbillon was back. He showed Charles the new herbs from Siam, but Charles only had eyes for Dan-Mali.

"What do you think, Father Gerbillon, would it be a good idea for me to practice French with Dan-Mali one day a week?"

Father Gerbillon hesitated. "I'll think about it," he said finally.

A few days later, a letter came from the court. Charles expected it would be another order for an execution, but it was a summons to another trial demanded by the marquise. Antoine had been right. The lady was bored, spent all her time in amusement parks, and would never stop suing. She had enough time and money.

Charles had another suit of green cloth tailored in time, and appeared wearing it at the court. Antoine came straight toward him. "That's a friendly color," he joked, "but did you know the marquise says you'd be wearing blue. Does she have trouble recognizing colors?"

"There are people who can't tell green from red, and we call them colorblind. But I've never heard of anyone who couldn't see the difference between blue and green."

"And you'd know that better than I would, of course," Antoine said in a serious tone, "because you're smarter than I am." Then he patted Charles patronizingly on the shoulder. "I'm not angry with you, Charles. Thanks to you I have a new client who's rich and malicious, and needs legal counseling every day. You know, a sort of relationship develops in that way in the course of time between a lawyer and his client. The marquise gets involved in a case, starts giving advice to her friends, and thus she always needs me. I have you to thank for that. Oh, by the way, let me win today, or I won't be able to bed her down today after the trial." He

burst out laughing. It wasn't spontaneous, but tense and malicious.

The marquise entered the courtroom and headed straight toward Antoine without deigning to look at Charles.

Even before the session began, the court president was yawning. He read the marquise's complaint in a monotonous voice and asked Charles for a brief statement. Charles explained to the court that he was of noble lineage, his father was the chevalier Sanson de Longval, and that he could not be deprived of his noble standing just because he was also the executioner. He was thus entitled to wear the color blue. In any case, regardless of the judgment of the court, he declared he wouldn't be wearing blue any more, as the color was not compatible with his complexion. That comment set off tumultuous laughter from the public. Many noblemen were present, among them the marquis de Létorières, who seemed delighted. With a smile, Charles turned to the public, but he froze instantly on seeing Father Gerbillon seated in the third row. Now there was no doubt the Jesuit priest knew that Charles was the Monsieur de Paris, and if he knew, so did everyone in the monastery. Never in a million year would Gerbillon introduce him to the secrets of pharmacy, never would he allow the hangman of Paris to give French lessons to Dan-Mali. The court declared the charge against Charles null and void, but for Charles is was a Pyrrhic victory.

Father Gerbillon waited for Charles by the exit. "I thought you hated your father's vocation and wanted to become a doctor," he said visibly disappointed.

"I still do," Charles replied defiantly, "but I was forced to do it, I didn't want to."

The priest nodded, and seemed lost in thought. Finally, he took him by both shoulders. "You have a lonely life, apart from society, Charles. It won't be a simple life."

"I don't wish to trouble you any longer," Charles said.

Father Gerbillon gave a conciliatory smile. "I, too, live apart from society, so how can I condemn you?"

"A Jesuit priest does not live apart from the world."

"Sometimes he does."

"May I still come and visit you?"

"You mean if you can still come and visit Dan-Mali?" Charles ran his fingers through his hair, embarrassed, as if he had just been caught lying.

"Maybe it's just as well that you don't come for a while," the priest said. "Everybody in town knows who you are, and soon we'll be returning to Siam. This second dispute wasn't necessary, Charles. You've been wearing green recently, in any case. One must know when enough is enough."

Shortly thereafter, the marquis de Létorières was seen in public wearing the same identical green suit, and soon this creation was referred to as the *mode à la Sanson,* and hundreds or perhaps thousands of Parisian men had themselves fitted for green suits, as if they wanted to say *we are all like Charles-Henri Sanson, we're with him, and he's one of us.* But that wasn't really the case. It was just a fetish of the bored, jaded upper class, and perhaps some noble offspring who wanted to shock their families. No one seriously wanted to be a Sanson.

Charles wanted to put Father Gerbillon's assertions to the test as he waited patiently in the street outside the Collège Louis le Grand. As the bell in the tower struck five, the pupils came streaming out of the building. It was impossible to miss the Siamese. They were considerably smaller than the other pupils, and always together. Dan-Mali was at the head of the little group, and when she saw Charles, she ran straight toward him. Suddenly, however, she seemed embarrassed to have shown her feelings so openly, and she slowed down. Her friends waited.

"I wanted to see you again," said Charles. Dan-Mali beamed with joy.

"Since the very first time I saw you . . ." Charles struggled for words. "I want to see you more often . . . every day."

Dan-Mali nodded and gently touched his arm. "I must return to my king, to Siam."

"You already speak our language very well."

"Language is like music. If you know the notes, you can speak."

"You could stay with me, live with me."

"Perhaps in another life."

Charles struggled to find the right words. The waiting Siamese girls were giggling.

Dan-Mali shook her head. "I belong to Father Gerbillon, I promised my mother. The priest helps my family in Siam, and I am grateful, I always obey Father Gerbillon, and my family would starve without him. My family needs me, Buddha sees everything, Buddha knows everything."

"Is Buddha a good God?" Charles asked.

Dan-Mali crossed her arms over her chest and lowered her head reverently. "Buddha has many faces."

"Does he sometimes place curses on people?"

"Buddha can punish you if you do something evil."

"Has he cursed you? Does he place a curse on anyone for their entire life?"

"Buddha can punish someone for their entire life." Dan-Mali was preparing to return to her friends.

"Wait," Charles cried out. "When can we meet again?"

"In another life. I am returning to Siam."

"Then will we never see one another again?"

Dan-Mali shook her head emphatically. She looked distraught. Then she turned and ran toward the monastery, where friends awaited her and tried to console her. She did not look back.

Charles needed no one to console him. He had learned many time how harsh life was, and that fate was merciless. Life feeds on sorrow. He didn't know where he'd read those words, but at that moment they came back to him. It was possible there were people in Paris who led happy and carefree lives, but that was not normal. Life was full of hardships, broken dreams and bleeding hearts.

It took Charles months to recover. The more he tried to come to terms with the fact that life with Dan-Mali was not possible, the greater became his longing for it. He tormented himself. Eventually, however, after countless sleepless nights, the realization came over him that they would forever be apart. He tried to console himself with the thought that the cultural differences had been too great, while at the same time knowing he loved her more than he'd ever loved anyone before. The only person he could have unconditionally committed to was his mother, who had died early, but now, for Dan-Mali, he would have given his life.

165

CHAPTER 7

When he went riding in he forests around Montmartre, Charles was always alone. No one wanted to go hunting with the hangman. On the other side of the forest, vegetable gardens extended as far as the eye could see, and to the south, in the direction of Paris, were the simple homes of the peasants who leased their lands from the abbey of Saint-Pierre de Montmartre. On a small hilltop nearby stood the home of the gardener Jugier and his family, which was also a small tavern that Charles sometimes visited. The two daughters, Marie-Anne and Marie-Luce, were both around thirty. Day in and day out, the father sat in a rocking chair in front of the house, sleeping or watching the many gardeners working in the fields. On his right was a bottle of potato brandy that he emptied daily by nightfall. Sometimes he would jump up suddenly, walk energetically toward one of the laborers and show him how to do a task. "Listen to me: work harder and the time will go faster." Each time the worker would just nod. They knew what a bad temper the old man had. Sometimes when he'd had too much to drink he'd fall down in the field and the workers would struggle to lift him up again. Then he'd get really angry, for a man like him didn't need any help. His wife was very short and blabbed on and on, so most of the hikers who stopped there simply asked for water for their dogs, and kept moving. When the two of them were alone, they constantly argued about everything. The man was actually not quarrelsome, but his wife prowled

around his rocking chair like a venomous tarantula trying to stir him up about something or someone.

"Won't you ever give me any peace," he used to say, and walked back out into the fields. "Someday you'll get your peace," she called after him as she cleaned the tables once again, glancing inconspicuously back and forth and giving a swift kick in the ribs to a dog standing in her way. The dog yelped in pain and limped away. She hated dogs.

"They just make messes all over," she said. But without dogs she could not have practiced her religion: cleaning up, again and again.

When she saw Charles, she fetched a pitcher of water and a cup and placed them both on his favorite table, the one farthest away. He sat down and, lost in his thoughts, observed the arrival of a hunting party. It offended him that even here he was excluded. He could do without the theater and the opera. even though that was not easy for him, but he didn't want to forego the horses, the dogs, horseback riding in the countryside, but even here he was ostracized. Though he liked women, he hardly had a chance of finding a wife. As soon as he mentioned his vocation, they turned away. His vocation disgusted them. He had found the right woman— Dan-Mali—but she had made it clear to him that a relationship was not possible. He thought of her constantly, even when he was sitting here at the table looking out the door of the gardener's house. When he entered, the two sisters usually left the house together. Marie-Luce was a very friendly and good-natured person with a striking, fiery head of hair and an energetic gait. She was married to a noticeably older foreman with a deep tan from his hard work in the fields. He, too, was always cheerful, ready to help, and liked to sing and chat with the workers. Marie-Anne was nearly the opposite—quiet and with an authoritative disposition, like her father. It was hard to approach her, as she barely spoke a word, and it was hard to know what she was thinking. She

was slender, tall, and had a strangely penetrating gaze, always conveying an impression she wanted to say something but was holding back. Was she angry? Was she about to lose her self-control? In any case, she usually seemed tense. When she served a pitcher of water, she put on a gentle and friendly face, but when she turned away and thought no one was looking, her face darkened and her eyes again took on a piercing, hostile gaze, as if she was about to strike out. She appeared to be inconsolably angry for even having been born. That was it—inconsolable, inborn anger. There was something about her that attracted him, a mysterious aura. With her he didn't feel the erotic attraction, the primal urge he usually experienced with women. He felt no urge to see her naked body or to kiss her. It was nothing like that. It was something mysterious and magical that came over him. Sometimes he felt as if he was looking for consolation from her because of his loss of Dan-Mali. But she hardly ever spoke, she seemed only interested in her work. Thus, Charles bought fruit and vegetables from her until his housemate Gros was inundated with more food than he could ever use.

"Are you really going to eat all that?" she asked with a smile. Evidently she had seen through him long ago, but if it had to do with business, she could even smile.

"These are the best fruits and vegetables you can find for miles around."

She raised her chin haughtily and whispered, "I don't believe a word you're saying."

"I've rarely seen your father awake," Charles said abruptly, trying to change the topic.

"He sleeps a lot," she said, "I wake him up to eat, then he usually goes back to sleep again. That's what age does to you. He's already over eighty, a span of two lifetimes. Some day he won't wake up and sleep forever."

Dogs were barking, white hunting dogs with long ears, running ahead of the hunters who followed on horseback. Marie-Anne turned away from Charles and awaited the arrival of the dogs that jumped up on her, full of joy. She knelt down to pet them, and one dog began licking her ear, which seemed to amuse her. She seemed to know the dogs and be very fond of them. Charles had never seen her like that. How could anyone open up like that to dogs, yet be so reserved toward people? Perhaps it was his fault, perhaps she knew he was a hangman. Yes, that probably was the reason.

Charles mounted his horse and slowly started riding away. As he rode past the hunting party, the men silently looked him up and down, as if trying to drive him away by their gazes. None of them greeted him. Charles knew that from now on this was a place he'd have to avoid. They would tell Marie-Anne about the position he held and say all kinds of horrible stories about him. If he didn't want to remain single and childless, the only choice he had was to marry the daughter of a hangman. Or Marie-Jeanne Bécu from the Rue des Deux Portes. Charles resolved never to return to this place. He'd find another place to go horseback riding.

On arriving home, he handed his housemate the fruit and vegetables. Gros asked if the woman was really so beautiful, and said he could soon open his own market stand at home with all the fruits and vegetables Charles had brought back from his hunting trips.

He remained in the kitchen watching Gros wash the vegetables in a tub "She is pretty," said Charles after a while, "but she's completely withdrawn. You never know what she's thinking."

"If you want to know how girls are going to be when they grow up, you only have to look carefully at the parents." Gros laughed.

"The father is a good-natured fellow, dominating, drinks a little too much, but almost everyone is like that when they get old. But the mother is a witch, constantly complaining."

"And," Gros asked, "which one does she resemble?"

"Physically, she resembles her father."

"Don't let that fool you, Monsieur. Many people have been in for a surprise. Perhaps she has the physique of her father and the furious temper of her mother. And remember, every little character trait in younger years develops into something larger when the girl gets older. What you get now is not what you'll have in twenty years."

Charles took the two rabbits he'd slung over his shoulder and put them on the counter. "Cook the rabbits for us, Gros. I have a craving for real meat tonight."

"It's too late, Monsieur, tonight we're having chicken."

Barre, Firmin and Desmorets entered the kitchen and took their seats at the table. They were hungry, and ate their supper silently along with diluted red wine. Every evening they could feel the emptiness in the house. A woman was missing. Charles's melancholy tone had silenced the rest of them. None of them wanted to draw the ire of the Monsieur de Paris because of some silly remark. Charles made a firm resolve to look for a woman. He wanted a wife and sons—and daughters, why not daughters as well?

Whenever Charles could not sleep, he'd get up in the middle of the night and play the piano, and his assistants knew he was saddened. But soon the piano was as out of tune as he was himself. Since he yearned to play the piano, he summoned the German organ builder Tobias Schmidt, who had built the instrument.

Tobias Schmidt was a quiet, discrete man who lived in his own little world—a world of music and peculiar instruments that he invented and also constructed. Like all really creative men, he didn't just have one talent. He had heard that the

man who could some day build a machine to preserve food would conquer the world. He worked on methods of distillation and resinous adhesives that could be used to make glass containers airtight. He was around forty years of age and lived alone in an old factory building behind the Cathedral of Notre Dame. He was as skinny as a rail, nearly bald, and his face was always gray and bloodless because he didn't eat properly and seldom left his dark factory building. He was a man of the night, a tinkerer who enjoyed a very good reputation among experts ever since his invention of a hydraulic press. He had only once made any comment on the vocation of a hangman:

"Someone has to do it, Monsieur." Music brought the two men together and helped to create a silent agreement between them. They did not need many words. Once the piano had been tuned, they sat down side by side on the piano bench and played duets. Later, in the kitchen, they drank a glass of wine. Their mutual music-making had satisfied them like a sumptuous meal.

"You should marry, my friend," Schmidt said suddenly.

"After you," Charles answered with a laugh.

"I'm married to my machines, hydraulic presses, pianos, organs, and other machines yet to be invented. The problem is I don't know what the machines I invent can do, as I sometimes invent them before they are needed. The only one I'm quite certain of is the one for preserving food. Some sailors have taken glass jars with them, but unfortunately the glass often breaks on the high seas. If I succeed in conserving fruits and vegetables in tin cans, it will be not just a service to mankind, helping people survive years of poor harvest, but also revolutionize the conduct of war. Military campaigns can be planned to the end of time, because until now, armies are stopped more often by rotting food supplies than by opposing forces. With conserved food in their packs, any army can keep marching on forever."

"It will lead to world wars," Charles said.

"Once a need has been expressed, there is no stopping it. But you really should find a wife. You are not suited to a solitary existence. Your vocation is difficult enough. You need a wife waiting at home for you."

"I know," Charles replied, "but it is not simple for a hangman to find a wife."

"It needn't be for love," Schmidt said, "but rational. I know you love children and hope for descendants, and for that you need a wife."

Charles needed to think about that.

Several days later he received an invitation from the journalist Gorsas to meet him at the establishment in the Rue des Deux Portes. The woman in blue, Marie-Jeanne, greeted him in the doorway and accompanied him into the great hall with the glass dome.

"Have you found your prince?" asked Charles, in an inquisitive tone. Marie-Jeanne took him by the arm and beamed blissfully. "Yes, he's the Count du Barry, and he has great plans for me. He intends to present me as a mistress for the king, hoping to improve his own standing in Versailles. The king is old, but if I agree to it, I'll be set up for the rest of my life and won't need a husband. Why should I mind having to do a blow job on the old man every morning? I'd rather deal with that than with the young studs who want to bang me several times a day. And I've heard that your job, Monsieur, is not exactly a bed of roses."

Charles couldn't help laughing. In a sense, this practical outlook impressed him, but he warned her that without a title of nobility the doors to Versailles would forever be closed to her.

"The count will marry me off to his brother, and then I'll be the Countess du Barry."

"Oh, that sounds impressive—Countess du Barry."

"What are your wishes, Monsieur? This is my last night in this establishment."

"I am supposed to be meeting the journalist Gorsas here," Charles whispered. "Is he here?"

"He's standing right behind you."

"Madame Bécu, he's mine now." Gorsas laughed and Marie-Jeanne stepped back with a polite curtsy. "Come along," Gorsas said in an undertone, and led Charles toward a wooden door beneath a stone archway. Charles was skeptical. "Trust me," Gorsas giggled.

Together they descended a spiral staircase. Groans and shrieks of pleasure could be heard coming from down below.

"He likes it when people watch," Gorsas whispered, and winked. Carefully he pulled back a heavy black curtain, revealing a plain, vaulted room that looked like a dungeon or perhaps a torture chamber. It reminded Charles of Damiens. A large cross hung from a wall with a young man bound to it. Naked. He was about Charles's age, slender, and strikingly handsome with dark brown hair and an infectious, mischievous look in his sparkling blue eyes. He had a pale face and pointed chin, and his face was twisted into a sarcastic grimace. He seemed completely relaxed and unrestrained, and laughed with obvious enjoyment each time the whip struck him.

"The man on the cross is Donatien Alphonse François de Sade, and he is seeking new ideas for his pornographic novels. The other man is Sire de Fronsac, the illegitimate son of the marquis." Charles turned to leave, but Gorsas held him back. "We are one big, discreet family—you can join us. No one will ever betray you."

Two naked girls wearing black masks took de Sade down from the cross and forced him to his knees. While the girls sucked on his penis, Sir de Fronsac thrust his own phallus up his anus.

"Have you invited me here to see this?" asked Charles, turning to leave. He was climbing back up the spiral staircase toward the exit when Gorsas caught up with him. "I have something to discuss with you. Let's sit down in a quiet corner and drink a glass of champagne. You are my guest." He beckoned to a girl, and raised two fingers. Evidently he was a regular here—everybody knew him. They sat down in two large leather armchairs, on either side of a small table. Gorsas leaned forward with a conspiratorial gaze. "Monsieur, our society needs a culture of reason, and it must be preceded by a period of dechristianization, as reasonable man needs no God. He trusts what he sees. The place of God would be taken by the divine sun, the origin of all religions, for the sun is light, the light of God, the highest being. What do you think of a cult of the highest being instead of our statues of gods and patron saints? From now on we would do homage to nature, celebrate nature, but first we must destroy the clergy, as they will attempt to domesticize the highest being for their own purposes."

"Is this a conspiracy?" Charles asked suspiciously. He clearly felt uncomfortable about being dragged into this.

"There are people from all social strata thinking about it. They call themselves the Grand Orient de France and meet secretively. They wear red caps, the cap of Mithras, the Sun God, the God of prehistoric hunters, embodiment of divine nature, and origin of all religions. The brothers of the Grand Orient de France believe that all men are equal by birth. We believe in freedom, brotherhood and equality."

"Do you advocate a revolution?" asked Charles, "or are you just attempting to learn my views?"

"No, no," Gorsas demurred, "I observed you back then in the courtroom and have been directed to contact you. You are the hangman—but that doesn't concern us. You have courage, stamina, and a sharp, analytic mind. We need men like you. Women can also become members of the Grand

Orient de France, because in the future, men and women will have the same rights."

"I'll consider it, Monsieur Gorsas," said Charles, to end the conversation and leave this place as soon as possible.

"But don't take too long, you must decide. Something is brewing in Paris, Monsieur, and every storm has its harbingers. I've seen the first of them, there is something in the air."

Charles resolved never to set foot in this house again nor to ever again ride out to the gardener's house. Nevertheless, he did, telling himself he liked the area. His hunting trip to Montmartre had been a success. He'd shot a deer. On the way home, he stopped at the house, as his dogs needed water. The house was empty, but he saw some people standing together at the far end of one of the rows. He recognized Marie-Anne Jugier, evidently giving instructions to a crowd of seasonal workers. He tied up his horse, checked that the deer's carcass was securely tied on, and sat down at one of the tables in front of the house.

Marie-Anne came quickly, and asked Charles if he'd like a glass of water or some wine. Charles asked for wine. It couldn't hurt him, considering what he intended to do.

She returned with a carafe, sat down across the table from Charles, and told him her father had died the week before.

"Last week?" Charles repeated. "I am so sorry." Then they silently drank their wine.

Marie-Anne stared dreamily into the distance. She seemed to love the sweet pain of melancholy. When Charles put down his glass, she looked at him briefly, intending to look back into the distance again, but her eyes locked on him instead. "One cannot live forever," she said, as if to herself. "Now let's drink his favorite wine that he put aside for special occasions. That's the fate of all good wines. They are too costly to drink except on special occasions. And for this

reason, they are eventually consumed by the heirs on trivial occasions."

"This occasion is perhaps not so trivial," replied Charles, then continued after a pause. "Have you ever thought of marrying?" He looked at Marie-Anne with wide-open, friendly eyes.

She smiled self-consciously. "Sometimes," she said. "If God wills it. He has taken my father and will perhaps send me someone now."

"If God sent you someone, would you recognize him?"

"I don't know. He would have to give me a sign, otherwise there would be no point in His sending me someone."

Charles nodded pensively.

"He'd have to give me a marriage proposal, as I never know when men like me. I always learn years later, when these men are married, have had children, and I am still standing in the middle of my vegetable garden."

"Do you miss having someone to love?"

"But Monsieur, you surely haven't come here just to have this strange conversation with me."

"Actually, I have. I wanted to ask you if you could imagine marrying a man who does his work faultlessly but is not of your social class, or of anyone else's?"

"It would have to be an odd vocation . . . but if this man really loved me . . ."

"But I do, Mademoiselle."

Now both of them turned deep red and didn't know how to continue.

"I shot a deer," Charles blurted out. "I'll take it home now, and my assistant Barre will gut it. If it's not too great an imposition, I'll bring the best piece back to you tomorrow morning. The back. I'm sure you'd be able to prepare a wonderful meal with it."

"I could only accept if you come to share the meal with me and my mother."

"Good," he said, "Then I can ask your mother for your hand."

"Is there something else you wanted to tell me?" she asked.

"Yes, I am the hangman of Paris."

"I know—I've always known that."

Charles-Henri Sanson married Marie-Anne Jugier, six years his elder, in the church of Saint Pierre de Montmartre on January 20, 1765. He was barely twenty-six. Charles didn't know if he had married out of love, or for practical reasons. He loved the intimacy with Marie-Anne, her quiet, gentle manner that was always infused with a charming melancholy that wakened his sympathy. He longed for her embrace, though he didn't know whether he wanted to protect her or seek peace in her arms. She didn't speak very much, and sometimes it seemed to him she spoke more with the dogs they kept in the yard than with him. It was as if she had achieved a silent intimacy with these hunting animals that made her very happy. Her other passion were the beds of herbs and vegetables that she tended patiently and lovingly. She loved Charles, too, but in a different way. She cooked what he liked, and always awaited his return late in the evening. When she felt desire for him, she darkened the room and lay down on the bed. He groped his way to her and kissed her. She seemed to like it, but she wouldn't let him kiss her vagina, as she considered this unclean. It seemed basically that she was ashamed of her nakedness. When she had reached her climax, she simply whimpered softly and dug her fingernails deep into Charles's shoulders. One morning when he was standing in the courtyard next to the water trough, she asked him with surprise and concern what had happened to his shoulder. Had he been attacked by a falcon? At first, Charles thought she was joking, but Marie-

Anne had no sense of humor and didn't like speaking about her feelings. Though they made love often, Charles learned it was almost a sacral act for her, performed in the darkness, and something he shouldn't talk about.

They were both delighted when she became pregnant, but it was a very difficult birth. They were twins—Henri, a plump little fellow weighing almost eleven pounds, and Gabriel, a scrawny, underweight baby with strangely misshapen feet. The midwife said they would get better, but they didn't. They stayed clumpy and twisted, and Gabriel was moving around on all four long after Henri had started waddling about on two legs. For Marie-Anne it was a shock. She imagined she had somehow failed, she felt demeaned, and developed a strangely aloof attitude toward Gabriel. She didn't want to accept this handicap.

Charles, on the other hand, loved both sons above all else. "It's not your fault," Charles kept saying, "Not every tree grows straight as an arrow, Marie-Anne. That's natural. We have two sons. Rejoice in that."

But Marie-Anne found no joy, and secretly reproached this innocent child with the deformed foot. She never said so, but it was obvious.

The two boys grew up, and Marie-Anne continued trying to be the perfect housekeeper and wife and pamper her husband with her cooking. But she no longer wanted to sleep with him. At first, she had all kinds of excuses, until he finally understood that she no longer wanted to.

"Perhaps that's the curse," she mumbled one evening after the children were in bed and she was drinking red wine with him. At first he didn't know what she meant. Then it came to him. Apparently, she couldn't let go of that feeling. "Because you are a hangman. That brings nothing but bad luck. My mother warned me, and said God would punish us."

"I'm not so sure anymore that God can plan everything. He no doubt loses track of everyone, with all the people involved."

"Enough of your sarcasm!" she shouted, and poured herself another cup of wine.

Charles took the jug from her hand. "It's the wine, Marie-Anne. You must stop now and go to bed."

"I'll drink all I want to," she snarled, grabbing the pitcher again.

When she drank in the evening, she was hung over and unbearable in the morning, running around, shouting, and not paying attention to the children. Henri and Gabriel would then run away to the pharmacy, where Charles would stop work, take them to the piano in the living room, and teach them how to play. Henri was not especially interested, but Gabriel was fascinated by the melodies he could coax out of the instrument. In this way, they started making music every evening while Marie-Anne sat in the dark kitchen drinking her wine. She abhorred the light, feeding and nurturing her melancholy spirit like a potted plant.

Charles was appalled; he had exchanged his loneliness for hell. Increasingly he slept in his laboratory, as he was sick of getting into angry discussions in the early morning hours. Every attempt at reconciliation ended in an outpouring of criticism ending with the assertion that Charles was responsible for Gabriel's misshapen feet. Charles could put up with the criticism, the shouting, and the drinking, but what he couldn't stand was that Gabriel and Henri could hear their mother's words resounding through the house. He knew that animals sometimes rejected their offspring, but the fact that it occurred even among humans was new to him. For this reason, he cared for his sons all the more, and started designing splints in his laboratory for Gabriel's feet, and building a leather frame that turned his feet to the right position and offered sufficient support. Henri was delighted,

and helped his brother get onto his feet, spending hours outside in the yard with him teaching him to walk. In time, they ventured out onto the road, but the pavement was so uneven and there were so many missing paving stones that it was almost impossible for Gabriel to get around. He felt most comfortable at the piano, with help from his brother.

For Henri, the situation was complicated. Again, and again his mother chastised him, telling him he was responsible for his brother's affliction, because he had taken too much room away from him in the womb. In time, he no longer took his mother seriously, and when he got angry said that neither he nor Gabriel had asked to be born. These words irritated Marie-Anne all the more, and she shrieked that their father was responsible for it all. He had impregnated her, no, raped her, since he'd never asked if she wanted children. Henri avoided her from then on, but that was not possible for Gabriel. He took refuge in his music and developed a very fine musical ear. Now and then he'd ask for Tobias Schmidt to come to tune the piano. Marie-Anne didn't like the German and considered his work as superfluous as music itself. In this matter, however, Charles didn't relent. He had given up his research in the laboratory, for the most part, in order to take care of Gabriel in his free time, and called for Tobias Schmidt whenever Gabriel asked.

One evening, on finishing his work, Schmidt was as usual enjoying a glass of wine with Charles.

"Monsieur de Paris," he said, "I've seen Gabriel's splints, and it's possible to improve on them. Let me try, and it won't cost you anything. The leather must be reinforced so there is more support for the heel. My father was a shoemaker. He taught me a thing or two, but I was more interested in inventing new things. But I understand feet, and have never forgotten what I learned. Gabriel has fallen arches, a hollow foot, and in addition a splay foot. We must make special

shoes for him to elevate the foot on the inside. That would give him a more stable footing."

Charles nodded.

"But I'd have to consult a shoemaker," Schmidt said. "He would cost something."

"That doesn't matter," Charles replied. He was so excited at the thought Gabriel's feet could be treated that he was scarcely able to sleep that night.

From that evening on, Marie-Anne withdrew for the most part and Gros took over in the kitchen again. She spent most of her time with her mother at the farm, and when she returned one morning without saying a word, Charles knew right way her mother had died. She withdrew to the bedroom, closed the shutters, and lay there in the darkness. A few times he heard her steps at night when she went to the kitchen to fetch some wine. She remained withdrawn, in her dark world, and Charles assumed this would quickly pass. But it didn't. It got worse. After a few days, she left her darkened room to take care of her dogs, concerned that Charles wouldn't be able to feed them. From then on, she spent most of her time in the yard talking with her four-legged friends. She wandered among the herbs and vegetable beds, plucking off a dead leaf now and then, and watering the plants. When Charles came out into the yard, she put on a grim face full of contempt, and if one of the dogs went to greet Charles, she hissed some command to bring it back. Then she smiled to herself because the dog obeyed and returned to her. But the dogs still wagged their tails. Charles tried to speak with her a few times, but she declined, and he wondered if she had perhaps become mentally ill.

A few months later, her bad temper returned, and she often got into arguments with neighbors over trivial things. She also criticized Charles for not loving her enough, and when he tried to show his affection she recoiled, as if he had

the plague. Charles was surprised and saddened by Marie-Anne's strange transformation. He couldn't believe he had exchanged the freedom of his bachelorhood for something like this. Marie-Anne began visiting her sister, though they constantly quarreled over their inheritance. The only point of contention Charles had expected in their marriage, in fact never came up: his vocation as a hangman. She completely supported him in that—the good pay was reason enough. She could never get her hands on enough money. She hoarded it, but never enjoyed anything, not even her two boys, who prospered and flourished. Charles loved the two of them beyond measure, and for them was willing to continue practicing his vocation, at least for a while, to assure they had a good education later in life. The welfare of his two sons was more important to him than the fulfillment of his own dreams. Henri soon towered head and shoulders above his friends the same age. He loved swimming in the Seine, horseback riding, and going hunting with his father. He was really proud of his father, and felt more and more drawn to him, as his mother's coldness was hurtful. She never embraced or kissed her sons like she did her dogs, and in the course of years lost the boys completely to Charles.

Henri increasingly took an interest in his father's vocation. He had never been troubled by the sight of blood. For him it was no more frightening than a puddle of wine. And when Barre disemboweled a deer out in the yard that had been killed in the hunt, the boy watched with interest while his school comrades held their hands up to their faces in horror.

Girls were smitten by Henri, as he had a handsome, masculine face and very broad shoulders from his daily swims in the Seine.

Gabriel did not have broad shoulders. The special shoes with inserts and supports that Tobias Schmidt had made for him in month-long sittings made it possible for him to move

about freely, but he seldom took advantage of this new freedom. He had become accustomed to sitting down and playing the piano with a neighborhood girl his age. His years of disability had turned him into an anxious homebody, and even though the disability had now been at least partially remedied, his anxiousness had remained. He was afraid of large animals, had never touched a horse's nostrils, and was afraid of water, avoiding rivers and lakes. He only felt secure was he was at home at the piano.

When Henri announced he would like to become a hangman, too, Charles kept waking up at night bathed in sweat. Had the curse returned? Marie-Anne supported Henri, but Charles was not completely sure she'd said it out of conviction or just to annoy him. Like her mother, Marie-Anne had recently made a habit of always choosing the opposite side in an argument. She'd become argumentative, and nothing was so insignificant that she couldn't quarrel about it all day, or just remain completely silent. She didn't seem to suffer from it, as she didn't bottle it up inside her. The woman who was once so melancholy smashed dishes or threw the food out into the yard, if she didn't like it. For the entire family, Marie-Anne was a tempest within their own walls. She denied saying she was bad off. No, she had no financial worries, was never hungry, and had four dogs she loved above everything else. What more could one ask for these days in the starving city of Paris?

Marie-Anne had no need for human company. When the family gathered for meals with the assistants in the large dining room, she scarcely spoke a word. Sometimes when she glared at Charles, he had the impression of looking into the eyes of Grandmother Dubut. He shuddered, but the more he tried of avoid confrontation, the more imperious Marie-Anne became, as if taking the place of the deceased grandmother. Charles consoled himself with the thought that

one day his son Henri would take over as the leader of the household.

Charles devoted himself increasingly to his laboratory and his patients, while his assistants took over the work in the house. That displeased Marie-Anne. She began talking again, about money, and Charles used this opportunity to improve the mood in the house and try to normalize relationships in the house. It almost appeared that Marie-Anne had used the period of her self-imposed isolation in order to pull herself together again. Time had apparently helped her to accept the fact that Gabriel's feet were simply as they were. She began to prepare the meals again, and expressed pleasure when Charles, Henri, Gabriel and the assistants complimented her cooking. When Charles returned from work late at night, seized her around the waist and tried to kiss her, however, she turned her head aside, resisting any physical closeness. Charles felt offended. He didn't understand what was wrong with Marie-Anne. Demons had taken possession of her soul, and one could never know which demons one would encounter the next morning. Eventually, Charles decided to accept it and withdraw into his own world.

One evening he took his pillow and a blanket to the sofa in the laboratory, and from then on they slept in separate rooms. The alienation continued and Charles became absorbed even more in his studies while Marie-Anne pursued her obsession for perfection and order, and broke out in a rage if anyone disturbed this order in even the slightest. Since Charles was good-natured and didn't like to quarrel, he simply nodded. His good-naturedness nourished her obsession, and no one questioned her authority any more— she had usurped the freedom of opinion.

Charles felt no compelling need to leave her, as he didn't desire any other woman, and life in his laboratory was pleasant, since this was a place Marie-Anne never entered, resolutely avoiding any place he frequented. If she had

something to tell him, she asked Desmorets to convey the message. Once, on the day after Easter, a wave of sentimentality came over her after two glasses of red wine, and she touched Charles's shoulder with the tip of her finger. That was the most passion and affection she was able to summon up.

There were days when this situation troubled Charles. After a tough execution, it wasn't easy to return home and feel this coldness in the house, and in these depressing moments Charles longed for his father. Since he'd already been gone for a few years now, Charles went to visit his last resting place in St. Laurent's Church. His vault was behind the last row of pews, with no inscription on the stone slab, but Charles knew that the remains of his father lay beneath one of the slabs. Here he could sit and think clearly about his situation. Everyone needs a friend to keep him on a steady course, he thought. It can even be a silent friend, or even a dead friend. The friend does not need to reply, but simply be there to speak to in one's imagination and hear his advice, even if those imaginations are just self-made. One must be able to pour out his heart in words—to a river, a horse, a wooden cross, a diary, a head of cauliflower—and only then can they take shape, so that one can process and shape them like a lump of clay. Charles believed that all sorrow held within it the solution.

A homeless man was dozing on one of the stone slabs, and was startled when he saw Charles.

"Do you know who is buried beneath you?" Charles asked.

"A pious man, monsieur, who never passed by me without giving me a pittance."

"Just how much did he give you?"

"A pound," said the man.

"And so shall I," said Charles, handing him a few coins. "My father would have wanted me to."

At that moment, the old man recognized Charles as the son of the generous hangman Jean-Baptiste. "Monsieur," he lamented, "men are dying of hunger, and no one cares about them. Is our Lord then only the God of kings and noblemen?"

"I don't know," said Charles, "perhaps God has left us on our own for a while."

Charles sold the house on the Rue d'Enfer. He was now in his late forties and wanted to have part of a house for himself. And there was another reason. He would make money on the sale of the house and could put money aside for Gabriel. They moved to the Rue Neuve Saint-Jean. The house was not as large as the previous one, but had a yard similar to a Roman atrium that one could cross through to reach the large kitchen and the living room, and on the left a separate entrance to the office where he could care for his patients. Behind that was his laboratory that hardly anyone was permitted to enter. Across from the entrance to the yard was the washroom, servants' rooms, stables, toolshed, and woodshed. On the top floor on either side were bedrooms for Charles, Henri, and Gabriel as well as for the assistants. Marie-Anne had her own room.

Charles was very happy with his decision and felt quite comfortable in the new house, but conditions in Paris were deplorable. The previous winters had been very hard, the crops had failed for the most part, and bread was expensive and scarce. Very scarce. The people of Paris were hungry and seething with anger. No one took note of this anger—not King Louis XVI nor his extravagant Austrian wife, the hated Marie Antoinette, or the clergy or the nobility. Until the day Jean-Louis Louchart suffered an agonizing death.

CHAPTER 8

Jean-Louis Louchart gave a face to the fury. He killed his alcoholic and violent father in self-defence. The two had quarreled once again about Benjamin Franklin, the inventor of the lightning rod and one of the fathers of the American Declaration of Independence, which proclaimed all men free and equal. His portrait was for sale everywhere in the streets of Paris. Paris loved this former diplomat as well as his fellow countryman and successor Thomas Jefferson who presently resided on the Seine as the American ambassador. Both were intelligent and modest. There was nothing pompous about their clothing—no powdered wigs, no gilded buttons—and their simple, modest black suits underscored their affinity for the simple people.

In a violent argument, father Louchart had brandished a hammer and threatened his son, who then left the barn shouting he'd look for work in the city and never return. The father now threw the hammer, just barely missing his son's head. Jean-Louis, in a fury, picked up the hammer and threw it back. Unfortunately, it struck the old man on the bridge of the nose and crushed a part of the brain. For that, the court in Versailles ordered him executed publicly, as old Louchart was once the stable master at the palace. These people enjoyed special protection and any attack on one of them was regarded as an attack on the court.

Charles was unhappy with this death sentence. He knew that Louchart was feared as an extremely brutal and violent man who spared neither man nor beast, but Charles also

sensed that the Louchart case was something more than a family tragedy. It was the herald of the impending storm. People were increasingly and openly critical of the deplorable state of affairs, quickly losing respect for the monarchy and the forces of law and order. Nothing could be expected from the church, and people had nothing more to lose.

On the day of the execution, two wagons left the prison yard at Versailles in the early morning hours. A great crowd of people were awaiting them outside the gates, but when Charles-Henri Sanson's wagon appeared, there was neither derisive laughter nor shouting. The crowd turned silent. With dark and threatening gazes the people stared at Charles, who was standing upright in the first wagon like a general heading into battle. He was wearing a dark green buttoned frock coat and a black top hat in accordance with the English fashion, and his hair was carefully combed and powdered. Though other hangmen in France still wore military-style boots and blood-red cloaks, Charles tried through his clothing to bestow additional dignity on his office and suggest he was not just a butcher with an ax, but an official of justice. Behind him sat Desmorets, Barre, Firmin, and his son Henri, who had begged to come along.

Soldiers on horseback cleared a path through the crowd for them as they made their way in a slow procession through Versailles to the Notre Dame Cathedral. The crowd remained silent, but Charles could feel a strange crackling in the air, presaging the disaster to come. He could clearly feel the explosive force seething through the crowd as he helped Louchart down from the wagon and took the written sentence out of his pocket. The condemned man was barefoot and was wearing a blood-red shirt with a noose around his neck. Clenching a candle in his hands, he knelt down before the main portal of the cathedral, his head lowered. "Jean-Louis Louchart is hereby condemned to have his back, arms, legs,

thighs, and legs broken, and then be placed alive on a wheel and tortured to death. The execution is to be carried out on the Place Saint-Louis." A murmur passed through the enormous crowd of onlookers, and there was a rustling in the crowd that Charles could clearly see reflected in their faces. He cast a short glance at his son, but Henri remained expressionless. Even though the execution had been scheduled for five o'clock in the morning because of security concerns, thousands of people were present. They were angered because it was clear to everyone that the defendant had acted in self-defense. Everyone knew the story of this ruffian who had been killed by his own son. As the assistant Barre summoned Louchart to get in the wagon, the murmuring in the crowd became louder, like the snarling of a beast as it prepares to strike. Normally there would have been applause and the defendant would have been jeered, but this time the huge crowd appeared enraged. The people clearly felt something like pity. That was something new. It was as if they had all read Rousseau. Never before had such a mass of people felt pity for a condemned man, possibly because of their increasing bitterness toward the king. Poor Louchart falsely assumed the anger was directed at him, and he squirmed restlessly. The priest who was already in the wagon embraced him and pronounced absolution. "Let him know that the judges have allowed a retentum," Charles whispered.

At the end of the Rue de Satory, the road was blocked and the procession of wagons came to a halt. Soldiers attempted to clear the road, without success. Suddenly, a gentle voice rose above the mumbling and jeering of the mob. "Adieu, Jean-Louis, my love." It was young Hélène, the condemned man's lover struggling to make her way to the wagon through the crowd. Her innocent and despairing voice was heart-rending, and no one attempted to stand in the way of the frail young woman. Finally, she reached he wagon and clung to the wooden bars. She stumbled, but didn't let go, and was

pulled along by the wagon. Suddenly a huge man appeared out of the crowd, strode briskly to the wagon, jumped up onto the shaft and declaimed loudly, "Jean-Louis, no one has the right to kill an honorable man like you." It was a colleague who worked in Versailles as a blacksmith and knew the old drunkard Louchart. A man on horseback pushed him aside, and they argued as the wagon moved on to the Place Saint-Louis, where the scene threatened to become violent. The mob crowded around the scaffold and tore down the board fence around it. Charles, along with Henri and his assistants seized Louchart and hurried toward the steps to the scaffold, but the huge man got there first and was smashing the wheel to pieces with a battle ax. Charles rushed to protect his son, though the latter was even larger and more powerfully built than his father and showed no signs of fear. The crowd applauded the man with the battle ax and started to dismantle the scaffold. "Stay calm, hangman, then nothing will happen to you." The huge man untied Louchart's shackles and lifted him up onto his shoulders. Triumphantly, he headed back down the stairs while the people cleared a path for him. "Let the hangman and his assistants pass. Woe to anyone who even harms a hair on their head."

Even before Charles and Henri had left the Place Saint-Louis, the remains of the scaffold were ablaze. They waited anxiously for the assistants who were struggling to make their way through the crowd. Pale as ghosts, they were still holding the reins of two horses. They'd had to leave one of the wagons behind, as it, too, was in flames.

"What happened there, Father?" asked Henri.

"What you saw was an old order beginning to totter. This was just the beginning, and no one can stop it now."

They all climbed into the undamaged wagon and drove back to Paris.

"They have overthrown the throne of justice," said Desmorets after a while, "and soon the throne of the king will

be cast into the flames. I don't understand why the king doesn't do anything. He has enough soldiers."

"Shall he slaughter all of Paris?" asked Firmin.

Barre nodded and stared gloomily into the distance.

"These things must be nipped in the bud," Desmorets insisted, "if he shows weakness, Paris will lose respect for him."

"There's no stopping an idea whose time has come," said Charles. "It's unthinkable that Paris could starve while the queen spends two hundred thousand pounds for her wardrobe."

"Do you think the king is responsible for the bad harvest?" asked Desmorets.

"Not for the bad harvests," Firmin bristled, "but for the cost of bread."

The city lay in darkness. People no longer had money for candles or firewood, and lived on chestnuts. The price of bread had exploded again, and the king, who confiscated half of the cost, did nothing to ease the suffering of his people. Out in the countryside there were frequent uprisings and looting. Gangs terrorized remote villages and even attacked small castles, venturing as far as Paris and plundering the flour and bread markets demanding the *king's price,* that is, the price of the bread minus the taxes for the king, and stormed and looted more than a thousand bakeries within the city limits of Paris. Most people, however, remained indoors if they had a roof over their heads. As the last of the candles burned down and flickered out, their hopes also vanished. It seemed as if the devil in person had arrived in the city and blown out all the lights. Paris sank into darkness.

By May 1789, the collapse of the monarchy was clear for all to see. Overseas wars in the previous decades had depleted the king's finances. Whatever remained was squandered by the queen in all-night orgies costing more than four hundred

thousand pounds per night. Payments she used to cultivate friendships became even more expensive. She gave over a million pounds to the duchess of Polignac, a year's rent of thirty thousand pounds to her lover—all so they would come and take part in the festivities. The king sat by idly, or rather he looked away, hesitant as always, tentatively, indolently, devoted only to his hobby, hunting, and his strange passion for door latches. He fabricated artistic door latches even as the crown took out loans for more than a billion pounds and even considered raising the taxes again for peasants, craftsmen, and workers. The clergy and nobility almost never paid taxes. The poorest of the poor financed the life style of the richest. Since only the representatives of the entire nation —the clergy, nobility and commoners—could approve the raising of taxes, there appeared to be no way out of the impasse until the demand went out once again, after one hundred seventy years, for an assembly of the Estates General.

The outraged people in the streets spread fear, chanting "Death to the Rich" as they stormed the palaces, but it was the nobility that brought about reforms, knowing that if they didn't give some ground they would lose everything. For this reason, they joined the commoners and the reluctant clergy, abolishing the three estates and declaring themselves the only representatives of the nation, the National Assembly.

Charles went about his work as usual, obediently hanging and beheading those condemned to death, branding thieves for misdemeanors, and carrying out his usual duties to the complete satisfaction of his superiors. He no longer heeded the applause of the crowd. Why should he be proud of branding a half-starved man who'd done nothing more than steal a piece of moldy bread?

Since moving into the new house, Charles had started thinking again of Dan-Mali, and once again, his longing for

her grew. He often wondered what she looked like now and what her life was like in her homeland. In his memory, he had glorified her, although he'd only spoken to her once or twice. Suddenly he was obsessed with the thought of seeing her again.

A few days later, as he was approaching the Jesuit monastery, he could hear shouting from far off. Acrid smoke came pouring down the street toward him, and he saw a group of ragged people tossing stones and burning bales of straw at the building. The excited mob cursed the clerics and demanded they hand over their supply of food. When mounted police appeared at the other end of the road, the attackers fled. An angered priest stormed out of the house and took the reins of one of horses. "The crown has the duty of protecting us and our property," he shouted at one of the policemen.

"Why? Do you perhaps pay taxes?" The horseback rider laughed and pulled his horse back.

"Where are the girls from Siam?" Charles shouted to the priest, who turned around in surprise. When Charles rushed toward him, he raised his hands defensively and ran away. Charles chased after him and seized him by his cowl.

"Where is Dan-Mali?" he shouted.

"She hasn't lived here for a long time," replied the priest, flailing about with his arms. Dismayed, Charles let him go. The priest then darted up the last two steps and disappeared behind the monastery walls. Charles realized it had been almost three decades since he'd last seen Dan-Mali, and he seriously wondered if he'd gone completely mad.

Dazed, he returned home and sat down at the piano alongside Gabriel, but the music could not calm his anger. Finally, he withdrew to his laboratory and took out the diary. But he didn't write about her—even after all those years it was still too painful. He wrote about the uprisings that were gradually taking on the scope of a revolution. The people had

declared the wealthy as their enemies. "If someone does not give, it will be taken," wrote Charles. "Now everyone is stealing from everyone else."

The attacks on the monasteries and the wealthy increased daily. If there were a dozen people passing through the streets in the morning, by evening there were hundreds chanting "Death to the Rich." Ironically, the wallpaper manufacturer Jean-Baptiste Réveillon had to suffer for this, because he was once a worker himself and paid social benefits to his employees, something that no other Paris businessman did. Since a few dozen guards were protecting his house, the mob moved on to the next city residence, destroyed all the furniture and burned it in the street. It's remarkable that none of them thought of simply taking the furniture and selling it. What drove them on was blind, destructive fury, pure hatred. The mob followed whoever shouted the loudest. A week later ten thousand demonstrators stormed Réveillon's mansion again, police reinforcements appeared with firearms, and when the battle was over three hundred were dead in the garden of the villa. It was a heavy loss, but men were becoming aware of their power. When they all marched together, no army on earth could stop them. It took only a spark to get them on the move again.

On July 14, 1789, Charles invited Henri to accompany him to the Palais Royal. Marie-Anne had left a few days earlier on one of her frequent and long visits to her sister. She was not even there for the twenty-second birthday of her two sons. By now, Henri had become a handsome young man, taller than his father—in other words, a real Sanson. Women turned around and giggled when they passed him in the street, just as they used to for Charles. He gladly told anyone who asked that he was the hangman's son and would soon be the Monsieur of Paris himself. He was brimming with self-confidence. The Palais Royal was just a stone's throw from

les Halles, the marketplace where thousands of sacks of flour were stacked against the walls of houses and splattered by human waste from chamber pots that the residents dumped out their windows. For this reason, the flour in the sacks rotted while elsewhere in town people were starving.

The Palais Royal had been the residence of the Duke of Orléans, who assumed temporary rule as the regent after the death of the Sun King in 1715, and drove the entire country into bankruptcy with an uncontrolled experiment with paper money. Just like the Sun King, the duke loved women, wine, and gambling and maintained a lavish and decadent life style. He opened the palace to the public, and since then it was regarded as the greatest amusement park in Europe. For a few sous, one could gaze at the allegedly fattest woman in the world, marvel at men from foreign lands with huge penises, view pornographic drawings behind a curtain, listen to bawdy songs, attend theater presentations, see a magic lantern show, or admire the waxworks of the Bernese physician and modeler Philippe Curtius, who at the invitation of the Prince von Conti had made his home in Paris. Curtius had also brought his alleged niece Marie Grosoltz along with him from Switzerland and taught her the trade. It was always unclear if the girl was his lover, his illegitimate daughter, or actually his niece. In the Palais Royal, there were no hierarchies—rag pickers, prostitutes, wealthy middle-class matrons, and nobles all came together here. No police were allowed on the premises, adding to its enormous popularity. Nowhere else in Paris were so many illegal publications opposing the king for sale, and nowhere was it easier to learn what was going on in Paris and Versailles.

On this day, Charles wanted to discuss the matter of his succession with Henri. He was ready to resign his office and from that point on devote himself exclusively to the healing arts. To provide the proper setting for this conversation, they took a seat in one of the numerous cafés. It was exceptionally

loud there, and Charles wondered if this was the appropriate place. At the adjacent table, one man suddenly became agitated, saying that King Louis XVI had summarily fired his finance minister Jacques Necker from Switzerland, and as if on cue, all the patrons began chanting the name Necker. They wanted him back. After all, he'd provided two million pounds from his own private fortune to give bread to the starving people—something not even the church had done.

"Necker made himself very unpopular at court with his great generosity," Charles said to Henri, "putting a lot of pressure on some of the nobles and church authorities to offer an explanation. If just one of them can give away two million pounds for bread, why can't the nobles and the church do the same?"

Someone shouted that the king had intentionally planned Necker's dismissal on a Sunday because the National Assembly was not meeting that day.

"This will end badly," said Charles. "Without Necker, French government bonds will become worthless, France will go bankrupt again, and many of the nobles will lose their entire fortunes." He rose to his feet. "Come, Henri, let's go somewhere else." As they tried to leave the premises, hundreds of people suddenly appeared before them standing in front of the wax museum and blocking their path. There, too, people were chanting "Necker, Necker" and demanding the wax bust of the finance minister so they could carry it through the streets of Paris in a triumphal procession. A delicate young woman appeared in the doorway holding the wax bust of the finance minister, and handed it to them, but now the crowd demanded the head of the Duke of Orléans. In a piercing voice, the young woman shouted this was not possible as the head was inseparable from the figure's torso. The crowd surprisingly accepted her explanation and moved on, leaving behind only the resolute, seventeen-year-old woman, Marie Grosholtz. A man came stumbling out from

behind her, the engineer François Tussaud. "Hurry up and get home," he barked at her. He was having a problem with his balance and sank to his knees, but when he reached out for her arm, she pulled away and returned to the wax museum.

"Won't you marry me?" Tussaud wailed. "Don't you want to become Madame Tussaud?"

Outside, the wildest rumors were flying about, and thousands had gathered on the Champs-Elysées to celebrate the start of a new era. They were joined by almost a hundred cannoneers who had deserted from the Hôtel des Invalides. No one intervened, and the city seemed to be slipping into utter chaos.

At that point, Camille Desmoulins, a young attorney twenty-nine years of age, stepped up onto a table and gave a fiery speech. Like his cousin Antoine Fouquier de Tinville, Desmoulins was generally regarded as a failure in life. Everything he'd put his hand to until then had been a failure. "Citizens," he shouted, "you know the nation has demanded that Necker stay, but now he has been dismissed and driven away like a dog. Is there anything more insulting and shameless they can still do to you?" Before his speech was drowned in the wild applause, he shouted "To arms, to arms!"

Like a wildfire, the brazen cry spread through the labyrinth of narrow lanes and stinking sewers clogged with cattle, wagons, and coaches of the nobles. Beggars bore the news to other parts of town to merchants who passed it on to their customers. Soon, forty of the fifty-four customs houses at the city gates were burning. An uncontrollable mob stole the merchandise and set fire to the tax receipts and registers stored in the tax offices. The monks in the Saint-Lazare Monastery, and others, also had some uninvited visitors. Their storerooms were overflowing with wheat, wine, and casks of butter and cheese. The books in the library were tossed out into the street, and burned. Finally, the entire room

was torched. As night fell, the uprising took an increasingly violent turn as a procession of torch-wielding men moved through the streets like a stream of molten lava from one bakery to the next, from one gunsmith to the next, stealing bread, muskets, pistols, pikes, and swords. Half of Paris was busily plundering the other half. A new rumor started spreading: troops loyal to the king were on the way. Drummers moved through the streets, calling on men to sign up for the militia. As their insignia, they would all wear a blue and red cockade, the colors of Paris. The storm bells were ringing.

Charles and Henri followed the enraged mob pushing its way through the Rue Saint-Honoré. Near the Place Vendôme, they were met by the royal German regiment of the Prince of Lambesc and immediately attacked the soldiers while deserted members of the guard hurried to support the people. Shots were fired, but they didn't intimidate the crowd—on the contrary, the mob became even angrier. Charles and Henri followed the rebels to the Hôtel des Invalides, where they hoped to acquire weapons. They beat down the door as the guards offered no resistance. Like lemmings, they rushed into the underground armory, without considering there was no way out for them, as more men came streaming in from the street. The looters panicked, attacking their own people with bayonets on the narrow, winding stairway in order to clear their own way back to the street. Several dozen men, some with deep cuts and stab wounds, stormed out of the barracks, screaming and moaning as if they were emerging straight from hell. Weapons were distributed and some men hauled cannons out into the courtyard, among them an especially valuable one with silver fittings. The crowd worked itself into a rage, like a leaderless, headless Fury.

Charles and Henri were watching with curiosity as a dozen men pulled the silver cannon out into the street, when suddenly a woman appeared in front of the impressive

weapon. Her skin was darker than that of French women, and her black hair reached to her waist. As she stood there shouting and waving, she reminded Charles of Dan-Mali, and as she came closer, he saw it really was her. He could hardly believe his eyes. She still had the same delicate facial features and mysterious body language signalizing humility and strength. When one of the rebels seized her by the hair and pulled her to him, Charles at once rushed forward and threw the man to the ground. When the man tried to get up again, Charles slammed his fist down on the top of the man's head. Stunned, the man staggered and fell to his knees. Dan-Mali stared in disbelief at the huge man who had come to her aid, then rushed forward tearfully to embrace him. "I knew we would see each other again some day. *Kun-kwaun*."

"Dan-Mali," Charles whispered.

"Watch out! Father, watch out!" Henri shouted as he ran to confront the men who were rushing to their friend's aid. He rose to his full height to meet them, grinning brazenly. The attackers were rattled at so much self-confidence.

"Are you going to lay hands on a defenseless woman?" Charles shouted, punching the closest one in the face, who immediately collapsed and lay motionless on the ground. His nose was broken and the blood flowed down over his chin. His friends now formed a circle around Dan-Mali, Charles, and Henri.

"Who are you?" one of them shouted theatrically, so that other rioters stopped and looked.

"The Bastille is over there," Charles shouted in return. "If you want to storm it, then do so." Dan-Mali clung to him, trembling, and he wrapped his arms protectively around her.

The two Sansons enraged the rebels. How could one even dare to stand up to an entire mob? A huge man pushed his way forward.

"Leave him alone—I know this man. It will only bring misfortune to your cause to do him any harm." It was the

blacksmith from Versailles. Gradually, the group dispersed, and the men moved on with the cannon they'd looted.

Dan-Mali wanted to stop them again, but Charles held her back. "The cannon is a gift from my king to yours. No one can steal it, that would be a great offense to Siam," said Dan-Mali. She looked shyly up at him, and an embarrassed smile darted over her lips. "*Kun kwaun,*" she repeated.

"*Kun kwaun?*" asked Charles with a smile. She wiped the tears from her eyes.

"You have learned our language," he said with admiration.

"Because I knew that we would someday meet again."

Henri followed the aroused crowd, and because Charles didn't want to leave him on his own, he said to Dan-Mali:

"Come, let us go to the Bastille." As he wrapped his arm around her shoulder and held her tight, a feeling of warmth he had never known before swept over him. He had found her again.

The Bastille, in the eastern part of Paris, was originally a castle built into a city gate. With eight towers rising up into the sky like stone monsters, it now served as a gigantic fortified prison, the hated symbol of royal power. The castellan, or keeper of the castle, was the marquis Bernard-René de Launay who commanded around eighty wounded war veterans and more than thirty Swiss guards. Charles pointed at the roofs of the market stands set up along the massive outer walls. The merchants didn't seem to mind that hundreds of rebels were trampling over their tables and merchandise—indeed, they even helped some of them climb the walls. In this way, the men made it over the first perimeter wall and were able to let down the drawbridge. Launay quickly lost control and ordered the cannoneers to fire directly into the crowd, which confident of victory now stormed into the inner courtyard and directed their efforts to lowering the next drawbridge. A dreadful bloodbath ensued.

Charles, Dan-Mali, and Henri tried to step back a bit, but it was too late. Two deserted companies of the guard approached and set up their cannons in the street, blocking their way. Suddenly, Launay appeared on the ramparts waving a white flag, and soon thereafter a Swiss guard thrust a pike through an embrasure with a message from the commander offering surrender in return for free passage out for its inhabitants. The rebels agreed, but as soon as he'd exited the last drawbridge they began poking him with their bayonets from all sides. Launay walked bravely on, though he was already bleeding from numerous wounds. Suddenly he let out a wild shout and started punching and kicking those around him. He hit a cook in the abdomen, who pulled out a gun and shot him dead. The cook called for a sword and tried to cut off Launay's head, but the weapon was too dull, so he finally took out his knife and cut the head off like a piece of sausage. Blood spurted out like a wild fountain into the sky. Then the cook impaled the head on a pike, and the crowd move forward, holding it up ahead of them. The street was open now.

Dan-Mali kept her eyes closed, and it was well she did, as they passed mutilated corpses and other heads impaled on pikes along the way. Charles glanced at Henri, who seemed unmoved. He was no doubt shocked by the grisly atrocities, but they seemed to upset neither his mind nor his stomach. He just said, "You were right, father, this is not an uprising, it is a revolution."

The rebels had expected to find more than a hundred prisoners in the dark dungeons of the Bastille, but the cells were all empty. They found only a handful of prisoners—seven petty thieves—in the upper, brightly lighted and comfortable cells: Donatien Alphonse François de Sade, who had been begging the people for weeks to come to his aid, was not among them. "Help us! They are slaughtering the prisoners!" he had cried over and over. It was all a

fabrication. For that reason, he had been taken from the Bastille a few days earlier to the insane asylum of Charenton-Saint-Maurice. The only thing remaining, written in tiny letters, was his manuscript entitled *Les 120 journées de Sodome*, The Hundred and Twenty Days of Sodom.

Suddenly, Charles saw blood on his left hand. It was Dan-Mali's. Someone had nicked her with a pike. "Come with me, I'll care for your wound," he said.

Dan-Mali looked up at him and asked incredulously: "You can relieve pain?"

Charles was surprised. Didn't she know he was the hangman of Paris? Had he possibly been mistaken when he thought he'd seen her after Damiens' execution?

He returned to the house with Dan-Mali, while Henri decided to stay behind. They walked across the yard to the laboratory and Dan-Mali lay down on the bed. She appeared exhausted.

"You must remove your shirt," he said.

Unashamedly, she removed it. The pike had struck her under her left breast, but the wound was not deep. Charles disinfected the area and applied a clean bandage.

"I have waited a long time for you," he said in a soft voice, and sat down alongside her.

Dan-Mali nodded, as if to say she, too, had been waiting.

"We have both gotten older, I have a wife and two sons, but not a day has passed that I haven't thought of you. Sometimes I stood waiting outside your school."

"I know. At that time, I had to return to Siam. But I have come back; I wanted to see you again. This is our karma."

"You speak our language very well. You are very talented." Charles smiled.

"I can remember everything. If I hear a word once, I will never forget it again."

"Will you be here for a while now, or are you returning soon to Siam?"

"I shall probably never see my homeland again. My family is very poor and wants me to stay here in Paris. Without the regular payments from Father Gerbillon . . ." She hesitated, then tears started running down her cheeks. "It is hard for me. I would like to see my family again, but I must stay here. I came to Paris to learn, and now I am Father Gerbillon's maid. He loves Siamese food."

"Shall I speak with him?" asked Charles. "You could also stay here and work for me. We dry plants and healing herbs and make medicines with them."

She shook her head. "Don't speak with Father Gerbillon —that would anger him. He mustn't know we have seen each other."

Charles could feel something was wrong, but he didn't want to get her in trouble. "I'd like never to let you out of my sight again," he said finally.

Dan-Mali nodded. "I must leave now. Father Gerbillon doesn't like it when I'm gone for too long."

She rose to her feet with a look of regret, lowered her head, and put her hands together beneath her chin. She wished she could have stayed a while longer. Charles watched as she departed and kept staring after her long after she'd left the yard.

From this point on, Charles was like a man possessed. His thoughts constantly revolved around Dan-Mali. He saw her smile and her eyes, and smiled himself inwardly, lost in his thoughts. He wished he could see Dan-Mali every day, he wished she'd live with him. The desire was so strong that he didn't even contemplate how that could be possible.

In Paris there were signs of an enormous, impending upheaval. In one single night session, the National Assembly abolished tax privileges, hunting and fishing rights of the nobles, and their right to make and enforce laws. Everything was abolished, even tithing for the church. Europe was in

shock, for if the king of France tottered, all the others would follow.

The Marquis de Lafayette was the vice-president of the National Assembly and at the same time leader of the National Assembly, which was trying to rein in the rebels in Paris as well as protect the king. Lafayette was a seasoned military leader, thirty years of age, who fought alongside George Washington in the American War of Independence and was celebrated as a hero on both sides of the Atlantic. He prepared a first draft of a declaration of human and civil rights fashioned after the American model. He was assisted by none less than Thomas Jefferson. Newspapers printed the declaration with enthusiasm, and Charles copied it word for word into his diary. It was an extraordinary idea that all men had a right to freedom, equality, and brotherhood, but for the people, the disempowerment of the nobility and clergy did not go far enough. It wasn't enough for them to decorate a tree in red, white, and blue and call it a freedom tree. They wanted more. They were displeased that all power was in the hands of the National Assembly and not with the rebels who continued plundering, robbing, and torching stores and castles and spreading rumors that foreign armies were marching on France to save the king. Soon, a leaderless procession was marching on Versailles, where they overpowered the guards and even penetrated into the king's private quarters. They forced Louis XVI, who was at that moment dining with his family, to follow them to Paris wearing the tricolor on his hat. They wanted their king to be with them. No one was concerned about the soldiers' corpses on the castle grounds. It was as if suddenly anyone had permission to stab and kill the royal guards unpunished. Some of the rebels still demanded death for all rich people and confiscation of their property. A few who were even more radicalized demanded abolishment of private property

and the death sentence for any behavior the rebels viewed as unpatriotic.

In a triumphal procession of more than thirty thousand, the citizens of Paris led their king back to the capital. Louis XVI had been reduced to the level of a subordinate because he had always hesitated and never made decisions. But even as the king's power faded, he regained the affection of his people. Defeat had humanized him, Charles wrote in his diary. But there was one thought that preyed on his mind.

The new laws regarding human rights had inspired him to get up in the middle of the night and write a letter to the public prosecutor Roederer demanding change.

As often as time allowed, Charles visited the Jesuit monastery, but he was always left standing at the door and informed that Father Gerbillon was praying. A truly pious man. And Dan-Mali? He was told she was not allowed to receive private visitors during working hours. And when were working hours over? That varied a lot. He'd have to ask Father Gerbillon, but as they'd mentioned, he was praying.

One rainy Friday afternoon, someone knocked at Sanson's front door. Charles thought instinctively of Dan-Mali and ran to answer the knocking. To his great disappointment, a representative of the National Assembly was standing there, the shy Dr. Joseph-Ignace Guillotin. Charles felt honored by the visit, as Guillotin was close to the king's private physician, Dr. Antoine Louis. As a member of a royal commission, he was studying animal magnetism according to the teachings of Franz Anton Mesmer. He was also a founding member of the liberal free mason's lodge *Orient de France* and for this reason often the subject of wild rumors.

Charles invited him into his pharmacy and offered him something to drink, but the guest declined stiffly. Guillotin sat down opposite Charles and waited until he had Charles'

complete attention. "I have read your message to Roederer, the public prosecutor. You should have addressed your letter to Fouquier, too. He was very angry."

"Fouquier?" asked Charles. "Antoine Fouquier de Tinville?"

"Yes," replied Guillotin. "He too has a position as a public prosecutor—by inheritance. But for heaven's sake don't call him Fouquier de Tinville anymore. Now he calls himself just Antoine Fouquier to conceal his noble heritage. The people of Paris are unpredictable. Times are changing. But let's talk about your letter, Monsieur. It has aroused some interest, for we too are working on humanizing execution, irrespective of the background of the condemned person."

"That is scarcely possible," replied Charles. "Even if all the offenders were put to death by the sword, no execution would ever be like another. Most of them are trembling, their mouths become dry, they can no longer speak and suddenly start squirming so much that it's difficult to make a clean cut to separate the head from the torso. To perform a successful beheading, the executioner must be a master at his craft and the condemned man must remain absolutely still."

"That is expecting a great deal," Guillotin mumbled politely.

"Another consideration is the cost. The sword is unusable after each execution—the blade is nicked, becomes jagged, and must be sharpened and honed. Sometimes the swords snap, which can lead to serious injury if the point of the blade breaks off, striking one of the assistants or onlookers. It's a very barbaric type of execution. If the first blow of the sword fails, the head will remain attached to the torso by individual tendons which then need to be severed with a knife by one of the assistants until the head finally falls off. That's a ghastly scene. In my first year as an executioner, I once had to try

four times. I was sure the people would lynch me if the fifth one failed."

"Which kind of execution is the most humane? Which one is more in keeping with the ideals of our revolution, and shortens the suffering?"

"The best would be a machine that guides a falling blade —every criminal would suffer exactly the same punishment. The executioner would only have to pull the pin blocking the blade."

Guillotin smiled briefly, showing his brownish teeth reminiscent of a rotted garden fence.

"I could design a model," said Charles, "and Tobias Schmidt could help me."

"Do that," said Guillotin, "and I will take the liberty of stopping by to see you again in two weeks."

The next day, Charles's persistence outside the Jesuit monastery seemed to have paid off. A coach arrived, and Father Gerbillon climbed down. He had aged. Charles immediately called his name and rushed toward him.

"Monsieur de Paris!" Gerbillon smiled, pointing at the liberty tree alongside the staircase. It was decorated with blue, white and red garlands and topped with the red liberty hat. "Do you know what that is up there?"

"No," Charles replied impatiently. "I must speak with you."

"That's a Phrygian cap. The revolutionaries believe mistakenly that this cap was worn in ancient times by freed slaves. That's wrong, just made up by this Dr. Guillotin," Gerbillon lectured as they entered the hallway of the monastery. "The people planning the revolution have no education. It's the cap of the sun god Mithras! The Free Masons don't believe in God, they believe in a divine power, the sun, as the origin of all life on our planet. Actually, they are not completely mistaken, as all religions have gods of

light. Even Buddha wears a corona, a halo. But you can't get very far with just the sun—religion also needs a face, and a face needs a life story. The Marquis de Sade could confirm that for you. Do you know his books?"

"I wanted to talk about Dan-Mali."

Father Gerbillon invited Charles into his office. "Very well, I'm boring you. How can I help you Monsieur de Paris?" he asked with an amused look.

"I'm looking for someone to help me in my laboratory," said Charles, straight out, "and I thought of Dan-Mali."

"Oh," replied Father Gerbillon with a smirk, "the hangman is in love? Am I mistaken, or are you married?"

"Would it be possible for Dan-Mali to work for me?"

"Unfortunately no," Father Gerbillon said, "the King of Siam gave her to me personally, and she is all I have left after the National Assembly decided to confiscate all church property in order to pay off the national debt. Now the rebels are printing government bonds, they call them assignats, and cover them with confiscated church property. But who is going to trust the paper, or, as Voltaire said, 'All paper currency eventually is reduced to its real value: nothing.' You see, I'm reading Voltaire these days."

"I'd pay her," said Charles in an earnest voice. "So you could hire another maid."

"What are you going to use to pay me—assignats? They have already lost a third of their value. At first, the economy was stimulated by the fresh supply of paper money, but now they have already stopped paying the interest on the assignats. So how can you pay me—with gold? Possession of gold has recently been forbidden, and no one can protect himself from inflation."

"Keeping slaves is also forbidden, Father Gerbillon!"

Gerbillon broke out in a loud laugh. "Since when is it forbidden to serve the church? And in any case, our rebels aren't concerned about women. Equality, freedom, and

brotherhood are not extended to them. Admittedly, that's not very logical, but that's just the way our rebels are. What do you think, actually, about our revolution?"

"I wish our king would recognize the signs of our times and accept a constitutional monarchy according the English model. In this way, he could survive the revolution as the figurehead of our magnificent ship of state."

"Do you know what I'm doing now, Monsieur de Paris? I'm drinking my best wine, just like all my colleagues in the monasteries of France. We don't pray any more, we drink." He rang the little bell on his desk and shortly thereafter the door opened and Dan-Mali entered. "Make me some coffee with cinnamon," he said without looking up. He was still looking at Charles. "But wait—stay here until Monsieur de Paris leaves our premises, or he'll come up with the idea of kidnapping you."

Dan-Mali tried to catch Charles' eye.

"Monsieur de Paris," Gerbillon said, pointing toward the door, "it was a pleasure seeing you again, but the pleasure would be even greater if we never saw the hangman again on these premises."

Charles ignored Gerbillon's snickering, looked at Dan-Mali again, and smiled warmly.

He left the monastery and sought refuge in the laboratory. Shortly there was a knock, and Marie-Anne's head appeared at the door. "I'm taking the dogs tomorrow and going to visit my sister. She needs help, and perhaps I'll stay a few weeks."

Charles nodded. Marie-Anne remained standing at the door a while, but he didn't reply. After the sound of her footsteps had disappeared down the hall, Charles reached for his diary. Paris is drowning in paper money, he wrote, I am being paid with it, but my assistants don't want paper money. The rebels are printing more and more of it to finance new debts, and so the assignats lose even more in value and people are starting to hoard food again. Prices are out of

control, and no law can prevent it. It's not possible to create money from nothing. Paper is just paper.

When Charles heard the sounds of a piano, a smile spread across his face. He put the diary aside and sat down in the living room alongside Gabriel. They started playing together, and no more words were necessary.

The next day, Charles paid a visit to Tobias Schmidt's workshop. He knocked, but even though he could clearly hear hammering inside, there was no answer. He entered the old shop, stopped, and called out to Schmidt in a loud voice. The owner was still dressed in his bathrobe, and flinched on hearing his name. The walls of the shop were hung with wood and metal parts, belts, straps, cast-iron steam boilers, toothed wheels in all sizes as well as oversized sketches of strange machines whose purpose could only be surmised.

At once, Tobias led Charles to the back of the shop. "I think I've told you I'm working on a device to preserve food. How can you stop the decomposition process without losing either the taste or the nutritional quality? The man who finds a solution to that . . ."

". . . can conquer the world, I know." Charles grinned.

"You're right," Schmidt insisted. "I'm trying to cook vegetables and fruit and conserve them in tin cans, but I still don't have a device to seal the cans. It's also not easy to figure out the optimal boiling temperature for the individual ingredients. It will take years. Years!" Schmidt was stirring a large pot with apples floating around in boiling water. "I need thousands of cans for my experiments, but I still can't figure out whether to preserve vegetables in oil, vinegar, alcohol, or sugar syrup. It takes at least two years before you find out."

"I'd like to discuss a smaller project with you," Charles said.

"I'm sorry. Am I boring you? I haven't seen a soul for weeks." Schmidt, befuddled, shook his head and shuffled stooped over through the shop to a torn sofa with chicken feathers sticking out through the fabric, where he collapsed.

Charles followed him. "I had a visit from Dr. Guillotin."

"That free mason. I'm telling you, they'll start a revolution. It's coming. First, we abolish the clergy, then God, because now everything has to be rational. That will be our revolution's next achievement. Robespierre will demand a civil cult of reason, a festival of the highest being. And who is the highest being? Nature! Robespierre will insist. We will worship nature just as our forefathers did six thousand years ago, and soon we will be kneeling down at sunrise to thank the sun for its light."

"Monsieur Schmidt," Charles persisted, "I must speak with you about Guillotin's machine."

"Yes, yes, I've read about his ideas in the newspaper— the humane killing machine. I have ideas about that, too. The whole world wants my ideas, but no one wants to pay for them. Artists like me always go away empty-handed, and I earn just enough with my piano tuning to afford new tin cans."

"If you invent a machine that will kill all men in the same way, you will become a rich man. Would you care to prepare a sketch that a layman can understand?"

"Yes, yes," said Schmidt petulantly, "I have ideas, and it would be wonderful if I could make a presentation to the court. After that I could explain to the king how to preserve food, and he could march into Russia, Africa, or India with his armies, and his troops would always have something to eat. He enjoys so much waging wars."

"Monsieur Schmidt, for now it will just be about this killing machine. If your design is accepted, you might be able to build such a machine for every precinct in Paris."

"Oh, that would be my life's dream! I have so many ideas for new machines, but no money for the material. I'd be eternally grateful to you, Monsieur, and I'd even give you a share in the earnings."

Charles smiled. "Your friendship is reward enough for me."

"And how is Gabriel?" Schmidt asked.

"He's not making great progress anymore, but he's not getting any worse, either. Since he's walking more, his muscles are becoming stronger and his stride more stable."

Schmidt pulled on a cord hanging down from the ceiling. The cord led across the ceiling, along the wall, and from there through a small hole drilled in the wall to the adjacent room. In the distance the sound of a little bell could be heard, and shortly thereafter a corpulent woman about sixty years old appeared. She waddled as she walked, and Charles immediately noticed that her hips were injured.

"Bring us some red wine," said Schmidt.

"But you haven't eaten a thing since yesterday morning."

"Are you my doctor?" Schmidt growled. "I have hired a maid, and now I need a piece of bread, and quickly. I've ruined my stomach."

"Again?" sighed the woman.

Charles had filled up his school notebooks with writing, and needed more books for his entries. He had to keep track of so many criminals: a button maker, a horse trader, a manservant, a locksmith . . . he filled two pages with names. That was Monday. On Tuesday, there were already three more. The many death sentences were intended to act as a deterrent, but they were ineffective. The misery in the streets of Paris and the surrounding countryside was simply too great. Poverty created a whole army of criminals. The number of condemned men rose sharply. Charles carried out the sentences stoically, but he was anything but indifferent to the

men he had to execute. On the contrary, he had sympathy for them. He couldn't understand how the public standing tightly packed around the scaffold so rarely showed any compassion. After all, they shared the same fate. If it weren't for Henri, Charles would have quit, but if his son actually wanted to take over the job someday, he reasoned, he should pass it along to him properly and remain as executioner until the public prosecutor approved the transition.

One afternoon, on returning home after work, they found Tobias Schmidt and Gabriel in the living room playing a duet on the piano. "He has a lot of talent . . . that is what I call a gift," Schmidt said with admiration.

Charles was delighted to hear that. He greeted his son with a fatherly kiss on the forehead and invited Schmidt into the laboratory, where Schmidt took a book out of his pocket and opened it. "Look, Monsieur de Paris, this is an engraving by Achille Bocchi dated 1555, showing a wooden scaffold built with two parallel, perpendicular wooden posts. Between the posts is a sharp blade hanging on a rope to prevent it from falling. When the free end of the rope is untied, the blade will come hurtling down between the posts and behead the unfortunate person whose neck will be lying right in the path of the blade."

Charles examined the sketch closely and after a while said "That isn't satisfactory. The problem is that the condemned man can't hold still in view of his impending death. On his knees, he will quickly lose his balance, and thus the body must be tied down securely to assure a clean cut. Otherwise, you'll have nothing but a grisly slaughter that won't appeal to the public, either." Schmidt nodded. Charles could see he was already thinking of a solution, and added: "It's urgent! If we do nothing, doctors Louis and Guillotin will come up with something, but I'm the one who will be standing up on the platform and be responsible if it doesn't work. I trust you, Monsieur Schmidt," he said.

Schmidt smiled. "Very well, I'll work on it—tonight. But we can't end this evening without some music," he replied as he sat down at the piano with Gabriel. After the third piece, Schmidt stopped abruptly. "I have the solution! Let me go home now, I must prepare a sketch." And he rushed out into the street.

Charles sat down with Henri in his laboratory, where they drank wine and talked about the new machine. Charles explained the details.

"It will make our work easier," said Henri, "but you will always need someone to operate the machine and guarantee that everything is done properly."

"Yes, but it doesn't make it more just. You can execute them all in the same way, but perhaps there is one who is innocent, and the conviction was bought. When you kill someone, the act is irreversible."

"That's not our responsibility, Father."

"Perhaps so, Henri, and perhaps not. At the root of every judgement is the spirit of the times, and every country has its own laws. We apply the law, but we do not exercise justice." Suddenly he asked, "Do you remember the woman from the Kingdom of Siam?"

"The girl with the silver cannon?"

"She is no longer a girl, Henri. In Siam, people don't age the way we do here, they eat differently, they don't overeat, and their skin remains supple and young. Her name is Dan-Mali, and I'd like to see her again."

Henri looked at his father for a long time, then asked, "Are you in love?"

"Henri," said Charles, in an almost pleading tone, "For love, age is of no importance. Until now, I have known love only from hearsay. All my life, I've done what others—the family, society, and now the revolution—told me to do, and now that the revolution has broken out, the desire for freedom has also broken out in me. I, too, want a new life."

"Does mother know about that?"

"No, Henri, and it is pointless to speak with her about it."

Marie-Anne had been visiting her sister for weeks, and helped caring for her dying brother-in-law. No one knew exactly what was wrong with him. He was having great difficulty breathing, and in time couldn't breathe at all when sitting up in bed. It was a pathetic sight as he gradually wasted away.

Any puppy drowned in the horse trough died faster and easier.

When Marie-Anne returned to Paris to pick up her clothes for the funeral, Charles asked when the burial would take place.

"You're not invited, Charles. They don't want a hangman at the service.

He didn't answer, but helped her load a few things onto the horse, and she accepted the help reluctantly. When she had disappeared around the corner, Charles felt relieved. Life could be very peaceful, he thought, as he walked over to his laboratory to crush some laurel leaves. He caught himself thinking how he secretly wished that Dan-Mali would take a little detour to visit him the next time she went to the market. But no doubt she was afraid her family in Siam would lose the regular support by Father Gerbillon. Charles would gladly assume that role, but how could he ever let her know that? In his mind, he was always with her, and felt the same peace and serenity there that he'd known in his youth, even though all he had now was the image of her conjured up in his daydreams. There was really nothing Dan-Mali could do for him, but she still gave him everything he longed for. She only had to be there, nothing more.

CLAUDE CUENI

One day when Charles came back from the courtyard after bathing at the fountain, there she was in his laboratory, curiously studying the little jars of salves.

"How did you get in?" Charles asked in surprise.

"Through the door." She smiled mischievously.

He walked slowly toward her. Her eyes sparkling, she looked at him, then slowly lowered her gaze in shame. He wanted to spare her any embarrassment, and pointed to his clay jars. "These are the roots of yew trees. Here we have thyme, citronella, dill . . . and over here charred reeds for dead body tissue. The plants and herbs grow in my garden, and I crush them and mix them with oils and fats to make salves and tinctures. You could help me with that."

Suddenly she wrapped her arms firmly around Charles. "*Kun kwaun*," she said, "I have great pain." She had tears in her eyes.

Charles had her sit down on the bed where she removed her shirt and closed her eyes as he examined her. He cleansed the wound that was slightly infected and covered it with an ointment. He could smell the sweet oil she had rubbed over her entire body. She sat down on the edge of the bed, reached out for his hand, placed it in her lap, and pulled him to her, smiling.

"That's good." They were both looking out into the yard.

"What does *kun kwaun* mean," Charles asked.

"Good man." After a while she added, "Father Gerbillon will be travelling back to Siam to bring some astronomical instruments to our king. He was appointed Royal Mathematician and will observe the stars in Siam in order to prepare new sea charts. Someday your country will use these sea charts to come to Siam in many ships and conquer our land. Our king thinks that your king's mathematicians are his friends, but Father Gerbillon is not interested in the starry skies, he loves young boys and girls, and that's the reason he's returning to Siam. He wants to take me along with him,

but I don't want to go. I hate him." She collapsed in his arms and wailed like a child.

Charles kissed her forehead. "You are not alone in this world, Dan-Mali . . ."

She didn't allow him to finish. Abruptly, she stood up straight, said "I'll be back soon," and ran out of the house.

CHAPTER 9

Early in the morning, Charles went to the Conciergerie, the state prison, to see if there were any executions planned for the afternoon. He climbed the winding staircase on the left side of the courtyard and knocked on the door of the new public prosecutor. He was eager to see Antoine again.

"It may take a while," someone said behind him. Charles turned around as the journalist Gorsas emerged from a windowless niche in the tower wall. "There's no one inside, and he loves to keep people waiting."

"Why are you here?" asked Charles, staring distrustfully at Gorsas.

"He summoned me. Probably he's displeased with my articles. In the future, he'll tell me what to write in order to comply with the demands of freedom of the press. I am going to write that he inherited a small fortune, and used it to buy the office of the public prosecutor. The rest of it he spent on women and drink. After he sobered up, he impregnated his rich cousin no less than five times, and since going bankrupt has had a passionate hatred of rich people."

"And you're going to write *that*?" Charles asked incredulously.

"Anyone who takes freedom of the press seriously, Monsieur de Paris, winds up on your scaffold. Do you know that many revolutionaries make an ideology of their personal failure, but someone like Antoine Fouquier could inherit a whole chicken farm and not a single chicken would lay an egg? Did you know that the incorruptible Camille

Desmoulins is his cousin, and managed to get him the position as public prosecutor?"

Charles knocked again on the door.

"Yes?" Antoine Fouquier shouted. When Charles entered the office, Fouquier held up his hand to make clear he would have to wait. He was at that very moment involved in a conversation with Roederer. Fouquier's appearance had changed greatly. His bitterness in defeat was written all over his face. It was not pleasant. He looked more like a gaunt bird of prey, with a long, hooked nose. His lips were no wider than the stroke of a pen, reflecting his mean spirit, and his narrow sideburns seemed to draw his face downward. Antoine Fouquier was much feared, like so many who have been a failure in life. When they also are given power, they become merciless and cruel. Now he was screaming at Roederer: "If you don't want to wipe out this scum, what will you do with them? Feed them for fifty more years in our prisons and at our expense? There are plenty of decent people in Paris who are less well-off and have to live on bread and cabbage soup."

"We'll send them to our colonies overseas. Why do you want to kill a man who's still able to work in our mines for forty more years?" Roederer glanced at Charles and signaled to Fouquier that he didn't want to continue the discussion in the presence of this man.

Like Roederer and Fouquier, most of the representatives in the National Assembly were also lawyers. It was incredible how many failed lawyers in the provinces had seized the opportunity to come to Paris to cozy up to the leading elite of the revolutionaries. Naturally, they all wanted to be leaders, not citizens, and they all wanted to use politics as their stepping stone to power and money. Most of them had no interest in the revolution, but gloried in the feeling of being important and enjoying the high life of fashionable society. That was their own personal revolution.

"Is that the hangman?" asked Roederer in a scornful tone. Fouquier nodded, looked at Charles, and grinned, visibly enjoying the situation. Roederer was one of those people, on the other hand, who never smiled, never befriended anyone, and went through life with a dour face. His expression was always the same, whether the news was good or bad, and his face always seemed to be saying, what do you want from me, you little piece of shit? He was very talented at getting that message across. His lips were always tightly squeezed together as if someone had just insulted him or interrupted him, and he looked tense and bitter.

Fouquier turned to Charles. "We have no work for you, Citizen Sanson, and by the way, the next time you send me a letter, please spell my name correctly. The next time I might take it as an offence—no, the next time I will definitely take it as an offence." Glaring at Charles, he added, "In the future you will be paid in assignats. We have so many of them, you know." He broke out laughing and pointed toward the door. "You may go. After all, we can't execute the entire city."

Charles wanted to reply, to somehow bring up old times again, but he saw that Fouquier wanted to be alone with Roederer and didn't want Roederer to find out that he and Charles had attended the same school in Rouen. As Charles left, he heard Roederer saying that the hangman in France would soon be unemployed.

Outside, Gorsas was still waiting.

"You can write that there won't be any more executions today," said Charles.

Gorsas laughed. "Since you're here anyway, perhaps you could answer a few questions for me. Are you for or against the death penalty?"

"I'm not paid to have an opinion."

"My readers would like to know that," said Gorsas in a tone of mocked anguish. "What does the Monsieur de Paris think? That's what they want to know. No hangman on earth

has such a terrifying appearance as you. You are an institution—so let's work together. Perhaps someday you'll need my help."

"I'm sorry," said Charles, "I carry out my duties according to the rules, but otherwise I've no interest in publicity, and don't like being the focus of general interest."

"Then you reject my friendship," Gorsas declaimed theatrically.

"No, Monsieur, I am not rejecting you."

"Oh, but you are, you are! You are refusing my friendship." As Charles descended the spiral staircase, he called after him "Perhaps you'll soon be standing closer to the focal point than you care to."

Charles did not go directly home but took a long detour through the forests of Montmartre toward the banks of the Seine, where he sat down along the river. He was now fifty-two years old, had two sons, and was married to a woman with whom he was now estranged. He was worried about the future, particularly that of his sons. He tried to get up his courage. If the death punishment was indeed abolished, he certainly wouldn't be unemployed, he mused. A hangman and his assistants would always be needed to brand convicted felons or tie thieves to the pillory. Someone would have to pick up the sentences at the Conciergerie in the early morning hours and carry them out in the evening. So he wouldn't be unemployed, but he would earn less and be paid in assignats. Life would be harder. Charles decided he'd rent out the little outbuilding that he never used to some young people. They'd asked him a while ago if they could set up their printing press and prepare handbills there. Handbills were much in fashion, and one could make a little money doing that.

Tobias Schmidt had prepared a new sketch that he proudly presented. "I have tried to build a very simple machine," he declared, "that any idiot can operate—because someday an idiot will be operating them. You, Monsieur de Paris, are the last great hangman."

"We must try it out," said Charles, unimpressed. "There are people with necks like a bull—so strong that even an ax cannot do the job."

"It's just a question of the weight of the blade, and how far it has to fall. If the falling blade is heavy enough, it will work. Can we try it on some corpses?"

The next day, Charles sent a message to Dr. Guillotin, who came over immediately and had them explain the sketch to him. With almost childish enthusiasm he approved the design. "What do you think, Citizen Sanson, is the separated head still conscious? Can a beheaded body still experience pain?"

"For a fraction of a second, the pain is so severe that the condemned man quickly loses consciousness. The enormous loss of blood does the rest."

"But will the machine work?" Guillotin didn't want to be embarrassed.

"Yes. It worked two hundred years ago, and will work now. I read that a similar machine was in use at the time of Julius Caesar. We'll try it out first on sheep."

Shortly thereafter, Dr. Guillotin presented the machine to the National Assembly. He praised its merits, stressing that by using it one would come very close to satisfying the demands of equality and humanity. The machine was an expression of humanity, it honored the demands of the revolution that each man was equal from birth. Everyone would die in the same way, and no one would have to suffer for long. "The condemned man will feel just a slight rush of air around his neck before his head flies off his shoulders," he said. "The

mechanism functions like a flash of lightning, the head rolls, the blood spurts out, and the man is gone." The gathering broke into peals of laughter on hearing these words. Dr. Louis, professor of surgery and the king's personal physician, was ordered to present an official report. The appeal of a young attorney was barely audible in the crowd. His name was Robespierre. He argued against the death penalty because it was unjust and a relic of the barbaric feudal system.

Gabriel was playing the piano while Charles and Desmorets prepared an inventory of personal belongings of men hanged the previous evening. It was noticeable that the hair and beards of executed men had become longer recently. Barre always cut them off and put them in a large chest in the Conciergerie given to a wigmaker at the end of the month. The proceeds went to poor houses, hospitals, and other needy causes.

"The hair is longer, but we're still making less money," Desmorets commented.

"Wigs are falling out of fashion," Charles mused.

"The court is becoming irrelevant. The true revolutionaries are those who reject all pomp and ceremony, like the two American diplomats in their plain black suits."

Suddenly, someone tapped on the window, and Desmorets stepped outside. Shortly afterward he returned with Dan-Mali.

"I'll do the rest myself now," he said, sitting down again on his stool.

Charles led Dan-Mali into the laboratory. "Is the wound dry now?" he asked.

"That's not the reason I'm here," said Dan-Mali, looking very serious. "I wanted to see you. May I lie down?" Without waiting for a reply, she lay down on the bed in front of the bookshelf. She was moving very deliberately, as if certain

motions were painful to her. She beckoned to Charles to lie down also, then closed her eyes. "Don't say anything," she whispered, squeezing his hand. They lay there for a long time on the bed, hand in hand.

Suddenly, a coach stopped in front of the house. Charles thought at once of Marie-Anne, but the sounds on the pavement were not at all familiar to him. He stood up to look out the window and saw a coach with the coat of arms of the king. Barre knocked on the door and called out: "Someone is waiting outside in a coach, Monsieur de Paris."

"Bring him in," Charles called through the doorway.

"He declined, and said he is picking you up," replied Barre.

"He said you had an invitation from Dr. Louis."

Charles walked out into the yard where Guillotin was sitting in a coach looking very agitated. "Get in, get in," he said, "we have an invitation from Dr. Louis in his office at the Tuileries. He wants to have a look at our new design."

Dan-Mali appeared behind Charles in the street.

"I'll come back later," she whispered, then quickly left.

The Tuileries Palace had in the meantime become the permanent residence of the royal family. A servant in a blue uniform led the guests through enormous ballrooms and hallways. The splendor had faded, and the palace seemed lifeless. Never had Charles felt so clearly the imminent end of the monarchy than here, in the deserted rooms. The doctor's office was, in contrast, richly decorated and appointed with furniture made of the finest wood. In this office, furniture and rugs were still being cleaned and cared for. Louis and Guillotin greeted one another cordially.

"And now I'd like to see the new sketches," said Louis.

Guillotin spread them out on the table.

Louis leaned down. "And who made these comments?"

"Citizen Sanson, the Paris executioner."

Louis cast a quick glance at Charles, then turned back to examining the sketch. The minutes ticked by very slowly. Suddenly, Charles heard a faint rustling, and on turning around saw a barely noticeable door opening in the wall. Louis rose to his feet at once as an imposing man entered the room from the concealed entrance. He strode confidently toward the table, picked up the sketch, tilted his head from side to side, and pursed his lips, but didn't even acknowledge the presence of Charles or Guillotin in the room.

"Now, Dr. Louis, what do you think of the sketch?" he asked.

"It's exactly what we were looking for."

"I doubt," said that man, "that a rounded blade is suitable for every kind of neck. Every neck has another shape and size."

Charles looked instinctively at the man's fat neck and thought that a round guillotine blade indeed would not be suitable for him.

"Is that the man," he asked, nodding toward Charles without looking at him.

"Yes," Louis answered, bowing respectfully.

"Ask him how he thinks the guillotine should look."

Louis turned to Charles. "You heard the question. And what would your answer be?"

"He's right," said Charles. "The half-moon shape could sometimes cause problems."

The man was without question King Louis XVI, though he was wearing no medals or insignias on his light-blue vest. He smiled with satisfaction, and made a few corrections to the drawing with energetic strokes, altering the half-moon shape to give it a diagonal slant that would cut crosswise on impact. "I may be mistaken," said the king with a smile, "but try it." He waved politely and disappeared through the half-concealed entrance as silently as he'd come.

Charles was enthusiastic about the king's changes. Now the blade would even cut through the neck of a bull, he thought.

All parties urged Dr. Louis to speed up the process. Some wanted a speedy introduction of a humane method of execution, while others demanded more machines in order to execute a growing number of condemned men.

In September 1791, a few young people moved into the Sansons' vacant outbuildings. Charles was happy about the extra income from the rent, as modest as it was. They brought with them a printer, boxes of ink, and a great deal of paper. Charles watched as they moved in and asked one of them "What are you going to print? Assignats?"

The young man laughed and unrolled a flyer. "These are lyrics to the revolutionary songs. We sell them in the Palais Royal, and they are in great demand."

"Very well," said Charles, "that's fine. Just pay the rent in time on the first of the month."

Gabriel was fascinated by the printing press. When he wasn't reading, playing the piano, or helping Charles in the pharmacy, he'd cross the court to visit the young people. They liked him and helped him after he slipped once and fell on the wooden planks that had warped and come apart in the course of the years. Usually one of the young men would hurry out to take him by the hand when they saw him coming across the courtyard.

Charles appreciated that very much, and even noted it in his diary. He hoped that after he himself had passed away, his son would have a strong network of friends. He even noted in the diary that Louis XVI called himself Citizen Capet now and had taken an oath to the new constitution. He had lost his power. He could perform ceremonial duties and play the part of the king, but he had no authority. This was the vacuum in which the representatives struggled to gain

power. They were all trying to call attention to themselves in search for higher political office with speeches that were often absurd and promises that could never be kept—all for just one reason: to be reelected. There was a veritable deluge of new regulations, ordinances, and laws, but the people in the street did not want to share the power. Thousands of them continued rioting, plundering and murdering. The rule of law had broken down, and very few people dared to confront the angry mobs. The nobles in the National Assembly curried favor with the Radicals, trying to avoid suspicion of being Royalists, and in this way came closer to the radicals, the s*ans-culottes*, who controlled the streets. The sans-culottes were radical workers and journeymen who, in contrast to the nobles did not wear sporty knee-length breeches, but practical, long trousers, giving them the name *sans-culottes,* 'without breeches'.

No one was left to protect the rights of individual liberty that had once been so loudly proclaimed. People were again subject to arbitrary abuses just as at the time of the monarchy. The anarchy of the streets replaced the old order. No one had any interest anymore in Voltaire, Rousseau, or Montesquieu, and anyone who wasn't out in the street shouting and gesticulating wildly was under suspicion.

Denunciations and a police-state mentality flourished, and many long-standing disputes between neighbors were settled in that way. Austrian and Prussian troops were approaching the French border, and the king tried to flee and make his way through to the advancing armies. He failed. Once again, he was put under arrest, and as a punishment suspended temporarily from his official duties.

"What are you writing in this book?" asked Dan-Mali, lost in her thoughts, as she pulverized dried bark in a mortar.

"Things I cannot entrust to anyone."

"Are you writing about me, too—about us?"

"No," said Charles, "those are things I wouldn't entrust to this book."

"Can I sleep here for an hour?"

Charles nodded. "Can't you get any sleep anymore in this Jesuit monastery?"

Dan-Mali smiled wearily and sat down on the bed. Once again Charles noticed how she avoided certain movements.

"Are you feeling pain anywhere?" he asked.

Dan-Mali looked surprised. She shook her head and lay down while Charles continued writing in his diary. There were so many things he wanted to record. "Paris is starving," said Charles, "that's what I'm writing about now."

"Nobody is starving in the monasteries," said Dan-Mali. "The priests have full pantries, but they are not sharing it with the needy. They preach water and drink wine. Now I understand that saying. In the evening, the priests even drink much wine, are often drunk, and argue loudly. They fear the future, the revolution, the starving masses in the streets, the foreign armies at our borders, the devaluation of money— they are afraid of everything. Except God, because they don't believe in him. Sometimes I pray to their God, and Buddha isn't jealous." She smiled. "Lie down with me and close your eyes, for I must leave soon." Charles lay down and held her hand firmly. All his writing had made him tired.

When he woke up again, Dan-Mali has disappeared, and for a moment he seriously wondered if it had all been a dream.

Gabriel was standing in the laboratory. "Mother is back," she said excitedly, "and she's outside in the yard."

"Where has Dan-Mali gone?"

"When she heard the horses in the yard, she quickly left the house."

Charles walked out into the yard, where Marie-Anne was grooming the horse, and washed his face. Briefly, she looked up at Charles, but didn't greet him. "Did you sleep well?" she

asked sarcastically. Since she herself got by on just a few hours of sleep, she despised everyone who needed more. Charles didn't reply. He knew this little game.

Marie-Anne regarded him skeptically. "Was that your Siamese girlfriend?"

Charles nodded and went into the kitchen, with Marie-Anne close behind. It didn't bother her at all that the assistants were present.

"How old is she?" Now she was standing in front of him, looking him right in the face.

Gros had already served the soup to everyone, and Charles took a seat at the table.

"I never asked her," Charles said. He picked up a spoon and set it down again. The soup was too hot.

"Is she young?"

"You saw her yourself," he mumbled, putting a spoon to his mouth. "Why all the questions?" The soup tasted fine. He was about to thank Gros, but changed his mind. "Her name is Dan-Mali."

"Dan-Mali? Who ever heard of a name like that?"

"In Siam, our names probably sound just as strange."

Marie-Anne sat down at the table. The mood was tense and the assistants were exchanging glances and starting to feel uneasy.

"For a long time now we haven't lived together as man and wife," Charles said. "That never seemed to bother you, so why does it matter to you if I have someone? You have your dogs."

"You're unhappy with me, aren't you?" she asked angrily.

"I don't know any man who would be happy under these circumstances. A kind word is sometimes worth more than a warm bowl of cabbage soup."

Marie-Anne jumped up from her chair enraged, and left the kitchen. Barre grinned from ear to ear and looked over at

Firmin who was bent far down over his soup trying not to laugh. Desmorets pushed his bowl aside and picked up the *Courrier de Versailles,* looking very concerned.

"What is it?" Charles asked.

"Do you know Gorsas, the journalist?"

Marie-Anne entered the kitchen again.

"Oh, are you back already?" asked Charles.

Marie-Anne pulled a loaf of bread out of the wood stove.

"If I don't watch it, you'll just let it burn." The bread had a wonderful fragrance and spread a pleasant feeling of warmth around the room. But the mood remained frosty.

"How much do you pay her?" she asked. When Charles remained silent, she added, "or don't you pay her at all?"

"Did you come all the way here just to ask me these questions?"

"No I brought you the paper, so you're no longer the only person in Paris who hasn't heard."

Desmorets pushed the newspaper across the table to Charles. "Read the lead article," he said with an emphasis that got Charles' attention. "Gorsas writes that the royalists are planning an overthrow in order to roll back the revolution."

"They all write that," Charles said, "to keep us on our toes."

"But he writes that the ones planning the overflow are the hangmen of France. And who is the leading hangman in the country?"

Charles looked up at his wife, and she stared back at him with a penetrating, accusatory gaze.

"He writes that the counterrevolutionary flyers are being printed in your outbuildings," Desmorets said.

Now Charles picked up the paper and read. Indeed, Gorsas suspected him, and was announcing his intention to report the hangman of Paris to the authorities. Marie-Anne

poured the coffee, without saying a word. She looked as if she was choking.

Henri and Gabriel entered the kitchen. Alongside his athletic brother, Gabriel seemed delicate and frail. He hesitated before sitting down alongside Charles. Henri quickly stepped behind him, as he knew that Gabriel sometimes tensed up when there was too much excitement. Then he would lose control of his legs and fall.

"If anything happens to me," Charles said, "Henri will take over my duties as the hangman. You," he added, looking at the assistants, "will do your duties as always, and will obey him, as you have me." He took Henri by the hand. "And make sure nobody takes the victim's clothes for themselves. That could cost us our job."

Desmorets nodded earnestly. "We'll keep an inventory of all the items, as usual, and give everything to the authorities. You can depend on us."

"Why are you talking like that?" Marie-Anne asked in a nasty tone, "have you done something wrong?" She stared at him scornfully.

At almost the same moment there was a loud knock on the door, and Barre got up to open it.

Soldiers of the National Guard burst into the kitchen and surrounded Charles. "You're under arrest," said the leader of the group, "by order of the public prosecutor Fouquier, accused of subversive royalist activities."

"Can I at least finish drinking my coffee?"

"No," replied the captain. "Where are the printing presses?"

"Desmorets will take you there." Charles gave a nod to his assistant and made a point of drinking the rest of the coffee, burning his lips. Desmorets led some of the soldiers into the courtyard while the others took Charles away.

They led Charles to the Conciergerie, visible from afar with its barred windows and huge, blackened walls rising up like a prehistoric monster at the end of the Quai du Nord. It had never occurred to him how threatening they appeared, but now, with his hands tied behind him, the feeling was palpable. If you are afraid, everything seems threatening. As they proceeded through the iron gate into the courtyard, the soldiers grabbed him by the arms.

"That's not necessary," said Charles, "I have no reason to flee."

Like a hardened criminal, they led him into the office of Antoine Fouquier. The chief prosecutor looked up briefly and with a dismissive gesture signaled to the soldiers that they could leave. Antoine leaned back in his chair and regarded Charles coldly, without offering him a seat.

"The hangman as a suspect in my office—who could have imagined?" Fouquier mumbled.

"What are the charges, Antoine?" Charles snapped.

"Antoine? Have you once again forgotten the proper form of address?" Fouquier stared into space, disappointed that Charles showed no fear. His face had become even more haggard, although it was well known that like most revolutionists he was always well disposed toward a bottle of red wine and generous helpings of food. "Citizen Sanson, we have seized in your shed a printing press used to print defamatory propaganda against the revolution."

"I have no need for the shed, and have rented it out."

"Citizen Sanson, the nation is threatened from all sides. Foreign troops are standing on our borders, and their governments fear that our revolution will spill over into their countries. Rightly so. Our revolution will conquer the whole world. One cannot stop ideas whose time have come. And internally, aristocrats are seeking the return of the monarchy and plotting against us. But the monarchy will never return. So why, Citizen Sanson, are you abetting those trying to

destroy the achievements of the revolution? Is it true what Gorsas suggests in his newspaper, that all the hangmen in France are united in opposing the revolution?"

"No, the hangmen in France are not pulling on the same rope."

Fouquier laughed. "How true, each hangman has his own rope."

"I had no idea what the young people were printing in my shed. They spoke of revolutionary songs they intended to sell in the Palais Royal. And there is no reason that should interest me. I am the Monsieur de Paris and not a spy for any public authority."

"You're wrong there. Vigilance is the order of the day, and whoever is not for us is against us. But tell me, Citizen Sanson, is your salary so inadequate that you must rent out your shed?"

"I am being paid in assignats, my salary is just enough to get by, and even before I get home, the paper has lost its value. More and more condemned men are being sent to the scaffold, so my expenses increase, but not my income. I now have sixteen people to provide for: my family, four assistants, servants, and wagon drivers—and the blacksmith is already charging fifty pounds for shoeing each horse. Bonuses and pensions I pay from my own salary. In addition, it is the tradition in our family to help the poor, and for years so many beggars have come to me pleading for help that I'm happy for any additional source of income."

"Do I detect veiled criticism in your words of the rising number of death sentences? Citizen Sanson, once the revolution is underway, there will be tens of thousands. We must purge Paris and root out the aristocracy. Every revolution, like an infant, is born in blood, and its children will wade through blood until the revolution is complete."

"I hope there will be someone still left to carry out the sentences," said Charles.

Fouquier's face was inscrutable. "If necessary, I'll do it myself. Be careful what you say, Citizen Sanson, your position offers you no security."

"I intend to sue Gorsas and the *Courrier de Versailles*."

Fouquier shrugged. "That's up to you, but don't forget your machine. We'll need it. We're nowhere near finished yet. In the meanwhile, you'll spend a few nights in the Saint-Lazare Prison. Perhaps then you'll think of something that you can confess to me. There are so many rats in the underground dungeons that it's almost impossible to sleep. So think about it."

"About what?" asked Charles, without showing the anger boiling up inside him.

"We are interested in all counterrevolutionary plots. Do you know any royalists? Surely. So give me some names."

"You know very well . . ."

"My office requires a more respectful answer. Were we best friends in elementary school?"

"A hangman has no friends, he shares his meager rations with dogs and horses, and no one wants to be his friend."

"That may be," Fouquier replied, "but you are not just the hangman, but the Monsieur de Paris, and many people have a high regard for your knowledge of healing. By the way, I sometimes have a tugging on the left side of my chest, like little pinpricks. Could it be my heart?" Fouquier's cool tone took on a tinge of concern.

"Nervousness, it's absolutely harmless."

"Very well," Fouquier replied with a sigh of relief. "I'm sure some names will come to you in Saint-Lazare. He reached for a sheaf of assignats lying on his desk.

"The paper money of the French Revolution," he said, fanning himself with them. "A shame they're counterfeit," he added. "Where do you think these fake banknotes were printed?" he said, grinning. Now Charles really did blanch. "It may be that your renters were publishing revolutionary

songs—but not just that. It was a camouflage." Fouquier laughed "You see, Charles, I always warned you. You were a model student in Rouen, but I knew we would meet again someday and you would come to the painful realization that someone who comes from the gutter will always smell like shit, and someone with noble blood in his veins will always be superior. It's a special satisfaction to me to throw you in the dungeon."

"What did I ever do to you, Antoine?"

"Antoine? Again? I am Fouquier, the supreme prosecutor of the Republic. I accuse, and you carry out the sentences. You are the butcher."

In the former leper's hospital of Saint-Lazare, men were imprisoned, tortured, and killed without a trial. There were no private cells. The prisoners were crowded by the hundreds into dark, endless subterranean dungeons wearing the same clothing they had when they were arrested. Despite the dreadful accommodations and gloomy prospects, there were still many inmates who whiled away the hours playing cards, singing, or attempting to seduce prisoners of the opposite sex. Young women, in particular, desperately searched for a man to impregnate them, as a pregnancy would save them from certain death.

After a few days, Charles heard his name called. He walked to the door and searched for a familiar face behind the barred window. Suddenly he saw Marie-Anne before him. She had brought him some sausage, a loaf of bread, and a mug of wine.

"When are they going to let you go?" she asked.

"I have no idea," Charles replied, and took the food she had pushed between the bars in the window.

"I made the sausage just the way my mother always did."

"I always hated her sausage," Charles said in a soft voice.

"You never told me that."

"You didn't want to hear it, but I'm very grateful you've brought me something to eat. I didn't expect you to."

"Are you criticizing me?"

"I stopped criticizing you years ago, Marie-Anne. We hardly ever see each other anymore."

"What did the prosecutor accuse you of doing?"

"Nothing."

"Why did they arrest you?"

"I don't know."

"Is there an indictment?"

"No, that's what the revolution has accomplished. We don't need an indictment here anymore. Men are rotting away down here, some of them slandered by children."

"Desmorets is going to get you a lawyer."

"I have no right to a lawyer, Marie-Anne. Now even the fathers of the revolution are wasting away down here, the authors of the declaration of human rights. The whole thing has gotten out of hand. The pressure from the street is so intense that every moderate person has to defect to the radicals in order to survive. The National Assembly keeps giving in to them, so they won't be accused of being too moderate. Everyone is afraid of being arrested."

They both fell silent, then after a while Marie-Anne said, "If we don't have anything more to say to each other, I'll go now."

Charles nodded. "We had more than twenty years to say something to each other, Marie-Anne, and we didn't. But there is something I want to tell you."

Marie-Anne looked at him quizzically.

"If I ever get out of here, Dan-Mali will come to live with me. The only thing we two have in common is the roof over our heads, and that can remain."

"A woman knows when she has lost her husband," she replied. "My wish for you is that you rot away forever down here, then I'll see to it that your Siamese tramp leaves our

country." She turned around and disappeared among the visitors in the gloomy hallway.

A week later, Charles was again brought to Antoine Fouquier.

"Do you have any names?" he asked, getting straight to the point.

"I'm working on it," Charles said, playing for time.

"Did you know the contents of the flyers printed in your outbuilding?"

"No," said Charles. "As I told you, they said they were printing revolutionary songs. Frankly, there didn't seem to be anything suspicious about that. On the contrary, I thought it was better for these young men that they had work to do and weren't hanging around in the streets."

"Why didn't you go and check on them?"

"Why should I have done that? I'm the landlord, and a landlord doesn't spy on his tenants. Should I have stopped by every night to read what they were printing? Is this the oversight of which I'm being accused? Why would I have suspected they were counterfeiting assignats and printing verses mocking the revolution?"

Fouquier shook silently, suppressing a laugh. "The people have no money for bread, but you think they are going to buy song lyrics? You're offending my intelligence."

Charles shrugged. "I'm just telling you what my tenants told me."

"And it didn't make you wonder?"

"If they have crazy ideas in their heads, then so be it. If I'd known what they really were printing, I wouldn't have rented the building to them, of course, and would have reported them to you right away, Monsieur."

Fouquier smiled. He was flattered that Charles had addressed him now as *monsieur*. He scrutinized with a certain amusement the huge man before him who was so

dependent on his goodwill. Though the whole world feared him, he was here now fighting for his freedom.

"Very well," said Fouquier, "almost all the young men escaped when we stormed the building. We found a large number of assignats, but we still don't know if the counterfeits are from England or were printed in your outbuilding. We consider it unlikely that young people have so much paper money, and the result of the ongoing investigation naturally depends somewhat on whether you can come up with a name or two for us. So don't take the matter lightly, or your son Henri will suddenly have the unpleasant duty of executing his father. Think about it, ask around, and give me names."

Charles nodded.

"You're free to leave—for the time being. And hurry up with your new machine. We have new convictions coming along every day now."

Charles nodded again, and turned to leave. Just as he was about to open the door, Fouquier asked, "Did you know Hentz?"

"The hangman from Alsace?"

"Yes, he was executed last week. Even the hangman's job is no protection for anyone."

Charles went down the stairs to the courtyard of the Conciergerie and asked the stable boy for his horse. He was familiar with the story about Hentz. Fouquier hadn't told the whole story. Several times Hentz had raped the bodies of beheaded women.

The stable boy handed him the reins, but just as he was preparing to mount his horse, a coach drove up, blocking his way. A servant opened the door, and Dr. Louis stepped out. "Oh, Monsieur de Paris," he said, "we can build the machine, but the carpenter Guédon is asking almost six thousand pounds for each, and the public prosecutor's office finds that

too expensive. Guédon says that nobody would want to build a machine like that, and that's why the price is so high."

"Tobias Schmidt will build the machine for three hundred pounds," said Charles, "though for the linen sack he wants twenty pounds more."

"Tell him to start today," said Dr. Louis, and started up the stairway to Fouquier's office. He didn't want to be seen tarrying with the hangman for too long.

Charles went about his work again. At night, if he couldn't sleep, he wrote down the day's events in his diary, though it no longer helped to put his mind to rest. He wondered if he should simply burn the diaries—their contents would be enough to set off a criminal investigation—but he needed them. While the citizens of Paris were paralyzed with fear and tried to stay out of sight, Charles often took up his pen and secretly recorded what no one dared to say anymore. He entitled his notes *Mémoires des Sanson: Sept générations d'exécuteurs*, (*Memories of the Sansons: Seven Generations of Executioners)*.

One day, Dan-Mali was waiting for him in his laboratory. She looked somewhat lost, peering into the bowls containing crushed blossoms and roots. When she saw Charles, she ran toward him with open arms, embraced him, and kissed him. After a while she said, "I have pain." Charles asked her to lie down. The wound had healed, but suddenly he noticed black and blue marks on her waist. When he took off her dress, he noticed many bruises, as if she'd been whipped.

"Who did that?" Charles asked, trembling with anger.

"I fell," Dan-Mali lied.

"I can read wounds, so don't lie to me."

"Father Gerbillon, but it's my fault. I cried when he told me I could never see you again. Now I must always stay with him, cleaning, cooking, shopping, and at night I have to sleep

in his bed. That is not the will of my king in Siam. The priest forces me to do things that are unclean."

"Don't any of the other priests help you?"

She shook her head. "No, they drink as if there will be no tomorrow, they await the Day of Judgment and are afraid of Father Gerbillon. He has too much influence. He socializes with powerful men in the Chateau of Madame Gourdan."

"Father Gerbillon," mumbled Charles, as if to himself. Dan-Mali nodded. "What are you going to do?"

On the same day, Charles visited the establishment on the Rue des Deux-Portes.

"Any special wishes, Monsieur?" a Spanish woman asked in broken French.

"Father Gerbillon?" Charles whispered.

"Madame Gerbillon?" she asked, leading him into an unfamiliar room. The people here were not wearing dark robes, but formal clothing for a soiree. The Spanish woman pointed discretely to a woman who was conversing with a young, naked blond woman.

"That's a woman," said Charles.

"He prefers to wear women's clothing," said Gorsas, who suddenly appeared next to Charles. "Nobody knows what happened to the king's mathematician in Siam, but it's certain he didn't spend his time observing the night sky and preparing new nautical charts. He enjoys protection because he provides Siamese girls to our revolutionary higher-ups." Gorsas followed him. "Monsieur, I hope you are not offended by my little article about the Royalist's printing shop. Readers like such stories." Gorsas beckoned to the Spanish woman to leave. "You can entrust your guest to me," he continued, sucking on his pipe. "Look over there, it's Robespierre. He can't stand that Saint-Just is running after the same woman as he is, and if this rivalry doesn't stop soon, the revolution will fail, all because of a cheap bitch."

Charles eyed Gorsas skeptically. He'd changed, and his gaze now was full of mockery and contempt.

"There ought to be things more important to a man, Monsieur de Paris, than a young whore. His clay pipe, for example." He took the pipe out of his mouth and coughed. "You can share a whore, but not a clay pipe."

Charles had lost most of his respect for the journalist and watched the clumsy courtship contest between Robespierre and Saint-Just.

"Do you know Saint-Just?"

Charles shook his head.

"I've heard some of his fiery speeches in the National Assembly. He comes from back in the provinces, and his ambition is boundless, but his talent wretched. He's a worthless failure, just like Robespierre, whom he idolizes. Look closely—is he a real man? He's just a child with an old face. Come along." Gorsas led Charles to Saint-Just and Robespierre.

"How are you coming with your writing?" asked Gorsas, grinning straight into Saint-Just's face. "You could issue a decree in verse form, ordering the Paris publishers to print your poems."

Saint-Just cast a disapproving glance at Gorsas.

"Watch out, Citizen Gorsas. Even if you are not a royalist, you're far from being a court jester with a fool's freedom to say whatever you like."

"Oh, are our revolutionaries as untouchable now as kings used to be?" Gorsas reached into his pocket, pulled out a document, and set it down on the table in front of Saint-Just. "Olympe de Gouges wrote this pamphlet with the title *Declaration of Rights for all Women and Citizens*, based on the principles of human rights, and is distributing it now in the streets of Paris."

Saint-Just mumbled a few lines: "*Women are born free and equal to men in all respects*. She must have misunderstood something."

Robespierre ripped the pamphlet out of his hands and tore it to pieces.

Gorsas laughed. "I'm afraid you need to do more than that."

"Don't even think of printing that, or I'll send you . . ."

"What happened to freedom of the press, Citizen Robespierre?"

"Freedom of the press can also be abused in order to incite the people, Citizen Gorsas." Robespierre stared at him sternly.

"This conversation is over, Gorsas. Someday you'll be shocked."

"Then it will no doubt be my turn to lose my head." replied Gorsas.

"Gorsas," Saint-Just sighed, "the problem is that suddenly everyone wants to be a ruler, and no one wants to be just a citizen."

A curtain was pushed aside, and an imperial figure entered the room. It was Danton, the big man with the loud mouth, pockmarked face, and thick lips. He gave the woman in his company a slap on the rear and strode toward Saint-Just. "The reward for a victorious revolutionary must be a life of luxury, don't you agree?"

Saint-Just waved him off, whereupon Robespierre quickly seized a black-haired girl with a pageboy haircut, stood up, took her by the hand, and led her into one of the private rooms.

"The woman has chosen power," Gorsas said to Saint-Just, "not youth or money."

Saint-Just rose, as well, and followed Robespierre.

Danton turned away and headed toward the bar.

"This Saint-Just! He's a narcissist and unconsciously wants to take out his revenge on the monarchy because it has closed the doors to Versailles to him despite all his efforts. That's my theory, Monsieur de Paris."

"What do you know about the king's mathematician?" Charles asked discreetly.

"In Siam, they have made a transvestite out of him, and he evidently enjoys how the people there run around during the ceremonies. Then he returned to Paris with twelve Siamese exchange students. One of the little Siamese girls seemed to please him so much that he immediately took her for himself. That's the way it is with our revolutionaries. What they decide applies only to others—can you imagine that?"

"When you carry out death sentences, you can imagine anything. Some time ago, I executed Damiens . . ."

"I remember very well. My memory is my greatest asset." said Gorsas, "nothing escapes me, and this fake woman will have to take care. He'll be the next to land on the scaffold." He went to the bar.

As Charles watched Father Gerbillon flirting with a very young girl, he could feel the hatred welling up inside him. He turned away, shocked once again at the new abuses of power spreading in Paris. The revolutionaries had usurped the throne of the king, and in other countries there was already talk of *Robespierre's armies*.

"Charles!" someone shouted. He turned around and saw Father Gerbillon with the girl. "What a surprise. I thought you preferred Siamese princesses. Be patient. A shipload is on the way." The priest laughed. He had not the slightest inhibitions, certain that he enjoyed the protection of the revolutionaries, and that a hangman was too insignificant to cause him any embarrassment.

"What do you mean by that?" Charles asked uneasily.

"I told you, the revolution has impoverished the church. How can we finance our monastic life?"

"With respectable work," Charles replied sharply.

"What is respectable work, anyway? Is your work respectable?"

"Are you planning to sell Dan-Mali to this house?"

Father Gerbillon burst out laughing. "Would you think I'd do anything like that?" he chuckled. "I'm warning you—love is only of short duration, then the excitement of the hunt returns and you yearn for the illusion of a new love. God has created us in this way—by the way, in his own image. Can you imagine how much the big guy has screwed around?"

Charles showed no emotion. "I asked you once if Dan-Mali could live with me and work with me."

The priest shook his head and said emphatically, "I claim Dan-Mali for myself alone, she belongs to me. I love her cooking."

"I can pay you."

The priest looked as if he was hearing that for the first time. "Finally, a reasonable suggestion. The church urgently needs money to feed its sheep. I'll consider it, if you promise me one thing . . ."

"Yes?" Charles felt like killing the priest.

"Don't think badly of me. The revolution has swept God away, and now we can indulge in our most depraved fantasies because there is no one up there keeping the books." He put his hand on Charles' shoulder and whispered, "Without God, there are no more curses. Charles, the revolution has liberated you—you are free!" Again, he burst out laughing and departed with the girl.

CHAPTER 10

The gigantic contraption stood in the courtyard in front of the Conciergerie, its perpendicular beams thrusting skyward, casting narrow shadows on the little gathering of people who had come to observe the spectacle. It was April 15, 1792. Present were Dr. Louis and Dr. Guillotin, the public prosecutors Roederer and Fouquier, as well as Charles with his assistants and his son Henri. At some distance stood the prison guards. Gorsas arrived a bit late and was greeted by Fouquier with a cordial nod. First, the spectacle began with a mud-splattered sheep that ran madly around the device as Charles' assistants tried to catch it, in vain. Now, some of the jailers joined the chase, and together they managed to catch it, tie it down on the base board, and slip the board beneath the blade All Charles had to do was to pull the metal slide bar, and the blade came hurtling down, cleanly separating the sheep's head from its torso as blood spurted across the yard. Everyone was clearly astonished at the speed of the operation.

"Do you have any corpses?" Louis asked.

"Yes," said Charles, giving a sign to his assistants, who brought three corpses into the yard of men with powerful necks provided by the hospital. One had killed himself, the second was an alcoholic, and the third a musketeer of the king who was killed in a duel.

The first two corpses were beheaded quickly and cleanly, but when they got to the third, Dr. Louis wanted to exchange the blade for the half-moon shaped blade they had been

considering before the correction suggested by Louis XVI. The experiment was not successful, very much to the satisfaction of Dr. Louis who was pleased he could inform his king he'd been right.

"What are we going to call this device now?" Gorsas asked out of the blue. "There will be many new devices in the future, so we need a special name. Louisette?"

"Out of the question!" Louis said angrily, "I'm a doctor. What about Guillotine?"

"I'm a doctor, too," Guillotin objected. The two turned to Charles.

"Sansonette?" Gorsas laughed.

"I'm just the operator of the device," Charles replied.

Gorsas shook his head. "I like Louisette, it sounds so melodic."

"Why not, then?" Fouquier said. "After all, there are a lot of people with the name Louis." He laughed. Then he turned to Charles. "Citizen Sanson, I must speak with you, but first bring us Pelletier. The lucky fellow will go down in history as the first man executed with the Louisette."

In the Conciergerie, Charles cut the shoulder-length hair of the condemned man, Nicolas Jacques Pelletier, and removed his collar so the neck was clearly visible. Firmin and Barre helped the prisoner put on a blood-red shirt, tied his hands behind his back, then accompanied him to the tumbrel standing outside to take him on his last journey. Pelletier had stolen eight hundred pounds in a brazen robbery on the Rue Bourbon-Villeneuve, and for that had been sentenced to death.

Thousands of onlookers had already gathered in front of the Conciergerie, the wagon drove up, and finally Lafayette, the Commander of the National Guard, left the inner courtyard, pushed his way past the wagon, and took his position at the head of the procession as the crowd applauded enthusiastically. They were standing crammed together in the

streets and narrow lanes, leaning out of their windows, while the nobles sat on their balconies. The trip to the scaffold took more than two hours. A flyer described the scene as resembling a theatre performance. Between the arcades, merchants had set up sausage stands, and nearby restaurants had printed the name of the condemned man on the front of their menus. On each table stood one of Tobias Schmidt's miniature models of the device that could be used to cut up carrots or asparagus. As the tumbrel rolled by, jeers went up from the crowd, and wildest taunts were heard. Soon he would *spit in the sack*, that is, his blood would spurt out and his head fall into the sack of heads on the other side when the blade fell. He would be punished by "the nation's straight razor". A well-known local buffoon named Jacot jumped up onto one of Charles' horses, made funny faces, and ridiculed the condemned man. As the public applauded, Charles picked up his carriage whip and drove the clown back into the crowd. Wasn't death punishment enough? Pelletier was pelted with rotten vegetables and tried to seek shelter under the wagon, but Charles held him back. Those were the orders he had from Fouquier.

As they turned into the Place de Grève they could see the two vertical beams of the bloody device rising into the sky, its blade sparkling for a moment in the sunlight. Henri and his assistants had built an impressive scaffold and installed the Louisette atop it. Lafayette's horsemen surrounded the scaffold as Pelletier was led up the wooden steps. He appeared stunned as he looked down across the Place de Grève—so many people had come to see him die. Charles loudly called out Pelletier's name and enumerated his personal possessions as Henri, along with Gros, Barre, and Firmin, tied the condemned man onto the vertical wooden board, then tipped it so it was level and pushed it between the two vertical beams. Immediately the blade hurtled downward and the separated head tumbled like a sawed-off branch into

the wicker basket. The blood spurted like a fountain from the torso, and the onlookers cheered. Most of them were disappointed, especially the old shrews standing around the scaffold in order to mock the condemned man with vulgar words. Everything had gone so fast that it was hard to realize what had happened—no long agony in boiling water, no choking while the neck was hanging on a rope, no hissing when extremities were burned. Nothing. Henri took the head, dripping with blood, out of the basket and showed it to the crowd. There was scattered booing. "Give us back our gallows," some shouted, then louder and louder they chanted, "Give us back our gallows."

The blood was still flowing from the executed man's head. Charles stood on the top step of the scaffold and watched closely to see if there was any agitation in the crowd by people opposed to the machine.

Finally, Gorsas resumed the conversation in an earnest tone. "It may be brutal but it is just, and the speed of the procedure stands in harmony with humanitarian principles. What did you feel, Citizen Sanson?" said Gorsas, as he approached Charles. Let our readers know."

"I have carried out a sentence of the court," Charles replied, "no blood is on my hands. I'm beginning to like this device."

"The devise now has a name," Gorsas said. "Guillotine. The king did that to protect his personal doctor. Dr. Guillotin protested, but he didn't prevail. His descendants will no doubt curse him, as their name will forever be connected to this killing machine. I am always amused by the irony of fate. That is the raw material from which I make my stories." Gorsas raised his hand briefly in farewell. "Until we meet again, Monsieur de Paris. I must deliver my story before the deadline."

Charles watched as Gorsas left. sucking on his pipe and trying to look important as he made his way nervously

through the crowd, whom he secretly despised. Then Charles saw the little woman who slipped by him on her way forward toward the scaffold. It was Dan-Mali, and she had probably been watching the entire time. At the bottom of the steps she paused, and Charles climbed down to meet her. She folded her hands respectfully before her and lowered her head.

"Charles," she said, looking at him admiringly, "I didn't know you executed people and regret I haven't shown you the proper respect." He looked at her skeptically. "In Siam, only holy men may execute others," she continued.

"They become one with the condemned man and are united with the gods."

"Weren't you ever present for an execution? When Damiens was tortured?"

"No," said Dan-Mali, "you must have confused me with someone else."

Now the crowd around the scaffold became denser as more and more people gathered around the wicker basket with a shudder but not without fascination to see the cut-off head, and some dipped their handkerchief in the blood. The assistants loaded the corpse into a coffin-like wicker basket, placing the head between the legs.

"I must go to the cemetery," Charles told Dan-Mali.

"May I come to you tomorrow?" she asked.

"Stay with me, you can live with me, we have enough room." He took her hand and squeezed it. At that moment, it started to rain, and the crowd began to disperse.

Charles left his assistants behind to disassemble the guillotine, and asked Henri to take a seat in the wagon alongside the corpse. Dan-Mali took a seat next to Charles, who took hold of the reins, and some of Lafayette's guards cleared the way for them to the nearest cemetery outside town. At dusk, they reached the scene of the mass grave that Fouquier had specified in the Madeleine Cemetery. "Single

graves are no longer possible," he'd said, "for reasons of space. Too many will still be coming."

When they arrived, Henri jumped down from the wagon, opened the iron gate, and they proceeded to the freshly dug pit in the southern part of the cemetery, where they picked up the headless corpse and tossed it in. They sprinkled a mixture of ammonia, carbonic acid, and water over the corpse, then covered it with a good portion of slaked lime. Suddenly, a young woman appeared between the gravestones and called out, "Monsieur de Paris!" Charles took her for a curious onlooker who wanted to dunk her handkerchief in the blood or plead for body parts.

"Can I have the head?"

"No," Charles replied, "I'm forbidden to trade in body parts."

"I can offer you no money, so it's not a transaction. I need it for just a half hour."

"Why?" Charles asked impatiently.

"I'm the owner, along with my uncle Philippe Curtius, of the wax museum in the Palais Royal. I wish to make a model of the first head chopped off by the guillotine."

"Ask the public prosecutor Fouquier or Roederer, you're not getting heads from me," said Charles, seizing the head by the loose hair and tossing it in the pit.

"I'll get my heads," she said defiantly.

"Indeed, and no doubt more than you want."

"How long is this going to last?" Marie-Anne asked furiously, as she stormed into the laboratory without knocking.

"She's staying here now, we spoke about that," said Charles. "She will be helping me in the laboratory and doing the cooking."

"What's she going to cook?" Marie-Anne retorted sarcastically. "Grasshoppers, chicken gullets, and other bizarre things that burn your tongue?"

"In Siam they also eat dogs."

Marie-Anne turned red with rage. "That's more than I can take! I'm going to my sister's. I'm apparently no longer needed here." She stomped down the hallway, through the kitchen, and watched as Dan-Mali made a fire. She wanted to say something, something nasty, but then, without speaking a word, she went out into the courtyard and saddled her horse.

Antoine Fouquier was staring out the window, his hands clasped behind his back. Charles was still in the room, standing behind Antoine's desk, waiting. Fouquier was in a good mood and even overlooked being addressed by his first name. "Congratulations on the successful execution. Your machine actually works, but your friend, that German piano builder, still won't be given the job. Roederer prefers a relative of his who is much more expensive but—a member of the family. You see, here again something comes into play that I warned you about a long time ago, in boarding school. Noble blood trumps knowledge, and kinship trumps quality. You'll never have a chance, Charles. You live in a cave and will never be able to break through the rock ceiling over your head. but only heaven can set limits on people born free like myself."

"Is that all?" asked Charles, unimpressed.

Fouquier ignored the question, which seemed to him a bit insolent. "Have you in the meanwhile come up with a name?" he persisted.

Charles took a deep breath, and exhaled again.

"So, I am waiting for names. Give me at least one name." Fouquier turned to the window again and looked down into the courtyard. "By the way, the little woman in the cemetery complained to me. You ought to lend her the heads for half

an hour each. We want people to see the victims of the revolution—that's a deterrent. There will be many heads, as we intend to fill our cemeteries and not our prisons. Citizen Sanson, I'm still waiting for names, just a single name!"

"Father Gerbillon," Charles heard himself say.

"I didn't quite understand," said Fouquier.

"Father . . .?"

"Father Gerbillon," Charles repeated, "a Jesuit. He was sent to Siam as the mathematician of the king."

"I remember, Gorsas mentioned it recently. Our mathematician was to observe the stars there and draw up new nautical charts, but instead he observed the asses of young boys and little girls. King Rama I still plans to declare war on us . . ." He laughed. "Gerbillon always enjoyed the protection of the court, because he—" and now Fouquier shouted the words—"is a goddamned Royalist. I hate him, I've always hated him."

Charles briefly raised an eyebrow as if to say *Well, that's probably the case.*

"Now was that so difficult, Citizen Sanson?" As Charles was about to leave, Fouquier said, "Your friend, the organ builder can build the guillotine—eighty-three of them at nine hundred sixty pounds. If one of them fails, the remainder of the order will be cancelled."

"But you just said . . ."

"You gave me a name, so I'm showing my appreciation, and in this way you have a unique opportunity to understand he rules of the game. Who knows, Citizen Sanson, perhaps we can still renew our old friendship."

Tobias Schmidt was drunk. He was lying on a discarded sofa in his workshop babbling inarticulately. New sketches hung along the wall, one depicting a huge guillotine designed to cut off twenty-four heads all at once. When Charles entered the room, Schmidt jumped to his feet, but was immediately

overcome by a feeling of nausea and stumbled to the floor. He got to his knees, took a deep breath and gasped. "Just give me a minute." "Roederer is not going to give me the job," he wailed. "He claims I'm too expensive and the quality is bad. That would have been my dream job, more than eighty guillotines, one for each *departement*." Again, he gasped for air. He had circulatory problems.

"Can I help you, Monsieur Schmidt?" Charles held out his hand.

Schmidt waved dismissively and pointed at a board on the ground running along the wall, where dozens of scale models of little guillotines not longer than a man's forearm were standing.

"Toy guillotines" Schmidt sighed. "Is there anything more shameful for an inventor than to squander his genius on children's toys? I have invented hydraulic machines, new type of chimneys, and the famous piano that combines the effects of the viola, cello, and violin. I'm also working on a method to preserve fruit and vegetables and ruin my stomach by testing them on myself every day. Now I'm making toys. Tell me, is there anything more disgraceful? It's like giving a victorious general a hobbyhorse."

Charles helped him to his feet. "Roederer's cousin asked 5,600 pounds, but you only 340 . . ."

"And twenty-four for the linen sack. A wicker basket would be even cheaper." Schmidt seemed about to lose his balance, but caught himself and staggered through the room. "I'm going to throw it all in the fire," he shouted, "all of it!"

"That can wait until tomorrow," said Charles, but first built the guillotines at 960 pounds each—that's what Fouquier ordered, and Roederer agreed."

Schmidt ran toward Charles and embraced him fervently. "Eighty-three guillotines makes altogether—wait—almost eighty thousand pounds! Monsieur Sanson, I am deeply indebted to you."

"But it is also important to me that you still find time to tune my piano and fit Gabriel's leg braces. He's been falling more recently," said Charles.

"I promise," said Schmidt, nodding earnestly. Then his eyes began to sparkle and he nudged Charles to a tool bench where a number of open cans were standing. "At present, I'm trying to seal the cans with lead. They say lead is poisonous and that the ancient Romans died because their waterpipes were made of lead. I'm using just a small amount of it, however, and it barely comes in contact with the food. If I succeed, people will be naming streets after me everywhere." Schmidt collapsed again on his couch and groped for the opened wine bottle on the floor. He drank the rest of it, then watched it roll across the uneven wooden planks.

"Very well, but you must get started at once with the guillotines," Charles insisted.

When he arrived home, Dan-Mali was no longer there.

On the night of August 9 to 10, 1792, all the storm bells in Paris were ringing. It must have been after midnight, and Charles, immediately suspecting a large fire, jumped out of bed and ran out into the street with Henri. Everywhere, people were streaming out of their houses, most of them armed, and forming a large crowd, marched toward the Tuileries. A few weeks earlier, the same thing had happened, and they'd marched to the palace, seized Louis XVI and his family, and forced them to toast them with a glass of wine. This time, however, there was more to it. There was a rumor that Prussian and Austrian troops had crossed the border into France and were coming to save the king. Monarchs in neighboring countries feared a political firestorm of epic proportions. What was happening in Paris was a second revolution. The radical sans-culottes had set up their own city administration, thus becoming a counter-government in defiance of the legal, democratic National Assembly.

Tonight, the ten thousand sans-culottes on the march were ready to do anything to rid themselves of their king once and for all. When they were in sight of the Tuileries they began chanting "Death to the king." They marched as a man toward the approximately one thousand Swiss guards protecting the king. On seeing the enormous crowd, the two thousand soldiers guarding the king on behalf of the National Assembly immediately fled and joined the ranks of the furious sans-culottes. Many soldiers of the Swiss Guard were killed by the angry mob, shot, chased through the streets until they collapsed in exhaustion, then beheaded with machetes like chickens. There was no longer any legal government, no one could control the crowd, and the Paris underworld awakened to new life, running riot through the city, pillaging, settling old scores, castrating dying soldiers of the guard, and throwing their genitals into the street. The people no longer had any political goals, they used the chaos and the freedom of the streets to plunder and slaughter the hated rich people. It was a bloody folk festival in which anyone could publicly kill anyone else without fear of retribution. Louis XVI, Marie Antoinette, and their children were taken to the Temple as the National Assembly took even more radical positions, trying to placate the anger of the sans-culottes. The representatives were shocked, but powerless.

In August, a new criminal tribunal was established that could pronounce the death sentence without the right of appeal at the slightest hint of "conspiracy" People were fearful and hid in their houses.

"What's happening now is not right," Charles said to Henri as they were waxing their ropes after finishing the day's work. It was a comforting ritual that helped them forget the day's executions even though now, with the guillotine, they no longer needed the rope. Much blood flowed down onto the pavement between the wooden planks of the

scaffold, giving off a foul odor that only attracted dogs. People didn't protest the slaughter, but the stench. Charles and his assistants therefore set up the guillotine in the Place du Carrousel in front of the main gate to the Tuileries.

Robespierre demanded "people's justice" against the enemies of the revolution, trying to get the unleashed masses under control again, but instead, the armed rioters and members of the National Guard stormed the prisons and massacred more than a thousand petty criminals. The noble goals of the revolution had been upended and metamorphosed into something grotesque.

Despite the mass murders, Charles' workload increased week by week. He reported to Fouquier every morning in the Conciergerie to pick up the sentences to be carried out that evening. Sometimes there were just a few hours separating the trial from the sentence and execution. The revolutionaries insisted it was better to kill ten innocent men than let a guilty one off.

"Prussian troops have crossed the border," cried Chief Prosecutor Fouquier as Charles entered his office.

"We'll leave it to the people's justice to decide what to do with anyone not showing patriotism. At this hour, thousands of angry citizens are storming the prisons and relieving you of that task. They are slaughtering them all."

"What happened to the noble goal of human rights?" Charles ask sarcastically.

"Careful, careful, Citizen Sanson! Didn't I tell you once that every revolution is born in blood. The National Convention has deposed the king and taken him to the Temple. Would you have ever thought it possible that one day you might guillotine the king?"

"He's still alive," said Charles, "there is no sentence."

"The National Convention no longer has any power. The power now resides in the streets, the revolutionary commune." Fouquier handed him the current list of those

THE HANGMAN OF PARIS

condemned to death. Charles glanced at it—assignat counterfeiters, a journalist, a shoemaker. Suddenly a name caught his eye: Father Gerbillon. He also noticed a well-known tradesman of good repute who merely expressed his opinion. "Any more questions, Monsieur de Paris?"

Charles shook his head.

Fouquier sat up straight and suddenly appeared distant. "I have heard that the clown Jacot accompanies your procession now and then and entertains the crowd with his antics. They say you drove him away with your whip."

"That's right," Charles replied. "An execution shouldn't degenerate into a carnival. I am accustomed to carry out the sentences in a dignified way."

"Who told you to do that?" Fouquier asked, looking down disapprovingly at Charles. "Who are you? Do you represent the revolutionary regime? An execution is a carnival of the revolution. Put this fellow on your payroll, that's an order. We must keep the people in a good mood. Who knows all we will ask of them in the coming months? And don't perform the executions until nightfall, place torches around the scaffold, and let's see if the people like that more."

Charles nodded hesitantly.

"There's something else troubling you, I can see it in your eyes."

"I'd like finally to hand over my office to my son, Henri."

"Silence! I don't want to hear a bit of it! This is probably the worst moment to make that request. You will guillotine the king, you are the hangman of the revolution, and Henri is just your journeyman. You are the arm of the guillotine, and many people come to the executions just to see you."

Once again, Marie-Anne had had a falling-out with her sister, and suddenly she was standing there in the kitchen cooking pea soup. "Fortunately for you, I'm back," she said. "Without me, you drop the reins and nothing works here. Besides,

Gabriel belongs with you at the executions. He can't just play the piano all day." She served the soup.

"Gabriel is devoted to the fine arts," said Charles, stirring his soup dejectedly.

"You can't make any money doing that," Marie-Anne snapped. "The hangman's vocation is one of the most secure in our country, because we will always need one."

"Someday," Gabriel said, "the death punishment will be abolished, and we won't need a hangman anymore."

"You'll never live to see that day," Marie-Anne shouted. "Robespierre wanted to abolish it, but he couldn't. Who else could do that?"

"Leave him alone," Henri said emphatically. "He doesn't want to be a hangman."

"You stay out of this," his mother said, "you're just afraid that your father's successor . . ."

"Just stop fighting," Charles said, pounding the table with his hand. "Henri will be my successor in Paris, and that's final. If Gabriel chooses, I'll find him a position in another city, but if doesn't want to . . ."

"He should be there at least once on the scaffold, and then he'll know if he really wants to."

"Why did you come back, anyway? Nobody missed you," said Charles.

"I'm still their mother," Marie-Anne said defiantly, "whether you like it or not."

"Enough!" said Gabriel, pushing his plate aside. "Stop arguing, and tomorrow evening I'll be there on the scaffold."

Outside, the first snow of the year was falling, and a biting wind was blowing into the house through cracks in the windows. Desmorets lit a large fire in the stove and Charles sat down with Gabriel at the piano.

Darkness had fallen and it began to snow lightly. The scaffold was illuminated by torches, casting the execution

site into a ghostly, flickering light. Charles tried to avoid looking at Father Gerbillon, and it was only when they reached the scaffold that their eyes met. Charles helped him up, and Gabriel was the first to climb the ladder to the scaffold, to the applause of the onlookers. First, according to protocol, the counterfeiters were guillotined, one after the other while Charles stayed at the bottom of the steps looking up at his sons and assistants. As Gabriel held out the head of one of the victims for the crowd to see, Charles led a journalist to the scaffold, then climbed down again. Once again, Father Gerbillon was looking him directly in the eye, but his expression was melancholic rather than anxious, and Charles felt mean and shabby. He was ashamed this man had to die because of him, but he tried to convince himself there had been no other choice and, moreover, the priest had deserved it because of the way he'd treated Dan-Mali. The journalist's head fell into the basket, and now Charles led Father Gerbillon up to the scaffold. He had no sooner left the scaffold when he heard the huge iron blade hurtling down and the head of the Jesuit priest falling into the wicker basket. Gabriel picked it up by the hair and raised it up for all to see. The crowd applauded, hooted, and laughed—a human life had no meaning anymore. In the flickering light of the torches, Gabriel strode slowly across the scaffold, pacing back and forth as if he were measuring it. But suddenly something strange occurred: Gabriel disappeared, as if carried away by a gust of wind. He just wasn't standing there on the scaffold any longer. Charles looked up, searching for his son, and the people standing around the scaffold began to scream in horror, forming a semi-circle around Gabriel, who was lying on the ground. He had fallen from the scaffold in the darkness. The priest's hair had suddenly ripped out, Gabriel had tried reflexively to catch the head, and had slipped on the snow-covered wooden planks.

Charles pushed his way through the crowd of onlookers and knelt down alongside Gabriel. Putting his hand under his son's neck, he immediately felt that his neck was broken. "Gabriel," Charles whispered, then took his son in both arms and roared out into the night "Gabriel!" Tears streamed down his cheeks. "The hangman is crying," someone said, and suddenly voices could be heard everywhere saying "the hangman is crying." After a while, Henri placed his hand on his father's shoulder. "Let us go, Father. Gabriel belongs at home." Henri carried his brother to the wagon and drove alone across the snow-covered square stained red with the warm blood of executed men. For a long time, Charles remained sitting on the bottom step of the scaffold.

The square was already deserted by the time he set out for home. No one was waiting for him there, the house was empty, and apparently Henri and the assistants had taken Gabriel's corpse to be laid out in the chapel. As Charles entered the courtyard to go to his room, he saw a figure sitting on the bench alongside the snow-covered vegetable garden. It was Marie-Anne. He walked toward her, stopped a few steps away, and was about to touch her, but then decided not to. Too often she had rejected him. "I don't need you," she mumbled, glancing up at him. Her face was care-worn, her eyes stained with tears.

"You'll catch cold," Charles said. "Come into the house, it's going to be cold tonight."

"Then I'll just catch cold," she replied. "You think it's all my fault."

Charles was going to deny it, but then fell silent, as he was indeed convinced it was her fault.

"I never should have married you," she said. Her revulsion showed clearly in her face.

"My mother warned me, but I didn't want to listen. She said that there has been a curse on the Sanson family for generations. It turned out she was right."

"There are no such things as curses, Marie-Anne, that's only an attempt people make to give a meaning to things. We are free, and you, too, are free, Marie-Anne. I will resign my post and leave you.

"You can leave me, Charles, but the curse will follow you everywhere, so think it over. I will leave tomorrow for my sister's."

"She will be happy," he said, "and when I come home from work tomorrow evening, it would be good if you had left."

He went to his laboratory, sat down on the bed, and drank wine. Suddenly he felt infinitely exhausted, like a rudderless ship on the high seas. He thought of Gabriel with great affection, and was consoled by the thought he hadn't suffered. Shortly after that, he was overcome by a dreadful anger at his wife. Then came the thought that God had punished him, taking his son from him in exchange for the life of Father Gerbillon. He suddenly believed that God was watching him—it wasn't Gorsas who was watching, but God. He had been punished, the curse was back, and Marie-Anne was possibly right. Then he thought he saw a figure outside the window. Did God want to visit him? No, he didn't believe in such stories, it was Marie-Anne. She withdrew, and went back to the house. He drank and drank and finally fell asleep.

At noon the next day he was still sleeping. Nobody had wakened him. Henri had taken over for him, and Charles could hear the wagon leaving the yard. He turned on his other side and fell back to sleep. All he wanted was to sleep, and never wake up, but then he thought of Dan-Mali, and his breathing became steadier and his sleep more peaceful.

When he woke up again, he felt a small, gentle hand on his cheek. It couldn't be Marie-Anne, who hands were rough, dry, and always smelled like wet dog fur after her work in the garden. These hands smelled of almond oil. He pressed them

firmly and fell back to sleep. The next time he woke up, he was alone and didn't know what he'd actually experienced and what was just a dream. At one point, Desmorets brought him a bowl of soup. "Madame says you should eat something. She is gone now." Charles placed the bowl on the table.

Later, Henri came to waken him. There's a man on horseback outside looking for you.

"What does he want?"

"I don't know. Perhaps he's sick or injured."

"Show him in," said Charles, getting to his feet. The change would do him good. Despite all the dreadful events, he was glad someone was coming to see him. As a doctor. The man on horseback was wearing a hooded cloak and knee-high leather boots. Before entering the laboratory, he knocked the boots together to shake off the snow.

"Lay your coat on the bench by the stove where it can dry out."

"Thank you, Monsieur," said the horseman, removing his coat. Beneath it he was wearing an elegant, two-piece suit made of blue material. He sat down facing Charles, took out a leather purse from an inside pocket, and loosened the leather strap so Charles could see the coins inside. "I have very influential friends," the horseman began cautiously, "and they are loyal subjects of our king. An hour ago he was condemned to death, and we intend to free him on his way to the scaffold. We ask nothing impossible of you."

"Leave," said Charles, raising his hands defensively. "No amount of money in the world will convince me to join a conspiracy."

"I know," said the horseman, "and that's why I have been so bold as to approach you. I know you are a just man, and we only ask you to do nothing to foil the freeing of our king. Just sit calmly on your coachbox and don't move. Nothing will happen to you."

"I don't want this money," said Charles. "I may find the arbitrary laws today reprehensible, but I must follow them. I am an official in the justice department."

The rider stood up. "I'll leave the money here. If you don't want it, give it to the poor. May God save our king."

"God save our king," Charles whispered. The thought that the king was going to be beheaded by his guillotine broke his heart. On the other hand, Charles thought, the king had only himself to blame for his fate. He had never reciprocated his people's love for him and had done nothing—absolutely nothing—for his starving people. "That is the way he wanted it," Charles mumbled, "and he alone is responsible."

CHAPTER 11

On January 21 1793, Charles noted in his diary: *The Death of the King*. It was difficult to put this event in words, since up to then the king was considered unassailable, virtually sent by God.

Before the church bells chimed the eighth hour of the morning, Charles took a seat in the wagon with his assistants Barre, Firmin, Desmorets, and Gros, and drove away. The closer they came to their destination, the more people lined the sides of the streets, and finally dense crowds encircled the wagon, embracing it like a huge octopus. Charles and his assistants passed one military cordon after another. Thousands of soldiers armed with rifles and pikes secured the streets under the commander of the National Guard, Santerre. An eerie silence lay over the city—there were no jeers or shouts, simply silence, as if they had all come together for a sacred act. When they finally reached the Place de la Révolution at around ten o'clock, the bloody scaffold with the majestic guillotine atop it rose above the plaza. Once again, Charles was dazzled by the sight. The towering guillotine had a grandeur suggesting that here a sacrificial offering would be made.

Henri already awaited them on the platform and signaled to a mounted soldier to clear a path for his father. Charles felt his breathing become faster. His hand felt for the dagger, pistol, tin of gunpowder, and bag of bullets under his coat, making sure they were still tied securely. He was fearful. He'd received so many threatening letters in recent days that

he didn't doubt an attempt would be made to free the condemned king. He kept glancing in the direction of the Rue de la Révolution, but couldn't make out any movement in the crowd, no coach bringing the victim to the scaffold. Suddenly, however, he heard shouts and the sounds of hoofs, and a corps of men on horseback approached, towering above the crowd. When Charles saw the royal coach he sat down briefly on the board of the guillotine and took a deep breath. He felt faint, was sweating from every pore, and had to struggle to stand up. He could no longer feel the ground beneath his feet now, the wooden boards seemed to move back and forth, to drift away, and he thought of Gabriel, he thought of Dan-Mali, and soon he no longer could remember what he'd been thinking of, he was simply overcome by a terrible anxiety.

"Go back down," Henri said, "wait at the bottom of the steps, and give me the signal." Charles nodded. A deathly silence had settled over the square and one could hear only the hoofbeats of the horses.

The royal coach stopped in front of the scaffold, the soldiers broke ranks to form a square around the coach, then the king stepped out, calmly, looking dignified and sublime, and without a trace of panic. He appeared more regal and exalted than Charles had remembered as his Irish priest stood at his side murmuring prayers. Desmorets took the initiative as Charles and the other three assistants stared at the condemned man, petrified. With great reverence and respect, Desmorets explained to the victim that according to regulations he had to remove the man's clothes. He reached out for the king's robe, but the latter stepped back, indignantly. "Take my robe, but do not touch me," said the man who until very recently had been admired in all of Europe as King Louis XVI. "We must also tie your hands and remove your hair and collar, according to the rules, Citizen Capet." He actually called him Citizen Capet.

Suddenly, he looked Charles directly in the eye, and all Charles' energy and strength drained from his body. For a moment he wanted to kneel down and beg the King of France for forgiveness, but then then he thought of the dignity of his office. Thousands have died because of this king, Charles thought, hundreds of thousands, and thanks to the revolution we men have regained our dignity. Why in God's name didn't you renounce the throne earlier, and by your own free will? Because you wanted to have it all, you now have lost everything. The death of the king is the price for freedom, equality, and brotherhood.

Charles took a few steps toward the king. "Tying the hands is necessary, or we are unable to do our work," he said softly. The king nodded without looking at his executioner, but he didn't move. Charles asked the priest to help him. The priest understood quickly, and whispered something to the king. Visibly humbled, the king placed his arms behind his back, and Charles could now bind the hands that once held the scepter of the kings of France. Before Louis Capet climbed the stairs to the scaffold, he kissed the picture of Mary which the Irish priest held up for him. As soon as he had reached top, Citizen Capet turned to the people that were no longer his and declaimed in a firm, clear voice: "Citizens of France, you see your king before you ready to die for you. If only my blood could bring you happiness. I die guiltless."

Santerre made his way on horseback to the scaffold and gave the soldiers a sign to begin the drumroll. The king's last words were drowned out in the deafening sound. Charles turned toward the Irish priest, but at the same instant the heavy blade of the guillotine hurtled down and the royal head rolled into the basket. Charles hadn't even noticed that the king had already been strapped onto the board. Henri took the head from the basket as a virtual fountain of blood gushed from the rump of the body. For such a thick neck a slanted blade actually had been necessary. As Henri lifted up

the head to show the crowd, some people ran toward the scaffold with their handkerchiefs and there were scattered cheers of "Long live the Republic!" but an uneasy silence was dominant in the crowd. The people were troubled. They had in fact guillotined their own king.

Again Charles could feel dizziness coming upon him. Despite all attempts at rationalization, he regarded the deed as a betrayal, a deadly sin, patricide, and he was convinced the headless torso of this king would follow him in his dreams and from that moment on whenever he looked deep into his wine glass, he'd see this head with its strange expression of perplexity and astonishment looking back. At the same time, he would look back in defiance at this head, because it had deserved to be separated from its torso. It had scorned its people. Now more and more men began to chant "Long live the Republic!"

The assistants began dismantling the machine while Charles and Henri took the king's corpse to the Madeleine Cemetery in their wagon, escorted by soldiers. No souvenir hunters would be allowed to run off with the king's clothing.

Marie Grosholtz was already waiting at the cemetery. They gave her the head without hesitation and she set to work immediately while Charles and Henri unclothed the torso. Nothing about this dead body looked royal. It was pale and fat, without any dignity. Even his sexual parts were undistinguished. Nothing of all the worldly goods he had hoarded was he able to take with him to the other world—neither his gold, nor his hunting dogs, nor his hall of mirrors at Versailles.

Crazy Marie worked like mad but with great skill on the cast, her tongue pressed between her teeth. No one could say she lacked talent or passion, and she quickly finished the job. Her coach awaited her, and beaming, she bade them farewell. She seemed not a bit troubled by this bleeding, butchered head. She lived only for her wax figures.

As Charles was about to leave the cemetery, he saw a little man by the gate wearing mustard yellow trousers and sucking on his pipe. Gorsas. "I just wanted to see the little woman when she took off the death mask, but apparently I have come too late. It doesn't matter—many more heads will roll." Gorsas planted himself in front of the horse and wagon.

"Come with me, Monsieur de Paris, I'll treat you to a glass of wine. We must speak."

Actually, Charles had intended to drive to the Jesuit monastery, but he sensed that Gorsas had something important to tell him, and he had to go along. Perhaps he was in danger.

Together they rode to the 'Establishment' on the Rue des Deux-Portes. The house had many visitors, as was usual after an execution, who came to discuss the case and usually agreed that the condemned man had deserved death, thus demonstrating their loyalty to the Revolution. On these days, the services of the ladies were less in demand. They enjoyed the atmosphere and all the naked skin, but primarily they were here to publicly declare their allegiance.

In the middle of the main hall sat Robespierre and Saint-Just, now the most powerful men in France. With great self-confidence they stretched their arms out on the large pillows of the armchairs. They had the guillotine and the command over it, while Charles felt puny and exploited.

"I hear you're keeping a diary," Gorsas said softly. "May I have a look at it?"

Charles was disturbed at his question, and shook his head. "How can I find time to keep a diary? And for whom? I have no need for one."

"Well, in the print shops, diaries are practically sold out, but now no one is keeping a diary anymore. Why do people buy them?" Gorsas grinned knowingly.

"There can be many explanations for that," Charles said.

"I have been looking around in the print shops and have learned you are a regular customer."

"I need them for my record-keeping, my work demands that. I keep records of the names of the condemned men, their vocation, reason for their execution, and prepare an inventory of their personal possessions."

Gorsas nodded, and again smiled knowingly. He didn't believe a word Charles said. "We journalists, too, are under an enormous amount of pressure," he said. "The revolutionary government wants us to slander citizens all the time so they can be executed, but every citizen is a potential reader!" He leaned forward and whispered in Charles' ear "Just look over there, our new kings." He grinned broadly.

Robespierre had recognized Gorsas, and called out to him, "Gorsas, write this down: What the republic intends is the complete elimination of everything opposing it."

"Then apartments will soon be very affordable in Paris," said Gorsas, ordering a glass of champagne.

"We must punish not just the traitors in our land, but all those who are indifferent, passive, and not doing anything for the revolution," Saint-Just added, with a grave expression.

Robespierre agreed. "The Germans are on the march in the north, the British in south, and Marseille even asked for the help of British soldiers. We must wipe the city from the face of the earth and call it "The city without a name" as a warning to others. Only with terror such as has never been seen before can we stamp out the counterrevolution in our country and thus have a free hand to deal with the foreign enemies at our borders."

"Patriots!" said Gorsas with a somewhat cynical expression, "I have just learned that Lyon, too, is now in British hands, and two thirds of the eighty-three départements of our country already oppose freedom. Can you imagine!"

"Soon they will all be on our side," said Robespierre, "either out of conviction or fear, and whether it's one or the other doesn't matter to me. And anyone pretending to be moderate or undecided can start cutting their hair for the guillotine. It's possible we behead a thousand innocent people, but that's still better for the revolution than if we overlook just one undecided."

"Better overcrowded cemeteries than overcrowded prisons," Saint-Just said dryly.

"Have we met?" asked Robespierre, turning to Charles.

"Not yet," replied Charles, and left the room.

As Charles and Gorsas left the Establishment, neither spoke a word. They left silently, and didn't speak until they reached the corner. "Today was no day for a champagne toast. I must be careful," said Gorsas, "I've made too many enemies. Sooner or later my name will appear on a list and I'll have to spit in the sack. Have you ever guillotined a friend?"

Charles shook his head.

"It will happen sooner or later," Gorsas replied.

"Why did you invite me to come here today, by the way?"

Gorsas stared at Charles for a long time. "You never know these days who you can trust, and what happened this evening showed me that it's dangerous to trust anyone. Has the Grand Orient de France contacted you, by the way?"

"No," Charles replied. "Should he have?"

Gorsas shrugged. "People are afraid, Monsieur," he said, sucking on his pipe, "and fear is stronger than any law."

"What did you want to tell me tonight, Citizen Gorsas?"

"Me?" asked Gorsas in a sanctimonious voice.

"Yes," Charles growled, glaring at him.

Gorsas looked away and shook his head, looking uncomfortable. "I must go home, Citizen Sanson, it's late." Hastily, he turned into the dimly lit Rue de la Verrerie.

Charles followed him. "What are you afraid of?"

Gorsas didn't stop. "Should I be?" he said, quickening his pace.

"I don't know, but I can read people, Monsieur, and I see you are afraid. A hangman feels the fear of others." He placed one hand on Gorsas' shoulder.

"What are you so afraid of?" he asked, in an almost paternal tone of voice.

Gorsas shook his head nervously, as if trying to throw off this thought.

"I haven't seen you now for a while," said Charles. "Have you been in prison?"

"No, no," Gorsas quickly replied, glancing around anxiously, "I was in London, not a very safe place to be in these hectic times, Monsieur."

"Why did you return? That wasn't very smart."

"Oh, it isn't what you are thinking. I was in London on business, as a journalist. Do you know the bank Boyd, Ker & Co.? It was the crown jewel of young Walter Boyd, who was married to a very beautiful creole woman. Together they visited all the soirees attended by Paris nobility and acquired new properties. That displeased our revolutionaries, who confiscated his bank." Gorsas suddenly flinched and tried to determine in the darkness the source of a strange sound. It was just someone tossing garbage out into the street, then closing a window. "The young man had a sixth sense," he continued, "and in the night he was to be arrested, he fled to London. And do you know what he took along with him?"

"You're going to tell me," grumbled Charles, who actually didn't want to hear any secrets which might just put him in danger. Several dogs raced past them and pounced on the rubbish, which now lay strewn all over the little lane.

"Gold," Gorsas whispered, "the gold of the Parisian nobility. He brought the fortunes of the Royalists to England,

and safety. I went to London for discussions with him, and he showed me something, or rather he gave me something. . ."

"And that's what's making you afraid?" Charles asked suspiciously.

"Yes, very afraid, because if someone knows that I know, I'll be brought to your guillotine."

"Then I'd rather not know it," said Charles, stopping in his tracks as Gorsas hastened forward.

He turned into a dimly-lit lane while Charles turned around and headed in the opposite direction.

Charles didn't want to go home. He went to the Jesuit monastery where a priest opened the door. When Charles enquired about Dan-Mali, the priest said they had all assembled in the chapel holding a vigil for Father Gerbillon. Then the priest added, "It would be better if you didn't come here anymore. Visits are dangerous."

"I must see Dan-Mali," Charles insisted.

"It's too late for that," the priest said, "we're sending the Siamese girls back home. We will not continue the work of Father Gerbillon."

"But is she still here in Paris?"

"Please leave now." The father tried to close the door, but Charles put his foot in the doorway.

"I won't go until you promise me to tell her I have been asking about her."

"Very well," the priest finally agreed, "I'll tell her."

Days passed, and Dan-Mali did not stop by. Charles had an increasing number of men to execute, and he could see that his assistants had become hardened to this work. But also the victims seemed hardened to their fate, and hardly put up any resistance on the trip to the scaffold in the wagon. They had lived too long in fear of being denounced, and now it was finally over, and death was a relief.

It was the same with grief as it was with a muscle, Charles thought. One can grieve as long as one can or must, but in the end the muscle grows tired. Gabriel no longer occupied his thoughts from early morning till late at night, but he dreamed of him every night, he heard him playing the piano, and he cried in his sleep. When he woke up, his eyes were wet from all the tears he had shed in his dreams.

"Gabriel was a good lad, I shouldn't have taken him along. His world was music." He was sitting with Henri in the kitchen drinking wine.

"You're not responsible for every step a person takes; it's not your fault if he stumbles or slips," Henri said.

"But your brother fell from my scaffold. I'd told him to go up there, he wanted to please me, and died doing it. Didn't I show him enough love, and is that why he tried to please me by doing it?"

"It was Fouquier's fault, Father. Why did he want to have the executions at night by torchlight? I hope that some day I will have a chance to personally take him to the guillotine."

A few days later, Charles had decided to visit the Jesuit monastery again when he saw Dan-Mali walking up the street to his house. He could no longer restrain himself and began to run. She threw herself into his arms and whispered "Don't ever leave me alone again."

He held her tightly. "I was just about to go to the monastery," he said.

"I must go back to Siam," she said sorrowfully, "but I want to stay with you."

"Of course you can stay with me."

Arm in arm they walked away from the center of the city until they came to a low wall surrounding a large estate, with horses grazing in the adjoining meadow.

"I will be able to help you. We didn't just learn French back then," Dan-Mali said after a while, "we also learned

much about the human body, plants, other countries, and mathematics. Father Gerbillon was a bad man, but he also taught me a lot."

They returned to the house and talked for a long time in the laboratory.

"I won't ever leave you alone again," said Charles.

"Come, let's get something to eat. Much will change now. At the end of the month I plan to resign my office and hand it over to my son Henri. I will no longer be needed, I will be free."

Dan-Mali got up and shyly kissed Charles on the forehead. "I will come back tomorrow, but this evening I must go back. The padres are not happy when I don't stick to my schedule."

"Promise me you will not return to Siam. I'll be waiting for you.

"We mustn't delay any longer," said Dan-Mali. She ran her hand over his gaunt face, then unbuttoned his shirt and kissed him. "It's sad when we look to the past, but it's also sad when we look to the future," she whispered as she took off her dress, "but now, Master Sanson, we will be happy, in this moment we are free of sorrow, and for this reason the present is what is best in life."

They made love until late in the afternoon, until their love was sated, then they remained on the bed a long time taking delight in being together. As darkness fell, they drank some tea while Dan-Mali spoke of the teachings of Siddhartha Gautama, the Buddha.

"Is Buddha your god?" asked Charles.

"No," replied Dan-Mali, "Buddha is not a god and also not the bringer of a divine message. Buddha is the way, a philosophy. You don't have a philosophy. Buddha teaches how to overcome sorrow which requires an awareness, an awakening to the four truths. Human life is characterized by sorrow, sorrow caused by greed."

As Dan-Mali was explaining the Asian philosophy to the hangman, Robespierre ordered the conscription of all unmarried men between the ages of eighteen and twenty-five, an innovation for Europe, which until then had known only mercenary forces. "The situation demands total war," he proclaimed in a piercing voice, "against both external and internal threats." He dreamed of a Greater France extending to its natural borders—the Alps, the Pyrenees, the Rhein, the sea. The constitution would be amended as necessary, and would deprive the people of freedom, equality, and brotherhood. The king was to be replaced by a bloody dictator. Robespierre dreamed of a people cleansed of everything that was inferior.

In October 1793, the newly created revolutionary tribunal sent twenty-one Girondists to their deaths by guillotine. They were early members of the party who had courageously supported the ideals of the revolution. Now they were all sent to their deaths. The Hébertists would be next, followed by the Dantonists, until only Robespierre's party would be in power. Charles and Henri needed four wagons to take all the Girondists to the scaffold. It troubled him greatly that of all people they had to execute the fathers of human rights. All of them, before their death, swore their allegiance to freedom and the accomplishments of the first stage of revolution. It was moving to see how composed they were as they climbed the scaffold. Not one begged for his life—they knew their Robespierres and Saint-Justs all too well. Pierre Vergniaud, a Girondist who was barely known but important enough to die, called to Charles: "Now the revolution is eating its own children."

Charles wanted just one more thing: that it would soon be over. But the Sansons needed to call for more and more carts. As many as fifty people had to be brought to the guillotine every day. Henri was getting faster and faster at operating the

mechanism while Barre and Firmin quickly unbuckled the victim and dumped the corpse into their dump wagon like the carcass of an animal infected by the plague. Even before the head fell, Gros and Desmorets were already leading the next victim up the scaffold steps, where Firmin and Barre quickly seized him by the arms, tied him to the board that was immediately tipped down so it was horizontal, then shot forward while Henri at almost the same instant released the heavy blade, which then came thundering down. Charles, Henri, and their assistants were like cogs in a machine made of oak beams, an iron blade, and human arms that like octopuses kept feeding the machine. Someone named the machine the goddess of reason. If that was the case, the executioners were servants of this goddess bringing her human sacrifices. Charles was not the only one who found this abhorrent. He watched how Firmin always turned white as chalk, how Barre staggered across the scaffold as if his legs refused to support him any longer, and Henri's long, skinny legs trembled as if a whiff of death was shaking his whole body.

The people of Paris began to complain about all the blood flowing down the gutters and attracting stray dogs. Some suggested the use of a linen shroud and alternating execution sites. People living in the vicinity of the Madeleine, Errancis, and Piepus cemeteries also complained about the stench of the rotting corpses as well as pollution of ground water and the diseases it might carry. Paris needed more cemeteries. The vegetable garden around the old Madeleine parish church that had been tended by the Benedictine nuns was dug up, a pit ten feet deep was excavated, and wagonloads of unslaked lime brought in. For a time, beheaded victims were tossed into a mass grave like waste from a slaughterhouse.

With up to fifty victims, blood flowed in great quantities of nearly 80 gallons a day. When the spectacle was over, the onlookers stomped across the square, the blood sticking to

the soles of their shoes. In this way, they spread it all over the city and into their living rooms, and when the sun shone, the stench of the warm blood was sickening. The wicker baskets didn't last as long as they used to, as the bottoms became and weakened and broke after being dried out. A basket could carry no more than six heads, and Charles demanded funds for new ones as well as another assistant to clean the scaffold after every seven executions. The persons to be executed became weak and anxious from looking at all the blood, and it was much more difficult to tie them onto the board. But Fouquier thought it was part of the punishment for the condemned men to have to stare down at the heads dripping blood in the wicker basket while they were tied onto the bloody board in their final minutes.

Fouquier did not dismiss Charles. He wanted to see the great Sanson on the gallows. Charles' resignation might have suggested to the people that the regime of terror was losing support.

Charles performed many of his executions as if in a trance. He was too busy with routine matters to think about what he was doing at the moment. His grief and sorrow always returned at home late at night, when he was trying to sleep. Then he drank wine and started writing, trying to get his thoughts together, but his hands had become tired from all the killing. It lay on his desk like a piece of meat, and the new pages of his diary remained white as the sheet on his bed. He had wanted to write that only Dan-Mali could still save him from going mad, but they hadn't seen each other recently and the priest at the Jesuit monastery no longer even opened the door when he knocked. They had barricaded themselves in the monastery. They were afraid.

It hardly occurred to him that Gorsas no longer wrote for the newspaper. Perhaps he had fled abroad. Yet he met the little man again in his light-brown dress coat, his expensive piqué

vest and mustard yellow buckskin boots on the steps of his scaffold. Even though his hands had already been tied, he was still sucking on his pipe. "This is the first execution I won't be able to write about," he mused. Disconcerted, Charles seized him by an arm had led him to the board of the guillotine. "Just a moment," said Gorsas. Charles granted him this favor. "Do you what my crime is?" he whispered. Charles was silent, still clutching Gorsas by the arm and trying to calm him down. "Our Doctor Guillotin wrote a little book," Gorsas continued, "in praise of freedom of the press. The printing machines were turned off and the book was forbidden, and that's what I wrote about. What has the revolution done for us if we can no longer speak about freedom of the press?"

Charles nodded. He didn't want to hinder the condemned man from saying whatever seemed important to him. Charles knew that the hour of death brought regrets. One regrets things one has done and those he has failed to do. That was a foretaste of hell. At that moment, the thoughts of the condemned man were racing, like the chaos at the start of all things, before they became men, and what they became. One was defenseless against these things, one no longer had control.

Gorsas suddenly embraced his hangman and urinated, without noticing. "Adieu, Monsieur de Paris. We could have become friends." Silently, Charles also took the little man in his arms. Gorsas stretched up, looking for Charles' ear. "When you take off my clothes in the cemetery," he whispered, "look in my right vest pocket. I have something for you." Gorsas started to cry as he was placed headfirst on the board and looked down at the severed heads below him. "The pain is very short, isn't it?" he asked, then his head fell into the wicker basket.

After him came a number of washer women, handymen, and even a stable boy, all of them poor wretches who'd never

been interested in politics. Their only crime was having been in the service of a royalist. Perhaps the execution of people who were clearly innocent was a part of the plan, the deterrence of the Reign of Terror. Finally came two noblemen who had attempted to smuggle their fortune abroad. Everything went very quickly, the assistants went through the usual routine, and when the last head had fallen into the blood-soaked basket Barre and Firmin loaded the headless corpses onto the wagon. Henri tossed the heads after them. The severed head was placed between the legs of each corpse.

Silently, Charles and his men drove away to the cemetery. It disturbed him that he had to execute Gorsas. He remembered their first meeting after Damiens' execution. At that time, the little journalist had annoyed him, but eventually he had come to like him, and now he missed him.

At the cemetery they unclothed the corpses, threw them into the mass grave, and Desmorets spread lime over them. They tossed the clothes, as always, in a pile in the wagon, except for the trousers, which were separated at the cemetery, as most of them were stained with fecal matter. The moment the head was separated, all the muscles lost control and only a few nerves quivered wildly, giving a false impression there was still a bit of life left. Then that, too, passed.

At home, they carried the clothes into the barn. "Go to the kitchen and make yourself something to eat," said Charles. "We'll finish up here in the morning." Henri and the assistants were not unhappy to hear that. They had gradually been getting tired of all the blood, as well.

Charles remained back in the barn alone, and began looking for the piqué vest. When he found it, he also noticed something in one of the inside pockets, a document several pages long. He put it inside his vest and withdrew to his laboratory, where he took it out again, and stood there thinking for a long while. If this document had cost Gorsas

his life, he didn't want to read it. He put it aside, not wanting to know what was in it. What did he have to do with all this? He was just a hangman who followed orders. Now he wanted his peace and quiet.

That turned out to be not so simple. During the night, the dead came to haunt him. He heard them speaking their last words, he saw their helpless eyes beseeching him, and then he heard the guillotine roaring down, and he was suddenly wide awake.

On November 3, the valiant supporter for women's rights, Olympe de Gouges, was guillotined at the age of forty-five. "We are not allowed to speak freely in public," she said to Charles in a firm voice, "we are only allowed to die publicly, though all we ever asked was the same rights that men have."

Countess du Barry also had something to say to Charles. She didn't want to give up her life so quietly on the eighth of December. The execution had been postponed several times because the streets and bridges of Paris were covered with ice. Winter was back, and the cold season brought back memories of Gabriel. The countess awaited her death in the Conciergerie, but she was not like the others. She was not silent, she raged at the top of her voice, she attacked every one of the assistants, and when Barre tried to cut her hair, she rammed her knee in his groin and tried to scratch his eyes out. Not until Charles entered the Conciergerie did she settle down. "Charles," she gasped, out of breath, "save me, I have a little castle near Versailles and jewels belonging to Louis XV. I was his mistress."

"Madame, I am here to take you on your last trip," said Charles, holding out his hands. In his left hand he was holding a rope.

"Madame?" she shouted, "but it's me, Charles, Marie-Jeanne Bécu."

Charles was stunned.

"Charles," she pleaded with him.

"Now I remember, Madame. It was a long time ago. You told me then you would soon be taking the name du Barry."

The countess beamed with joy and fell down on her knees before him. "Save me, Charles, I am innocent." There was nothing left of her youthful beauty. Her movements were still those of her youth, but her face was that of an old woman. All the fatty food at Versailles had transformed her face into a shapeless batter of dough in which only her nose and eyes still appeared young. Her breasts, voluptuous at that time, were even larger and heavier now, and were her dominating feature, as if this body had been created only to bear these gigantic breasts.

Firmin entered the prison with a red shirt and Barre pulled the countess down onto a chair, crossing her arms behind her while Charles, quick as a flash, tied her wrists together. They were a well-rehearsed team. Now Firmin stood in front of them holding the red shirt. Charles untied the countess again, and together they tried to pull the red shirt down over the head of the hysterical woman. Finally, Barre gave her a stinging slap in the face. She fell silent at once and put on the red shirt.

The trip to the scaffold seemed to last forever, but it's possible it only felt that way to Charles and his assistants. Countess du Barry screamed, raged, and cried constantly. She jumped up, held onto the railing and shouted, "People of Paris, save me, save me, I am innocent!" Wildly, she shook the locked gate of the wagon and screamed so loud that her words could be heard even in the sidestreets. Her voice was louder that the hoofbeats of the horses and the squeaking of the wheels. "Save me, have mercy, save me!" Charles didn't try to stop her, as it would have been pointless. Perhaps he also wanted to keep her from attacking him, biting him and scratching his face in front of all the onlookers, as she had done with Barre. She was hoarse now, but still screaming as

loud as she could, and her voice cracked. As they turned the corner toward the Place de la Révolution, she almost fell, but she held firmly with both arms to the wagon's crossbar, crying so pathetically that the hoots of the crowd gradually subsided. It was something new that a condemned person was crying and begging for their life like this. People didn't want to hear this, they didn't want to see it, and many people left the execution site in disgust.

The countess didn't want to leave the wagon. Firmin and Barre tore here hands off the railing and pulled her out of the wagon. She put up such a fight that one arm or the other was always free, and she was beginning to hope she could break away. When she had almost succeeded, Firmin threw her to the ground. Barre tried to seize her legs, but she kicked like a horse, hitting him in the face several times and knocking out two of his teeth. Now Henri and Gros hurried over to help, and carried the countess up the stairs to the scaffold, where Charles was standing with a stoic expression. "Mercy, Monsieur de Paris, for just a few moments," she pleaded. The assistants glanced at Charles. He shook his head sternly but calmly without looking at them.

Now there a few cries of protest from the crowd. The people didn't like this spectacle. "Leave her alone," a few of them shouted. That was something new. It was hard to believe, but the people had finally had enough of these executions. The Parisians felt something resembling sympathy. Few had read the books of Voltaire, Montesquieu or Rousseau, but the time was ripe for it. The individual had gained importance, and the people had become more sympathetic to the fate of others. If people had reacted like this at the very beginning, Charles mused, it would have been impossible to execute so many people. Is a man free of guilt if he allowed atrocities in the past that were in conformance with the law at that time?

Danton's turn came on April 5, 1794. "Show my head to the people, it is worthy of that," he told Charles before climbing the steps to the scaffold. But he had tears in his eyes because he was thinking of his wife and children. Charles did not follow him, but remained below and gave Henri the sign to release the heavy blade, which came whizzing down. For half an hour, the head belonged to crazy Marie, who was soon to marry François Tussaud and thereafter be known to all as Madame Tussaud.

Antoine Fouquier kept giving Charles longer and longer lists of men, some of whom had already been condemned and others for whom no sentence had been pronounced.

"In Lyon, the hangman Jean Ripet the Elder was executed at the age of fifty-eight," said Fouquier, handing Charles a new list. "I hope you have sufficient carts and horses." Charles understood his meaning at once. Ripet had been a Royalist.

"The king is long dead," said Charles, unimpressed. "May I hand over my office to my son soon?"

"Not yet, Charles," Antoine whispered, "it is not yet over, but it soon will be."

Charles was in despair and he had lost his patience, as he hadn't heard from Dan-Mali for months. He rushed to the Jesuit monastery, determined to simply take Dan-Mali along with him. Forever. He wondered if he should leave Paris with her. Henri was old enough. When Charles finally arrived at the monastery, he was shocked to find out that not much was left of it—the sans-culottes had burned it down. Charles let out a cry of horror as he ran up to the charred front portal and jumped over the still smoldering collapsed beams. "Dan-Mali!" he shouted, rushing into the courtyard. The building was deserted. Next, he ran to the middle of the herb garden, looking in all directions, crying "Dan-Mali!" over and over.

"Why are you looking here?" said a voice, and a priest appeared from behind a column. "They have arrested Dan-Mali."

"Why?" Charles shouted furiously.

"Didn't I tell you not to come back again? You bring us only misfortune. We never wanted to attract the attention of the authorities. Who knows what they will think of next."

The news struck Charles like a dagger to the heart. Dan-Mali had been arrested for alleged Royalist activities.

The priest approached Charles, hissing. "Look what you have done here." He reached out for Charles, who brushed his hand away and hurried back into the street. He had to confront Fouquier at once.

The latter kept him waiting as people came and went. Several times Charles pleaded with the servant in front of the door in his blue livery to announce his visit, and finally, after two hours, the door opened again.

"Where's the fire, Citizen Sanson?" Fouquier asked, without looking up from his desk. "We spoke just a while ago."

"A woman from Siam living in the Jesuit monastery was arrested by your officials. For what reason?"

"Why do you need to know, Citizen Sanson?" Fouquier straightened up in his chair and leaned back, wearily.

"She is my patient," said Charles. "I'm sure there is some misunderstanding. She was never interested in politics."

"But the politicians are interested in her. She came here to learn our language, but what is she doing? Until just recently she was ironing Father Gerbillon's shirts. The shirts of a Royalist." Fouquier smiled, running his tongue over his incisors, as if trying to release bits of food from between his teeth. "Father Gerbillon," he continued, "was a good tip. We have noted with satisfaction the cooperation of Citizen Sanson, but as you know yourself, it's not sufficient to remove a diseased part of the body. One must make a wide

circle around the focus of the infection, removing everything in the surrounding tissue. After all, you studied medicine for a few semesters, didn't you?" Fouquier threw back his head theatrically. "I still have some things to do, Citizen Sanson."

"I need to speak with her."

"Citizen Sanson, everyone is expendable, even you, so watch what you say, and keep away from people engaged in Royalist schemes. We will destroy them, all of them, as well as their supporters, even if they just iron clothing or make shoes for them."

"I need to speak with her," Charles persisted.

Fouquier paused a while before responding, and it was obvious he enjoyed tormenting Charles. "Very well," he resumed after a while, "after all, you turned Father Gerbillon over to us. So be it." He rang the little bell on his desk, and a servant entered the office. "Prepare a permit for Citizen Sanson to visit a prisoner, a lady of Siamese origin."

"Which prison?" asked the servant.

"I could look it up, but I don't have the time." Fouquier grinned.

Charles knew at once that he was lying.

Charles first went to the L'Abbaye prison, then the Madelonnettes, where the director of the opera was awaiting his death along with thirteen actors. The Port Libre prison housed only women, who mocked their inevitable fate, chanting "Long live the king" and "Give us a man." Here, too, there was no sign of Dan-Mali. On the Rue des Droits de l'Homme there were two prisons, the Grand Force and the Petite Force, both standing under the direct control of Fouquier. By chance, Charles encountered him in the prison courtyard.

As he walked by, Fouquier mumbled "Try the Sainte-Pélagie on der Rue de la Clef."

The Sainte-Pélagie had room for around fifty prisoners, but housed three hundred and fifty, vegetating on straw sacks. They all sought the proximity to the duke of Biron, an imprisoned general of the Republican Army, who had enough money to reward the director of the prison for favors. There were exact tariffs for every favor: drinks, gourmet food, books, visitors—anything could be bought with money. Many of the inmates were prostitutes who had provided the noble Royalists with many pleasurable hours, or women whose only crime was having been the friend or mistress of a condemned man—for example, a Creole woman who'd had an affair with the English banker Walter Boyd and didn't even understand the reason for her arrest. At the time of her execution at the guillotine, her former lover was in London celebrating his successful escape. In some cases, the only crime consisted of being rich.

Charles was led into the cavernous, damp subterranean rooms that had been converted into cells for masses of prisoners. The damp walls were made of huge stone blocks and the whole area stank of mold and human excrement. Hundreds of bats hung from the vaulted ceiling like little, black raincoats. A number of women rushed to the door and clung to the iron bars. "Fuck me," one of them screamed in Charles's face. "Once I am pregnant, I'll be set free."

Charles ran along the bars behind which the women were crowded. "I'm looking for a woman with dark skin, from Siam."

"Long live the king," some of them shouted.

"There was one here," said a guard, "but I can't tell you if she has already been executed. But you, sir, must know—after all, it's your guillotine." The guard grinned, showing the few remaining stumps of teeth in his mouth. His face was strangely deformed, as if a battering ram had flattened his nose.

"Dan-Mali!" he shouted in despair, and listened for a reply.

"I am Dan-Mali," a prostitute called out, shaking the bars.

"Pay no attention to the slut," said another. "I am Dan-Mali."

The guard waved him off and pointed toward the door. "I am sorry, Monsieur de Paris."

Charles stopped and looked him straight in the eye. "You must have noticed her, Citizen, she was dark-skinned." The guard shook his head again and pointed toward the door. Charles took a few hesitant steps toward the door.

"Kun kwaun" he suddenly heard someone say.

Frantically he stared through the bars, but nowhere among all the women could he find Dan-Mali.

He heard the voice again, and now he saw the thin arm reaching through the bars and waving. It was Dan-Mali kneeling behind the bars. "I will wait for you," she cried.

Charles knelt down in front of the bars, took her by both hands, pressed them against his face and kissed them. "I'll get you out," he said.

"No," said Dan-Mali, "that won't be possible. We shall all die, but over there, in the other world, I will wait for you. Have no fear."

She pressed her head against the bars, opened her mouth, closed her eyes, and Charles kissed her without letting go of her hands.

"Can I stay overnight?" Charles asked the guard. He shook his head.

"You mustn't ask for permission, just about the price," said a sonorous voice. A uniformed man made his way toward the bars. "Duke de Biron, General of the Republican Army," the prisoner introduced himself proudly. He had gray hair, long sideburns, and his cheeks were somewhat sunken and weathered. He handed Charles a few coins. "That should suffice, Monsieur de Paris. No, no, don't thank me. A burial

shroud has no pockets, I have no heirs, so what use is the money to me?"

Charles gave the money to the guard, who put it discretely in his pocket, but otherwise did not react.

"And for me two more bottles of Bordeaux" the general called to the guard, "and for Monsieur a bale of straw, but make sure it's a dry one."

In the early morning hours, Dan-Mali and Charles had fallen asleep, each on their own side of the bars, hand in hand.

Charles had wanted to plead for Dan-Mali's life, but as he was standing in Fouquier's office in the morning reading the list of the condemned, his heart skipped a beat. Without asking, he slumped down onto the chair across the table from Fouquier.

"Have I offered you a seat?"

"Let the woman go."

"I know, Citizen Sanson, the little woman from Siam. You found her now, after all," he said, leafing through some papers. "Is there anything else you want?"

"I told you to let her go. Do me that favor, and I will repay you as soon as I can."

"Citizen Sanson," Fouquier said, "First of all, we have a valid judgement, which no one can overturn. Secondly, you can hardly offer the chief prosecutor a favor great enough to persuade him to violate his responsibilities. Are you trying to bribe the chief prosecutor of the Revolution? The Siamese girl will spit into the sack today, and tomorrow others will follow. And if you insist, Monsieur de Paris, I'll have you put in chains charged with supporting a counter-revolution. Am I making myself perfectly clear?"

Charles was silent, understanding that Dan-Mali had no chance of surviving the day. Leaning over Fouquier's desk he snarled, "I warn you, Antoine, if Dan-Mali dies, so will you."

"Oh," Fouquier replied sarcastically, "I've never seen you like this before, Charles. You really look furious. Even back in Rouen I asked myself what it would take to make you really angry. You never dared do that before. You see, the Revolution has made you free. Be grateful!"

Dan-Mali was driven to the scaffold in a wagon along with three prostitutes, Charles seated alongside her. This was not unusual, as he often did so to try to calm down convicts, but this time he held the tiny hand of the little dark-skinned girl during the entire trip. His assistants lowered their heads, but it didn't matter to Charles. He loved this woman above everything else. His heart was filled with love for her, and if he lost her, his life would be shattered.

As the wagon turned into the Place de Grève, there were shouts and applause. Suddenly, however, everyone fell silent. Dan-Mali had gotten to her feet, as had Charles. He towered two heads above her, and alongside him she looked like a child.

"No children!" cried out someone at the back of the crowd. Others joined in. "No children!" and soon the entire crowd was crying as if with one voice: "No children! Enough! Stop!" In the adjacent houses the shutters were closed, as if the Plague were passing by. Charles wished fervently that this trip would never end and hoped they would ride on hand in hand in this wagon, without a goal, to the end of the world. But then he saw the two posts of the guillotine towering into the sky. He looked around in the crowd. For a fraction of a second he believed there would be some salvation, a stroke of fortune, a miracle. But when the women descended the cart in front of the scaffold and he saw the court officials, he knew no one would stop this crime.

"Be strong," Dan-Mali said as she placed her foot on the first step. She paused and looked at him. "We'll meet again, *kun kwaun*, because we have Buddha's goodwill."

Charles tried to follow Dan-Mali up the steps, but she stopped him with a gentle push and an imperceptible shake of the head. "It's not good-bye for long. I'm not afraid, Charles. Our karma is good." Henri held his father back and gently led him underneath the scaffold. "Go home, father. Today's not your day."

Charles stopped and braced himself against a beam with both hands. He heard the snap of the lunette, the swift fall of the blade, the thump of the head. Blood. Everywhere blood. He remained underneath the scaffold as if paralyzed while the blood of his beloved flowed through the cracks in the floorboards and dripped onto his forehead, where it mixed with the blood of those who had been executed earlier. A dog came running over and started to lick the blood. Charles gave it a hard kick. The animal yelped, ran away with its tail between its legs, but returned a short while later. Charles had never felt a greater gap between him and the rest of mankind: an outcast, despised, humiliated, besmirched with blood of the innocent, and without hope. There was no way out of this hell for him. Dan-Mali's blood stuck to his shoes and would forever haunt his every step. More blood dripped onto his forehead. He felt as though the devil himself was christening him. Charles tried to wipe the blood of with his hand but only smeared it all over his face. His breathing became heavy. He pushed himself off the beam and stumbled out from under the scaffold, directly into the crowd, which made way for the blood-smeared hangman instantly. When Charles had finally made it through the crowd on the square and reached the first houses, he paused and leaned against the nearest wall. Then he began to make his way from house to house, pausing from time to time, occasionally sitting down on a doorstep before continuing on. He felt as though he was walking on the back of a brown whale that wouldn't hold still but pitched and tossed in the waves, the sea spray hitting Charles' face. It had started to rain. He no longer managed to focus his eyes and

he saw double, which made him feel even dizzier than he already was. The houses around him suddenly appeared evil to him, and they started to bulge as if they were pregnant. He tried to walk faster to avoid falling, but stumbled nonetheless.

At dawn, Charles was sitting at the bank of the Seine. The blood had dried. A barge was delivering goods to the city. On the opposite bank, Paris was waking up. Merchants pulled handcarts or urged on their emaciated horses toward the market squares with fresh wares. Charles picked up a rock and squeezed it tight. He felt as though the rock was becoming soft and pliable like a sponge. But the rock wasn't changing its shape. Charles clenched his jaw, his teeth grinding. He felt an iron clasp trying to snap his neck like the lunette on the guillotine. I'm turning to stone, Charles thought. My punishment will be to remain the guillotine's arm for centuries, and my brain alone will work as normal so it can torture me.

"Monsieur de Paris!"

"Father!"

Frightened, Charles threw himself to the ground. Now he saw them. They were running across the meadow, toward him. His assistants Gros, Barre, Firmin, Desmorets, and his sons Henri and Gabriel. Something was wrong. Why could Gabriel run? Charles sprang to his feet and hurried along the Seine toward the burnt-down customs gate forty-four. He was smiling. He had seen Gabriel, so his son couldn't have had a fatal accident. He must have dreamt his death. But why were they running toward him? And why all six of them? One would have been enough to speak with. But there were six of them. Because they wanted to restrain him. But why? Then Charles understood. They were going to take him to the scaffold. But where was the written verdict? "Where?" Charles shouted.

"It's only a bad dream, father," Henri said.

Charles pushed off the blanket and sat up, looking dazed. "Gabriel is dead," he said, questioningly, giving Henri a pleading look.

"Yes," Henri said. "Gabriel fell off the scaffold and broke his neck."

Charles nodded.

"Fouquier has been looking for you," Henri said. "You must get up."

"Again?" Charles sighed. "Is it ever going to end? With every sentence they cut another little piece off my brain. They steal my happy memories, and all that remains are rolling heads that tumble across the wooden planks, silently accusing me. And everything I touch turns red, red as blood. How are my hands?"

"Your hands are fine. Lay back down, father, our assistants and I can cope."

Charles sunk back onto the bed. Henri covered him with the blanket.

"Do you know what an empty barn looks like?" Charles mumbled.

Henri nodded.

"When they have taken everything from you, you're as empty as a barn. The harnesses, the carts, the horses—all gone. They only leave the pincers so can keep torturing yourself."

Henri didn't know what to reply.

"I'm going to ride out," Charles said. "To the Seine. No, no, I've already been there."

"That was a dream, father."

"Go, go now to the guillotine. She's waiting for us."

"Father, it's just a wooden structure with a sharp blade."

"No, no," Charles protested, "they created me, they created me for the guillotine alone. And all the blood the

guillotine sheds brings her to life. You just wait, soon she'll turn up on our doorstep."

"Dan-Mali," Charles said when he shared a glass of wine with Henri late in the evening. "I loved her like I never loved anyone else. I wouldn't have thought man capable of such emotions, emotions stronger than the wind, water, or bullets."

Henri scratched his ear, feeling embarrassed.

"She was unique," Charles continued softly. "I gave her my heart. You can only give your heart away once, you can only love once, then your love is spent. Whatever you try to give afterward is something else, but you can't call it love."

"It doesn't have to be love," Henri said. "One can live without."

"But not once you've had a glimpse of paradise." Charles pulled an amulet from his pocket and placed it on the table. "This is the broken bell of the Sansons, a bell without a sound. It was a gift to one of our ancestors. It was cast in silver in the New World. Now it's yours. I have died many deaths, Henri. Death can't be any worse than the misery I have suffered on earth. I die without fear."

"But father," Henri exclaimed, "it's not your time to die yet!"

"End the dynasty of hangmen," Charles said. "Release our lineage. Let your descendants become bakers, carpenters, printers—anything but hangmen."

"Are you feeling unwell, father?"

"Life is draining from my body," Charles whispered. "It's doesn't want to go on. At some point everything must end, Henri."

Charles had fallen asleep with exhaustion. But after only a few hours, the demons came and tortured him. He kept dreaming that Dan-Mali wasn't dead, that she was alive somewhere. But she only lived in his dreams. "She's dead,"

the people in his dreams kept shouting at him, but he ignored them and dragged Dan-Mali's body behind him in the search for someone who could confirm to him that she wasn't dead. But no one would confirm it to him. And when he woke up, he knew Dan-Mali was dead. He stepped out into the courtyard and stared up at the night sky. He felt lonely.

He waited for the tiredness to return. Sometimes he drank wine. Then he returned to his laboratory and laid on his bed, but couldn't find restful sleep. He merely dozed. Suddenly he started up, and then he heard the voice again that had torn him from his dream. "*Kun kwaun.*"

Charles held still. "Is that you, Dan-Mali?"

"*Kun kwaun.*"

"Are you on the other side?" Charles asked. He didn't dare move. He felt a slight breath of air and he inhaled the scent of her skin. "Are you with me?"

"*Kun kwaun,*" she repeated tenderly.

Charles felt tears streaming down his face. "Is it really you? Dan-Mali, I thought the dead don't come back—but some do, don't they?"

Dan-Mali didn't reply.

"It's just a dream, isn't it?"

Dan-Mali remained silent.

Charles saw light underneath the door to the laboratory. Although it was dark in his room, he also saw the blood. It was flowing fast, as if a dam had burst. Now it was forcing down the door and breaking the windows, and huge amounts of blood came flowing in, and a few severed heads, too. The heads were emaciated with skin like parchment and eyes like charred apricot pits. The flood carried Charles away, outside. At the end of the road he saw the guillotine floating toward him. The tall structure pitched but didn't tilt—it was coming for him. The guillotine was coming for him.

"No!" Charles screamed. "I'm not wearing a red shirt, you can't take me. It's the rules. No one climbs the scaffold without a red shirt."

A dwarf wearing a black tricorn tugged at Charles' sleeve. "Monsieur de Paris! The national assembly has decided that shoemakers are only allowed to work for friends of the nation, and whoever contravenes this law has all their shoes confiscated. That's why more and more people are wading through the blood barefoot. We can no longer control the streams of blood. The ground doesn't want to soak up any more blood. The blood is as deep as a lake already. It sticks to the shoes, it sticks to the wheels of the carts and the hooves of the horses. It's not raining anymore. The sun is shining. It stinks. It stinks of rot. God is not happy about all the executed shoemakers. We'll have no more shoemakers tomorrow. I'm telling you, we're running out of shoemakers. Then we'll all be barefoot in the blood."

"Stop!" Charles screamed and tried to kick the dwarf. But he only kicked air. There was no dwarf.

On June 17, 1794 a caricature appeared in the paper, showing Charles-Henri Sanson lying down under the guillotine and pulling the iron bolt securing the blade. "Why is the hangman executing himself?" was written underneath the image. "Because he is the last citizen of Paris. Finally, Paris is cleansed."

In June, Charles, Henri, and their assistants had to execute six-hundred-eighty-eight people. A new law prohibited citizens from defending themselves in court. The radicals around Robespierre, Saint-Just, and Fouquier had become so far removed from their people that they could no longer see their own madness. They guillotined everyone: assignat counterfeiters, soldiers, officers, generals, priests, youths, cloth merchants, war veterans, invalids whose bones had to

be broken so they would fit on the board, fragile elderly who couldn't walk the steps to the scaffold on their own. The revolutionaries weren't bringing equality and fraternity, but death and misery and full cemeteries.

Robespierre now ruled the land—Robespierre, who had abolished the monarchy to free the people. King Robespierre. Abroad they were speaking of Robespierre's campaigns, Robespierre's troops, Robespierre's laws, and Robespierre's ambition for the crown. His enemies rejoiced in those rumors because they made Robespierre sound like a tyrant who needed to be brought down. When someone plucked up the courage to speak this in public, Robespierre tried to run. He knew the ways of terror too well. Pushed into a corner, he shot his jaw during a failed suicide attempt. Used to working at a desk, the man was very clumsy with anything practical, and anatomy had never been his strength. Charles thought it wasn't a surprise when he watched Henri and his assistants lead the mass-murderer Robespierre to the guillotine on July 28. Between the decree from June 10 and Robespierre's downfall, 1376 people had been guillotined.

"Only one is still missing," Charles said when Henri descended the steps of the scaffold.

"Just leave it, father, I don't want you to end up in a red shirt up there. The Reign of Terror is almost over."

"I'm longing for the day I'll be finished."

"You are finished, father. You handed over to me."

"There's still one verdict missing," Charles insisted. "And I'm going to continue visiting the conciergerie until the name is on the list."

"You're wasting your time, father." Henri gently touched his arm.

"I know Henri, but maybe it's the last thing I'll do."

The following day already Charles went to the conciergerie and straight to Antoine Fouquier's office.

"No longer knocking, Citizen Sanson?" Fouquier leaned over his papers. "Your son has already picked up the list."

"I read your list, Antoine. One name's missing."

Fouquier looked up. "Oh, you've got another name for me?"

"Yes," Charles said, stepped behind the desk, and grabbed Antione by the shoulders. "Antoine Fouquier de Tinville!"

"Let go of me, you're hurting me!"

"That's precisely what I came here for, Antoine. To hurt you. I was trained to inflict pain on people, even though I wanted to heal."

Antoine pulled himself free and tried to get up, but Charles forced him back on his chair and held his neck in a iron grip. "I also did some research," he said softly. "Just like you back in Rouen, Antoine Fouquier de Tinville, remember?"

"I'm calling the guard," Antoine shouted, trying in vain to wriggle out of the hangman's grip.

"They're already on their way," Charles reply. "You don't need to call them."

"What is all this about, Charles? Let go off me!"

"You had Gorsas guillotined when he returned from London, because he brought something back with him."

"Is that so?" Antoine waved his arms about helplessly.

"Yes, Antoine, it is."

"Charles, where are you going with this? What do you think is going to happen? You'll never get out here alive. So let go off me!" Antoine began to panic and tried once again to free himself.

Charles turned the chair around and started punching Antoine hard, again and again, as if he was trying to avenge every single man he'd had to execute. The blows hit Antoine like the hooves of a horse that has been kept in the stable for too long. Charles didn't stop when the lawyer was lying on

the ground, blood-smeared and squirming in pain, and kicked him again and again. When Antoine stopped moving altogether, Charles sat down on the chief prosecutor's chair. His foot rested on Antoine's neck.

"You issued a law that forbids the possession of gold so you can continue to swamp the country with your worthless paper money. Anyone who doesn't hand in their gold in exchange for useless assignats gets imprisoned for six years. But you and your entire family are right at the top of the list Gorsas received from Walter Boyd in London—you broke your own rules and shipped millions in gold out of the country. So, you're going to be convicted and executed according to your very own laws."

"You'll never get away with it," Antoine whispered. He tried to get up, but Charles held him down. Antoine stared at the giant of a man above him in shock. "are you insane? They'll put you on the guillotine for this!"

Charles grabbed Antoine and yanked him up. He threw him onto the desk and punched his face again, then he pulled him closer by one leg and battered him mercilessly. Antoine tried to crawl under the table, but Charles pulled him back onto his feet. With one quick movement, Antoine grabbed the little bell on his desk and hurled it against the door. At almost the same instant, the door was pushed open and four soldiers of the guard entered the office.

"Arrest him!" Antoine ordered.

The guards surrounded both men.

"I said, arrest him! I want his head chopped of today."

One of the soldiers grabbed Antoine's arms, another bound them.

"What's the meaning of this?" Antoine screamed and tried to free his arms.

"We're only following orders, Citizen Fouquier. You are under arrest for the unlawful possession of gold and for

smuggling it into enemy territory. You have compromised the revolution and collaborated with the enemy."

"See you on the scaffold, Antoine Fouquier de Tinville. I can't wait to see the color of your blood," Charles said.

"God hates all of you!" Antoine shouted as the guards led him out of the office.

Charles was already waiting by the steps to the scaffold when Henri and the assistants arrived with the cart. They only had one single prisoner. He was going to be one of the last ones to spit in the sack at the end of the Reign of Terror. A huge crowd had gathered, and every last square inch of the plaza was packed.

"Fouquier!" someone shouted at the top of his voice. The condemned man turned. Tobias Schmidt was making his way through the crowd. He staggered toward the steps and fell flat on his face in front of Fouquier. He was drunk. "Let me know how you liked the guillotine. Perhaps you'll have ideas for improvements. The nuts and bolts should be made of iron, not wood, right? And what do you think of painting it yellow?"

Fouquier turned away and climbed the steps to the scaffold on his own. Firmin and Barre stopped Schmidt from following. Charles placed himself behind the guillotine, between the two vertical beams. Charles' face was the last thing Fouquier saw when he was tied to the board and tilted forward.

The blood spurted onto the wooden planks, but none of it hit Charles. He knew where he needed to stand.

Fouquier's death made Charles take out his diary one more time. It would be his last entry. He had nothing more to say afterward, and his hand was too weak to hold the quill. It was too much for the hand that guillotines three thousand people. The last words in his diary read: *There is no curse. There*

never was a curse. Curses only exist if you believe in them. But I no longer believe in them. Man is free to decide for himself.

Charles-Henri Sanson never saw a scaffold again. He spent a lot of time sitting by the river, staring into the water. He wondered whether it was possible for one of the victims to return. Something like a spiritual encounter. He had beheaded so many men and women, maybe just one of them would manage to come back. Whenever someone approached him, he became terrified because he didn't know whether they were real or someone returning from the dead. Whenever someone looked at him sadly, he was reminded of the many sad looks he received from condemned men. Their eyes seemed to say, why do I have to go while others are allowed to stay? They will follow, Charles thought. He started at ever noise, because every noise reminded him on the machine to whom he'd been enslaved—the creaking of the floor boards, the awful screeching when the tilting board was pushed forward, the snapping of the lunette, the release of the bolt, the swooshing of the blade, the dull thud of the head in the wicker basket.

The kitchen seemed to be full of similar noises. Sometimes they would sit at dinner, and he would suddenly jump up, his heart racing, all blood drained from his face. He'd stare intently at Marie-Anne, as though he was trying to read in her face whether he had imagined it all. She'd smile and walk toward him. He didn't understand why she was suddenly there for him and smiling. She'd gently place her hands on his shoulders, and sometimes she even spoke to him. She'd tell him everything was fine, or ask him if he'd like more soup. If he was still hungry, he'd nod his head. It was a special head, bald, haggard, and when he wasn't starting at noises, he exuded great calmness and dignity. His assistants couldn't help but notice the change in him, but

CLAUDE CUENI

their respect for Monsieur de Paris was still as great as ever. Henri always sat to his right and placed his hand on that of his father whenever it started to tremble. He'd hold his father's hand tenderly and stroke it with his thumb.

Charles rode past the gardener's house of his deceased in-laws, past the endless vegetable beds, until he reached the forest. He took the narrow track that had formed in the course of the years and followed it uphill until he reached the lush meadow at the foot of a rock wall. The shady part of the meadow was so wet that his horse's hooves sunk into the ground. He jumped off and trudged through the soft ground until he spotted some mushrooms. They were about as high as a hand, and when Charles picked one, the stem turned blue where he broke it. He rode back into the forest and down to the river. Along the bank, the ground was dry. He unsaddled his horse and placed the saddle on a fallen tree trunk. Then he sat down and ate the mushroom.

At first, he only heard the chirping of a few birds, but then they became more and more, until it sounded like the whole world was singing for him. The sky began to breathe, but Charles was afraid of getting squashed because he felt as light as a feather. From the books his father had left him, Charles knew that in ancient times, this mushroom was used to consult fate, which was why it was also called *flesh of the gods*. He felt God entering his body. He felt the tingling of ants in his shoulders, felt how they slowly crawled down his spine until they filled his entire body. Then the cold set in. He tried to stand up but staggered as if he was drunk. Even his horse backed away from him. The colors and lights around him started to sparkle and spray, and suddenly he saw something approach him as if through a kaleidoscope. He laid back down and felt a whiff of eternity.

"Father," Henri said, "what's the matter?"

"I ate God," Charles whispered. "But God is just a mushroom," he added regretfully, "just a mushroom."

Henri emerged from the kaleidoscope and kneeled in front of his father.

The river, Charles now said thoughtfully, is life's true schoolmaster. "Everything flows. Nothing remains the same. You can't stop the river, Henri. The water flows through your fingers. That's life. You swim along and no single drop has a meaning, but all drops together might have one. But it doesn't matter. Have you ever tried to remember a drop of water in the river? At the end of the day, it's of no importance. Whether you had a long life or just a short one, eternity relativizes the number of years you spent on this earth. And in the end, this river is of no importance, either."

"Father," Henri said, "why are you speaking thus?"

"Death is liberation and the end of all our suffering. Our misery ends with death. We're returned to the same state of peace we were in before our birth."

Charles sat among the herbs in his courtyard. He wore brown breeches, gray socks, black leather shoes with large claps, a brown shirt, and a black tricorn. He thought about riding back up to the forest and searching for mushrooms, but then he forgot the thought and couldn't remember for the life of him what he'd just been thinking about. Had he been thinking about the heads at the cemetery? Was he supposed to dig them out again? That was the least he could do for them. Maybe they were already waiting for him.

"Death visits everyone," Charles whispered. "Some live long, others die young. That way, death comes to people of all ages, just like with animals and trees, and no one lives forever."

A hand was placed on his shoulder. It smelled of wet dog. After hesitating for a moment, he touched the hand and held it. It was time for supper.

EPILOGUE

On March 18, 1847, and old woman wearing a black veil entered the Saint-Laurent church in Paris and stopped in the middle of the nave. The gothic windows only let a little light in, but the woman saw someone kneeling in the first pew. That must be him. She had been told she'd find him here. Her steps echoed on the stone floor. When she reached the first pew, she kneeled next to the man and folded her hands in prayer.

"Are you Henri-Clément Sanson, grandson of the great Charles-Henri Sanson?" she asked softly.

The man didn't stir. His face was unshaven and bloated from alcohol. He was around fifty years old. "Don't come any closer," he mumbled. "I only bring ill-fortune. My family is cursed. You better go, God has no time for you, anyway."

"God always has time," the woman said without conviction. "Or, let's say, most of the time."

"Perhaps," Henri-Clément said, "but today I need him all to myself." He fixed his gaze at the mosaic above the altar depicting the resurrection of Jesus Christ.

"Do you believe in the resurrection?" she asked.

"No, madame, I fear it. All my ancestors have feared it, because they fear the dead. The return of the dead. First you feel a slight breath of air, and then they're there, staring at you. The last look of a dying man burns into your memory like a branding. We branded many shoulders. I still smell burnt human flesh wherever I go. I used to rub lard and gunpowder into the wounds. I didn't just kill, I also relieved

pain—I healed. Like all my ancestors." He lowered his head and tried to pray. After a few moments, he snarled at the old woman: "Can't you find somewhere else to pray?"

She didn't reply.

He tried to see her face, but in vain. He ran his fingers over his black stubbles and whispered: "My grandfather never wanted to become a hangman. Neither did I. I always hated my profession."

"No hangman ever became one against his will, because the pay was too good," she replied with contempt in her voice. "There was never a curse. I came to Paris to buy your grandfather's diaries, monsieur. He kept a diary during the revolution, didn't he?"

"Yes," he said. "My grandfather was Charles-Henri Sanson, the great hangman of the French revolution. They called him Monsieur de Paris. He told me everything. My father wasn't really interested, and history will forget him. But my grandfather won't be forgotten."

"Where are the diaries, monsieur? I want to see them. I want to read what the great Sanson wrote about me."

"About you? Whatever the case: I doubt you'll enjoy the read. But if you insist, madame—it'll cost you, though. I need money. Do you know d'Olbreuse? A man of the quill. He's looking for memoirs for his print shop. He's looking for scandalous diaries. Balzac is supposed to help him with the editing—it's too much for one man alone. Three thousand murders, no man can bear that on his own ..."

"But one man did," she cut him off.

"He did it, but he never found peace again." Henri-Clément laughed softly and looked closely at the woman. "What do you know about the Sansons?"

"Quite a lot," she replied ambiguously. "But that's not important now. Has d'Olbreuse read the diaries already?"

He gave her a suspicious look. A cold shiver ran down his spine. Suddenly he had an idea who the woman might be.

THE HANGMAN OF PARIS

Hadn't his grandfather told him about crazy Marie who used to wait for him at the Madeleine cemetery at night? If this woman survived the revolution, she must be ... He calculated. It was more than fifty years ago. More than half a century. She must be well over eighty.

"I want the machine and the diaries," the woman said with determination and took off the veil. Now he could see her face properly. Her bony nose stood out from her haggard face like a rock. Her skin was as white as the slaked lime they used to scatter over the bloody torsos of the guillotined at the Madeleine cemetery. Her stare was as rigid as that of a mummy, as if she had just climbed from a vault, her eyes as glassy as marbles. And now, with anger coloring her face, she looked as pink as an old wax puppet. Like a wax figure from her chamber of horrors.

"Oh God," Henri-Clément said with fright, running both hands through his hair. "Are you crazy Marie from the madeleine cemetery? You're Madame Tussaud!" He was a poor actor. Years of alcohol had ruined him. "I sold everything, madame," he continued without awaiting her reply. "The locks of Louis XVI, Marie Antoinette's shoe, Danton's stained collar. We didn't keep anything of Robespierre's—expect perhaps a bloody kerchief, though I'm not sure who it belonged to. So many people used to run up to the scaffold following an execution to dip their handkerchiefs in the blood. It was supposed to be lucky. I was left with nothing but the machine and the diaries."

Madame Tussaud jutted out her jaw and pinched her lips to a thin line. "I want the machine and the diaries," she repeated. "I want it all."

"Oh God," he sighed and thought about what to say next. He threw up his hands, tried to get up, but couldn't. He hadn't the strength. And he still wanted to pray. He needed to pray. Like all his ancestors, he needed to pray a lot. For all the souls the machine severed from their bodies. "I'm here to

pray," he called out in despair. His words echoed through the empty church. Again, he stared at the mosaic above the altar, as though trying to make sure God had heard that he had come here to pray and that it wasn't his fault he was still on the first rosary. Not his fault again.

"Monsieur," Madame Tussaud said, unmoved. "Your ranting and raving is inappropriate. You're here to pray, and I came from London to buy the machine. I'm paying cash. Ten thousand francs."

"Twenty thousand for the machine," Henri-Clément replied without a moment's hesitation.

She didn't react, her eyes fixed on the altar.

"All right, Madame," he relented. "Sixteen thousand and the cursed machine is yours."

"You'd be happy with half as much," she muttered.

He glanced at her with contempt. The old woman was used to doing business, profitable business, and she'd been able to tell from half a mile away that he needed money. She could humiliate him all she wanted and push the price—there was nothing he could do. He knew how to separate heads from bodies tidily, but he knew nothing about business. "Agreed," he eventually replied defiantly. "But you only get the machine for that. No diaries."

"Tell me the story of the Sansons first, and then I'll decide whether to buy the diaries or not. I'm not paying a sou for nonsense."

"I'm the last Sanson. The dynasty ends with me. I'm the last who can tell the story, but I need money—I'm in a lot of debt. On top of that, my wife left me today. That would never have happened to any other Sanson. I'm not a proper Sanson. I'm a failure. The Sansons were strong, tall, and charismatic, imposing and dignified, commanding. It was them against the rest of the world, no storm could bring them to their knees, no force on earth rattle them, but I am weak, a coward, I have no ambitions, I drink like a fish and frequent the most

disreputable establishments in Paris. I chase after every skirt. And … not just after skirts. No, madame, I have none of the great qualities of the Sansons. I'm merely the last of their kind, the disgrace of the dynasty. I withered away in the shadow of the guillotine, while my grandfather, the great Sanson is going down in history."

"Let us go, monsieur," Madame Tussaud replied coolly. "I'm not here to console you."

"Don't you have any empathy, madame?"

"Empathy? If you want empathy, get a dog. Paris is full of stray dogs. Where is your machine?"

"It's not my machine," he replied. "It never belonged to the Sansons. We merely carried out the verdicts. We neither invented this goddamned machine nor built it. The doctors Louis and guillotine did—you might say it's a surgical instrument. But what on earth do you want it for?" He sprang to his feet.

"I'm going to take it to London," she said calmly and stood up, too. Slowly. He could hear the creaking of her joints.

"May I help you?" Henri-Clément asked with concern.

"Don't touch me. I only want your machine."

"And what are you going to do with it in London?"

"I'm going to exhibit it amidst the Robespierres, Dantons, Marats, and so forth, because I fished them all from the bloody wicker baskets of your grandfather's by the hair and molded them in wax." She sat down on the bench. "Just like you, the Sansons, have passed the executioners sword down the generations, I, too, intend to complete my work and pass it on to my sons. But first, I want the machine. It's the only piece still missing, together with its story. Your grandfather is long dead, monsieur, but my wax figures are still going to be a living reminder of the people of the French revolution in a hundred years' time. I alone mold those memories, and I alone am going to decide what history is going to say about

their creator, Madame Tussaud. That's why I want to hear the story and perhaps purchase the diaries. Madame Tussaud has become an enterprise, and I won't tolerate any harm to come to my life's work. You are going to speak, monsieur, and you are going to answer my every question, and I swear to you, young man, if I catch you lying to me at all, I will find the branding iron in your shed and brand your shoulder—and I won't rub lard into the wound."

"All right, all right," Henri-Clément replied, now sitting beside her. "I'll tell you about this curse, about my family's fate."

"Stop it, I told you there never was a curse or a hangman who had been forced into his position. Tell me the story properly, my ship back to England is leaving this evening."

"Sixteen thousand francs for the machine? I can trust you?"

She nodded.

"But I warn you, too, madame, the curse is going to follow you and your museum will go up in flames. Your figures are made of wax, aren't they?"

"Start talking already! There is absolutely nothing I'm afraid of. I survived the French revolution—and two husbands."

"Madame, I'm going to make you cry."

"No one's died of that before. Start already!"

"I need wine, madame. I can't bear it without."

"I know. I was warned." She produced a bottle of red wine from her coat and placed it next to her on the bench.

Henri-Clément snatched it, yanked out the cork, and emptied half the bottle in one gulp. Then he began to talk: "My grandfather Charles-Henri Sanson died in 1806 at the age of sixty-seven years. My grandmother survived him by eleven years ..." He took another swig.

"Monsieur," Madame Tussaud said impatiently. "You're a pathetic drunkard. Give me the diaries. I'll buy them off you. I can't listen to your maudlin drivel any longer."

"There are none," he replied. "There are records about who was executed when and why, and inventories of the victims' clothes. I added to the text with newspaper articles from the time, eye witness accounts, memoirs of emigrated Frenchmen—"

"I know there's an original manuscript. Your grandfather kept an inventory of horrors."

"Yes, but I had to embellish it somewhat. I was paid thirty thousand francs for it. D'Olbreuse, the journalist, helped me, for seventeen thousand. And when the printer's engaged Balzac, five new volumes came out. You'd have to cut that man down with an ax before he stops writing." He rummaged in his pocket and pulled out an amulet. "My father gave me this talisman: a cracked bell. But it brought me no luck. You can have it for another bottle of wine."

"I don't give a damn about your amulet or your memoirs, monsieur. It's nothing but a bunch of lies, anyway. Now show me your guillotine."

"I don't have it," he mumbled and hung his head.

"Where is it?" Madame Tussaud was aghast.

"I lent it."

"Lent it?"

"To the pawnbroker, just around the corner. I needed the money. Can't you understand? You can have the guillotine, but you need to get it from the pawnbroker's first. It's quite easy—I've done it many times. A few times Canler had to do it, the head of the Paris sûreté. He said I'd be dismissed if it happened again, and now it's happened again. So we better hurry before he finds out. When does your ship leave for London?"

AFTERWORD

Henri-Clément Sanson was dismissed on March 18, 1847. He had indeed pawned the guillotine. His wife left him, and he was addicted to alcohol and young dancers until his death in 1889 at the age of eighty-nine.

Madame Tussaud's museum in London was destroyed by a fire in 1925, re-opened three years later, and destroyed again in 1940 by a German bomb, whereby the bust of Adolf Hitler was spared by coincidence.

Charles-Henri Sanson kept a diary during the French revolution, writing with a dry, sober style that makes the modern-day ready shudder. His grandson Henri-Clément Sanson sold these records to the journalist d'Olbreuse, who was looking for interesting material at the behest of the young print shop owner Dupray. Dupray was a visionary: he revolutionized typography and the publishing industry, and wanted a bestseller to make his print shop known throughout France. It is also proven that the young Honoré de Balzac, who knew and interviewed Henri- Clément personally wrote part of the *Mémoires de Sanson* as a ghostwriter, borrowing from his own manuscripts from the *Comédie humaine*, for example from *Une messe en 1793* and *Scènes de la vie politique et militaire*. Most likely, Balzac invented the 'curse' of the Sansons. He was a novelist, and he embellished and dramatized the facts accordingly.

With the exception of Dan-Mali, all characters named in this book are historical figures and their dialogue contains original quotes that were printed in newspapers or recorded in contemporary letters and diaries.

The French Revolution is one of the most significant events of modern European history. Inspired by the American War of Independence (1775–1783), it paved the way for other western democracies, enlightenment and human rights being its greatest accomplishments. From the view of a contemporary, however, the French Revolution didn't just bring personal rights to the French citizens, but also terror and mass executions, especially in 1793 and 1794. Only during the third and final phase from 1795 to 1799 did life slowly get back to normal, once it was too late for any of the revolution's opponents to turn back the wheels of time.

The terror during 1793 and 1794 was equally bloody and cruel as the tyranny of the Khmer Rouge in Cambodia during the 1970s. Under the leadership of Pol Pot, they tried to extinguish the middle class and—just like the revolutionary French Jacobins—punished even minor crimes and vague suspicions with the death penalty. They justified the murder of an estimated 1.7 million Cambodians with the argument of wanting to create the 'new human', which may require 'wading through a sea of blood'. Like Robespierre and Saint-Just, the Khmer Rouge became so paranoid that their waves of cleansing spilled into their own ranks and dragged down comrades from the Khmer Rouge's beginnings.

The French Revolution influenced our recent history like hardly any other event and brought personal freedom to the people of the Western world. Many third world countries are yet to experience a similar kind of revolution.

ABOUT THE AUTHOR

Claude Cueni, born in 1956 in Basel, Switzerland, has written novels, psycho thrillers, plays, audio plays, and over fifty screenplays for films and television series. His historical novel *The Great Gambler*, about the inventor of banknotes, John Law, reached the top of Switzerland's bestseller list and has been translated into numerous languages. His biographic novels, including those about Gustave Eiffel in *Giganten* (Giants), the discovery of the Philippines in Pacific Avenue, and the dramatization of the Gallic Wars in *Cäsars Druide* (Caesar's Druid), have helped Cueni secure a loyal readership.

E-MAIL: claude@cueni.ch
WEBSITE: www.cueni.ch

(c) Foto Mirko Ries, 2016, Agentur EQ Images

ABOUT THE TRANSLATOR

Translator Lee Chadeayne was a former classical musician, college professor, and owner of a language translation company in Massachusetts. He was one of the charter members of the American Literary Translators Association and has been an active member of the American Translators Association since 1970. His translated works are primarily in the areas of music, art, language, history, and general literature. Deceased in 2017.

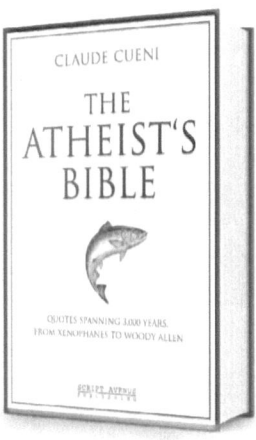

Claude Cueni
The Atheist's Bible
Quotes spanning 3,000 years, from Xenophanes to Woody
Allen
Paperback: 190 Pages
Script Avenue Publishing
ISBN: 978-1973766605

This pocketbook contains a collection of quotes from famous
atheists – from Xenophanes to Sigmund Freud to Woody
Allen. Out of the many hundred of the past 3,000 years,
sixty-six quotes were selected for this book based on their
originality, brevity, as well as the author's relevance.
Presented chronologically, these quotes provide insight into
the development of atheism across multiple centuries. The
twenty-four-page prologue describes the birth of religiosity
and sun worshiping, and the progression of later forms of
religion.

Bestseller on Amazon Germany for 54 weeks.

CLAUDE CUENI

THE

GREAT

GAMBLER

Womanizer, murderer,
speculator, genius.
The true story of
the man who
invented
paper money.

Script Avenue
Publishing

THE GREAT GAMBLER

Sneak peek: Read the first chapter of *The Great Gambler*!

In this colorful historical novel set in 17th and 18th century England, France and Italy, bestselling author Claude Cueni tells the story of John Law of Lauriston, the man who invented paper money. He was also a mathematical genius, a masterful gambler, a duelist, murderer, womanizer and lover. But he is best known as the inventor of modern finance and architect of the most catastrophic financial crash in history. At the height of his career, Law was an advisor to the the King of France, Louis XIV, The Sun King, and also owner of the Mississippi Corporation, with vast holdings in the Americas, and thus the wealthiest man of his time.

Translated from German by Lee Chadeayne.

PARIS, 1683

"Am I going to die?" the Scotsman asked. His nose, raw from constant wiping, dripped down onto the scarlet cape he had wrapped tightly around him. He pushed three gold coins across the dark, stained oak table as if offering a bribe to death. Then he leaned back in his chair and stared at the doctor wide-eyed. A wave of bitterness and anger swept over him. "Am I going to die?" he repeated in his strong Scotch accent.

"You didn't make the long trip from Edinburgh to Paris just to die here," Cartier smiled. "Don't be concerned, Mr. Law. You're in good hands." Cartier's head was covered with patches of reddish eczema, and in some places his hair had fallen out in clumps. He'd covered his head with thick, bright makeup to hide the disfiguring pock marks. Then he pointed at a glass bowl full of strangely colored stones standing in the middle of the huge table. "Those are gall stones, Mr. Law. Terribly painful to our patients who are now free of pain now that we've removed them. These people..."

"What is the probability that I'll survive, Dr. Cartier?" the Scotchman interrupted. He was accustomed to getting precise, straight answers to his questions. He was after all wearing the scarlet cape of the goldsmith bankers of Edinburgh.

Dr. Cartier leaned over the table and stared him directly in the face. "Mr. Law, I'm a surgeon and not a mathematician. I don't think much of these new sciences that have come into fashion recently. The whole world is trying to figure out probability. Please, Mr. Law, that's nonsense. God alone decides, not mathematics. For centuries, those Swiss mountain farmers attacked us with their pikes on the battlefields of Europe, and now they let the Bernoulli brothers loose on us with their probability theories. All truths

are now suddenly cast in doubt and need to be explained again and interpreted—in public, where everyone can take part. Today every stable hand is supposed to understand everything. That's a new sickness, Mr. Law, a plague. But your problem, Mr. Law, your problem is curable. For more than two hundred fifty years we've been performing gallstone operations according to the same rules. But these rules are secret, Mr. Law, and for good reason. What would it come to if everyone could form his own opinion? If even farmers in Holland could perform episiotomies on their livestock? Now everyone in the world wants to generate and publicize their own statistics, every patient wants to be something of a Bernoulli, a mathematician, a prognosticator. That's a sin against God and the monarchy! Numbers, facts, relationships! Predicting the future! Figuring out God's plans! They want to play God! I'll tell you something, Mr. Law. Calculating probability is something for gamblers." Dr. Cartier stopped and took a deep breath. He was even surprised himself that he'd become so emotional.

William Law nodded politely and leaned down now over the table, as well. "Dr. Cartier, I am William Law, goldsmith and coin inspector from Edinburgh in Scotland, and counselor to the royal mint. Of my seven sons and five daughters, only four survived childhood. Statistically, that's average for Edinburgh, according to my son John. I just want to know what the statistics are in your hospital so I can decide whether or not to take the risk. At home in Lauriston Castle, which I acquired a few weeks ago, my wife and my sons John and William, await me." For a moment the two men sat staring at each other, suspicious and threatening.

Then Cartier sighed, stood up, and pushed the *louis d'or* back into the middle of the table. "Mr. Law, for thirty-one percent of patients, the operation ends in death. But if you die, Mr. Law, your death is not thirty-one percent; your own

death is always one hundred percent, and that's why I care nothing for these probability calculations. It takes very little poison to destroy a body; sometimes it takes no more than an idea. The new mathematics is worse than the plague. If it prevails, nothing will be the same as before."

"The world will be different, that's all, Dr. Cartier," the Scotchman replied wearily. "The old will die and the new will be born. The entire organism never dies." William Law smiled politely. "Actually I asked you about statistics only for the sake of my son John.. It wasn't my intent to call your abilities as a surgeon into question. In case this is the impression I have created, I'm sorry, and I sincerely beg your pardon."

Cartier stretched out his arm and patted Law's hand affectionately. "Don't worry, Mr. Law, we won't let the coin inspector from Edinburgh die. In these times of high emotions that could easily lead to a new war, and that is something Europe has already seen too much of."

Law pulled back his hand and took out two brown, sealed envelopes from the inside pocket of his crimson cloak and put them down hesitantly on the table. "This letter is for my wife and the other for my older son, John. John Law. Just to be safe. It's still thirty-one percent."

Shortly after, as the two men walked toward the operating rooms, their steps echoed loudly through the high-columned halls of the Charité. "So your eldest will probably also become a goldsmith?" said Cartier, in an attempt to make a little conversation.

"In Scotland every goldsmith is also a banker. The Law family has been active as goldsmiths for generations—or as pastors. Some of them even became cardinals."

William Law was afraid, he was even sick with fear. Dizzy spells came over him again and again and he had the feeling that the very next step would find him falling into the

void. The Scotchman had caught a cold and high fever during the long trip by coach from Edinburgh to Paris. He was freezing. A shrill whistling in his ears startled him and his heart raced as if it were about to burst out of his chest and run back to Edinburgh by itself.

"Well?" Cartier asked in a markedly friendly manner. "Will your eldest become a goldsmith or a cardinal?"

"John is only twelve," William demurred with embarrassment. "He is not good at working with his hands ..." He struggled for breath, he needed air.

"Then he'll be a cardinal," the surgeon laughed, putting his arm around the man's shoulder comfortingly.

With quick, deft movements, twelve-year-old John thrust his penis between the throbbing loins of the servant girl Janine. The girl was resting on the wooden chest in front of the window of the tower room. She had thrown her head back into the window recess as if wanting to look up into the overcast sky. "I'll teach you everything, John," she moaned, "every move, every trick in the art of seduction, abandoning yourself to your lustful impulses, the art of keeping a mistress and spoiling her." With lightning speed the twenty-year-old seized John's hips, pushed back softly, turned, and knelt face down on the chest facing the window. Looking down toward the river, she saw a woman walking beneath the trees and approaching quickly. John shoved his penis in again, like a puppy who knew nothing else, impetuous and violent. He was unusually large for his age and looked almost like a man. Only the mischievous gleam in his friendly, dark eyes gave a hint of his young age. Janine had once said to him she had never kissed such a beautiful mouth.

For John, Janine was not the chamber pot of husbands, the pisspot of the lord of the house, as the French contemptuously called them. Quite the contrary, for him Janine was like a window on the wide world. Janine had

worked as a maid in Paris for a goldsmith who had been broken by his passion for gambling. Janine had taught John not just the card game Pharao, but also the things people talked about in the salons of the rich and mighty. And people spoke about just one thing. *Fais-le-bien*, the French said at the court of the Sun King. "Do it well," and John wanted to be the best, a real lecher, a hero for his time, a cardinal of the erotic.

"John!" came the furious voice of a woman from down below. She sounded impatient and tired. The seventy hectares of land on the south shore of the Firth of Forth belonged to Lauriston Castle, a three-story, imposing building with two small watchtowers. Drawing nearer, the woman stopped below the tower on the left supported by a corbel. "John, I must speak with you," she shouted, looking up at the tower window. The boy stuck his head out and shouted back. "What do you want now, mother? I'm working."

After Janine had served the food in the great dining hall— vegetable soup, bread and cheese—Jean Law recited a short prayer. The twelve births had left their mark on her. The once fiery red, shoulder length hair, which she had tied together with a red ribbon, had become brittle, her face was gaunt, and her eyes told of all the sorrow she had known and borne. Jean Law was thirty-six. After finishing the prayer, she added softly: "And may God protect William Law and see that he is healed and returned safely to his family."

Until a few weeks ago the family of six had been living in Edinburgh in a small apartment on Parliament Square, but now they were the proud owners of Lauriston Castle. William Law stood at the apogee of societal acceptance, and if he retuned healthy, then their happiness would be complete. Jean Law was fearful of this thought. She distrusted fate, but not because she had already lost eight children. In Edinburgh, where people lived closer together

than anywhere in the world, that was nothing special. Childhood death was so ordinary that people didn't think it necessary to baptize children before the age of seven, or lavish any special affection on them. No, Jean Law distrusted fate because she knew that a cloverleaf seldom had four leafs. And now that they had assumed ownership of Lauriston Castle, the absence of her husband worried her greatly. She was both religious and superstitious, in equal measure.

Janine first served Jean her soup, then John, and finally his brother William, younger by one year. The two girls, six-year-old twins, ate as usual out in the kitchen. As Janine served the soup, John Law gazed again at her well-rounded breasts covered with a stomacher. John wanted nothing more than to rush back into the tower room at once. Janine had really cast a spell on him. He couldn't help thinking of her bottom and her white thighs, and his erect penis absolutely drove him wild. Often he closed his eyes during class at school in order to inhale the fragrance of her hair, her breast, her sweaty skin, and her wet thighs. And when he opened his eyes again, his lips uttered a soft sigh.

"So, John," his mother began, "Your teacher wanted to speak with me today. He thinks you are very intelligent and have a special gift for numbers. Sometimes you even have a touch of –genius. Those were his words exactly..."

John's brother William began to laugh out loud, but John didn't seem to notice.

"But mother," John replied with a charming smile, "do you really think my teacher is in any position to recognize genius?"

"What is that supposed to mean?"

"He doesn't know very much about mathematics," John replied, "and since he is my teacher, he's quite aware of that."

"Pride cometh before a fall," shouted William, "Arrogant as a Frenchman!" But again John paid no attention to him. He spoke like a grown-up, Janine noticed with silent satisfaction. After all, he was the one who showed her how to conceal every emotion in a card game and match the spoken word with the appropriate gesture.

"John! God will punish you someday for your arrogance!" his mother scolded.

"Excuse me, mother, but is it arrogance if I point out errors to my teacher? Shall I humbly fall silent only because he's my teacher? Respect has to be earned, mother, through knowledge and accomplishments, not by virtue of office and titles."

"Aren't office and titles based on knowledge and accomplishments?" his mother inquired. Her voice sounded tired. More and more she lacked the strength to engage in such arguments.

"We stand on the threshold of a new day, Mother. The cards are being reshuffled ..."

"Stop it, John!" she cried, pounding the table with the palm of her hand. "With such ideas you offend God and the King. Whoever does not accept divine order stands outside the Christian community."

"You are right, Mother. But don't we owe our progress to exactly those people who don't accept the existing order and have deliberately set themselves apart?"

With a sudden motion, Jean threw her spoon on the table and shouted: "It's not for you to judge your mother and say she's right or wrong!"

"I beg your forgiveness, Mother. I didn't wish to offend." And with a smile so typical of him he softly added: "If you wish, mother, I'll even say the earth is flat, if I must, in order not to lose your love."

Jean wanted to scold her son, but John's smile moved her heart. Secretly she was proud of her little John, who had suddenly become so grown-up. She picked up her spoon again, dipped it in the soup, then paused again. "Your teacher says you're very temperamental, and that upsets him."

"Everything he doesn't know and therefore doesn't understand upsets him. Perhaps we should change teachers." The boy grinned.

"John," his mother said in a very serious voice, "When your father returns, I'll suggest he send you to Eaglesham ..."

"Renfrewshire? To this befuddled preacher? They say the devil's behind him."

John cast a pleading look at Janine, but she'd already turned her back and was on the way out the door. And John thought God had given her this wonderful ass just as He had given him his gift for mathematics.

"Father will surely want to keep me here near him," John smiled. "I'm certain of that."

"Certain?" his brother joshed. "How certain, master?"

"One hundred percent certain," John hissed, poking his brother in the thigh with his two-pointed fork. William let out a shriek.

William Law's screams echoed through the corridors of the Paris Charité. One of his Cartier's assistants pressed Laws' shoulder down onto the wooden bed. To the left and the right of the patient stood assistants holding his arms and legs securely. Cartier pushed the scalpel even deeper into the thigh muscle directly adjacent to the anus and tried once more to feel the gallstone with his fingers while William Law screamed and struggled to sit up. Cartier widened the incision and tried now to shove the speculum to reach the stone in the kidney. The surgeon was spattered with blood like a butcher in a slaughterhouse. The stone was still inside the kidney, and it was huge. An hour later his cries had stopped, and Dr.

Cartier looked in shock at the blood-covered abdomen of the Scotchman. Then he took the man's warm penis in his hand and introduced the stiff probe into the urethra, trying to locate the opening to the bladder. He couldn't comprehend was had happened.

"Doctor Cartier," whispered his young assistant Dutronc in a calm voice. "Doctor Cartier. The patient is dead."

Cartier paused, staring at the penis in his hand. Then he let it go. As he washed his hand, the bowl of water shook in the hands of his assistant. The bloody water spilled over the edge of the bowl and onto the floor.

Shortly after, Cartier sat exhausted in his paneled study. William Law, the Inspector of the Edinburgh Mint, had bled to death in the year 1683 during a lithotomy, the oldest known surgical procedure. It was out of the question to ship the body to far-off Scotland. He would be buried without ceremony in the Scottish Seminary in Paris. Cartier stared at the heavy red seals on the two brown envelopes the Scotchman had given him.

"He knew the risk, I kept nothing from him, isn't that right, Dutronc? The Scotchman knew the risk!" Cartier looked up at his assistant Dutronc who was standing patiently in front of the desk, evidently awaiting some order.

"I'm your witness, Doctor Cartier. You informed him."

Cartier smiled. "And it's still in God's hands who lives and who dies, isn't that right, Dutronc? We struggle as best we can, but God decides."

Dutronc was silent, and Cartier looked up at him again.

"What's wrong, Dutronc? He's dead. Accept that and turn your endeavors back to the living. Believe me, I'd rather Law were still alive and we wouldn't have to take these two envelopes to the post office."

"His death was perhaps avoidable," Dutronc said softly, without looking Dr. Cartier in the eyes.

"What are you saying?" Cartier asked crossly. "If it had been the will of God ... Or are you trying to say I did something wrong?"

"No, no, Dr. Cartier, you did nothing wrong. All of us may be doing something wrong."

"Do you want to perform gallstone operations using steam engines? Or with mysterious magnets?" Cartier asked, laughing contemptuously.

"Dr. Cartier, for more than two hundred years ..."

"You're right, Mr. Dutronc! For more than two hundred years gallstones have been removed in this manner. People suffer from their stones, some can be helped, and others die. But nothing has changed in the way the operation is performed, because there is nothing to change. Human anatomy doesn't change, nor do the stones, and it's for this reason that this operation will be done exactly the same way a thousand years from now in exactly the way it is today."

"No, Dr. Cartier," Dutronc flared up, unable to contain his youthful temperament any longer. "We have to share our knowledge, Dr. Cartier, with the doctors and surgeons from Italy, Holland, and England ..."

"Just cut it out, Dutronc! If there's something I can't stand, it's a hothead."

"It's not just gunpowder that's changing Europe! People are discovering new things all over the world."

"You just watch out what you say, Dutronc. You can strain a muscle just so far, and then it tears!"

"Have we strained that muscle because we don't live in caves any more and eat raw meat?"

"Listen, Dutronc, I know it's become the fashion in society to listen even to children and women, but I won't listen to you one minute longer. Take these letters to the post office! And then, as far as I'm concerned, take the next coach for Amsterdam to Brother Jacques de Beaulieu. He just had a

shoemaker make him a new tool for operating on kidney stones. A shoemaker!" Cartier shouted , pressing the two envelopes into Dutronc's hand. Dutronc took them and nodded. He could see there was no point in continuing the conversation with Cartier. Bowing briefly, he turned and hurried out the door.

"Dutronc!" Cartier called out, and Dutronc whirled around, his long blond hair whirling. "You want to play God, Dutronc! You want to create an immortal man in the image of God, and for that God will punish you!"

Dutronc's eyes glowed as if fired by black magic or a great love: "Yes!" he rejoiced, with passion in his voice. "Yes, Dr. Cartier, and the question whether or not there is a God must also be asked once again, and some day even the seat of your almighty God will be occupied by a man, and we will make men in our own image. And machines will do the work, while we happily fly through the air and visit cities deep beneath the sea!"

"Dreamer!" Cartier roared. "You're a dreamer possessed by the devil! A goddamed dreamer!"

www.ingramcontent.com/pod-product-compliance
Lightning Source LLC
Chambersburg PA
CBHW050549260626
47157CB00002B/485